A COURT
This
CRUEL
and
LOVELY

STACIA STARK

Map by Sarah Waites of The Illustrated Page Design
Cover by Cover Design by
Moonpress, www.moonpress.co
Interior Design by Imagine Ink Designs

KNOWN KINGDOMS

THE BARREN CONTINENT

THE SLEEPING SEA

THE CURSED CITY

ASRIC PASS

MINARET MOUNTAINS

NORMATHE MOUNTAINS

DYTUR RIVER

MISTRUN

EPROTHA

CRAWYTH

LESDRYN

FAE LANDS

GROMALIA

THOBIREA

For mum.
Thank you for believing in me.

1

PRISCA

There were few things more unsettling than watching ashen-faced Abus stand on the high platform in our village square, several of the king's guards directly behind him.

"Ten copper coins says he vomits."

I slammed my elbow into my brother's gut. "Quiet."

Tibris gave me a rare grin, and the vise around my chest loosened a little at his attempt to distract me from the guards.

I'll take that bet," his friend Natan muttered on my right. A chilly breeze rustled the tree branches above us, and he hunched his shoulders, shoving his hands into the pockets of his cloak.

"You're both terrible," Asinia said, but her lips twitched.

The frost-speckled ground sparkled beneath the weak winter sun as we stood in the middle of our tiny village, our breaths turning to misty clouds in the frigid air. Abus had reached twenty-five winters, and today, he would receive his allotment of his power back.

From my position near the back of the crowd, I could observe everyone. The guards, wearing maroon and gold and dotted among the villagers. The priestess in blue robes, preening under our attention. The king's assessor, dressed in black, his large silver brooch denoting his power.

To them, our faces probably all blurred into a mass of poor, barely educated peasants dressed in rough homespun.

Abus was quiet and thin, and he wrung his hands, clearly nervous. While most of our magic was sacrificed to the gods days after we were born, the whisper of power he received back today would help him contribute to our village.

The king's guard standing behind Abus looked bored, his uniform covered in dust from traveling. But the three guards surrounding Abus's family were resting their hands on the hilts of their swords. If Abus was found to have somehow defied the gods, his mother, father, and sister would be instantly slaughtered. Right before Abus was taken to the city to burn on Gods Day. I shivered, wishing I'd brought a thicker cloak.

One of the guards glanced toward our group, and my shivers turned to a full-body shudder. My heart stumbled on its next beat, and my breaths turned to shallow pants.

"It's not that cold, Prisca." Natan scowled at me. But

his face was pale too. Anyone with a shred of intelligence feared the king's guards.

On my left, Tibris was quiet, his eyes dark with sorrow. We didn't often talk about what would happen when I disappeared in a couple of years. I was going to have to figure out my future—and soon.

Because this kingdom meant death for me.

The king's assessor stepped forward, dark eyes narrowed in his strongly carved face. His knife-sharp cheekbones, hard mouth, and wide shoulders made him a powerful, intimidating man—one who was known to enjoy his work immensely.

It was his job to check whether Abus had somehow hidden his magic all these years. That power made the assessor—and others like him—infinitely valuable to the king.

The assessor watched Abus. His smile was slow as he held his hands close to Abus's face.

You'd have to be blind to miss the disappointment in the assessor's eyes when he shook his head. Abus was indeed powerless—his sacrifice accepted by the gods when he was a newborn. Something unwound in my chest, and I could suddenly breathe easier. We'd never had an assessor find one of the corrupt during a Gifting ceremony in our village. They were usually discovered as children—when they accidentally used their powers for the first time. Or they were captured while attempting to flee before they reached twenty-five winters.

Behind Abus, three more villagers waited for their

turn—each of them recently having celebrated twenty-five winters, and all three of them displaying varying levels of excitement and terror. Jaelle looked like she might faint, while her twin brother Wilkin was expressionless. Lina shifted on her feet, clearly eager to receive her own power. She nodded to her grandparents, who were standing at the front of the crowd, smiling proudly up at her.

The king's assessor stepped back. The priestess held up her hand, and we bowed our heads.

"As infants, we gift our magic to the gods, so that they may be pleased with our offering and grow it under their care. Today, Abus will reap his reward, the gods acknowledging the sacrifice he made, so that they may watch over us and protect us from those who would threaten our way of life."

She practically spat the last words, her hatred of the fae palpable. They were the creatures who had caused the need for such sacrifice. The monsters who would prey on us if our king hadn't found a way to protect our kingdom from their cruelty.

The priestess raised her other hand, displaying a blue oceartus stone, glowing with power. She turned to Abus. "Your sacrifice has brought fortune to us all. Now, the gods return what was yours, which they have blessed. And they will further bless you for your sacrifice when you leave this world."

The stone began to glow brighter. And brighter. Abus stiffened, cheeks flushing. And the stone went dark. Inert. Empty.

I couldn't help but smile. Abus had received his gift back.

The priestess held her hand to his temple. A moment later, the blue circle marked him as someone who had reached twenty-five winters and completed the Gifting ceremony. That blue mark meant freedom. Several whoops sounded from the villagers surrounding Abus.

It was the twins' turn next, and they stood together on the high platform, waiting to be assessed. I gazed up at the freestanding wooden structures that had been purpose-built for the king's guards. Several of the guards were currently poised on those structures among the thatched rooftops surrounding the square, crossbows in their hands.

Fury rose, sharp and swift.

It bubbled in my chest, tingled in my fingers, sparked along my skin.

Usually, I attempted to bury it deep beneath grim acceptance of our lives. Today, I embraced it like a lover.

The gods needed our magic to keep us safe from the fae. But why did it have to be this way?

Why did our kingdom's sacrifice also have to mean terror and death?

Tibris elbowed me, and I took a deep breath, refocusing on the ceremony and ensuring my expression was blank. Any strange behavior could mean a surprise visit from the assessor. And then we would both be dead.

Wilkin and Jaelle stepped down, their wisp of power restored. Lina practically danced past them, obviously more than ready for her own gift. The guards left the twins' parents and encircled Lina's grandmother and grandfather.

The priestess reached for the oceartus stone. The king's assessor held his hand over Lina's head.

And smiled.

I could feel the blood draining from my face. Next to me, Tibris stiffened, slowly shifting his weight as he glanced around. My brother was searching for a way out of the square. But the guards above us would spot anyone attempting to flee.

"The magic of *luck*," the assessor announced. "Right here, where it shouldn't be."

Lina frowned. "I don't— I'm not—"

"Silence!"

I closed my eyes. Luck was a passive power. The kind of power that Lina may not have even known she was using.

Her grandparents began to beg in high, desperate voices.

I opened my eyes just as both of their heads rolled to the ground.

The king's guards had dispatched them in an instant. Behind me, someone gagged. To my left, a woman let out a high shriek. I stared, my mind unable to accept what I'd just seen.

Lina swayed on her feet. And then she began to scream.

The sound pierced the silence. And the crowd

instantly responded.

Someone shoved into me from the right. Someone else hit my left side. Pure panic. A child went down to his knees, crying out for his mother, and Tibris hauled him up by the back of his shirt.

The king's guards were moving toward Lina. She'd stopped screaming and was backing away from them, as far as she could move on the wooden platform.

Several chickens broke free of their cage at the side of the square and flapped across the guards' feet. The guards tripped, falling to their knees.

The gift of luck.

The village butcher turned to run. The first arrow took him between the shoulders. The second and third hit him in the spine, and he dropped to the ground.

"Nobody move!" a guard roared above us.

The entire crowd seemed to freeze. All I could see were wide eyes and stunned faces. Bile climbed up my throat as I slid my gaze back to the platform.

The assessor turned and backhanded Lina across the face. She dropped to her knees, and he kicked her square in the back, gesturing for another guard. Striding up the steps, the guard hauled her to her feet, clamping heavy irons to her wrists.

Lina hung her head, clearly dazed. Her only family was dead, with no husband to fight for her. There was a reason the legal age of marriage was twenty-five winters.

The assessor turned to us. "The corrupt, who were either rejected by the gods or who prevent the gods from taking their power—who choose *blasphemy* instead of truth—will be made to burn for their sins. Our king is so committed to protecting his kingdom from the fae that he has recently announced a bounty."

The priestess nodded. "One hundred gold coins to anyone who informs us of one of the traitors."

A few foot-spans to our right, a woman sucked in a sharp breath. I couldn't blame her. One hundred gold coins, and she'd never have to work again.

The assessor surveyed the crowd, his gaze burning with fervor as if he could seek out magic lingering where it shouldn't be.

Surely he could hear the thud of my heart. Could smell the fear-sweat that clung to my skin. The world receded until his face was all I could see.

He stepped down into the crowd, which parted for him. He seemed to be walking directly toward me, as if he *knew*.

Tibris stepped between me and the assessor. He made the move look casual, as if he was excited to congratulate Abus. But I stumbled backward, tripped on the hem of my cloak, and slammed into a hard male chest.

Strong arms caught me. The man held me suspended for a long moment, and we both froze, watching the assessor.

But he'd already sauntered through the crowd, likely readying himself to travel to the next village.

I glanced up at the man, and my breath caught in my throat.

The sun sliced across his eyes, which glittered with annoyance. The rest of his face was hidden by a black woolen scarf, and he wore the hood up on his cloak, covering his hair. I couldn't tell his age, if he was clean-shaven...*anything* about him.

But I knew him.

At least once a month, I dreamed of a man with green eyes. No, not just *green*. The word didn't even begin to describe them. Those eyes were haunting. A dark yet vibrant green with flecks of silver that seemed to attract the light. In my dreams, the man looked back at me as if patiently waiting. Some days, the dreams left me anxious. Other days, I felt a deep contentment—almost...safe.

"Watch where you're going," he snarled, lifting me back onto my feet.

"Charming," I muttered. "Well, thank you for—"

He'd already turned and walked away.

I stared after the cold, rude brute and shook myself out of my daze. Of course I didn't know him. The events of this morning were rattling my mind. I turned to find Tibris watching the guards as they climbed down from the rooftops surrounding the village square.

"Pris? Are you okay?" Asinia squeezed my shoulder. Her eyes were dark, her face pale, lips bloodless.

I likely looked just as shaken. While it was always a possibility that one of the corrupt would be found, no one had expected to see what we'd seen today.

"I will be," I said. "Are you?"

She just nodded. We stared at each other for a

long moment. Someone laughed, the sound entirely inappropriate as it cut through the somber crowd, and Asinia flinched. We both turned.

Abus's face was flushed with color as he embraced his family. His mother smiled, while his father slapped him on the back. Now, the family would take their five silver coins—a gift from the king. Tradition dictated that the entire village was invited to the celebration in this square—each villager bringing whatever food they could.

Abus's father had even managed to barter for a pig, which had been roasting on a spit since the early hours of the morning. The scent of the meat drifted throughout the village, curling into open windows and beneath closed doors.

My stomach clenched uneasily at the thought.

Tibris eyed me and opened his mouth. But Natan was already shoving his way toward us.

"So...that was awful. Who's staying for the celebration? I need a drink."

The sun had barely risen, but I was willing to bet half this village would be in their cups by noon after what had just happened.

Tibris watched Natan wander toward the wine. Then he turned back to me. "You should go check on Mama," he said carefully. "I'll stay here."

I knew what he was saying. He didn't want to stay for the feast. Probably wanted to be alone. But one of us had to stay and pretend to celebrate or our household would draw attention. Truthfully, it was difficult to understand how anyone could sit and eat only foot-spans from where Lina's grandparents had just died. Both her grandmother and grandfather had been popular in this village, yet their bodies had already been removed, the blood washed away, as if they'd never existed. Soon, most of our neighbors would loudly be giving thanks to the gods that one of the corrupt had been found and taken from our village.

And Tibris wanted to spare me from that. Gratitude swept through me. "You're right. I'll see how she's feeling."

It was difficult to receive an exemption from the Gifting and Taking ceremonies. My mother only had one because her visions could strike at any time, disturbing the peace.

"I'll walk you home," Asinia said. "Just let me tell my mother."

She walked away and my gaze met Thol's. He stood near Abus's family, looking ruggedly handsome as always. He smiled at me, and despite the roiling in my stomach, my cheeks heated. I'd never been this self-conscious with a man before, but wings fluttered in my chest each time I looked at Thol. His sister Chista leaned over and murmured something to him, and I turned away, forcing myself to stop staring.

Nearby, Kreilor was practically shouting as he talked to a group of his friends, ensuring everyone in the vicinity could hear his conversation.

Tibris shook his head and stalked away, likely to get a drink of his own. He'd never liked Kreilor. I couldn't blame him.

All the men in our village were required to learn how to fight—ready to be called to march on the fae if our borders failed. The boys were trained from a young age, and the only way they could be excused from training was if they chose the path to the gods. Kreilor had done exactly that and was studying as an acolyte to our village's priestess.

"And then the priestess showed me the inner sanctum," Kreilor announced, a smug little smile on his face.

I went completely, utterly still.

If Kreilor could get into the inner sanctum, he'd have access to the empty oceartus stones. Maybe I could follow him and...*borrow* one.

I'd memorized the priestess's chants. What if I could make the stones work for me? My pulse thumped faster, my mind racing in a hundred different directions.

One of his friends snorted. "*You* were allowed into such a holy space?"

Kreilor's chest puffed up. "Of course I was. I will, after all, be performing ceremonies within the next three years."

I shuddered at the thought. Kreilor had been a bully since we were children. He smirked at beggars, chose the only position that would allow him to skip training with those he considered beneath him, and used his family's wealth and reputation to get whatever he wanted.

Thol walked past, easily drawing attention from

Kreilor.

The two men loathed each other. Their fathers were good friends, and both had been given every privilege found in this village as they'd grown up. But while Thol had remained kindhearted, Kreilor had become obsessed with proving himself.

Asinia stepped up next to me, winding her arm through mine. "This is awkward," she murmured as Thol ignored Kreilor completely. "Let's get you back to your mother." She tugged me, and we walked toward my house. My boots scuffed on the cobblestones, but all I could see was Lina's grandparents' blood, pooled on the stones in the square.

What would Asinia say if I told her that unless I managed to get out of this village, it would be me on that platform one day, watching Tibris and Mama be slaughtered—their bodies dragged away as if they were nothing?

If she kept my secret, and the assessor found out, Asinia would die too.

We walked in silence for most of the way home. Finally, Asinia took a deep breath.

"That was some moment with you and Thol," she said.

She was attempting to cheer me up. I could do the same for her. "It was just a smile. I lose the ability to speak around him."

"You forget, you may be terrible at flirting, but it's one of *my* best skills. And I know when a man is interested."

"Don't placate me. It's even more depressing."

She squeezed my arm. "I'm not. You'll see."

We took our usual route home from this side of the village, walking past the large, spacious, *warm* homes behind the thick metal gate separating them from the rest of the village. What must it be like to live in those homes? Not to have to watch every coin or huddle next to the fire in winter because the glass in the bedroom windows was broken?

"Prisca?"

"Sorry. Daydreaming. What will you do after the feast?"

"I'm helping my mother with some work."

Asinia's mother was a seamstress, and her daughter came by her talent naturally.

I glanced at Asinia. We had different dreams. I wanted nothing more than to be able to stay right here, while she longed for a life in the city. Regardless of how much magic Asinia received back when she finally came of age in two winters, she hoped the reputation of her work would spread, until the news reached someone in the city who would come and hire her.

It would happen. No one sewed or designed like Asinia.

Wherever I ended up, I'd find a way to let her know I was safe. Maybe, if she could forgive me, we'd even be able to exchange a letter or two. My chest ached at the thought of not seeing Asinia every day. Would she ever be able to forgive me for such dishonesty?

"You should come for dinner tomorrow night," Asinia said.

I hid a wince. Asinia and her mother weren't quite as poor as us, but they definitely didn't have much food to spare either. And yet, they both kept trying to feed me.

"Asinia."

"My mother loves you, Prisca. She knows how things have been since your father died."

"I'll think about it."

Asinia raised her eyebrow in that way she did when she knew exactly what I was thinking. "Your mother would do the same for me."

She waved and turned back toward the square. I continued along the dusty path and unlocked our front door.

"Mama?"

Our house was quiet.

Unnaturally quiet. Eerily quiet.

Sprinting into her room, I dropped to my knees next to her. Her eyes rolled, and she gasped for air.

My mother was in the midst of a vision.

2
LORIAN

"Feels like a trap," Rythos muttered, shifting on his horse as the sun flickered over his dark skin. He ducked his head, barely missing a particularly low-hanging branch. Mountains towered to our east, their jagged, snowcapped peaks stabbing into the sky.

"Of course it's a trap." Marth scowled, pulling his cloak tighter around himself with a wary glance at the ruins of the city in front of us.

The Cursed City had once been the capital of Eprotha. Centuries ago, when humans invaded what was now known as the Barren Continent, they were unprepared for the retaliation they would face.

Now, the capital was Lesdryn—on the other side of the kingdom.

After so many days of travel, most of us could use a good fight. But we had little time to spare. Already, we'd had to ride hard from one of the smaller villages in the east for this meeting.

My skin felt too tight. This was,

indeed, guaranteed to be a trap.

As usual, Cavis was quiet. His wife had just had their first child, and he was longing for home. But he hadn't complained. Like all of us, he knew just how important the next few weeks would be.

"What about you, Cavis?" I asked. "Do *you* think the stone hags will actually behave honorably for once?"

Cavis sent me a wry smile. "Even men like us should be wary of the Cursed City. And the creatures who roam there."

Few knew that the Cursed City was now inhabited. Fewer still came anywhere near this part of the kingdom. And yet, here we were, at what were once the gates to this ruined city.

"Come out, hags," I ordered.

"Come innnn," a voice called back.

I shook my head. Walk into a city of rubble, when the stone hags could wield that rubble to bury us alive? "We have a bargain. Break it and accept the consequences."

I allowed a hint of my power free. Mostly because a hint was all that was left. Grinding my teeth, I held up a hand, my magic sparking in the sunlight. Soon. Soon, my power would be returned in full.

"You dareeee threaten usss?"

Rythos's horse shifted under him. He jumped off and pulled his sword. "Don't make us come in there."

"They *want* us to come in there," Marth muttered. "That's the point."

We didn't have time for this. I let my power strike

at the closest pile of rubble—one that had likely been a watchtower. From the shriek that pierced my ears, one of the stone hags had been using it to spy on us. I smiled. Hopefully *that* would reduce the time we spent in this place.

Several hags appeared from the rubble. All of them moved slowly, their gray skin wrinkled and dry as dust. The one in the center wore a crown of tourmaline.

I dismounted and waited for them to come to us. I'd always found power in silence. Rythos lazily swung his sword in his hand. I gave him a warning look, and his mouth curved in a feral smile. All these years, and I still didn't know why he loathed the hags.

"The bargain has changed," the queen hissed. "We will require more gold."

Galon jumped off his horse next to me, offense flashing over his face. Once agreed upon, deals were never to be broken. Behind us, Marth and Cavis guarded our backs, although I knew both men well enough to know they were hoping for a fight.

"And you believe we will comply with your demands?"

The queen smiled, a grotesque display of crumbling stone teeth. "I believe I know why you need this little ingredient." She held up a vial containing the specific moss we required. "And if I am correct, you will need secrecy. Because if the king learned of your plans, all of you would *burnnnn*."

I watched the queen until she dropped her gaze. She

immediately lifted it, but it was too late. We both knew who was more dominant.

I smiled. "And you believe you are safe here in this cursed land that was once a city? You believe Sabium wouldn't send his guards here—with all of the magic at their disposal—to turn this stone to dust?"

She studied my face. One of her sisters murmured in the queen's ear. I kept my expression blank, despite the restlessness that itched at the base of my spine. This was the weakest part of our plan. Without the hags' cooperation, and the moss in the queen's hand, my revenge would stay forever out of reach.

"We will agree to the original deal," the queen said finally.

"Then why waste our time?" Rythos muttered. The hag ignored him, and he mounted his horse, his sword still in his hand as he approached her.

Marth went with him. Rythos held out his hand for the moss. Marth offered the coins. All of us waited in tense silence. One wrong move, and there would be bodies on the ground. I didn't particularly mind if I had to wiggle that vial free of the stone hag's cold, dead hand. In truth, a part of me ached for the fight. The queen met my eyes and gestured to her underling. The moss hit Rythos's hand, the coins were snatched from Marth's palm, and it was done.

The hags sneered, drifting back into their stone city. The first part of our plan was complete. Grim determination simmered through me. If I could, I would wage war right this second. But the next step would take even longer.

Above our heads, a falcon swooped. My brother had insisted on training the independent bird to send his messages. Hopefully, the tiny piece of parchment it would be carrying contained good news and we could move on to the next stage of our plan.

The bird landed on Marth's shoulder, its claws tangling in his blond hair, and he winced, untying the message.

"Our contact says we need to meet him at the Gromalian border."

The antithesis of good news. I went still. "That's the opposite direction. It means going *past* the city."

Marth sighed. "I know. According to your brother, his contact says he can't risk traveling into Eprotha right now. Security is too tight."

"This will cost us at least two days of travel." If we took too long on the road, we would cut into our time in the city—and our search for what had been taken from us. That search would need to be carefully executed. Methodical. And yet, without the other vial, we wouldn't get anywhere near the castle.

We needed to risk it.

I forced myself to take a deep breath. My revenge was so close, all my plans falling into place. If this was the worst calamity we faced over the coming weeks, I would gladly welcome it.

Marth handed me the other note in his hand.

Unfolding the parchment, I scanned it.

Dear L,

My sources tell me you will be forced to travel back to the border in order to find the package. I can practically hear you grinding your teeth, but it must be done. As long as you travel quickly, you will still be able to make your meeting.

Riniana has been asking after you. Shall I tell her you're thinking of her?

Your older, extremely patient brother,

C

Shaking my head, I took the quill Marth handed me and scrawled my reply.

Dear C,

I suppose you think the situation with Riniana is amusing. We can't all be happily married and sickeningly in love. Nor would most of us want to be.

We'll travel to the package. Although I suggest next time you organize a meeting like this one, you consider just who we're dealing with.

Your younger, much more handsome brother,

L

"We leave now," I said. "Nothing else must delay us."

We would need to ride all night without stopping to make up for the time we would lose. Because we were heading back in the same direction we'd come. My teeth clenched at the wasted hours.

Marth nodded. Rythos slitted his eyes at the stone behind us. "Better traveling through the forest than anywhere near this place."

PRISCA

Hands trembling, I reached for a pillow and shoved it beneath Mama's head. There was nothing we could do when the visions took her, only keep her safe.

"I'm sorry," I murmured, my stomach twisting. "We shouldn't have left you alone."

Long moments later, my mother went limp. I stroked her gray hair back from her face, the same way she did for me when I was sick or upset.

"Prisca?" Her voice was groggy, her movements slow, as if she were half asleep. I closed my eyes for a brief moment. I still wondered if one day she would become lost in a vision and I'd never see that spark of recognition again.

"I'm here, Mama. Do you want me to help you into bed?"

"A few hours of sleep. Just a few."

"Okay." I kept my voice low and soothing.

Only the gods knew why they'd given my mother visions that came randomly, usually about people she didn't know. She'd once told me her power had been useful when she was younger, ensuring some of the wealthiest people in the kingdom came to her for advice on their marriage contracts and business dealings. But little by little, the helpful visions disappeared. Now, she was often left like this, shuddering on the floor in the aftermath of a vision she either couldn't—or wouldn't—understand.

Mama's eyes closed as soon as she lay down, and I spent the rest of the afternoon sitting by the window, picturing Lina, alone and terrified in the back of a barred carriage. I would never forget that excited, hopeful grin she'd flashed. My eyes flooded.

She hadn't even known she still had her power. So she hadn't known to run. I scrubbed the wetness from my face.

"Prisca?"

Mama was lying in bed. Thankfully, some of the color had returned to her cheeks.

"Help me up, darling."

I obeyed, helping her sit. My mother was losing weight. I needed to make sure she ate more at dinner tonight.

"That was a bad one," I said quietly.

Her glazed eyes sharpened, and she nodded, reaching her hand up to cup my cheek.

"I love you so much. And everything I did was to keep you safe."

My heart tripped at the way she looked at me. It was as if she was already in mourning.

"I know, Mama. Believe me, I know. Now let's get you settled before Tibris comes home and fusses."

She smiled. "He does so love to fuss."

I helped her clean the sweat from her face, settled her at the table with a cup of tea, and heated some of the soup she'd made yesterday.

"I love you so much," Mama murmured. "I just need you to know that."

Whatever she'd seen in that vision had obviously shaken her. It wasn't like her to be this emotional. "I love you too. Hey, what's this? It's going to be okay."

A solitary tear trickled down her cheek, and I reached out with my other hand, wiping it away. She caught my hand in hers.

"You know you can't stay here, Prisca."

My chest hollowed out. For her to talk so openly about it…

I had obviously featured in her vision.

"What did you see, Mama?"

Silence.

I took a deep breath. "I know the plan was always for me to leave, but I have an idea."

Mama just shook her head. "Whatever you're

thinking, it won't work."

The dismissiveness in her tone pricked at my temper. I couldn't just give up and flee. If I ran, I would have to keep running for the rest of my life. How could I resign myself to such a fate?

I couldn't.

I *wouldn't.*

I would snatch at whatever hope I found, no matter how small that slice of hope was.

Kreilor had access to the oceartus stones. I could follow him to see where the entrance was. I'd pay attention to how he got in and steal a stone myself.

I sucked in a deep breath, and my words came out in a rush. "What if I could just store my magic in the stone temporarily? Until the Gifting? The assessor would see I had no magic, and I could—"

"Your magic doesn't work like that."

I stiffened. My magic didn't work at all. Except at the worst possible moments. But this time would be different. It had to be.

Mama studied my face, amusement warring with weariness in her eyes. "You have your father's stubborn nature. It will help you in this life—when it's not making that life so much harder than it needs to be."

Grief made my throat tight. I still sometimes woke up thinking I'd heard Papa's voice. "It's all going to be okay. You'll see."

She just nodded. But her expression was still forlorn.

When Tibris returned, Mama was sipping the soup

I'd warmed for her.

"How was the feast?" I asked.

He gave me a faint smile. "Fine. Natan insisted on playing King's Web."

I rolled my eyes. Of course he did.

The game was based on myth. According to the old stories, the king's great-great-grandfather was so sneaky, so sly, he slipped his people into foreign courts when they were children. Those children were unknowingly spelled and called "sleeping spiders." When they were *awakened,* they were called to supply information or assassinate the old king's enemies. I was still learning how to keep my face carefully blank, but last time we'd played King's Web, I'd almost won.

I studied Tibris as he pressed a kiss to Mama's forehead and took a seat at the table. The crease between his brows told me he was angry. And the paper clutched in his hand told me why.

Ever since Tibris's friend Vicer had passed his Testing—with enough magic to be plucked from our village and sent to the city to apply for work, my brother had been even quieter than usual.

The letters he sent and received from Vicer were written in the same code we'd created as children. Back then, Vicer and Tibris had included me in all their plans, and I'd been privy to every secret note and hushed word. I'd trailed after them—usually with Asinia at my side—and Tibris had tolerated us with the put-upon sighs perfected by older brothers everywhere.

But these letters were different. For reasons he wouldn't explain, Tibris refused to allow me to read them. Of course, the more secretive he was, the more curious I became. If Vicer was in trouble, I wanted to help.

I watched Tibris frown down at the letter in his hand. Now, he would likely brood for days. "I'll go bathe." He wandered out.

I attempted to get some answers from my mother one last time. "Mama…is there something I need to know?"

Water sounded from the other room. Tibris was filling his bath with cold water.

Mama would tell me if the king's assessor was going to come looking for me. So what had she seen? Why was she so shaken?

Her eyes filled, and she shook her head mutely.

Seers had rules in place. Because sometimes, to tell someone their future was to bring about a fate that was much, much worse. Dread flowed into my gut and stayed there.

"I'm tired," Mama said.

"Let me help you to bed."

"I can do it. Good night, darling."

I made my way back into the main room, which also served as Tibris's bedroom. From the splashing coming from the bathing room, I knew he was still busy. But he'd left the letter from Vicer on the small, rickety table near his bed.

I shouldn't. We weren't children anymore. Tibris deserved his privacy. And yet…clearly, something was seriously wrong. It was my *duty* as his sister to help him—even if he didn't particularly want that help.

Besides, my brother had no problem pushing his way into my life whenever he felt the need. He was forever trying to protect me, but maybe this time, I could actually help him for once.

I peered down at the letter, hands behind my back. But it had been too long since I'd last read our code, and translating it would take some time.

I did recognize one word, though.

"Prisca." Tibris plucked the letter from the table and glowered at me.

I jolted. My brother could occasionally move like a cat.

"Why is Vicer writing to you about Crawyth?"

Tibris's face went white with fury. "Stay the fuck out of my things."

Stung, I reared back. Tibris had *never* spoken to me that way.

"Children?" Mama called from her room.

I stared at my brother. "I'm coming, Mama."

Tibris shoved a hand through his hair. "I'm sorry."

"Forget about it."

"Pris—"

"It's okay." I had, after all, been invading his privacy. He could keep his secrets.

He grabbed my arm. "Are you free for training tomorrow after you finish at the bakery?"

I attempted a smile. Tibris had insisted on teaching me

what he'd learned as soon as he'd begun training himself. I'd spent more hours than I could count wrestling with his friends and learning to use the element of surprise.

"Sure."

The rest of the evening passed quietly. Both Tibris and Mama fell asleep earlier than usual, and I lay awake, continually picturing the king's assessor knocking on our door.

When I did finally sleep, my dreams were unsurprising.

The man had blazing green eyes and a full mouth that curved into a feral grin. He stared back at me with one eyebrow raised as if in challenge. Yet every time I reached for him, he drifted farther away. And when I could no longer see him, it felt as if my heart might break.

I woke with the sun, restless and…sad.

Hauling myself out of bed, I dressed, ate breakfast, and stared out the window, my eyes gritty and dry.

Tibris was already in the kitchen. He'd be out healing in a few hours unless someone came to him with an emergency.

My brother had passed his Testing two winters ago, and thanks to his ability to heal small wounds and sicknesses—along with my work at the bakery—we'd almost paid off our debt to our creditors. As soon as that happened, we could start saving for our future, and our family could leave this village. My chest ached at the thought.

He reached out and ruffled my hair. I gave him the

look that deserved, and he smiled.

I leaned down and pulled on my slippers–light, comfortable shoes I preferred to wear while cleaning.

"You're not wearing your winter boots?" Tibris asked.

"I'm only walking to and from the bakery. Look after Mama, okay? That vision really shook her."

He nodded. "She'll be fine, Prisca. We'll make sure of it."

A knock sounded on the door, and I jolted. Tibris and I glanced at each other. He pulled the door open, and my heart skipped several beats.

Thol grinned at me. The breeze ruffled his light-brown curls, and he looked so handsome I wanted to sigh.

"Hello, Prisca."

I managed to smile back. Inane, but coherent. I was getting better at this.

Thol's grin widened, and he glanced at my brother. "Hi, Tibris."

"Hey." Tibris liked Thol, but he still gave him a warning look. I elbowed him, and he rubbed at his stomach with a smirk, disappearing into Mama's room.

Stepping out of the house, I closed the door behind me.

Already, my cheeks were heating again.

Thol smiled at me as if he found me particularly cute.

It was mortifying, that's what it was. I wasn't some innocent, inexperienced young girl who'd never spoken to a man before. I'd had more than one lover over the years.

But something about Thol turned me into a stuttering fool.

He stepped closer and clasped my hand in his. His hand was large and warm and everything I'd imagined. "Prisca. Will you take a walk with me tomorrow morning?"

I smiled. After all the time I'd spent thinking about Thol, at least this part was easy. "Yes. I will."

"I'll be waiting for you in the square." With a final grin, he released my hand, tucked his hands in his pockets, and strolled away.

I watched him go, my body suddenly lighter than air.

But reality intruded, bringing me sharply back to the ground.

Thol's father was head councillor for our village.

He'd traveled to the city multiple times. And according to rumors, he'd even met the king.

The king who would happily burn me alive on Gods Day.

Thol was the kind of man who never walked past a beggar without dropping a coin. The kind of man who hunted—not just for his family, but for some of the poorest families in our village. The kind of man who never used his father's reputation to make his own life easier.

I could lose myself in fantasies about what it would be like to stay in this village and marry Thol. Both of us knew how to work hard. Together, we'd work until we could afford to live in one of those big houses. Then we'd have children and grow old together. A nice, *quiet* life.

Except, that life will never happen. Because staying in this village will mean you die. Painfully. And your family too.

My shoulders slumped. Mama was right.

There was no point in even spending time with Thol. It would just make it harder when I left.

The village was awakening as I walked toward Herica's bakery. Villagers brushed their stoops, gossiped with neighbors, called their children in for breakfast.

I attempted to push Thol out of my mind and contemplated Tibris instead. Poking my nose into his business was the perfect distraction. What was my brother keeping from me with his letters to Vicer? Why exactly had Vicer mentioned Crawyth?

The ruin lay directly inside our southern border—close to the fae lands. Just decades ago, it was known as a place of learning—where those from all kingdoms came to study, to live, to thrive.

Then the fae came. No one knew why they'd turned the city to rubble. I'd heard multiple theories, but the most popular was that the mad fae king wanted the city for himself. When our king chose not to comply, the fae king's vicious brother burned the city to ashes with his horrifying powers.

Halfway to the bakery, I began shivering. I'd left my cloak at home. I picked up the pace as the bakery came into view. The squat wooden building had been continually patched up over the years, but for me, it was a second home.

Herica would be gone already today after beginning her baking before dawn. I'd clean the floors and surfaces, while Thol's younger sister Chista sold the remainder of today's bread.

The bakery door was cracked, and I pushed it open. Kreilor stood with his back to me, but I'd recognize that thick neck anywhere.

Dull panic spread through my belly like mold. "What are you doing here?"

He glanced over his shoulder with a smug smile. Someone moved behind him, and I took a step closer, craning my neck. Chista. Kreilor's hand encircled her wrist, and her face was wet with tears.

Fury punched into me, and I swiped the broom from where I'd left it leaning against the wall.

"Chista, go," I said.

Kreilor just laughed. This was yet another way to strike out at Thol. But Kreilor was too much of a coward to challenge him directly. Instead, he was targeting Thol's sister.

It was all just a game to him.

He pinned me with a predatory stare, and I took a deep breath. "Think carefully, Kreilor. I'm not afraid of you."

His gaze dropped to my throat, where my thumping pulse betrayed me.

"Oh, Prisca. We *both* know that's not true."

Kreilor stepped closer, dragging Chista with him. I readied my broom, prepared to use it like a staff.

"Think about this," I told him. "Think about what you're doing here."

"You think I'm behaving abnormally? Thol has *everything*," he hissed.

My gaze met Chista's. She was a few years younger than me. We'd never talked much, but in that look, I caught wild hope. I was the one she was counting on.

Maybe I could make Kreilor focus on me. I let my voice drip disdain as I sneered at him. "That's what this is about? You're jealous of Thol?"

Kreilor's hand tightened around Chista's wrist, and she winced.

"Be careful how you speak to me, Prisca. I know about your creditors. I know just how much it cost to keep your father alive, and how you and your family barely have enough to live on after paying those creditors each month. What do you think will happen when I tell everyone I caught you attempting to steal from this bakery? When no one else will offer you work, and your family is begging in the village square?"

Something dark rippled through my entire body. I bared my teeth. "Let her go."

He laughed again.

And then he was swinging one meaty fist toward her face.

The world narrowed, until all I could see was his hand. His hand, and the terror in Chista's eyes as she attempted to duck.

Time stopped.

And I was already moving.

Darting between Kreilor and Chista, I pushed her

aside, using my forearm to sweep his hand away from her.

The world resumed once more.

And I prepared for Kreilor to begin screaming. To summon the guards. A dull hopelessness spread throughout my body—the inevitability of my own death.

Kreilor's face turned purple, and he stumbled. His surprise allowed Chista to pull her wrist from his hand.

I watched his eyes for any recognition, anything that would tell me he knew just what I'd done. But there was nothing. He'd been focused on Chista and hadn't seen me move. My limbs went weak, my legs unsteady. Was I... safe?

Movement flashed out of the corner of my eye. And my eyes met Chista's. She'd backed away and stood next to the open door, her eyes on me. Her face was white as death, and she turned, sprinting from the bakery.

My knees quaked, and my whole body went numb. Chista had seen exactly how I'd frozen Kreilor. How my power had tugged at the thread of time.

Kreilor moved closer to me, his lips pulled back from his teeth, face almost purple. He was a large man, and he stood between me and the door.

Another step closer.

If he got his hands on me, I was done.

Darting to the side, I struck him in the face with the broom handle.

He cursed, rearing back.

I dropped my hand, angling the broom up between his legs. Kreilor folded in two, his face draining of color as he clutched at himself.

Our eyes met. It was as if I was floating above my body, staring down at myself.

"If you go near Chista again, I will kill you."

Kreilor's eyes widened. "You crazy whore."

He finally managed to straighten, although his face had that green tinge once more. It wasn't an attractive look on him.

"You'll pay for this."

"You're right," I said, thinking of Chista and the terror in her eyes as she'd looked at *me*. "But not as much as you will if you don't leave me alone. Try me, Kreilor. I have nothing left to lose."

He cursed and stumbled out, still bent in two.

I sat directly on the ground. My hands shook, nausea slid through my body, and I suddenly couldn't breathe.

My last words hadn't been true at all.

I still had plenty left to lose.

I wiped my wet face with the heels of my hands. I didn't have time to sit here rocking and sobbing. I had to fix this.

Where would Chista go? My only hope was to find her. To beg for her silence.

Even just long enough for me to steal a stone from the priestess.

I choked on my next sob. It was far too late for that. It was only a matter of time before the village was locked down, the king's guards summoned, and my family slaughtered.

Then I'd be taken to the city to burn.

I made it to my knees. And then to my feet. My entire body was numb. But I stumbled out of the bakery.

My legs barely worked, and I had the odd sensation of my limbs turning to water. The world spun dizzily around me, until my vision narrowed and all I could see was the route to my house.

The few options I had battled within my mind. Find Chista, find the stone, warn my family.

Family first. I had to find them.

I ran faster, ignoring the stares and whispers from the villagers.

Someone caught my arm, and I spun, arm raised, hand in a fist.

Not a guard. And not the king's assessor.

My knees went so weak, I almost stumbled.

"Mama?"

Safe. She was safe. We still had time.

"Quiet, Prisca." Her face was ashen. "Come with me, and don't draw any more attention."

No one who had seen my mother recovering from a vision would recognize her now. She strode with fierce determination, walking purposefully, almost dragging me with her toward the forest bordering our village.

A strange metallic taste filled my mouth.

"You need to go find Tibris, Mama." We had plans we'd made over and over throughout the years. If the worst ever happened and we were separated, we would find one another again.

Mama had a particular plate she would leave out on the table. One we never used. If Tibris ever came home to find that plate out, he was to flee. But we hadn't discussed those plans since we were children.

"They're already looking for you. Tibris knows what to do."

Already looking.

I'd had nightmares about this day my entire life. And yet even in my nightmares, it hadn't happened this quickly.

"Where are we going?"

Mama ignored that, pulling me faster, until I had to trot to keep up. I winced as a bramble slid between my slipper and my foot. I'd left both my winter boots and cloak at home, never imagining I wouldn't return straight from the bakery.

I'd lived in fear my entire life. And yet I'd also somehow gotten complacent.

"They're coming," Mama said. "Faster, Prisca."

Thoughts raced through my mind as she led me deeper into the forest, urgency in her steps, panic written across her face.

Shouts sounded in the distance. I tugged on her hand. "Mama—"

"The king's guards," she said.

My breath caught in my throat as terror seized my entire body. "Already?"

She nodded, hands fluttering. Beneath the determination was sheer terror. Even her lips were white.

"Chista has been flirting with one of the guards these past months. She's already speaking to him now. I saw them and came straight to you."

"Are you sure Chista told him?"

"I watched her tell him yesterday."

She was talking about her vision. She'd seen this happen and hadn't warned me.

I had a bag packed for just this situation. A bag with warm clothes, food, weapons, even a few coins I'd tucked away over the years. If Mama had told me, I would have grabbed it. Without it…how long would I last?

The world spun around me, and my lungs seized. It took several tries before I could talk. "You're going the wrong way," I got out. We weren't far from the cliff overlooking the river. We had nowhere else to go from there.

By the time we stood on the cliff, I was shuddering with fear. "You need to go warn Tibris. I'll run."

My mother was shaking her head. "Tibris will be okay. I left him a note explaining—"

"A note? Mama, they'll come for him."

"He's smart. He knows what to do." She took a deep, shaky breath. "I thought when the time came, it would be easy to do what needed to be done."

Something about the way she said those words, about the way her face tightened in grim resolve…made the top of my spine itch.

"We don't have time to waste here, Mama. I need to get to the next village to buy supplies." Thoughts spun through my head, plans created and discarded within seconds. "Then the city. And I'll stowaway on a ship…" A ship south to the other human kingdom of Gromalia. Before I left Eprotha, I'd create a false trail, make sure the guards thought I was going elsewhere. Distract them from hunting my family.

Mama just shook her head. "Listen to me carefully. I had hoped we would have more time, but fate had other plans."

My heart thumped faster in my chest, and I watched as she turned to pace, too close to the edge of the cliff.

I couldn't think. Couldn't *breathe.* "We need to run."

"Wait. There are things you need to know." Her voice had turned eerily calm. Her face was blank, and the color had returned to her cheeks. It was as if we could have been discussing the weather.

Shouts sounded in the distance. It was too late. We'd taken the wrong path. It was only a matter of time before they cornered us both here. My mouth went dry, my entire skin itching as I practically danced on my feet, desperate to *move.*

"Mama, please. We have to…to hide."

Hiding would be no use. The king's guards were trained for exactly that. My chest clenched until my lungs felt like stone.

My mother took my face in her hands, forcing me to focus on her. "While you have always been the daughter of my heart, I did not birth you."

"What are you talking about?"

She gave me a trembling smile. "I didn't expect to love you as I do. I…I did what I could to protect you. I'm sorry I took you from your family. But I could never be sorry for saving your life."

The breath froze in my lungs. "You…you *kidnapped* me? When?"

"I knew you had to live, so you could save us all. But first, you must find the prince," she told me. "Find him and meet your fate."

I just shook my head. The prince had only seen nineteen winters. King Sabium—his father—wanted me and anyone like me dead. What could the young prince possibly do for me? How would he help?

"The prince," she insisted.

"We're wasting time."

"Promise me you'll find him."

My mother's mind was breaking. It happened often with seers.

"I promise." I grabbed her hand. I'd drag Mama with me if I had to. I would find a way to save us both.

My mother struggled, lashing out wildly. Despite her thin frame, I could barely hold her still. What would Tibris do when he arrived home from healing and learned we were both dead? When he became the only surviving member of our family? When he learned his life was forfeit?

"Please," I managed to choke out, as the shouting increased, the guards approaching. I gazed around wildly. We could head east if they hadn't blocked that route yet.

It was our only chance.

Immediately, more hollering sounded from that direction. We only had one choice left to us. I choked on guilt as it thickened in my throat. I should've known Mama's mind had given out. By not taking control of the situation, I'd doomed us both.

"We need to hide," I snapped.

But it was too late. Three of the king's guards had already found us. One of them stumbled over a tree root as he burst through the tree line, and any other time, I might've smirked.

The guards were panting, but there was no mistaking the grim satisfaction in their eyes.

"Submit to arrest," one of them ordered.

It was over.

My mother held out her arms. I nestled close. One last embrace before we were both slaughtered as a warning to those who would attempt to hide from the gods.

"Swim, my darling. Swim."

Mama stood back and shoved me with both hands. A scream ripped from my throat.

I felt nothing but air beneath my feet. Then I was engulfed in a cold so all-encompassing, my lungs stuttered out the scant breath I'd been holding.

I kicked out desperately, fighting against the current. My arms strained as I thrust them through the water. But the river carried me away. I lifted my head, choking, and pulled in one precious gulp of air, angling my body toward the bank.

Something hit my back, driving the air from my lungs. A rock. Water closed over my head. I kicked up, reaching for the surface. But something else held me down. Sharp pain radiated from my shin as my leg smashed into another rock. The urge to inhale was almost inescapable.

My dress was caught. Caught in the depths of the river. A *stupid* way to die.

Oh gods, oh gods, oh gods.

I tugged at it. Nothing. I would drown here.

My lungs screamed for air. Was drowning a better death than being burned alive?

My vision dimmed at the edges.

Fury burned through me. I couldn't die like this. I refused.

I bent at the waist and kicked out with my free leg, reaching for my dress with both hands.

I pulled.

Nothing.

My panic was turning dull, my body becoming sluggish, already losing the battle against the cold water. My fingers were stiff, numb, almost useless.

My lungs contracted.

I clawed at my dress. One final, desperate pull. Yanking upward with all my might, I smashed my elbow into another rock. And then I was spinning, floundering as the river carried me farther from the cliff. From my home. From my family.

I gulped one life-saving breath of air before I hit a

fallen tree branch, my body shoved beneath the water once again.

Each time I managed to lift my head, I caught glimpses of trees on either side of the river. A slice of blue sky. A blur of greenery. I was traveling so fast. Too fast to keep track of where I was.

Cold. It was so cold.

My movements became slower. Lethargic. I sucked in another breath, but it was mostly foam. Inhaling more water, I choked as I was pulled down once more.

Maybe it would be quick. Maybe I would just…fall asleep.

Something wrapped around my arm. I pushed against it weakly, but it only tightened.

And then everything went black.

3
PRISCA

Cool air, rushing into my lungs. A warm body above me. A mouth on mine.

My lungs burned. I choked. Large, strong hands eased me onto my side. A man. I coughed up what felt like half the river.

I opened my eyes. Above me, the sky was a vibrant blue. Somehow, I was alive. But my rescuer could be a guard who had saved me just so the king could watch me burn.

The man who'd saved my life had a rugged face with nut-brown skin and dark, slightly upturned eyes. His nose had been broken more than once, and his scowl told me clearly that he didn't want to play savior, and he resented me for putting him in that position. It was an impressive scowl.

Not a guard. That didn't mean I was safe. And yet…he'd saved me.

"Ah, thank you. Who are you?"

"My name is Galon." He touched my cheek, and my body was suddenly dry, my clothes crinkled from the river water but no longer soaked.

I jolted back, staring at him. To have that much power…

I turned at the clop-clop-clop of horses' hooves. Guards? I scrambled in an attempt to get up, and one of those boat-sized hands pushed down on my shoulder, easily holding me in place. A group of men broke through the forest. Dressed well, in fine leather boots and thick cloaks. Not guards but not necessarily safe either.

I counted five of them, including the man at my side.

My eyes grew heavy. I was dry now, but I was still freezing.

"You found a selkie," one of the men said. He grinned at me, his teeth incredibly white against his dark skin. For a man who might be planning to kill me, he had a ridiculously compelling smile.

Galon shook his head. "A village girl. Drowning in the river, Lorian."

Horses parted, and my mouth went dry as I took in the man Galon was speaking to.

This was the man who continually haunted my dreams. The one who'd snapped at me just yesterday in the village square.

My eyes drank him in. He was a huge man, with broad shoulders and muscles that rippled when he moved. Dark hair fell past his shoulders, a few small braids worked in to keep it off his face. His jaw looked like it could take a punch—and anyone unlucky enough to hit it would break their own bones.

He lifted his hand, shading his eyes. White stripes decorated his knuckles. Scars. He wore several knives and a sword. A mercenary, then. Likely a brutal one. The kind of man who would sell me to the guards the moment he learned they wanted me. Whether he was the type of man who would harm someone who presented no threat to him remained to be seen.

His features were masculine, as if carved from stone, although his high cheekbones gave him an almost feral beauty. He was sickeningly handsome, and I took a shaky breath.

Green eyes met mine, cool and indifferent. I was right. I knew those eyes. And I'd looked into them at the Gifting ceremony.

But how? *Why?*

We stared at each other for a long moment, and I waited for any glimmer of recognition. How was it possible that I'd *dreamed* about this man? Was it because he was destined to save my life?

But he was already glancing away. "Leave her, Galon. We don't have time for this."

My heart stumbled over its next beat. If they left me like this, I was dead. Not only would the guards be spreading out, searching the forest surrounding my village, but I had no clothes, no food…

"Please," I croaked.

The beautiful man ignored me, turning his horse. I was so inconsequential that his expression had already turned thoughtful, his mind clearly elsewhere.

I memorized that harshly beautiful face.

My temper burned bright when provoked. But I'd

never felt this ice-cold rage before. This *need* to see someone hurt the way I was hurting.

One day, some way, I'd make him pay. If I lived through this. I'd make him regret leaving me here.

Galon threw me his cloak. If he felt any guilt for leaving me, it wasn't visible on his face. "Good luck," he said. He turned and mounted his horse as I made it to my knees.

They rode away. And all I could do was watch them leave, my mind shutting down.

I wrapped the cloak around me, my eyes heavy once more. I had to get up. Had to keep moving.

My eyes drifted shut.

When I finally opened them again, the air had cooled further.

My body felt like one big bruise. I'd lost my thin slippers, and my feet were still bleeding from the many times they'd struck rock.

I hauled myself to my feet, biting back a whimper. The moon was bright, giving me enough visibility here next to the river. But beneath the cover of the forest, I was likely to get hopelessly lost. Panic unfurled in my chest. I couldn't stay here.

A howl ripped through the night, and I shivered beneath the cloak. I never should have allowed myself to sleep. It was a miracle that I'd woken. That I hadn't slipped off to a much more permanent sleep.

But I was alive.

And now I had a list of things to achieve.

Most importantly, I had to get away from here, before

the guards found me. The fact that they hadn't stumbled across my unconscious body was a miracle. Since I was sure the gods didn't habitually provide mortals with such miracles—and since they'd never taken the time to help *me* before—I needed to take advantage of my good luck.

Tibris would find me. He wouldn't care that it would put him in more danger. And as much as I wanted to shake him for it, I was swamped with relief at the thought of seeing him again. I couldn't think of Mama. Of the king's guards. Maybe…maybe they hadn't killed her. Maybe they'd taken her for questioning and Tibris would find a way to free her. We'd all get settled somewhere new.

I just had to get to the city. I'd find Vicer and arrange for notes to be sent to all of our planned meeting spots. While there, I'd research passage out of the city.

We'd find each other again. If there was one thing I knew, it was that my brother loved me.

Except, he wasn't truly my brother.

My breath caught in my throat, instant denial coursing through my body. No. Tibris would always be my brother, even if we weren't bound by blood. And he'd expect me to survive. He'd know my only hope was to go to the city, to try to board a ship leaving the continent. Before the king learned that I'd denied the gods what they were owed. Before I was burned as one of the corrupt. But if it became too dangerous, I would leave Tibris here if I had to. He was smart, and he'd be able to lay low. I would make sure he lived even if it meant I never saw him again.

I had a plan. I just had to start walking.

And one day, I'd find the man who'd ordered Galon to leave me for dead. I'd find him, and I'd make him pay.

LORIAN

"We could have helped that woman," Cavis muttered. I slid him a look. The usually affable man was wearing a dark scowl. Children, women, animals…Cavis had always been obsessed with saving the innocent. And witnessing the Gifting ceremony in the last village we'd visited had put him in a dark mood.

"We did," I said. "Galon saved her life."

"And how long do you think she'll continue to survive out here in the wild? It might've been kinder to let her drown."

I didn't bother pulling rank when we were traveling together. Those who were afraid to hear any criticism made for piss-poor leaders. Cavis's pouting made me wish I'd taken a different approach.

"When you rescue half-drowned wildcats, you have to be prepared for them to slash you to ribbons," I said. The last thing we needed was attention, and a woman who'd somehow ended up in the river would draw far too much of it. She was trouble. I'd known that the moment she'd stumbled into me in her village, almost drawing the assessor's scrutiny.

A few days spent escorting her back to her village could be the difference between finding what we were seeking and losing it forever. The interest we'd receive from those villagers—and any guards in the area—would also jeopardize our plans once they began asking questions. And realized we were not where we should be.

I surveyed my men. Galon rolled his eyes. Marth grinned, while Rythos just shook his head.

"Pretty wee thing," Marth said.

She *was* a pretty wee thing. While she'd been pale, her skin had enough color to tell me she enjoyed spending time in the sun. A wealth of curly white-blond hair had tumbled over her shoulders as she'd glared at me. Her eyes had burned into mine—a strange but not unattractive amber, more gold than brown. Her mouth was lush, with a pillowy bottom lip. That mouth had twisted, her sharp little chin jutting out when she'd realized we were leaving her.

Rythos snorted. "Sometimes it's a damned shame you're so cold, Lorian."

I rolled my eyes. If my brother could hear my men sounding like a group of kindhearted old women, he would mock me ruthlessly.

"Was I the only one who saw through her helpless act?"

Rythos gaped at me. Cavis frowned.

I just shook my head once more. The wildcat had been half drowned and clearly bewildered to find herself still alive. But she hadn't been helpless at all. I'd caught the way she'd sized us up. She likely hadn't even been aware she'd been doing it. But it had told me that she'd survive just fine on her own. Besides, we *didn't* have time to linger on this trip. Everything I'd worked so hard for was within reach, and I wouldn't risk it because some village girl had been stupid enough to fall in the river.

A village girl who'd been wearing nothing but a wet white dress, which had clung to her like a second skin. Running my hand over my jaw, I shook my head. Clearly, so many days of traveling were taking a toll.

If I'd had any second thoughts about leaving the village girl, those had been quashed the moment I'd seen the cold retribution in her strange amber eyes.

"Those with nothing left to lose make the most dangerous enemies of all," I said. I should know.

Rythos's eyes turned to slits. Clearly, he was on Cavis's side.

I glanced at my closest friend. "And do you agree with our softhearted friends, Galon?"

He merely frowned. "I liked that cloak."

My lips trembled as I suppressed a chuckle. One glance at Rythos's appalled expression and I ruthlessly firmed them. "We need to move faster if we're going to cross the bridge before sunset. I want a hot meal and a deep sleep," I said.

Rythos sniffed and faced forward, nudging his horse until he was no longer riding next to me. The man would sulk for days, and he was our best cook. Thanks to the village girl, whatever meat I ate next would either be charred black, raw in the middle, or both.

Heaving a sigh, I urged my own horse onward.

4

PRISCA

If I survived the next few days, I would look back with a kind of befuddled wonder. The odds of staying alive were so low, if I thought about those odds, I'd be stuck here for what little remained of my life, frozen in fear.

And so I trudged on, following the Dytur River east. I'd need to find a place to cross and continue to work my way farther southeast toward the city.

If I'd been prepared for this trip, I could have crossed the river near my own village. It would have added a few days to my trip, but I would've avoided most other travelers. But the cooler temperature and lack of food would be a death sentence. So I needed to get to Mistrun—one of the few settlements large enough to be called a town north of the river. There,

I could steal food, a weapon, maybe even some boots.

The last time I'd visited Mistrun, I'd been a child. My parents had both been alive. At least, the people who'd called themselves my parents. Guilt, fury, sorrow, all of it wound together until I pushed that thought away.

At the time, they'd been debating where we would move next, and Papa had thrown up his hands, declaring he would be happy wherever his family was.

Grief curled under my ribs and kicked out at the thought of my affable father. I missed him like a lost limb, and yet my entire childhood was a lie. I wrapped my arms around myself and rocked.

No. I would fall apart later. If I gave in to the yawning hole opening up inside me, I'd lie down here and never get up again. My ability to survive would depend on making smart decisions. One wrong move out here, and I was dead.

I had to get away from the river soon. The king's guards would expect me to stay close to it if I was still alive. Although, surely, after learning I'd fallen into that freezing river, they *wouldn't* expect me to have survived. The sun was slipping down behind the trees, taking the last of the late-afternoon warmth with it. Soon, I'd have to find somewhere to curl up and hide for the night.

What had happened to Mama after she'd pushed me off that cliff? The king's guards flashed into my mind, and I forced them out. Where was Tibris? My brother had always inspired loyalty, thanks to his insistence on healing anyone—regardless of their ability to pay. Maybe one of the people he'd helped had given him some food or directed him to shelter for the night.

Pain howled through my foot as I kicked a rock. I sucked in a breath and glowered down at it. My toe screamed at me.

"Well," a voice said. "Who do we have here?"

Dread coiled like a snake in my belly. I turned. Another reason to stay away from the river. It masked the sound of someone stalking me.

The man was tanned and clean-shaven. He stood several foot-spans taller than me, with broad shoulders and thick thighs. He carried a bow, his shirt straining over the kinds of muscles men attained when they spent their days hauling slaughtered deer back to their villages. He eyed me, and his hand drifted to the long knife on his hip.

A hunter. The fact that he was here meant I was closer to Mistrun than I could've hoped. It also meant that this man was well used to bringing down his prey and dragging it home for payment.

I was dead.

"I know who you are," he said softly. "News travels fast to Mistrun." His mouth twisted as he took me in, barefoot and shivering. "I'll make it fast, little lamb. You won't even know it happened."

Standing still, I let him approach. My shoulders

slumped, and a tear trickled down my cheek. Some of the tension left his face. He likely thought I'd be easier to slaughter than a deer.

I was weak, weary, and weaponless. Unless I came up with a plan in the next few moments, I'd be his easiest kill yet.

A dull fury took up residence in my chest. I'd survived that river, only to die *here?*

The world narrowed until all I could see was his face. The hunter took a step toward me, and beneath the pity, I caught the feral pleasure in his eyes. This man had been bred for hunting. Even if he promised me an easy death, he'd still enjoy it.

I wouldn't make it easy for him.

Something moved to my left. His horse stood just foot-spans away. I brushed my foot against a rock to my right. My eyes met the hunter's.

I'd learned a few things during my lessons with Tibris and his friends. The most important was that no matter how much I trained, if one of the men pinned me, I was finished. They simply weighed more than me. This hunter was much larger than Tibris and his friends. His muscles made theirs look almost feminine in comparison.

"There you go," the hunter soothed me. "It will all be over soon." A sick light entered his eyes. He was probably mentally spending the gold he'd receive for my death. He'd get more gold for bringing me to the king's guards alive, but I had a feeling this man wouldn't be able to restrain himself from killing me for that long.

Another step closer. The blade of his knife glinted in the last of the sunlight.

Now.

I crouched. My hand found the rock. It was rough, heavier than I'd imagined. The hunter bared his teeth at me and took another step.

I launched the rock in the direction of the horse, careful not to hit it.

Distantly, I was aware of the horse rearing, of the hunter's curse as he whirled. But I was already turning, desperately scanning the forest floor.

There.

The branch was too heavy. Long and unwieldy. A bad choice. But the hunter was still turned, torn between seeing to his horse, which was trotting away, and immediately killing me.

He pivoted back in my direction, and I swung the branch.

It hit him in the side of the face, enough to make him stumble.

Screaming, I hit him again. He fell to his knees, one hand coming up to protect his face, the other pulling his knife. Blood poured from his nose.

I hit him again.

He fell onto his back. My chest heaved. His eyes

rolled back in his head. Was he truly unconscious? I lifted my branch once more.

I hesitated.

Bile crawled up my throat. I couldn't do it. I wasn't a killer.

He groaned.

I let the branch come down.

Sobs shook my body as I hit him once more. Blood sprayed from his nose. I dropped next to him, and my hand found his knife.

It was him or me.

I buried it in his throat and pulled the blade free. Liquid hit my face, and I gagged and jumped away. Leaning over, I vomited bile. Tears streamed down my face.

Stumbling, shaking, I slipped down the bank to the river. My feet didn't hurt anymore. Nothing hurt. I barely felt the icy water as I splashed my face and washed the knife clean.

Feeling began to return as I climbed back up the bank to the hunter's body. I didn't have the time or the strength to bury him. The ground was half frozen, and I needed to move.

His face had already lost its color. Even in the dim light, it was obvious he was dead. And that he'd died a bad, bloody death.

My stomach roiled again, but I pushed it down.

Crouching next to his body, I found his coin purse and cut it free.

Apparently there were no depths I wouldn't sink to in order to stay breathing.

Rustling sounded, and I froze, tightening my hand around the knife.

Dark eyes met mine.

The horse.

"Uh, I'm sorry about the whole rock thing. It was all I could think of at the time."

If a horse could scowl, this one did.

I slowly got to my feet. "You and I? We could be a team."

I'd travel much, much faster with a horse. Approaching slowly, I made soothing sounds as I shuffled through the forest. It was getting so dark now that I could barely see.

"There's a pretty boy." I ducked my head. "Girl. Sorry. Either way, you're gorgeous."

The horse didn't exactly look like she trusted me, but she allowed me to stroke her. The knot in my gut began to unravel, even as my hands continued to shake.

I reached into the hunter's saddlebag, pulling out his food stores. Bread. The hunter had bread, an apple, and— wrapped in a soft cloth—a valeo.

My breath caught. The sweet fruit was rare, often almost impossible to find. Papa used to travel to other villages a few times a year when I was young. I'd loved it when Papa had gone southeast, because the villages near the coast were much more likely to have my precious valeo available.

Tibris had liked it best when Papa went north, where some of the best woodworking artisans lived. Papa would always bring back tiny wooden animals, and by the time he died, we'd each had a collection on the small tables next to our beds. I'd give almost anything to have one of them in my pocket right now. Just one small wooden piece to remember him by.

Lifting the fruit to my nose, I inhaled. Memories rushed at me. My father's smile, the way he'd pretend he hadn't been able to find any valeo and then pull one from his pocket. The time right before he'd died when I'd spent a precious few coppers on a valeo for *him*.

What would he think of me now?

The horse shuffled, and I pushed the memories away. I now had bread, fruit, water, and a horse. All it had taken was for me to murder a man.

Enough.

Grimly, I pulled the saddlebag completely off the horse. I'd eat just enough to get me through the night, and then I'd lead the horse on foot. I couldn't risk traveling far in the dark. If the horse broke a leg, I'd be back where I started.

"We'll get along just fine," I murmured. "I'll eat,

we'll walk far enough to find shelter" *—and away from the body behind me—* "and then we'll rest. Tomorrow will be better than today."

Something snapped behind me. I jolted.

The horse bucked to the right. Cursing, I reached for the reins, but it was too late.

The horse bolted. She had already been spooked, and I'd scared her further. Now she was frantic, galloping in the dark.

She wasn't coming back.

I sat on the forest floor and sniffled, tearing off chunks of bread and stuffing them into my mouth. The bread was stale, but in that moment, it was the best thing I'd ever tasted.

A dull fury took up residence in my gut.

I never asked for this.

I would have given the gods my magic a thousand times over.

They were the ones who'd rejected my offering when I was just days old, leaving me in possession of my power. I would never know the reason, but I'd now be hunted for the rest of my life solely because the gods had decided they didn't want my power.

The unfairness of it all took my breath away.

I fisted my hands and rose to my feet. I would stay alive simply to spite them.

I would live, and when I died, old and content in my

own bed, I would demand an explanation from those gods. And if they decided to make me burn in my afterlife, at least I would have sucked all the joy and sorrow and love from this life first.

Glancing up, I let out a shaky breath. Above my head, stars gleamed in the night sky. More than once today, I'd thought I'd never get to see them again. But here I was, suddenly in awe of the way they glittered.

I'd survived. It was all I could ask for.

Stalking back to the hunter's body, I rifled in the dark until my hands met cool wood. His bow. I was a terrible shot. Truly awful. But I took it anyway, along with his arrows.

My head felt as if it had been stuffed with Tibris's healing bandages. I was so tired I could no longer hold a thought for more than a few moments.

But I made myself move, counting my steps to keep myself awake. Word of the bounty on my head had already gotten to Mistrun. I couldn't risk stopping to steal more food or better clothes. But I could travel across the bridge. Now, when it was dark and cold, and there would be few people crossing. It was my best chance.

Finally, finally, the bridge came into view.

And so did the guard standing watch.

Despair rose, sharp and swift. I shoved it down. *Of course* they'd posted a guard on this bridge. Anyone planning to flee south would either have to attempt to cross the freezing river, traverse the Normathe Mountains, or take the bridge from Mistrun.

If only I'd washed up on the other side of the river.

You weren't going to wash up anywhere. You were half dead, remember?

Oh, I remembered. And I remembered the distant, bored look in those dark green eyes when the mercenary told Galon to leave me for dead.

If nothing else, my fury would keep me warm over the coming days.

PRISCA

The guard didn't look very old. He paced back and forth in an obvious attempt to keep himself alert. I studied his movements. The fact that the guard was young wasn't good for me. Young meant strong.

If I'd practiced more with a crossbow, I could've killed him from here. I sighed. I'd been on the run for mere hours, and already, I was contemplating murder as easily as contemplating breaking my fast in the morning. I should probably be concerned about that.

Unfortunately, my odds of hitting the guard from this far away—in the dark—were about as high as Asinia winning a game of King's Web.

My heart ached at the thought of my best friend. Did she think I was dead? Did she hate me now for being... corrupt?

Later. I'd think about that later.

The guard had a sword on his hip, and he moved like he knew what he was doing. But he was alert enough that he was clearly new to this kind of posting. And new guards were more likely to be paying attention.

But *this* guard had likely been recruited by force from one of the poorer villages and sent to the city for basic training before being deployed. With any hope, he'd see a poor, defenseless young woman and picture his sister. I surveyed the bridge. The railing was just above the guard's hips.

Okay.

I shoved the hunter's knife into the saddlebag. The crossbow wasn't a problem—I looked like any desperate woman who'd gone hunting and gotten lost.

Taking a moment to think about all the ways life had recently wronged me, I allowed my eyes to fill. It didn't take much to give in to the sorrow that wanted to drag me down.

I choked out a sob. "Excuse me?"

The guard jolted, blushed, and frowned in quick succession. His hand slid to his sword, and I held up my hands, another sob leaving my throat.

"Are you okay?" he asked.

That told me all I needed to know. Just a few years of service would have toughened the guard until his first words would have been *Who are you?* A few more years, and he would have immediately ordered me to lie down on the ground before stripping me of my weapons.

"N-no."

I'd always looked pitiful when I cried. It was one of the reasons I hated it so much. I let my lower lip tremble, and the guard took his hand off the hilt of his sword.

"I was in the f-forest, looking for food for my f-family," I sniffled, stepping closer. "I got lost. And then…"

"It's okay." The guard took in my torn clothes and the blood on them, and I saw the moment he came to the logical conclusion.

"There's a healer in this town." The guard leaned against the bridge railing and nodded toward Mistrun. Even as young as he was, he didn't offer to take me there himself. Instead, he reached for the pouch hanging from his belt, pulling out a green trowth stone.

Fuck.

He would use that stone to contact his commander, who would immediately order my arrest.

My hand itched for the knife in my saddlebag.

And the hunter's shocked, accusing face flickered through my mind.

Real tears spilled from my eyes. I didn't *want* to hurt this young guard.

"Please don't," I said, nodding to the trowth stone. "I…I'd prefer privacy."

He frowned, but his hand drifted away from the stone.

"I would escort you to the healer myself, but I can't leave my posting."

"I think I would prefer to find a healer in the next village." I nodded to the other side of the river, still inching closer to the guard.

He frowned, clearly wondering why I would continue walking in my condition.

He looked at me again. Realization flickered through his eyes, and his hand landed on his sword.

But I was already launching myself at him.

If he'd been a woman, it wouldn't have worked. We had a lower balance point. And if the guard had been standing a single step farther from the railing, he would have used that sword to run me through.

But I dropped into an almost-squat and pushed up and forward.

He let out a cry as he fell.

Splash.

Regret instantly froze my every muscle.

No. I'd survived. He would too.

You survived because one of those brutes fished you

out of the river.

No. The guard was bigger than me. More body weight meant it would take him longer to freeze.

I didn't have time to make myself feel better about his odds of survival. The noise he'd made had cut through the night, over the rushing water below, and anyone within hearing distance would likely come to investigate.

Turning, I thundered down the bridge toward the forest on the other side. When I didn't hear an immediate shout, I sucked in a deep breath but continued running anyway, at least until the canopy above my head blocked out the stars.

It was dark, I was so exhausted I was stumbling, and I needed to find somewhere to hide. But the guard's disappearance would be noted. If he survived, that little green stone could lead to my death.

So I kept walking. I knew when I strayed from the path, because the undergrowth would scratch and tear at my ankles. Time lost all meaning, until I fell to my knees.

"Just a little more," I mumbled. Pushing myself up, I scanned my surroundings. It was so dark, all I could do was step off the trail and crawl through the undergrowth until I found a spot to lean against a tree trunk. Wrapping my cloak around me, I waited for dawn.

5
PRISCA

As soon as the sky lightened the next morning, I was on my feet once more.

If you're ever lost, look for higher ground. From there, you can more easily navigate. And you'll have a better chance of finding water. Tibris's voice sounded in my head, calm and sure.

Where was he right now? Had he spent a terrifying night out in the cold? Was he hiding in someone's barn or loft?

I refused to think about the other option. That he was already dead. Instead, I scanned my surroundings. No mountains to be found, but to the right was a small hill. I trudged up it, attempting to stay as quiet as possible. My efforts were useless, though, as I stumbled over branches, slammed into a tree, and grunted when my bleeding foot hit a rock. I paused with each misstep, flinching at every noise, my gaze darting around me as I strained my ears for the smallest sound.

I surveyed the area below me. To

the north was the river I'd crossed last night. My heart rate quickened at the memory of just how close I'd come to death.

Turning to face the opposite direction, I looked south. Another river—much narrower than the Dytur River. I would need to cross it.

My palms began to sweat at the thought of more freezing water. I took a deep breath and forced myself to focus. If I'd stayed on the road that led from the bridge, I would have followed it southwest, eventually finding my way to the kingdom's capital—Lesdryn. There were larger towns dotted along that road. Towns where I would have a greater chance of blending in until I could steal a horse and get to the city. But I was a mess. My feet were bleeding, I was limping, and my condition would only draw attention.

So, I'd keep to the forest until I was closer to Lesdryn. It was the only real choice I had. Hopefully by the time I was forced to use the road, I would have come up with a plan to keep myself safe.

I could do this.

After all, against all odds, I was still alive. I just had to keep reminding myself of that.

The river was only about knee-deep, but it was flowing fast.

My chest tightened, and I gulped in several shallow breaths as I stared down at my planned path.

One misstep and I would be in that freezing water. It may only be knee-high, but I could slip, hit my head, drown just the same.

Move.

I choked out a sob, loathing that I was even hesitating. I could do this. I *had* to do this, or I may as well turn back right now.

I strode into the frigid water, moving as quickly as I could without slipping. By the time I made it to the other side, my feet stung with fresh cuts from the sharp rocks.

Planting my hands on my knees, I leaned over until I stopped shaking. When I lifted my head, my surroundings seemed to rotate around me.

I walked all day. By the time the sun was setting, my stomach howled, but I was almost out of my scant food and would need to save what little I had left for tomorrow.

Red flickered in the distance. Flames?

I went still. I couldn't feel the warmth, of course. But for a moment, I imagined I could. Imagined I was lying in front of that fire, drowsy after a filling meal.

The king's guards probably wouldn't light a fire. Herica had once told me they usually traveled with an umber stone—a large black stone that could be charged with magic and would release heat.

Where there were flames, there was likely food. My stomach grumbled as if in agreement, and I kept my gaze on the orange-red glow through the trees.

Creeping closer, I peered around the tree and into the clearing.

I sucked in a sharp breath. I recognized that group of men, stretched out by their campfire without a care in the world. Grinding my teeth, I counted four of them. One of the brutes was hiding somewhere, likely on sentry duty.

Fury swept through me, along with a healthy dose of outrage. After everything I'd been through since Galon had pulled me out of the river, seeing them sleeping by the warmth of a fire, likely with full bellies and dry clothes…

It was a twist of the knife.

Galon was lying closest to me. Across the clearing, the leader—*Lorian,* they'd called him—was stretched out, eyes closed. Behind him, their horses rested near several packs of supplies.

Likely, some of those supplies included food. My skin prickled with anticipation.

Where, exactly, was the sentry?

Lorian rolled over and glanced to his left. My mouth stretched in my first smile since I'd fled my village. The tyrant was unable to simply let his man do his job. He had to breathe down his neck.

And he'd just given his sentry's spot away.

Fool.

I'd take their food and leave them with almost nothing. The way they'd left me.

Painstakingly slowly, I began to move to Lorian's right. I had more visibility here, but I couldn't afford to rush and snap a branch.

One of the men coughed. I used the sound to cover a few quick steps.

It felt as if it took hours. I knew my strengths, and skulking through the woods was not one of them. But

I refused to allow my impatience to lose me that horse. Those supplies. All the food.

Finally, *finally,* I was just a few foot-spans from the horses. I slowly sucked some air into my lungs, and with a final glance at the resting men, I prepared to—

I froze. Lorian was gone.

His voice sounded behind me. "Did you really think we didn't know you were here, village girl?"

Ducking down, I whirled, avoiding his attempt to grab me. Surprise flashed across his face, and he charged me.

I tripped him, my own leg tangling with his. He cursed and we fell, rolling toward the fire.

By the time we came to a stop, my blade was at his throat and my heart was beating so hard, it felt as if my ribs would snap. He'd pinned me with his huge body, but all it would take was a flick of my wrist and he would be dead.

He stared down at me, those forest-green eyes lit with amusement.

A trap. The bastard had looked at the sentry to lure me close and ensure I went in the opposite direction. So he could track me. He'd likely known I was here before I'd even seen his fire.

Dismay swept through me. I had to do better. Had to learn fast if I was going to make it to the city and get on a ship.

"Did you really think we'd let you take one of our horses? What did we do to deserve your theft?"

Fury punched through me. "You left me for dead," I hissed.

"You survived."

"No thanks to you!"

He heaved a sigh. As if *I* were inconveniencing *him*.

I imagined my blade splitting him open. Visualized the spray of blood. I wasn't usually bloodthirsty, but this man brought it out on me.

His expression had turned bored. I'd been through hell over the past few days, and this man could have lightened my load. Instead, he looked moments away from yawning.

Fine. We'd see how he liked it when *I* left him for dead.

A sharp blade was suddenly nestled against my skin, right next to the spot where my pulse thundered. I wedged my own knife closer to Lorian's throat.

"Put it down," an amused voice said.

My skin turned clammy, a heavy weight pressing on my chest.

I stared into Lorian's green eyes, and I made a silent vow to myself. If I lived through the next few minutes, and the gods ever decided to make our paths cross once more, I would ensure this man regretted leaving me to die.

His gaze sharpened as if he were reading my mind. A huge, callused hand clamped around my wrist, until I was forced to drop the knife.

Lorian rolled off me, but not enough for me to *go* anywhere. Who knew what they'd do with me now? They could rape me, kill me, turn me in to the king's guards. The things these men could do to me would make that hunter's quick death seem like a gift.

My desperation may have just cost me my life.

Lorian's friend dragged me to my feet, reaching for my hands. The rough texture of the rope he carried scraped against my wrists.

My skin heated, and a sharp, insistent shriek filled my mind until there was only one outlet for it.

Stop.

Time froze.

Sweeping up my knife, I turned and sprinted toward their horses.

I had moments. If I was lucky.

I untied the closest horse.

And my body hit the ground.

"What did you do?" No amusement filled that silken voice now. I was once again helpless. I went still, frustration coursing through me. I was so fucking tired of this day.

"Let go!"

"Use your magic on me again, and you will regret it."

"My magic?"

"Do *not* feign stupidity."

He flipped me over, and I panted, desperate for breath. His gaze dropped to my heaving chest and then flicked back up to my face.

Lying was stupid since the mercenaries had seen what

I could do. In this case, the truth was my best defense. "I don't. Not like you mean. I can just do this one thing. And only sometimes. And not for long."

I was rambling now, desperate to make him understand. I never should have come here. Should have known better than to think I could steal one of their horses. I was tired enough and hungry enough that I'd allowed my desperation to overrule my logic. Now, they'd hand me over to any guards who came for me, and then they'd enjoy the king's reward.

Lorian studied the empty spot on my temple, where the blue circle would have been if I'd reached twenty-five winters. His expression was inscrutable, and yet I could practically feel his mind racing as he attempted to understand exactly who I was.

My own gaze slid to the blue mark on *his* temple, resentment sliding through my veins. But the brute was already speaking once more.

"How did you end up in that river? Lie," he purred before I could speak, "and I'll throw you back in. But not before ordering Galon to tie rocks to your feet."

Fear punched into my gut, and for a long, endless moment, I couldn't breathe. The thought of that water rushing at me, into my mouth, flooding my lungs…

Lorian was still studying me. He knew just how well his little threat had worked. I attempted to wiggle away from him, but all I was doing was moving my hips closer to his.

"Speak," he growled.

"My mother...she pushed me into the river. Because the guards learned I was one of the corrupt. They were coming for me."

My lower lip trembled, and I ruthlessly clamped down on it with my teeth. I'd been attempting to deny it since the moment Mama had pushed me, but it was time to face the truth.

My mother was dead.

The guards would have killed her instantly. Perhaps brutally since they'd watched her defy the king and help me escape.

My eyes burned, but I refused to mourn my mother here with Lorian staring down at me.

This close, I could see all the different shades of green in his eyes. This was the man I'd dreamed of over and over again, and I still didn't know why. A small part of me had hoped...

I killed that thought. The reality of the man was nothing but disappointment.

"I suppose your plan is to get to the city."

"Yes." I definitely wouldn't be telling him about my plan to get to a ship. The less he knew about my life, the better.

"Can you use your magic whenever you please, or must you be in peril?"

This man was obviously trying to keep me shaken with the unexpected way he asked his questions.

"I've only used it a few times in my life."

Galon took a step closer and shook his head. "Tell

me you're not thinking what I think you're thinking."

I blinked at that. Lorian tightened his hands around me. Then he was getting to his feet, hoisting me up with him like I was a sack of grain. He planted me on the ground.

The casual demonstration of his strength was scary. Likely, that was his intention.

"I have an offer for you." Lorian's expression had turned contemplative. Any offer from him was unlikely to bode well for me. And while I'd made some desperate— albeit necessary—choices so far, getting involved with a group of mercenaries would be the worst choice of them all.

Since it didn't seem as if these men were going to kill me, I took a big step back.

"I don't want anything you're offering. Remember that time you left me to freeze to death?"

He sighed. "Are you always this dramatic?"

One of his men snorted, and I trembled with the need to punch Lorian in the mouth. He merely raised his eyebrow at me, as if reading my mind.

"Yes. Yes, I am. A great reason for you to let me go."

"I don't think so. You haven't listened to my offer yet."

I clenched my teeth. Maybe the smarter move was to listen. To study their weaknesses. "Fine. Talk."

"We are also going to the city."

It was my turn to snort. Of course they were. The mercenaries were either returning to a client, their job done, or heading to the city in search of work. The kind of work that would involve someone ending up with a much lighter purse—or worse…dead.

"And?"

"And," he ground out, "we could use someone like you to help us arrive…undetected."

Ah. Someone with magic like mine would be *very* helpful to mercenaries who needed to sneak into a city. "What exactly is it that you're offering?"

"Three meals a day, a horse, blankets, and whatever clothes we can find to fit you. In exchange, you'll help us at the city gates."

"Wait. You want me to use my magic on purpose? In front of the king's guards? Are you mad?"

My future flashed before my eyes. It featured flames, a jeering crowd, and my own agonized screams as I burned.

One dark brow lifted. "If you use your magic properly, no one will know we were there."

"I don't *know* how to use it!"

"I will teach you."

"You…can do that?"

What if I could learn to wield my power? I could use it to keep myself safe. With my gift, I'd have a much greater chance of staying alive.

Oh, he was *good.*

I snarled, pushing him away from me. "A pack of mercenaries who can't be seen in the city? I get caught with you, and I'm *worse* than dead." Their enemies wouldn't just include the king's guards. I'd wager plenty of rival groups would be pleased at a chance to take out the competition.

His eyes met mine. They were surprisingly clear. "Have you ever seen anyone burned at the stake?"

I swallowed. "No."

"You don't want to. And you certainly don't want that death. If we get caught, I'll give you a fast death myself."

What a charming offer. "I don't need you." My voice was high-pitched. Desperate.

I didn't *want* to need him. That certainly wasn't the same thing.

Lorian waved a hand, his expression bored. "You just tried to steal my horse. That impulsivity? It tells me you know nothing of surviving outside of your village. The very fact that you managed to last this long is a miracle."

I hated that he was right.

I'd made it this far on stubbornness, rage, and blind luck. But traveling with the mercenaries meant food, warmth, and learning about my powers.

He was still studying me. I had a feeling those eyes of his could see far too much. "You wouldn't have killed me." He caught my chin between his finger and thumb. "You don't have it in you to kill a man when he's looking you in the eye."

My mind flashed me back to the hunter's last gurgling sound, and I took a deep, shuddering breath.

No. Focus.

"I made it this far. Alone."

"Congratulations, you lived. But we both know you'll never make it to the city by yourself."

Gods, I loathed this man. I yanked my head. His fingers tightened on my chin.

As much as I wished I could deliberate, it wasn't like I had many choices. I either died out here alone, I got caught by the guards who were trailing me, or I took my chances with these men.

He wanted a deal? I'd let these mercenaries teach me everything they knew about magic, and then I'd use that magic to abandon them close to the border. The way they'd abandoned me.

Sometimes, you had to take your revenge where you could find it.

"Okay," I said finally.

He released my chin and took several steps away from me. "We need to eat and then get a few hours of sleep. We'll be up before dawn."

As soon as Lorian stepped away from me, his friends seemed to relax. Galon still looked displeased, but I picked up his cloak from where I'd dropped it, wrapping it around me. Narrowing my eyes, I gave him my best hard stare.

The cloak was mine now.

The corner of Galon's mouth twitched, but he said nothing, merely wandering away to collect wood. From the surprised look one of the younger men shot him, that wasn't his usual task.

I needed to watch this group carefully. Needed to figure out their strengths and weaknesses so I could exploit the latter.

"Come, have something to eat," one of the men said. I'd nicknamed him Smiley in my head, and he flashed it once again as he gestured for me to sit next to him.

I wandered over to him, taking a seat a few footspans farther from the spot he'd indicated. He merely held out a dish for me, already laden with some kind of meat. My stomach growled in response.

I took it, and he passed me a bladder of water. "You can keep that," he said.

"Thank you."

"My name is Rythos."

"Prisca."

We ate in silence. I inched closer to the fire, still feeling cold deep in my bones. Most of the other men went back to sleep, but Rythos said he was going to be on sentry duty soon so was happy to cook for me.

Maybe it was his way of making me lower my guard around him. That wouldn't happen, but I'd happily eat his food.

Lorian prowled restlessly around the camp, checking the horses, throwing an extra bedroll on the ground, and sending me the occasional narrowed-eyed look. I restrained myself from making any comments designed to alienate him even more than I had. It was clear that he was the leader here, and his little band of mercenaries didn't do anything without checking in with him first.

I wolfed down the meat, gulped half the skin of water, and gathered my courage. My next task wouldn't be enjoyable.

Leaning over, I examined my filthy feet. A few of the cuts still oozed blood, one of them dark with grit. Risking infection would be the height of stupidity. I poured water over one foot until it was clean enough to bandage. Since I could feel eyes on me, I heroically didn't wince at the sting. Examining my filthy dress, I attempted to find the cleanest part to tear from.

"Here," Rythos said, holding out a handful of clean strips of linen. Mercenaries would have to travel with medical supplies. From what I'd heard from the men in my village, they were always fighting and killing and doing various other morally bankrupt tasks for coin.

"Thank you."

"We have salve too."

I raised my eyebrow as he handed it over. I could scent the brackweed, which had been ground into a paste and mixed into the salve. It would prevent infection. So far, Rythos seemed the kindest of all the men. Although, like all of them, he'd simply watched as Lorian had threatened to have me drowned. I wouldn't forget that.

"Do you need help?" a rough voice asked.

I glanced over my shoulder. Lorian was watching me. A strange awareness prickled my skin as our eyes met.

I shook my head. "My brother is a healer."

Surprise flickered across his face, immediately replaced by his usual inscrutable expression. "He heals small cuts and scrapes, and helps with the occasional mild sickness?"

"Yes."

He shook his head and stalked away. I glanced at Rythos, who just shrugged, watching as I tended to my feet.

I didn't know what Lorian had against healers, but I'd seen my brother burn himself out time and time again, attempting to heal vicious wounds and chronic sickness. When our father got sick, Tibris lay next to him for weeks, channeling everything he had into him until he'd been little more than skin and bones himself, too weak to summon his own power.

I'd nearly lost them both.

Now, Tibris was either in incredible danger or…

No. My brother was a survivor. He had people in place for just this scenario.

I studied the men as I finished slathering salve on my feet. Other than Galon, none of them had displayed any hint of their own power. I wasn't sure exactly what Galon's gift was, but he hadn't used it again since I'd stumbled across their camp.

Since they knew what I could do, I needed to find out what kind of threat each of them presented.

As soon as my feet were bandaged, I took the blanket Rythos offered me and lay down on my bedroll, curling into a ball as close to the fire as I could get without getting singed. I was still freezing, but my belly was full, my wounds were bandaged, and my eyes burned with exhaustion.

I'd planned to stay awake, because these men couldn't be trusted. I felt movement to my right and managed to crack my eyes open, only to find Lorian's gaze on me.

Something about the assessing look in his eyes made a chill slide over my skin. He looked at me with predatory focus—as if I was a new, unexpected pawn and he was deciding which move he would play.

I shivered and closed my eyes.

6
PRISCA

shook my head at Lorian. He gestured toward his mount once more, his lips thinning when I didn't immediately move.

I ignored his imperious gesture. "You didn't tell me we'd be sharing a horse."

Lorian crossed his arms. "Did you see any spare horses with us, sweetheart?"

I sucked in a breath, squinting into the early morning light. "Don't call me that." Planting my hands on my hips, I attempted to look threatening. "I can share with one of the other men."

Maybe Rythos. He'd been nice so far. And unlike with Lorian, my hand didn't itch to wrap itself around his throat every time he spoke.

Lorian leaned closer, his eyes narrowed. "My horse is the largest and the most suitable for carrying two people, even if one of them is as scrawny as you."

"We can't all be oversized brutes."

He flashed his teeth at me. "Get in the saddle before I put you there myself."

I sniffed and swung my leg over the horse's rump, almost kicking Lorian in the face. Unfortunately, he stepped out of my foot's path.

Next time, I'd swing wider.

His huge body landed in the saddle behind mine. I should've told him to mount first. I'd much rather be the one holding on to him than have his huge arms caging me in.

Lorian didn't give me the option. His arms came around my waist and gripped the reins. His body was so big, I was instantly surrounded by him. His masculine scent wound up my nostrils, and I forced myself to breathe through my mouth, ignoring the way he leaned close as he stroked his horse.

The man was oversized, with biceps larger than my thighs. From what I'd seen so far, he wasn't exactly a lumbering oaf either. No, he moved panther-silent and far quicker than a man of his bulk should have been able to.

That made him exceptionally dangerous.

For now, at least, it meant he was a lethal threat to anyone who would stop me from fulfilling my end of our bargain. Somehow, he'd become the man most likely to keep me alive—at least for the next few days. How ironic.

With a nudge of Lorian's heels, we were immediately moving back down the narrow forest path.

This part of the forest was dark and overgrown, with the vines intertwining and fighting for space. The tree limbs were like gnarled hands—broken fingers grasping at the denser foliage.

It was dead quiet except for the occasional creak of a branch or the snap of a twig. As if the forest was holding its breath, waiting.

"You need to relax," Lorian told me. "You're annoying my horse."

I blew out a breath, the tightness in my chest letting me know I'd held it for too long. "We need to travel faster," I muttered.

"The king's guards don't know about this route. Yes, we need to move quickly, but we don't need to panic. The faster we travel, the more often we need to rest the horses."

I knew that. But I also knew that if we were caught, *I* was dead. These men? They had *survivor* written all over them. Anyone taking one look at them would know they were made to get out of the worst kinds of situations. And I'd be an idiot to imagine they wouldn't sacrifice me if it gave them even a few minutes of extra time to run.

Me? It was a miracle I was alive. If not a miracle, then a string of luck. But neither miracles nor luck could be counted on. And neither could the mercenaries, who were somehow convinced I could help them achieve their own goals. *I* was the only one who was going to ensure I kept breathing.

Eventually, my muscles began to ache from holding myself so stiffly. I rolled my shoulders and forced myself to relax as much as I could.

At least I had clothes now. The men had come up with shirts, a pair of breeches that I'd rolled up until they no longer dragged on the ground—even some massive boots that I could barely walk in. Thankfully, Rythos had given me a few pairs of socks to push into the bottom of the boots so I wouldn't fall on my face.

I was in a better position than I'd been yesterday—despite the oversized annoyance on the horse behind me. I could at least be thankful for that much.

Once the path had widened enough, one of the men pulled his horse up next to ours. He was younger than most of the others, likely around Rythos's age. His hair was slightly longer than Rythos's and carelessly pushed back, displaying a broad forehead. He rode like he'd been born on a horse, and his dreamy brown eyes made me wonder exactly what he was thinking.

He gave me a surprisingly sweet smile. "I'm Cavis."

"Prisca. Where are you from?" I asked, suddenly curious. He had the slightest accent.

I was watching him carefully, so I caught the flicker of his eyes toward Lorian.

"If you're going to lie to me, don't bother," I muttered.

"Prickly woman," Lorian murmured in my ear.

I shrugged, craving my own space.

He obviously caught on, because he leaned even closer into my personal space. "Cavis's wife just gave birth to their first child."

Cavis beamed, and if a man could burn with pride, he would have lit the forest around us on fire. "A daughter."

I couldn't help but smile too. "Congratulations. Do

you mind if I ask what kind of magic you have?" Subtle. But I may as well ask now, while the man was answering *some* of my questions.

Lorian tensed behind me, but he didn't stop Cavis from answering.

Some of the brightness left Cavis's smile. "I'm good at languages."

"Good at languages?"

Marth laughed behind us. "He means he can understand every language spoken in this kingdom—and every other."

"Now that sounds like a helpful skill for a mercenary."

Cavis's eyes widened slightly, and he glanced past me to Lorian. Whatever he saw on the brute's face had him nodding and falling back.

Marth took his place. "And what can you do?" I asked him. He gave me a slow smile.

"I get glimpses of a person's past."

Curiosity prickled at the base of my neck and I opened my mouth, but Lorian had already gone still behind me.

"Enough," he rumbled.

More secrets. I gave up, turning my attention to my own thoughts.

Unfortunately, those thoughts consisted of imagining Mama's last moments and picturing Tibris in all kinds of terrible situations, my mind asking questions I couldn't answer, over and over again.

We stopped before sunset. Lorian swung his leg over the horse, offering me his hand. I was so stiff, I took it, and he slid his other hand around my waist, helping me dismount. I'd expected to feel repulsed at his touch, but his huge hands were oddly comforting.

The bank to our left was high and steep. It would give the horses some protection from predators, while the tall oaks would shelter them from the elements. To our right, the river beckoned. We'd be able to bathe, although I knew just how cold that water was.

"Why have we stopped?" We could likely have traveled for a few more hours. My skin itched with the need to put more distance between us and the guards.

The other men began setting up camp, Rythos and Marth disappearing into the forest—likely to find wood and hunt for dinner.

Lorian eyed me. "This is a good clearing for us to rest. Besides, you need to practice with your power."

I flinched, my gaze swinging around the forest behind us, as if someone would hear the word and arrest me for treason.

Lorian waited until I'd glanced back at his face. "Sit for a few minutes while I see to the horses, and then we'll get started."

I nodded, watching as Rythos returned, carrying a pile of wood. "Can I help?"

Rythos slid me his easy grin. "Nope."

I watched as he strode to his horse, bringing the tiny lantern he carried everywhere back with him, along with a small bucket. Both hung off the side of his saddle.

"Why do you carry that with you? And more

importantly, why does the fire in the lantern never go out?"

"It's fae fire," he murmured. I stared at him, and he shrugged, as if carrying around something the fae used was a normal occurrence. "People from Gromalia use fae gifts every day without being labeled sympathizers."

What must that be like? Such a thing was unimaginable in Eprotha.

I couldn't help but sidle closer to Rythos, intrigued despite my efforts to ignore the flames.

"What does fae fire do?"

He smiled. "Once it catches, it never goes out."

"Sounds dangerous." It also sounded incredibly helpful.

"It is. It's also one of the best ways to ensure you can always light a fire when you're traveling. Some people even use it in the city—right beneath King Sabium's nose."

Those people were literally risking life and limb to do such a thing. I couldn't understand it.

"If it never goes out, how do you douse it each morning?"

"A plant called damask weed, dried and ground into a fine powder." Rythos picked up a tiny bag. "Just a pinch mixed into a bucket of water, and it's extinguished."

Dangerous, indeed. And a good way to accidentally burn a village or town to the ground.

"How do you know if it's fae fire and not normal fire?"

He smiled and lifted the lamp. In it, the flame burned like any other. But as I peered at it longer, the center of the flame appeared almost...purple.

"That color is impossible to fake," Rythos said.

In my village, we'd been taught that anything to do with the fae was...sinful. After all, the gods had helped us humans in our war against them.

"Let's go." Lorian jerked his head, and I got to my feet, my stomach roiling with nerves. Rythos sent me a sympathetic look, and I chewed on my lower lip as I followed Lorian toward the river.

He stopped a few feet from the water and surveyed me, his green eyes so dark they appeared almost black. "Tell me about the last time you used your power. What went wrong?"

I licked suddenly dry lips, considering how much to tell him. "I worked in a bakery in my village. A man named Kreilor had a...feud with another villager, and he was threatening the villager's sister. He was...hurting her."

The backs of my eyes burned. Now, my mother was dead, and if Tibris was still alive, he was in just as much danger as I was. I'd made the situation so much worse.

"Focus," Lorian demanded. "We don't have time for your self-pity."

Gods, I'd never known such a cold, vicious bastard. My tears dried up, replaced by fury.

Lorian just nodded. "Good. How large of an area did you freeze?"

"Freeze?"

He gave me a look that told me he was attempting patience, but my stupidity was making it difficult. I wondered what his nose would look like if I broke it.

Lorian smiled slowly, as if reading my mind. He gestured for me to sit on a large rock and stood in front of me.

"You may be ignorant about your power, but by now, you know you can stop time. An incredibly rare gift that would be in great demand if you were captured."

I frowned at that. "I can…stop time for a few seconds at the most."

"For now. Tell me more about what led you here."

"Chista saw me. She was the one I was trying to help. She ran to one of the guards. I'd always been good to her," I muttered. "My brother taught her to defend herself."

"Never underestimate what people will do when it comes to coin. Expecting others to uphold your moral standards will leave you disappointed every time."

Life lessons from the mercenary.

"Your power manifests when it senses a threat," he said.

That made sense. Each time in the past had been when I was suddenly surprised or in tremendous danger. "Is that normal?"

He shrugged. "Small children come into their power that way. You likely would have displayed it as a child when startled or afraid."

I was silent. Speaking about my power didn't come

naturally. Part of me wondered if this was a way for him to gather more information before he sold me out to the guards.

He just watched me with those cool green eyes. "You did, didn't you?"

I turned my gaze to the water. Lorian took a step closer. "You need to tell me everything if I'm going to help you learn how to wield your magic. Your history with it is important."

I sighed. "Yes, I used it when I was afraid. It was one of the reasons why we moved villages so frequently when I was a small child. My mother is—was—a seer, and my father was a mind healer, so we were always welcome."

My eyes prickled at the thought of my family, and I blinked quickly. I could fall apart later. Alone. In the dark.

Lorian's brow was lowered, as if he was either annoyed or deep in thought. With the mercenary, it was difficult to know.

I took a deep breath. "I need you to explain why I still have my…power."

He narrowed his eyes at the way I whispered that last word, but thankfully, he let it go. "Are you sure you want to know the answer to that question? Once you understand just how you and others like you have been lied to, there is no turning back. Something tells me someone like you would much prefer ignorance."

Someone like me. As if I'd *wanted* to grow up with power I couldn't understand, knowing that any day, I could lose everything. I shot to my feet and slammed my hands into Lorian's chest. "You *don't know me*," I hissed.

He stared at me. Then a slow smile crawled across his face as he shook his head. "You're not ready."

"You don't get to determine that." Knowledge was power, and I needed as much power as I could get.

"I'll tell you what you want to know when you've mastered your power."

I gaped at him. "You can't be serious."

Lorian just leaned down and picked up a stone, throwing it into the air.

"Freeze it."

It hit the ground with a thump.

He tutted, the sound filled with impatience, and lifted the stone once more. "*Try.*"

I tried. I truly did. I focused on the stone, attempting to find that place inside me that would make them freeze. Lorian threw the stones up again and again, until I was so exhausted, my hands shook. But nothing happened.

I was a failure. My power was my only bargaining chip—the only way I could keep myself safe—and I couldn't wield it.

Lorian picked up the stone. And this time, he threw it at me.

I ducked out of the way. "What in the—"

Another stone. Slightly larger this time. It bounced off my right breast.

"*What* is your problem?"

He looked bored. But his eyes glittered with amusement and something darker. "If you need to feel afraid, I can make that happen."

"By throwing *rocks* at me?"

This was useless. He was useless. And *I* was the most useless of all.

I turned and stalked away.

LORIAN

As much as I usually enjoyed being out in the wild, away from my brother's expectations, traveling with a woman was a new and entirely unwelcome experience.

She'd insisted on bathing in the freezing river that morning, almost turning blue. Her body was so slight compared to ours, even Galon had scowled at her shivering when she'd returned. If he'd had another cloak, I had no doubt that Galon—the man with one of the highest kill counts of anyone I knew—would have tucked it around her shoulders himself.

Then there were the endless questions. Always, always the questions.

Why the wildcat seemed to think she was owed answers to those questions was the biggest mystery of all. Finally, when she'd worn herself out, she'd fallen silent, likely sulking.

I frowned down at her. It had taken her entirely too long to realize we hadn't turned off to travel east to the city. Her head lolled, and for a moment, panic slammed into my gut. Was she…dead?

We needed her power at the city gates.

And…if I was being honest with myself, the thought of her dying was…disconcerting.

The back of my neck itched at the thought.

Oh, she was *good*.

The only reason I cared was likely because she'd been continually poking at me, implying I was the worst kind of man for leaving her by that river.

I surveyed her. No, she'd fallen asleep in my arms. What an unusual creature she was. Likely, she'd exhausted herself with useless fantasies of her revenge against the cruel mercenary. People were, after all, entirely predictable. I'd spent enough time traveling across this continent to know that much.

She began to slip sideways. I debated letting her fall off the horse. It would do the woman some good to have her bones rattled. Already, she was taking up far too many of my thoughts, when I needed to concentrate on our own plans. Her body leaned some more, and I sighed, tightening my arms around her. If those bones broke, it would only slow us down.

She nestled her face into my chest, and Marth threw me a wide-eyed look as his horse drew even with mine.

He opened his mouth, and I shot him a warning glare. I wanted to enjoy the precious silence for as long as possible before the harpy woke up and realized we weren't going directly to the city.

A bird shrieked, and Prisca jolted in my arms.

I sighed. Perfect.

Her eyes flew open, and for a moment, they were clear, dazed with sleep. Those strange eyes met mine and immediately filled with rancor.

She pulled away. "Sorry." She cleared her throat. "I didn't get much sleep."

Sitting up, she gazed at the forest around us. Then she looked up toward the sun. "Why are we traveling south?"

"We have something we need to do before we go to the city."

She let out an interesting hissing sound. My horse's ears pricked. "This isn't what we agreed to. I don't have time to go run your errands. I need to get to the city and—"

Her mouth clamped shut. I just shook my head. Did she really think we didn't know her plan? Her only option was to get on a ship and flee.

"You're breaking our agreement," she growled.

No one annoyed me like this woman. The urge to dump her off my horse struck again. Rythos cleared his throat and gestured at his own horse, silently offering to ride with her.

I ignored him. "Our agreement was for three meals a day, a horse—" I gestured to my mount "—and lessons to help with your power. Your side of the agreement is to use that power *when* we cross into the city. No time frame was ever specified."

"Let me off this fucking horse right now."

My mouth twitched. There were few things more

amusing than seeing this woman riled.

"We made a deal. You'll uphold your side of it."

She struggled, pushing at my arms. I pressed my mouth to her ear, loathing that her scent was so intriguing. "Continue to annoy my horse, and I'll tie you to the saddle and make you walk behind us."

"You'll pay for this," she hissed.

I just shrugged. We rode in blissful silence for several hours. Finally, she turned her head and scowled at me. "What is it that you have to do anyway?"

"None of your business."

"Of course. A mercenary's gotta mercenary, right?" Her upper lip curled, and she turned to face forward once more.

My hands itched to wrap themselves around her neck and squeeze. Her pale throat was tempting me enough that my hands tightened on my reins.

Now, *I* was the one annoying my horse.

7

PRISCA

The days flew by.

It was strange—I was inarguably in the worst situation of my life. I could die at any moment if we were discovered. And yet, for the first time in twenty-two winters, I felt...free.

It was as if I were a puppy, gamboling through the forest. We were heading in the *opposite* direction of the city, a fact that terrified me. But Marth had pointed out that taking such a route could help. It was likely that the northern gates were more heavily guarded.

I had a feeling Marth was telling me what I needed to hear. But I'd accepted that I had no control over this situation right now. At least, that was what I told myself.

The mercenaries were still closed-mouthed about where they were going and why. But they certainly weren't on a mere *errand,* as I'd assumed. No, from their hushed conversations and the tension that seemed to radiate from all of them—especially Lorian—

wherever they were going and whatever they were doing was significant. I itched to know what it was.

I was also desperate to know more about their power. I knew they had more magic than I'd ever seen before, but they rarely talked about it, even when encouraging me to use my own. Although, one night–after drinking too much ale by the fire–Marth had told me a few details about his magic.

While Mama's visions could strike at any time, Marth could control his, specifically looking into a target's past.

A very helpful skill for a mercenary.

I'd asked him exactly how far into the past he could look, and he'd shrugged. Obviously, I wasn't to be trusted with that information.

Then Lorian had sat next to us, and I hadn't bothered asking Marth anything else.

Rythos had an easy charm that could've been annoying, but he was the one who constantly coaxed a smile out of me when I would drift into the fog of fear and dread. His wide grin made me want to smile back, no matter how lost in worry I was.

Cavis was a quiet man, prone to staring dreamily into the distance—likely thinking of his family. The only time he truly came alive was when he spoke of his wife and their daughter.

And Galon? He was the oldest. Intensely loyal to Lorian, and continually evaluating potential threats, his gaze forever scanning the forest. He'd explained his power last night—he had an affinity for water. The day he'd dried my clothes, he'd pulled each drop from the fabric with just a thought.

Putting my safety in their hands was difficult. Even if I'd likely be dead by now if I were alone. With no other choice, I rode with them each day, slept next to the fire each night, and practiced my magic at every opportunity.

So far, that practice had been in vain.

In spite of the uselessness of my power, I was almost…enjoying myself. Of course, I still wanted to stab Lorian—enough that Galon had taken to searching me for weapons each night before we went to sleep.

These men might be untrustworthy, but for now, at least, I could be myself. I didn't have to hide the spark of power that wanted to jump out into the world. It was as if I'd been holding my breath for all these years, and with one long exhale, I could breathe freely once more.

It wouldn't last for long. As soon as I got to the city, I'd be hiding once more. The thought made a hot ache sweep up my throat. But for now, at least, I had a taste of what life would have been like if I didn't carry this secret.

And that taste was delicious.

"What are you thinking?" Lorian's voice was low, almost intimate, and I barely suppressed a shiver as his warm breath caressed the shell of my ear. I stiffened and shot him a glare.

The obstinate man merely tightened his arm around my waist.

My thoughts were still my own. And Lorian was entitled to none of them. "I'm thinking about my magic."

"Good. Perhaps if you think hard enough, you'll figure out how to wield it."

I tensed. "Your teaching methods leave much to be desired."

"I take offense to that." Amusement curled through his voice.

"You told me everything I knew was a lie, refused to tell me *why*, and threw rocks at me!"

Each practice session had been a repeat of that first day. And each time I asked just what he'd been referring to when he'd called me ignorant, he'd shrugged and suggested he'd maybe be willing to tell me once I was useful for more than just decorative purposes.

His body moved behind me as he shrugged those enormous shoulders. "You're not trying hard enough."

I *had* to learn how to wield my power. Because I knew Lorian well enough to know that if he didn't think I was ready, he would camp in the forest near the city walls until he decided I could be trusted at the gate. The sooner I could use my power, the sooner we could go our separate ways.

A cool breeze was coming from the north, bringing with it the smell of rain and newly cut pine. The sun had gone down, and I shivered, sucking the cold air into my lungs. "We'll need to find shelter soon."

"We're stopping at the next village for the night."

My mouth went dry. Villages meant people who would be on the lookout for anyone they could hand over to the king's guards. Even the most kindly innkeeper could be bought for a hundred gold coins.

"Is that safe?"

"I'll keep you safe."

He said it casually, and I just shook my head with a laugh. Sure, I was trusting him with my safety *to a point*. But if he thought I would just blindly believe his word, he was insane.

I could practically hear the brute grinding his teeth at my instant dismissal. But if he thought I was going to forget about him leaving me to either freeze or burn to death, he could think again.

I pulled the hood of Galon's cloak over my head as the village came into view. Night was already falling, and my stomach had awoken at the thought of a proper meal. My body longed for a real bed, even if it was only for one night.

Rythos disappeared to see if the closest inn had rooms available.

My heart pounded like a drum. My vision narrowed. I watched every face, paying careful attention to anyone who looked at our party for too long.

And yet, no one seemed to notice us. Their gazes flicked past us, and a few gave us a nod of greeting. But no one called for the authorities.

"You don't need to be afraid."

"I'm not."

Lorian snorted.

"Why would I be afraid, when I have so many big, strong men to protect me?" I simpered when I could unclench my jaw.

"My thoughts exactly."

"Was that what you were doing in my village when I saw you at the Gifting ceremony?" I asked. "Staying at the inn?"

A long silence followed, as if he was debating whether to answer. Finally, he nodded. "Your priestess insisted on even more blather than most."

Rythos returned. His expression was morose when he rode back toward us. "Only two rooms available," he said with a deep sigh. "It'll be bedrolls on the floor for us." He gestured to the other men.

"We'll arm-wrestle for the bed," Lorian said, and Rythos just rolled his eyes.

"Why waste the time when you'll trounce every one of us?"

What exactly were they talking about? "Surely if we're all spread over two rooms, it won't be *that* bad."

Galon scowled at me. "You can't sleep in the same room as us."

"Why?"

He just gave me a look that said he was doubting my intelligence.

"I've slept next to you big lumps every night on our journey. Why would being confined within four walls make it any different?"

Rythos shook his head. "That's not how they think in towns closer to the city. You'd get a reputation..."

I shook my head at him. "I'm a criminal who will be

on the run for the rest of her life. Such ideas are useless."

Lorian tightened his arm around my waist in the infuriating way he did when he had a decree to make. "Regardless, it would draw attention. The men will share, and you will have your own room."

If they wanted to suffer, then who was I to stop them? Besides, maybe some privacy would be a good thing. I could reevaluate if working with the mercenaries was in my best interest. And if it wasn't? An inn was a good place to separate.

"Fine."

"Fine."

The inn was located on the outskirts of town—the peeling white paint seeming to glow in the moonlight. The two-storied building boasted a thatched roof, a crumbling picket fence, and a huge wooden door with a brass knocker.

A drunk stumbled out of that door, laughing uproariously, and I flicked my gaze to the surprisingly large stable situated next to the inn.

People were coming and going, stable hands taking horses from those arriving. Once again, no one paid us any attention.

I slid off the horse, my knees twinging as I hit the ground. Lorian handed the horse off to one of the grooms with a few murmured words, and the others did the same. Within a few minutes, we were walking into the inn.

The warmth of the inn hit me, finally warming bones I swore were still half frozen from that god-awful river, and my eyelids immediately grew heavy.

Someone let out a screaming laugh. I jumped, gazing around blearily, and Lorian placed his hand on my lower back. I suspected he was attempting to calm me the same way he would calm his horse directly after he'd startled.

I didn't know whether to be offended or amused.

To our left, a fire roared. Its sparks escaping the hearth, the orange-blue light from the flames flickering on the faces of those dining at the scarred wooden tables. The tables in the center of the common room had been wedged so close together, it was as if everyone was dining as one big family.

Considering I was in hiding, I would much prefer a dimmer room and separate tables.

In the corner, the barkeep was boiling a cauldron of stew. The steam from the huge pot made its way over to me, carrying with it the scent of fresh-baked bread and some kind of gamey meat. My stomach howled.

Lorian took my arm and directed me to a table near the back of the common room, where he sat positioned with his back against the wall. I was too tired to protest the manhandling, and I slipped into the chair next to him, keeping my cloak over my head.

I tuned out the conversation as the men murmured to one another. My eyes must have slid closed, because a nudge from Lorian's elbow had them shooting open. Rythos smirked at me. "Sleepy?"

Someone plonked a bowl of stew and a cup of ale in front of me. I handed the ale to Rythos. I'd never gotten a taste for it. Now, wine, on the other hand…

I drank the last of my water, the warmth of the room and salt in the stew stoking my thirst. Tucking the skin back into my cloak, I got to my feet. Lorian's hand immediately caught my arm in that enchanting way he did, which never failed to make me feel like his prisoner.

"Where are you going?"

"To get water. Release me," I ground out, suddenly frustrated. I was almost desperate with thirst, and the sooner I finished my stew, the sooner I could crawl into bed.

Lorian let my arm go, and I crossed the inn, aiming for the barkeep. He nodded when I asked for water and pointed me toward a pitcher and several cups. I took a cup, relatively sure the men would much prefer their ale.

Still, I probably should have offered.

I turned, slamming into a giant chest.

"Well, lookee here." The man grinned at me maniacally. The lower half of his face was almost completely covered in a dark-gray beard which he'd let grow down to his chest. His hand shot out, pushing the hood of my cloak off my face. With my cup in one hand and my reflexes dull from weariness, I was too slow to stop him.

"We have a wee beauty in our midst. Where did you come from, lady?"

I could feel my heartbeat in my throat. Without my hood over my head, I felt naked. Would he recognize me?

I forced my voice to stay steady. "Nowhere you'll

know. Let me pass."

"Now that's not nice. That cloak is made of a fine material. Your dress could use a cleaning though. I'd be more than happy for you to drop it onto the floor of my room to be laundered—"

"Move," a low voice ordered.

I glanced past the bearded man to where Lorian stood, his irritation clear. Our eyes met, and my face burned. The next time I wanted to walk ten paces away from him, he would likely refuse, like the tyrant he was.

The unfairness of it all made my hands shake with fury. Some of the water sloshed over the side of my cup, and Beard dropped his gaze.

"Now see what you've done? You've frightened the little bird."

Lorian followed his gaze. Then his eyes met mine again. He knew I wasn't frightened.

"Move, or I'll move you." The words were flat, but I'd seen Lorian take that exact stance right before he trained with his men.

Beard spun on Lorian, his movements unsteady. I stepped back, but his elbow knocked the water out of my hand. I watched as my cup fell to the floor.

Perfect.

"Now, don't you be causing a scene." Beard swept his arm around him to the people watching in a way that made it evident he relished the thought of a scene. "I was just saying hello to your traveling companion."

Lorian watched him silently. His expression was

blank, but those green eyes were filled with an icy rage.

When he didn't reply, Beard reached out both hands to push him.

Lorian was standing in front of him.

And then he wasn't.

He moved so fast, my breath caught in my throat. Stepping to the side, he lashed out with methodical precision, avoiding the man's punch and slapping him across the face.

The *crack* of the slap carried through the inn, and all I could hear was the sound of witnesses sucking in a breath.

I sighed. Slapping the bearded giant was a calculated move. Lorian wanted to humiliate him.

Beard bellowed a garbled threat, swinging again, but Lorian was no longer there, his expression bored. I blinked. I'd never seen anyone move like that. It was as if *he* had the power to stop time.

He slapped Beard again.

"Lorian," I growled. This was just drawing more attention. If he didn't stop, someone would call the authorities. Lorian glanced at me, and his green eyes flashed. But some of the languid fury drained from his expression.

Beard stumbled. Lorian took a step back and crossed his arms. Beard's hand came up to his nose—now crooked and bleeding.

Lorian had broken his nose with that second slap.

"Leave," he said. His voice was so quiet, I had to

strain to hear it, and I was just a few feet away.

Beard spat on the floor. "Whore," he hissed at me.

I curled my lip at him but managed to keep my mouth shut.

Lorian took a single step toward Beard, and he stumbled back, turned and fled. I slammed my hand into Lorian's chest. "Enough."

His gaze dropped to my hand, and when his eyes met mine, they were still feral. I glanced at the people watching us, and Lorian slowly turned, raking his gaze over the room. Everyone suddenly found other things to look at.

My eyes burned.

"You're hurt?" Lorian's voice was rough.

I shook my head, and to my intense embarrassment, a tear threatened to spill over. I sniffed.

"What is this?" His eyes narrowed. "Do you want me to hurt him some more?"

"No, I don't want you to hurt him some more," I hissed, my eyes drying. "I'm upset because the water spilled, and I wanted that water!"

He cast a disinterested look at the water on the floor. Then he glanced back at my face. "After everything you've been through since you left your village, this is what makes you teary?"

"I'm exhausted, you brute."

With a sigh, he stalked over to one of the barmaids, who immediately handed him a fresh cup and an entire pitcher of water.

Typical.

I stalked back to my seat, digging into my lukewarm stew. The group was silent, and I raised my head. "What?"

Lorian placed the cup in front of me and filled it with water. I gulped at it. The water was cool, and it soothed my dry mouth and throat. Rythos glanced at him and quickly dropped his gaze back to his food.

"Nothing."

"We haven't seen you cry before, that's all," Marth said. "We wondered if maybe you were on your woman time."

I snarled, but Lorian clamped his hand on to my arm, leveling a warning look at both of us. "Quiet."

I spooned up more stew, taking the extra piece of bread Lorian slid me. It felt almost like a silent apology.

"We need to teach you to fight," Galon said after a long silence.

"I know how to fight."

The silence became thicker, and I glanced up from my bowl. "Just because I haven't demonstrated the best of my abilities since I met you giant ruffians doesn't mean I can't protect myself. My brother and his friends taught me to fight."

And I missed them with such a wild longing, it felt as if someone had carved a hole in my chest. My eyes stung once more.

Galon scratched at one eyebrow. "I'm sure they did a good job of it. But there's a difference between fighting for fun in your village and fighting for your life. We'll make sure you at least have a chance of survival when we leave you in the city."

I lifted my gaze once more. Galon was talking as if he actually cared. I opened my mouth to snap at him, but a long sigh came out instead. If he was offering to help me stay alive, I'd take him up on that offer.

"I'd like that."

8
PRISCA

After making my way up to my room, I paced, debating the merits of stealing a horse from the stables and striking out on my own. There were definite benefits to traveling with the mercenaries—including their hunting and cooking skills, and the fact that they seemed to know all the best routes to avoid the guards.

But there was no doubt that a single woman traveling with five men drew attention. I could pull up the hood of my cloak, but I couldn't disguise my build.

Finally, I fell into bed and slept the sleep of the half dead. Each time I stirred, awoken by a loud laugh from the hallway outside my room or the voices of angry drunkards below me, I immediately slid back into a sleep so deep, I could only hope Lorian didn't have us up before dawn.

A scraping noise sounded. My eyes shot open, my body tense. A hand slammed down over my mouth. A huge, callused hand.

I screeched, bucked, kicked, clawed.

"Uh-uh," the bearded giant from earlier snarled. Cool metal wedged against my neck. "Be nice, little bird, or I'll slit your throat and leave you to drown in your own blood."

My lungs burned, my throat screamed for air. I sucked deeply through my nose.

Beard pinched my nostrils closed.

I thrashed, hitting out uselessly. Black dots danced at the edges of my vision.

He lifted his hand. "Can't have you dying too early."

I panted, inhaling sweet, life-giving air. My limbs had turned weak. Blind terror punched into my gut. My heart stuttered. I couldn't die like this. In a cheap inn, far from home. I *refused*.

"Be smart," Tibris's voice whispered in my head. *"Wait for your chance."*

I slid my hand under my pillow and wrapped my fingers around the cool hilt of my knife. I breathed. Stilled. Waited.

The giant's eyes glittered. His nose was broken, one eye puffy and swollen. Clearly, he was holding a grudge.

And I was the one who'd pay for it.

He looped a rope around my wrist.

"I'm going to kill you and leave you hanging at the inn entrance." He grinned, leaning close, and his noxious breath made my head spin. "See how your man likes that."

I could see it—Lorian and the others looking for me in the morning, only to find my dead body strung up in the inn. Cold, slimy fear burrowed into my chest and stayed there.

Beard hauled me up from my bed as if I were a kitten. Now.

I slid my hand out from beneath my pillow and slashed at him.

The blade caught his ear, even as he ducked. He knocked the knife from my hand, the beginning of a yell leaving his throat.

He instantly cut it off with a glance at my door.

Within a second, the rope was looped around my neck, and he had me pinned to the bed once more.

I clawed at my throat like a wild animal, desperate for air.

A shriek rose in my head. The sound was high-pitched. Primal. Full of retribution.

It drowned out the couple arguing in the alley below us. It smothered the taunt of the giant on top of me. It consumed my fear and doubt, until only one word remained.

Stop.

The giant froze.

Sobbing, I ripped his hand off my mouth. But I was still pinned.

Roaring filled my ears. I tossed wildly beneath the giant, pushing with everything I had.

My right leg came free. I planted that foot in Beard's side and heaved.

Free.

Run.

Don't look back.

Scrambling off the bed, I sprinted toward the door, howling for help.

Pain erupted in my scalp, and I dropped to my knees.

"Magic, huh? You'll make me a rich man, you little bitch."

I fumbled, my hand sweeping along the floor for the knife.

Beard pulled me up by my hair, and I shrieked, my scalp burning.

I swung, slashing out with the knife.

He howled, his hands clamping over his shoulder as blood sprayed. I stabbed at him again, and he dropped to his knees. I screamed wordlessly, driving my foot into his gut.

And then my room was full of furious males.

Lorian took one step inside and threw the giant across the room. Rythos stepped in front of me, blocking the scene from my vision.

"Give me the knife, darlin'."

I stared up into Rythos's face. His eyes blazed with fury, but his expression was calm. His hand was gentle on mine, and still, I flinched as he unwrapped my fingers from the wooden hilt.

He handed the knife to Galon and then wrapped an arm around me. Safe. I was safe. I'd begun to shiver, and he tightened his arm. "Don't look over there. Come with me, Prisca."

I allowed him to lead me to their room. A few of the men followed, but I was dimly aware of Galon staying with Lorian. Other guests were flooding into the hallway. One of the women caught sight of my shirt and the blood staining it. Her mouth fell open, and she let out a wild shriek.

Rythos growled and I jolted, not used to such a sound from him. He reached out and brushed a hand over my hair, but his gaze stayed on the woman. She shut her mouth.

Rythos sat me on the lone chair in their room. I stared at the wall while the men talked in hushed voices.

"Don't do that." Rythos's voice was gentle as he pulled my hands from my throat. I'd been scratching at it, as if that rope were still wrapped around me. My cheeks heated, and I took a deep breath, burying my hands in the blanket he placed on my lap.

Lorian stepped into the room. His knuckles were bruised, and a muscle twitched in his cheek when he looked at me. "Tell me what happened."

My throat thickened until I could barely breathe. For some reason, a ball of shame was burning in my chest.

"Prisca." His voice was gentle, and he crouched in front of me, the remaining fury drained from his expression. "If you can't talk about it…"

The unexpected gentleness shook some of the fog from my mind.

"I-I was in such a deep sleep. I woke, and he was already in my room. How did he get into my room?"

I loathed how small my voice sounded. Lorian's jaw clenched. "It's likely that he stole a key from the innkeeper. The idiot's lying in a drunken heap by the fire."

I nodded, still feeling as if I were stuck in a nightmare. As if I were about to wake up at any moment.

"You don't need to talk about it," Lorian said.

Our eyes met and held. Not pity. Sympathy and banked fury, but he wasn't looking at me like I was a victim. That look made me steadier.

"No. No, I want to." I took a deep breath. "His hand was on my mouth, and he pinched my nostrils until I couldn't breathe. He said he was going to kill me. And then hang me up where you'd find me." Nausea made my stomach swim, and Marth let out a rough curse from somewhere behind me. "We fought. I used my...my power." I said the last word in a whisper, conscious of anyone who could be listening at the door. "He only froze for a second, but it was enough for me to take the knife and run for the door. Then his h-hand was in my hair, and he pulled me back. I slashed out. And I couldn't stop. *Wouldn't* stop."

I'd been like an animal. All I'd known was fear. Fear, and the knowledge that I'd do anything to survive.

Marth opened the door. I hadn't noticed him leave. He stepped back inside the room and handed me a cup of tea.

I took a sip. Peppermint. The scent both calmed me and cleared my head. "Thank you."

"You did everything right." Galon's voice was rough,

and he crouched next to Lorian.

"We need to leave," I said. "Surely the authorities were summoned?"

Lorian gave a disinterested shrug. "An attempted murderer was felled by a tiny woman. Everyone in this inn just watched him stumble away. No one will be summoning the authorities tonight."

I ignored the tiny woman part. "Are you sure?"

"The innkeeper is too drunk, and any guests have been suitably frightened by Rythos's glare."

Rythos snorted. The gentle ribbing between the men settled me more than the tea had. Some of the tension in my chest began to drain away.

"You'll sleep in here tonight." Lorian got to his feet. "We'll leave at first light."

I glanced around the small room, at the bedrolls that covered almost every inch of it. As much as the thought of going back to my own room made my stomach swim, I couldn't see *where* exactly I could sleep in this room.

"Uh…"

"Get in bed. Here." He took my empty teacup and handed me a clean shirt. I stared down at myself, suddenly revolted by the splatter of blood across Rythos's shirt.

"Sorry," I muttered to Rythos.

"Never mind about that."

Marth stepped forward, looking suddenly awkward as he handed me a damp cloth. "For your face."

My lower lip trembled. Who would've known this group of hard-faced, tough mercenaries had mother-hen tendencies?

I took the cloth and wiped at my skin, ignoring the rust-colored residue that transferred from my face.

The men all politely turned their backs as I changed my shirt. I climbed into the bed, and despite the fact that I was now surrounded by mercenaries, I felt strangely safe.

They somehow found room on the floor for Lorian, and within a few minutes, the lamp was dimmed.

I stared at the ceiling, unable to sleep. Each time I closed my eyes, my breath caught in my lungs, and I felt his hand over my mouth, felt his fingers pinching my nostrils closed. Felt the rope, unyielding and rough around my neck.

My eyes burned. I gave in to the tears that rolled silently down my face. And I wept. It was as if once I allowed myself to mourn, I cracked open the stone wall I'd erected between myself and the reality I'd tried so hard to ignore.

My tears dripped onto my pillow. For the village I'd never see again. For Tibris, either dead or running for his life. And for my mother, who was gone from this world. I'd forced myself not to think of her. Attempted to focus on the fact that she'd kidnapped me and then lied to me my whole life. But…

She also cared for me. She loved me. I knew that much. She'd done her best to ensure I kept my magic hidden as a child—continually moving villages to keep me safe.

And if the priestesses were right, Mama was now

drowning over and over again in the waters of Hubur. Because she'd helped me hide from the king's guards. Because she'd protected me.

I was the reason she was dead.

And I would have to live with that knowledge for the rest of my life.

Her face flashed in front of my eyes, and my shoulders shook with suppressed sobs.

All I'd been to my family was poison.

A warm hand came out of the darkness, and I jolted, swinging out.

"We'll work on your form tomorrow," Lorian said.

"What—what are you doing?"

"Can't sleep for your sniffling. Move over."

I moved automatically. When he sat on the bed, I froze.

"Figured you'd be going over it in your head," he said gruffly, grabbing a pillow. "Sleep, savage woman. I'll keep you safe."

My breath hitched again, this time for a different reason entirely. I lay down next to him, studying the ceiling. He fell asleep almost immediately, his soft breaths steadying me. Across the room, Marth began to snore, the sound a low rumble. I closed my eyes, trusting that if anyone else came for me, these men would keep me safe. At least for tonight.

9
PRISCA

stood in the common room of the inn, blinking again and again, as if, eventually, the scene in front of me would change.

The bearded giant who'd tried to kill me was currently hanging from a hook. Dead. The hook had been attached to the ceiling of the inn, near the fire. His teeth were broken, and a key had been shoved between them, glinting in the low light.

I would bet all the money in the hunter's purse that it was the key to my room.

The innkeeper stood frozen, several feet away from the body, his face so pale, it was impressive he was still on his feet.

Beard hadn't had an easy death. The skin around his neck was mottled and bruised, highlighting the cut I'd made in his neck. But that hadn't been what killed him.

No, that was likely the fact that his hands were no longer attached to his body.

I wasn't sure exactly when Lorian

had killed him—he would have done it himself, rather than sending one of the others to do it—but he'd either taken care of it last night right after I fell asleep, or he'd hunted him in the small hours of the morning.

The floor felt as if it were tilting beneath me. Nausea swelled in my gut, and my mouth had turned bone-dry.

"This was unnecessary," I managed to get out.

Next to me, Lorian stiffened. I glanced at him. He was watching the innkeeper, his gaze still filled with retribution.

Something told me the man wouldn't be passing out drunk without securing his spare keys ever again.

"It was completely necessary."

Sometimes when I looked at Lorian, I didn't recognize him. The man in my dreams had been approachable, like a sated tiger. The Lorian I'd first met had been all languid amusement and put-upon boredom. *This* Lorian looked wicked and wild, his eyes glowing with a strange, feral light.

He looked back at me, and I shivered.

Whatever he saw on my face made that light leave his eyes. "We're leaving. Now." He turned and prowled out the door.

Good. We needed to leave before someone decided to call the authorities.

A crowd was gathering around the body, many of them shooting terrified glances in our direction. This would draw attention. The kind of attention that was *dangerous*.

The thought clawed at my temper, and I stalked after Lorian. The others had already saddled up the horses and were waiting. I tensed as Lorian reached for my waist, and that muscle ticked in his jaw again. "You think I'm going to hurt you?"

"No."

His expression hardened. And then I was in the saddle. He was careful not to touch me as he reached for the reins.

"We got you a couple of dresses, a tunic, and some breeches from the market," Rythos said. "The boots might be a little big, but they'll be better than what you're wearing now."

My eyes stung. I hadn't dared to hope I'd get a chance to find some clothes. "That was so kind of you. Thank you."

"Our deal included clothes," Lorian grumbled in my ear. I ignored him.

All of us were low on sleep, and Lorian was in a particularly dark mood for the rest of the day. We were approaching the Gromalian border, and if there were no delays, we'd complete whatever task Lorian needed by tomorrow morning.

Soon, I'd be in the city and on a ship south. If the border itself hadn't been so heavily guarded, I could've traveled into Gromalia by land. But the king had set up numerous checkpoints on his side of the border, ensuring the corrupt couldn't escape. A ship was safer and could get me farther south.

I hadn't thought about what my life would be like when I started somewhere new. Truthfully, I didn't want to. But as soon as I got to the city, I would find Vicer. He could send Tibris a message in our code. We had a number of places to send such messages to. Surely Tibris would be waiting at one of them.

Sometimes, when I woke up and realized I wasn't at home with Tibris snoring in the next room and Mama safe in her bed, I wondered if that grief would drown me.

We stopped to water the horses, and Lorian sent Cavis to scout for spies or enemies or whoever it was they were watching out for.

I jumped off the horse before Lorian could help me down. He'd practically vibrated with rancor all day, and neither of us had said a word to each other.

Now, he leaned close, until I was trapped between his body and his horse.

"Last night was the second throat you've slit within the past few days, sweetheart. Not to mention the guard you pushed off that bridge." I felt the blood draining from my face, and he gave me a humorless smile. "Of all of us, *you've* been the most murderous lately. Perhaps you should think twice before judging us as savages."

My gaze found Marth's. He shrugged, but his face was slowly turning red. Of course he would've looked with that power of his. Likely at Lorian's order. Betrayal twisted my gut, and for a moment, my hands shook with it.

But Lorian was right. Not counting the way I'd contributed to the bearded giant's death, I'd killed two other men since I'd left my village. I'd even used the knife I'd stolen from the hunter to stab the bearded giant.

Lorian watched me. His eyes narrowed, and with a low curse, he turned and stalked away.

My feet were numb, and I stumbled as I made my way to the river. A half-rotted log lay a few foot-spans from the water, and I sat on it, rubbing at my throat.

I'd stared in the mirror at the rope burn this morning. The truth was, if not for the power I didn't understand—and the mercenaries who'd been kinder than I could have expected—it would've been *me* hanging in that inn this morning.

A branch snapped over my shoulder. I jumped at the sudden sound but continued staring at the water. "I want to be alone."

Of course, the giant brute ignored me. Lorian sat next to me on the fallen tree trunk.

If he refused to leave, then *I* would. I made it to my feet before he snagged my wrist and hauled me back down.

I *hated* him.

He let me chew on my wrath. We both watched the water.

"That man deserved to die," he said.

I glanced at him. His jaw was tight, brows furrowed. He truly didn't understand my reaction. If anything, he seemed…bewildered by me.

I frowned. One morning, Herica's cat had strolled into the bakery, a dead rat in its mouth. It had dumped the rat on the floor, gazing at Herica as if to say, "You're welcome."

Herica had screeched, chased the cat out with a broom, and buried the rat behind the bakery, her cheeks burning with embarrassment and fury.

The cat had stayed away for weeks, until Herica had burst into tears, wishing he'd return.

The way Lorian acted sometimes, it was as if he'd forgotten his humanity. Leaving a weaponless woman to die was a good example. He made life-and-death decisions so easily, always from a place of logic, depending on if it would help him with whatever task he was being paid to complete.

And yet, the only reason I could see for him to kill Beard—especially so violently—wasn't from logic at all. No, it had been rage that had driven his actions.

I couldn't imagine the things he'd seen as a mercenary. The things he'd *done*. Maybe in his mind, killing the man who had hurt me was almost like a…gift.

"I shouldn't have thrown that in your face," he said finally.

It took me a moment to understand what he was talking about.

A hole opened up in my stomach. "Why not? I *did* kill two men. Violently." As much as I'd hoped the guard on the bridge had been rescued the way I had, it was unlikely he'd survived the freezing river.

He rubbed at his jaw. His hand made a rough sound as it scraped against stubble. "Because you're a survivor. It's not fair for me to tell you to fight as if your life depends on it and then verbally flay you for it when you do."

I swallowed around the lump in my throat. "I see their faces. Every night when I try to sleep. I wake from dreams—"

Enough. That was enough.

Lorian turned until he was facing me. I kept my gaze on the river.

"It won't last forever," he said. "The first few times you kill, the guilt consumes you. Even if the kill was justified."

"And then what happens?" I whispered.

His expression turned cold. "And then you become numb to it. It's an animal instinct. Either they die, or you do."

"I don't want it to become easy. I don't want to become a monster."

Like you.

I didn't say it. Didn't even think it. But from the way Lorian stiffened, that was what he'd heard.

He moved. Turning, I grabbed his hand. I didn't have a hope of pulling *him* back down, but he went still.

"Thank you. For teaching me. I want…I need to survive. For my brother."

We were all each other had. Thanks to me, Tibris had just lost Mama. I would fight to find him again. Even if he couldn't forgive me.

Lorian studied my face. "Don't survive for anyone else. Survive for yourself. Survive because the thought of not surviving, the thought of letting those who would hurt you win, is so repulsive, you can't stand it. Survive because you *deserve* to survive."

I thought about that. After a long moment, I nodded. He angled his head.

"Time for another lesson."

"I don't think so."

"I do. And I'm bigger than you."

Standing, I leaned closer until I was right in his personal space. "I've killed two men since Galon saved me, remember? Just looking at you makes me murderous. So don't make me try for a third."

Had his eyes just dropped to my lips? Awareness shot through me, even as I stepped back. His huge hand closed around my upper arm.

"As cute as your little death threats are, right now, you have no way to back them up. You want me to fear you? Learn how to freeze me in place. Because that's the only chance you have of taking me down. And we both know it."

He was right. That didn't make it any easier to accept.

Lorian's green eyes gleamed as he angled his head. A lock of his dark hair fell over his forehead, and for a wild moment, I had to clench my hand into a fist so I wouldn't do something stupid like brush it back.

He'd probably rip my hand off the wrist if I attempted such a thing.

One dark eyebrow quirked. "What are you thinking about?"

"My power."

His gaze turned intent. But if he knew I was lying, he chose to ignore it.

"You used your power last night. It saved your life. But we can't rely on your instincts reaching for that power when we get to the city."

He dropped his gaze to my throat, and his expression hardened. Then his face went blank. That expressionless mask had never boded well for me before.

"Take your mind back to the moment you realized that man was going to kill you."

I didn't want to. But I tried.

"Close your eyes," Lorian said softly.

The clearing was so very quiet. I had a feeling Rythos and the others had disappeared for a while so I could focus. I could feel Lorian's eyes on me. Could feel his expectation.

"You're not remembering it," Lorian murmured.

My eyes flew open. He'd taken another step closer when I wasn't looking. A strange kind of anticipation turned my skin hot and my belly tight.

"Close them," he said.

I sucked in a breath, tense and annoyed for reasons I couldn't explain. But I closed my eyes again and forced myself to think about the bearded man and the rope in his hand.

"Good," Lorian said when I shuddered. "Now keep that image in your mind."

I opened my eyes to see a small stone flying at me.

The bastard had backed up a few steps again.

"We're back to this?"

"You need to feel fear in order to use your power. Visualize the man who tried to kill you."

I tried, but Lorian was too damned distracting with his intent expression and his stupid stones. Not to mention, most of the time when I thought about the bearded man, my mind showed me the way I'd seen him last—hanging from the roof of that inn, his body reflecting unspeakable damage, and the key he'd used stuck between broken teeth.

"You're not trying," he said mildly.

"I *am*." It wasn't my fault he'd removed any and all threat that the bearded man had previously presented.

Lorian's expression turned colder. Remote. It was the same way he'd looked at me when I'd been lying next to the river, coughing up water. That expression told me that he didn't see me as a fellow human. I was just a problem that needed to be addressed.

Back then, Lorian had left me behind. I knew he wouldn't do that now. After all, he needed me. Somehow, that knowledge made it worse.

"I didn't want to do this," he said, pulling Beard's rope from the pocket of his overcoat.

Black spots danced around the edges of my vision, and my heartbeat pounded in my ears. All I could feel was the rough rope around my neck. All I could see was the sick grin on Beard's face when he told me how he was going to hang me up.

Lorian stepped closer, and I reacted like a hunted animal, jumping a foot-span to my left. My hands shook, and I held them up in front of me defensively. Uselessly.

He was so fucking *big*.

My throat constricted, and I almost choked on my next breath.

A muscle twitched in his jaw. "Show me you can use your power, wildcat." He leaned down and threw another stone. It bounced off my thigh.

He held up the rope. My mouth turned dry. I backed up a step, stumbling over the rocky ground.

Obviously, we were wrong. Terror didn't help me use my power. If it did, that rock would be hanging frozen in the air.

Lorian followed me.

"Don't come any closer," I hissed.

All life had left his expression. He looked inhuman, his eyes glittering with an ancient knowledge.

I blinked, and he was Lorian again, his brow creasing. But he took another step. Turning my body, I prepared to run.

He moved so fucking fast. Screaming, I turned toward the clearing. Rythos and Marth appeared to my left, hands on their weapons.

Lorian's hand grabbed the back of my tunic, and the rope brushed my shoulder.

I went wild. Lashing out, I fought like a cornered cat, hissing and clawing and howling.

"Use your power," Lorian gritted out, but I couldn't.

I was nothing but terror. Terror and betrayal.

"Prisca." Lorian's voice was a dark warning. I was choking myself with the neck of my tunic. Dimly, I realized he wasn't moving, but I was also rooted in place, my feet kicking up dirt and stones.

The feel of the rope on the side of my throat was what did it.

A pit opened inside me. A pit filled with endless rage and icy vengeance. A scream burned up my throat, and something deep in my belly roared its wrath.

Rythos was running toward us, his mouth open as he bellowed at Lorian.

I pulled, desperate, hiccupping a sob.

The world froze.

Rythos paused midstep.

I wouldn't let time unfreeze until I was miles from these men. Until I was on one of their horses and several villages over.

My terror was married to fury in a way I had never felt before, and I could feel my power coiled within me. This time, I memorized the feeling.

I tore myself out of Lorian's grasp. My tunic ripped, but I was already pulling the rope from his hand and throwing it into the river. Then I hauled my foot back and slammed it between his legs with everything I had.

I was running when the grip on my power slipped.

Rythos was still frozen. But Lorian's vicious curses told me he now felt that kick. Dark satisfaction wrestled with grim determination.

Suddenly, Rythos was moving, and his eyes were wide as he came to a stop. To him, it must have seemed like I'd shifted places between one moment and the next.

"Keep him away from me," I choked out. "I'm leaving."

Rythos glanced past me, and his expression turned grim. For some reason, Lorian had shaken off my power earlier than Rythos. But how? I chanced a look over my shoulder to find Lorian bent almost in two, breathing through pain that likely would have driven a lesser man to his knees.

I should have kicked him harder.

Grabbing my cloak, I reached for my boots and sat on an overturned log, pulling them on. Marth strolled along the clearing. "You try to leave, and he'll just drag you back. You made a bargain."

"Fuck his bargain."

Marth grinned at me. I debated throwing my boot at him. His grin widened, as if he was reading my mind.

"Don't give him the satisfaction," he advised. "Lorian takes his deals seriously." Marth glanced over my shoulder, and I turned, my gaze meeting Lorian's.

Something vicious looked out at me. But a dull pride replaced it, and I wished I could turn back time and hurt him much, much more than I had.

LORIAN

It wasn't that I *enjoyed* terrifying women. But usually, it wouldn't occur to me to want to soothe one. Especially after I'd been the one to scare her.

For some unknown reason, I'd felt...guilt when Prisca's eyes had turned stark with horror.

"I think she should ride with me," Rythos muttered. We were both watching Prisca as she refilled her water skin, her mouth tight as she pretended I didn't exist.

"You overstep."

"You just terrorized her."

"You wish to fuck her? Fine. But I'm the one teaching her how to survive. Don't forget that."

I walked away, feeling like there was an itch beneath my skin, and no matter how much I scratched, I couldn't make it go away.

"We're leaving," I told Galon. He merely nodded. I narrowed my eyes at him. "You have something to say?"

He shrugged one shoulder. "You should be careful with that one. Rage can simmer for years before it explodes into vengeance. As you know. She could have killed you in that moment when she controlled time."

I should feel threatened by that. But for some reason, all I felt was a strange sense of...pride.

We saddled up. Prisca rode with Rythos, allowing me to focus on my upcoming meeting, and not the curvy ass she insisted on rubbing against me each time she shifted uncomfortably in the saddle.

The fact that I *missed* that curvy ass just darkened my mood further.

It had been far too long since I'd taken a lover if my body was fixating on the wildcat. As soon as I finished with our task, I would find a willing woman and rid myself of this need.

Time crawled by. All of us were silent—Prisca scowling into the distance—while I focused on the forest around us. This close to the Gromalian border was bandit territory. We had to be careful not to get much closer or we'd run into Sabium's checkpoints.

Finally, we came to the edge of the forest. The air seemed fresher here, or perhaps that was just my anticipation sharpening my senses.

Scrubland stretched out before us, much of it hidden by a thick mist, the fog lit gold by the rays of the setting sun. The wind that washed toward us carried the smell of soil and wild flowers.

"We'll stay here tonight." I slid off the horse. Prisca jumped off Rythos's horse next to me, and I caught the twinge of pain on her face as her feet hit the ground.

If she didn't want my hands on her, she could deal with the consequences.

I scowled at her, ignoring the vicious look she sent me in return. And the way Cavis shook his head at us. Given how everyone was reacting, it was as if I'd actually wrapped the rope around her neck and strung her up.

I'd paid the price for helping her with her magic. My balls still ached enough that I was grinding my teeth with my every movement. "You can thank me for my lesson whenever you're ready," I said.

Prisca held up her hand in a lewd gesture that made Marth snort a laugh.

That wariness when she looked at me…it would make our lessons that much more difficult. Regardless of what she'd managed under intense pressure, she still couldn't use her power reliably.

Finding someone with her power had been a boon. If one believed the gods had a stake in our world, it would be easy to credit them with the fact that Galon had saved her life. Her power presented us with a unique opportunity I refused to let pass me by.

Beyond that plan was one simple fact—the thought of Prisca being a victim in this world was quite simply intolerable. Especially considering she carried the potential to never be a victim again.

Rythos got to work building a fire. From the look he sent me, my meat would be black tonight. Prisca sat next to him, murmuring quietly, and I shook my head at Marth when he attempted to take my horse.

"I'll do it."

I busied myself feeding the horses, ignoring the way Prisca and Rythos whispered together at the fire.

Finally, Galon and Cavis returned with the rabbits they'd caught. With nothing left to do, I sat on one of the overturned logs Marth had pulled close to the fire, pulling out my blade to sharpen it.

"What's your magic, Rythos?" Prisca asked a few minutes later.

Rythos hesitated, and I struck. "Didn't you know, wildcat? Rythos has the power to make you *like* him."

Something that might've been hurt flashed in Rythos's eyes as Prisca turned an accusing look on him. "You— I—"

"No," he snarled. "I've never used my power on you."

Doubt crossed Prisca's face. Strangely, the chasm widening between them didn't make my mood any brighter.

Gods, I was a bastard. From the narrowed-eyed look Marth sent me, he was thinking the same. It wasn't often that Rythos's smile dimmed, but I'd made it happen.

Now everyone else was as miserable as me.

Prisca looked at me. And then she reached for Rythos's hand. Her skin was so pale next to his. They looked like they belonged together.

"It's okay," she told him, her gaze still on me. "I believe you."

He smiled at her. My hand tightened around the knife I was sharpening.

"How does your magic work?" she asked.

The rest of the night crawled by, with Rythos mixing truths in a way that impressed even me. At one point, our eyes met, and his expression turned defiant.

I just raised an eyebrow. Marth nudged me, while

Cavis ignored all undercurrents, likely lost in thought about his perfect family. Galon watched all of us, expression bemused. I couldn't blame him. Traveling with a woman had changed everything. And not for the better.

Finally, we crawled under our blankets. Prisca was close to the fire, and I positioned myself next to her, hoping it would irritate her. From the blistering look she sent me before rolling over, it did.

I couldn't help it. I watched her as she fell asleep. Just when my own eyes were becoming heavy, she jolted awake, panting. Something that might have been guilt tightened my gut. Was she dreaming of me chasing her with that rope? For a moment, I had the strangest urge to pull her close. To soothe.

She rolled to face me, likely feeling my eyes on her. I didn't bother pretending to be asleep. Her eyes slid to the blue mark on my temple and stayed there.

"Nightmare?" I whispered. It was strangely intimate, talking to her by the fire while the others were asleep.

She shuddered, and for a moment, I almost pulled her close until she stopped trembling.

But she was already blinking, long, slow blinks as if she was fighting sleep. When her eyes slid shut for the last time, I wondered if the solitude would eat me alive.

Then she spoke. "I used to see *you* in my dreams," she mumbled. "Now all I see is the men I've killed."

I stiffened. "What?"

But she was already asleep.

PRISCA

I'd never been this far from home before. Of course, that was going to change, just as soon as I got to the city and on a ship. But for now, I soaked up everything, ignoring Marth's teasing as I turned my head from side to side.

The forest had given way to yellow and green bushes, brown grass, and tall, thin trees that reached into the sky with gangly limbs. It was so…open here.

And we were being watched.

My mind kept providing me with images of the king's guards surrounding us, lying in wait, ready to attack.

I wasn't the only one who could feel eyes on us. The mercenaries had turned tense, quiet, speaking only when necessary. I kept my mouth shut, my hand occasionally straying to the dagger I'd stolen from the hunter.

It was too large for me, but the feel of the wooden hilt brought me comfort just the same. Galon no longer took it from me before I slept. He seemed to know just how much I'd come to rely on it. And maybe he was finally convinced that I wouldn't kill Lorian in his sleep.

Lorian must have recognized where we were, because he brought his horse to a halt and dismounted, his hands sliding to my waist as he hauled me to the ground with him. He'd insisted on my riding with him today, and I'd taken one look at the frozen wasteland in his eyes and known I wouldn't win that argument.

His eyes met mine, his hands still on my waist. "You'll stay here with Galon," he said.

To Galon's credit, he didn't sigh. Although, he didn't look pleased. "Not smart to split up."

"We won't be long."

"I would like to come," I said.

Lorian just shook his head.

Grinding my teeth, I glanced at Marth, who shrugged. "It's so if you're tortured, you can't talk about what we're doing."

Lorian let out a sound that might've been a growl, and Marth smiled, turning his horse.

Now I *really* wanted to know what they were up to. It was the first time I'd seen them tense with anticipation, and I was almost desperate to know why.

It was my turn to smile. Because, thanks to Lorian, I'd be able to do just that.

During his little game with the rope, I'd finally understood where my power lived. And I'd practiced with it over and over while we rode today, only able to achieve a couple of seconds at best while I focused on the terror I'd felt over and over since I'd fled my village.

I had no plans to tell the mercenaries I could now summon my magic until I absolutely had to.

Lorian had reminded me that the only person I could trust was myself. And if he'd known just how often I'd frozen time today, he wouldn't be looking so calm and assured.

He glanced at me one last time, and his eyes narrowed. I attempted my best bored expression, but from the way he studied my face, I didn't succeed.

"Watch her," he told Galon.

Galon heaved a sigh but nodded, giving me a look that said he would not be tolerating any games.

I waited with Galon while the others disappeared down the trail. I had to time this carefully. Too soon, and Galon would know what I was doing. Too late, and I'd miss their little meeting.

Crossing my legs, I shuffled in place a few times, sighing occasionally. When Galon threw me an irritated look, I shrugged.

"I need to duck behind a bush."

Galon hunched his shoulders. Of all the mercenaries, he was the most uncomfortable whenever he was reminded that I was a woman.

"Fine. Don't take long."

"It'll take as long as it takes."

His eyes widened, my cheeks heated, and we both glanced away.

I strode toward the slightly taller bushes near one of the strange, thin trees. My breath quickened, and I turned toward the trail Lorian and the others had continued down.

Glancing over my shoulder, I surveyed Galon. He was leaning over, checking his horse's shoe.

I wasn't going to get a better opportunity.

My sneaking skills hadn't improved much since the night I'd found the mercenaries in their clearing. Perhaps I could convince one of them to teach me their skulking ways before we reached the city.

Once I was far enough away from Galon, the dense bushes made it easy to hide. I dropped to my hands and knees, wincing as I scraped them along sharp sticks and stones.

The trail climbed up a small hill, and I followed it until I heard voices.

My magic came to me easier than it ever had before. During the long day of travel, I'd discovered that finding and using my power wasn't the challenging part. No, the part that felt almost impossible was holding the thread of my power in place for longer than a few seconds.

Taking a deep breath, I rolled my shoulders and pulled on the power inside me. My skin went hot, and the bird above my head froze in place, wings spread in preparation to fly.

I shuffled forward, well aware that this was where my control was the weakest. If I wasn't careful, time would resume while I was still getting into place.

But I was lucky. I released my hold on my power, and when the bird trilled a few foot-spans behind me, I was perfectly positioned above the mercenaries, crouched behind a thick shrub. I peered down, my heart thudding harder in my chest.

Lorian, Rythos, and Marth were standing in a tight group, clearly waiting. Cavis stood a few foot-spans away, surveying their surroundings. I ducked my head.

But not before I caught movement.

I leaned around the bush once more. Two men were approaching, and Lorian's rough growl reached my ears as he greeted the visitors. Both wore cloaks, their hoods covering their faces, and I frowned as one of them handed Lorian a glass vial. He slipped it into his cloak pocket with a nod.

Rythos said something that made one of the men laugh, and then they both turned. The cloak slipped off the stranger closest to me, and my lungs seized up.

His ears were pointed.

Fae.

A cold sweat broke out on my neck, and my vision speckled. The mercenaries were working with the fae.

Truthfully, I shouldn't be surprised. The whole point of being a mercenary was doing not-very-nice things for the kind of people willing to pay in gold.

But…

Something broke in me at the thought of them working with the fae. The very creatures who'd terrorized our kingdom for so many centuries. The reason our king had to bargain with the gods in the first place.

If not for the fae, I might've grown up as a normal child. All of us villagers would've been able to keep our magic. There would be no Taking ceremony, no Gifting ceremony…

Tibris would likely have much, much more magic. We all knew the gods kept the majority of our power.

Without Tibris's sacrifice, would our father still be alive?

Fury warred with the terror, and I jolted back into motion. I needed to get back to Galon. Marth's comment about holding up under torture made much more sense now. What would Lorian do to me if he knew what I'd seen?

I crawled back down the hill. Galon was already calling for me. Brushing off my hands on the underside of my shirt, I sauntered back toward him.

"Sorry, took a while."

He turned red. I no longer cared about potential embarrassment. I was too busy turning away to pace.

This whole time, Lorian had kept the upper hand in all our negotiations. He knew I still had my power, that the king's guards were hunting me, that I hadn't seen twenty-five winters.

Now, *I* had information on him.

Just how useful was that information? Was it useful enough to bargain with the king for my own safety?

My stomach roiled at the thought, but I shoved the guilt down deep.

The fae. I didn't know how they'd managed to get into our borders, but they were a threat to everyone in this kingdom. Buried beneath my rage and shock was a sliver of grief I couldn't seem to kill, no matter how much I tried.

I liked Rythos, with his charming smile and small acts of kindness. I liked Marth, with his lewd humor and devotion to Lorian—even if that devotion had allowed them all to know just how many men I'd killed.

I liked Cavis, with his dreamy eyes and stories of his wife and baby. And I liked Galon, who'd saved my life and never once asked for his cloak back.

I didn't like Lorian, but I could at least see the wisdom of keeping him alive.

They returned, and I attempted to look bored. Lorian took one look at me and snarled, his gaze taking in the dirt on my knees and the scraped hands I tucked behind my back.

He obviously knew I'd been up to something.

Surprisingly, he didn't say a word. That, more than anything, was what made true fear shudder through my body.

I wouldn't be sleeping tonight.

10
PRISCA

"Again," Galon said.

I sucked in a breath and hit the folded-up bedroll once more. Galon thrust his hand out toward me, and I slid to the side, knocking his hand away with my forearm before striking with my elbow.

According to the mercenaries, Tibris had laid a decent foundation with my training. But that foundation had no roof, and the walls were falling down around me.

Whatever that meant.

Galon's answer to my weaknesses was drills. Constant, never-ending drills.

Apparently, half of staying alive came down to reflexes. People who could defend themselves automatically—their body responding to an attack the same way it had a thousand times before—were much more likely to survive.

When I was finished warming up, and I'd completed Galon's drills, the men took turns attacking me in new and creative ways. Each of them had something to offer, although Galon was in charge of my physical training.

I tripped Marth and kicked him in the ribs. Since I didn't *really* want to hurt him, I kept the kick light. Galon scowled at me. "You don't just hit once. You hit them until they stop moving," Galon said.

I winced, but he was right. Once I lost the element of surprise, I was in big trouble. The only reason I'd managed to stay alive so far was because men continued to underestimate me.

Long may it last.

Lorian stood from where he'd been leaning against a tree trunk, watching everything through narrowed eyes.

"We need to leave," he said.

I panted out a breath, grateful for the reprieve. Although I didn't enjoy the fact that it had come from Lorian.

"You're riding with me," Lorian said. The expression on his face dared me to argue. If I protested, he'd throw me over his shoulder and dump me on his horse, making it clear that no matter how much I trained, I was useless compared to him.

I itched with the need to stop time and mount one of the other men's horses.

Curling my lip at him, I stalked toward his horse. "Hello, darling," I crooned, patting him on the neck. He lipped at my hand, and I laughed. Lorian still hadn't told me his horse's name. It was yet another way to annoy me.

I no longer felt like the days were disappearing

beneath me. Now, they'd slowed to a crawl as our horses trod on, day after day.

Even though the thought of the city sometimes made my mouth turn dry and my stomach churn, I still longed for it. Right now, I was stuck with no way back, only forward, and the sooner I got to the city, the sooner I could find a ship and a new life.

Mama had said she'd kidnapped me from my real parents. They'd probably assumed I was dead all this time. Didn't they deserve to know the truth as well?

"What are you thinking about?" Lorian's voice was low in my ear.

"You know, for a man who refuses to tell me anything about himself, you sure think you're entitled to my every thought."

He chuckled, and I attempted to ignore just how much that sound made me want to grin.

Surprisingly, Lorian hadn't said a word after his meeting with the fae. I'd struggled to stay awake that night, but I'd eventually told myself that if he wanted me dead, he could reach out and snap my neck while I was awake. Now, neither of us spoke of the fae they'd been meeting. I was pretty sure he knew I'd been spying. He'd definitely seen evidence that I'd been crawling around in the dirt, away from Galon's keen eye. But Lorian was tricky. He'd likely guessed that *not* mentioning it would make me crazed.

We approached the outskirts of the town Lorian had decided we would stop in tonight, and I pulled my hair over my face, flipping up the hood of my cloak. "We're staying at the inn on the other side of this town, closer to the city," Lorian said.

If I didn't know him better, I'd think that was an attempt to make me less afraid. But Lorian enjoyed my fear. He'd made that much clear when he'd pulled that rope out of his pocket by the river.

After this, we would be traveling for just one more night, and then we would arrive at the city gates. Nerves fluttered in my stomach at the thought.

My legs were aching when we dismounted. Lorian took my arm and I stiffened, but he ignored me, practically dragging me into the inn as the others followed closely behind.

"My wife and I need a room," he said.

I went still. This man was determined to keep me off-balance.

The innkeeper's gaze dropped to my empty wrist, which would have been encircled with a wedding bracelet had I actually been married. My hair was pulled in front of my shoulders and covering my temples, but the innkeeper still glanced at the side of my face, as if searching for the blue mark that would proclaim me old enough to be wed.

Lorian leaned close. "Is there a problem?"

"N-no. Of course not. You're in luck today. We have our best room available."

I closed my eyes, my cheeks burning.

Lorian's mouth curved as he wrapped his arm around my shoulders and leaned close. "Did you hear that, sweetheart? The *best* room." He turned back to the innkeeper. "We'll take it."

One day, I would make this man pay for every drop of mortification I'd felt in his presence.

The innkeeper handed over the keys, and I glanced behind me at the others, ignoring Rythos's snort, Marth's grin, and even the hint of amusement in Galon's eyes. As usual, Cavis was staring into the distance, deep in thought.

"Rooms include dinner and breakfast," the innkeeper said.

"Good," Marth muttered. "Please tell me it's anything but rabbit."

Offense crossed Rythos's face. "You don't like it? Maybe you should cook your own food."

Leaving the men to bicker, I checked the hood of my cloak and wandered into the main room, where a fire was currently roaring in one corner. Lorian prowled after me, practically breathing down my neck.

"What's the matter?" he purred. "I thought you didn't want to sleep alone."

The mercenary was in a playful mood. Clearly, I wasn't the only one looking forward to a roof over my head tonight.

"I don't," I said coolly. "But I'd prefer that no one thought I was stupid enough to marry a coldhearted brute like yourself."

He gave me a knowing look that made me grind my teeth. By the time we got to the city, my teeth would be little more than dust.

Dropping into his chair, Lorian pulled me down next to him and surveyed the inn. Across the room, a barmaid was pouring ale for a group of travelers who were just as dusty—and likely as road-weary—as us. She looked up and winked at Lorian, her tongue darting out to lick her lips. When I glanced at him, he was looking at me, the hint of a smile on his face.

"What?"

The smile disappeared, his expression falling into its usual neutrality. I sighed and got to my feet. He instantly clamped his hand around my wrist.

"Let go," I growled.

"You go nowhere alone."

I knew that resolved expression. The brute wasn't going to change his mind. After what had happened the last time we were in an inn just like this one...

Lorian waved the barmaid over, and she swung her hips in a way I knew I could never replicate. Not that I wanted to.

"Water," Lorian said.

"Please," I gritted out.

The barmaid didn't seem to have a problem with his gruff tone and lack of manners. She smiled widely at him and filled our cups.

"Food and ale?" she smiled.

He nodded, and she sauntered away toward the kitchen.

Marth strolled over, sending the barmaid his I-know-you-want-me smile. Her eyes lit up, and I shook my head at him.

I missed the company of other women so much sometimes. Missed my best friend even more. What would Asinia think of me now?

If not for the fact that I was one of the corrupt, she would likely find the fact that I was traveling alone with five men both hilarious and titillating.

"You're quiet," Rythos said.

"I'm tired."

Rythos just nudged me, hard enough that I wobbled on the rickety stool. Lorian sent him a warning look.

The barmaid returned with plates of some kind of meat, root vegetables, and bread, which she placed in front of us. The bread was fresh, and I took a bite, my stomach awakening as the other men sat down and began stuffing food into their mouths.

The barmaid leaned over the table, revealing the tops of large, round breasts, and gave Marth a saucy grin.

She shifted her attention to me. "Now which of these fine men is yours?"

Lorian snorted. That. Was. It.

"Well," I said. "This is a little…awkward…"

The barmaid's eyes lit up, and she leaned closer. "It is?"

"It's just that…they're *all* mine." I surveyed the men as I said it, grinning at their reactions.

A chunk of meat fell from Rythos's mouth. Cavis's eyes widened, while Marth choked on his ale. Galon closed his eyes and muttered something that sounded like "young enough to be my daughter."

Lorian just looked at me, irritation clear in his eyes.

I smiled a smug little smile that was guaranteed to annoy him even more. I had to get my enjoyment where I could find it.

The barmaid's mouth had fallen open.

"She's just joking," Marth ground out, obviously seeing his chances with her going up in smoke. "Tell her, Prisca."

"Don't say that, darling," I crooned. "I promise you'll get your turn with me eventually."

I didn't know what had come over me. From the horror on Marth's face, neither did he.

I'd expected Lorian to snarl. Instead, he leaned close. So close, my body hummed with awareness. So close, I could barely breathe.

"My *wife* has a…filthy mouth," he purred, his gaze dropping to my lips.

I licked my lips, and he leaned even closer. Galon slammed his cup on the table, and I jolted.

Lorian launched to his feet, pulling me up with him. "Are you finished?"

I glanced down at my empty plate and beamed at the barmaid. "I am. That was delicious, thank you."

The look Lorian sent me made it clear he wasn't talking about the food. I wrapped both my arms around one of his, determined that he wouldn't win. He stiffened, brow lowering.

"Let's go to our room." I winked at the others. "I'll

see you all *later*."

"Enough," Lorian said, hauling me toward the stairs. "You've had your fun."

I glanced at him. I was expecting him to growl at me. What I wasn't expecting was the way his shoulders shook, or the way he pulled me close, holding on to me as his chest rumbled with his laugh. "Did you see Galon's face?"

The older man's horrified expression flashed in front of my eyes, and I giggled. "His daughter," I got out, almost folding in two as fresh laughter erupted from me.

Lorian stopped laughing first, his gaze on my face. His expression had turned gentle, almost indulgent. He was so close that I could see the darker green flecks in his eyes. The moment stretched, and my heart began thumping erratically.

"What is it?"

He cleared his throat. "Nothing." Pulling the key from his pocket, he glanced down at the number. "Let's get settled."

I followed him up the rest of the stairs and to the right. Our room was on this floor at the end of the hall.

Lorian swung the door open, taking in the "best room."

The sound that came out of me was an embarrassing moan of pure *want*. Lorian stiffened, and I glanced up at him then back at the bath, which had been drawn while we were eating. He chuckled.

"I'll leave you to bathe." He dropped his bag on the

floor and gently pushed me farther into the room so he could shut the door.

I'd bathed in the river that morning. But that had involved shivering until it felt like my bones would break and cursing at the lack of soap. Now, I could laze in this cracked, clawed tub for as long as I liked.

My clothes hit the floor within moments, and I was stepping into the bath, sighing as I leaned back in the candlelight. The water was almost too hot—just the way I liked it—and whoever had drawn the bath had left behind vanilla-scented soap.

This. Was. Paradise.

I lathered every inch of myself, washed my hair, and leaned back once more.

Teasing Lorian, finally hearing him laugh...had been...*fun*. I'd thought I'd annoy him—and had been just fine with that idea—but hearing the rough mercenary truly laugh for the first time... Our eyes meeting without the usual rancor...

It had been nice. That was all. A nice, enjoyable moment in an otherwise monotonous travel day.

A moment that had—for reasons I didn't understand—reminded me of my parents.

Gods, they'd laughed so often. They'd rarely fought, unless it was over me. The worst was when my parents took us to a wedding in the village. It was before we moved to our last village. The one I'd just...left.

I couldn't recall who exactly was married that day, but I'd never forget the way the bride's smile lit up her face when they vowed to be true to each other for all time.

When the groom took her in his arms and kissed her, the whole village cheered. I'd sighed, laying my head against my mother's hip.

"I'm going to get married one day," I'd announced. "Here in the village."

My father had given me his amused, patient look. My mother had been battling a headache all day, and her voice had been sharp.

"No, you won't, Prisca. Such things are not for you."

My father's expression had tightened, and he'd wrapped his arm around me. "Vuena," he'd said warningly, and my mother had given him an impatient shrug.

"She needs to learn now. Better than to be disappointed later."

"Let her have her dreams," my father said softly. They hadn't talked for the rest of the day.

A few months later, I'd learned exactly why such things weren't for me. That was the first time I'd pulled that strange thread that had made time stop. But I'd vowed I would find a way to change my fate.

My mother continued to remind me I was different each time there was a wedding or a baby born or any of the other happy milestones of life.

"Prisca," she would say, when my father was busy elsewhere. "Remember, this is not for you."

And of course, like most people, the more I was told something wasn't for me, the more I wanted it.

A knock sounded on the door.

I startled, an embarrassing squeak leaving my mouth. "One moment."

Reaching for the bath sheet, I stood, wrapping it around me. The room was freezing, and I huddled by the tiny fire as I dragged on one of the mercenary's shirts. Sure, they'd given me clothes, but I'd convinced them to let me keep a few of their shirts for sleeping.

"Who is it?"

"Lorian."

"You can come in," I called, and Lorian stepped inside. His eyes went dark, and I glanced down to see the shirt clinging to my damp skin, my nipples pressed against the cloth.

"That's my shirt," he said. Was his voice hoarse?

"Well, you can't have it back."

He rubbed his hand along his chin, still staring at me, and my toes curled on the cold floor. His gaze dropped to them, and he jerked his head toward the bed. "You're cold. Get into bed."

I complied. He began to strip.

My heart jumped into my throat. "What are you doing?"

"There's still steam rising off that water, wildcat. If you think I'm letting a warm bath go to waste…"

That was my stomach swooping like I was on the edge of a precipice. "I can leave…"

"You're not going anywhere alone. Close your eyes if the sight of a male body offends a lady as meek and modest as yourself."

His tone implied there was nothing meek or modest about me. I glowered at his back. His skin was smooth, tanned, with thin white scars along his ribs, his back, his shoulders. He had the body of a warrior, and as his hands dropped to his pants, those muscles in his back rippled smoothly.

His shoulders were so…wide. I'd never seen a man built like him until the day I'd met the mercenaries.

The thought of that river should have dampened the strange, warm feeling in my stomach, but Lorian's pants dropped to the floor and I sucked in a breath.

He slowly turned his head, and our eyes met.

His smile was very male. And very smug.

Don't do it. Don't you dare do it.

My gaze dropped to his toned ass, and I swallowed, my mouth suddenly dry.

"See something you like?" Lorian purred.

"Nothing. Nothing at all."

He chuckled, turning to the bath, and I slammed my eyes shut. It wasn't fair that he was so annoying and yet so fucking perfect.

Splashing sounded, and I cracked my eyes open. Lorian wouldn't know I was watching him in the dim light.

I was pretty sure.

He reached for the soap. The thought of him smelling like vanilla was enough to make me smirk. But he ran his hands over his body roughly, until I practically itched to push those hands away and caress every inch of him.

What was I thinking?

I closed my eyes once more. "You did well today," Lorian murmured, his voice low. Intimate. As if we were that couple I'd watched when I was a young girl and we bathed in front of each other every day. "With Galon. Your fighting is improving."

It took me a few tries to reply. "Thank you."

More infernal splashing. I didn't understand how I could *loathe* someone on such a deep level…and then fantasize about his body this way.

It was a stress response. It had to be. I was alone, and my body was reacting to Lorian because it knew he would keep me safe.

I barely suppressed a snort. That thought was weak, even for me.

Lorian stood. I knew that, because I'd opened my eyes to slits once more. He stood facing me, his expression thoughtful as he reached for the bath sheet.

His chest looked like it had been carved from rock. He roughly swiped that bath sheet over his stomach and… lower.

Even his cock was disgustingly perfect. Long and thick and smooth and—

Stop staring at his cock.

I swallowed. Lorian arched his back in a stretch, and I closed my eyes, my body hot and feverish. Awareness crackled over my skin, my core throbbed, and I forced myself to roll over and face the wall.

I could have sworn I was too worked up to fall

asleep, but I somehow managed to drift off. Movement made me jolt awake. He was finally getting into bed. I had a sneaking suspicion he was still naked. The thought removed any hope of sleep.

I could feel his gaze on me, and I rolled over. His green eyes shone like a cat's in the dim light.

He leaned closer. His eyes were so dark they appeared black. I breathed him in. His gaze dropped to my lips, and every muscle in my body went weak. My core clenched. Heat pooled in my stomach...

But I had to know.

"Why are you working with the fae?"

He went still in that strange way of his. It was as if he channeled all his anger and frustration into turning his muscles to stone.

"Go to sleep." He rolled over.

I blew out a shaky breath and turned onto my side. I knew when a man wanted me. And Lorian wanted me. The thought was heady.

"Sleep," he ordered once more.

My cheeks blazing, I closed my eyes and willed myself to sleep.

11
PRISCA

I woke to the sound of bells ringing.

Ice crawled through my veins.

"No," I got out.

I turned to Lorian, who glanced at me. He was already jumping out of bed and reaching for his leathers. "We need to go."

The bells continued to ring, and someone slammed their fist on our door. I jumped. Lorian slowly turned his head in a way that spelled death for whoever was out there.

"Taking," the voice announced. "Everyone to the square."

My entire body seized. My lungs constricted. Black dots danced across my eyes.

"Prisca!"

Lorian was crouching in front of me, his hands wrapped around my upper arms as he shook me.

"King's assessor," I said through numb lips. "Here."

"I know." A muscle twitched in his cheek. "We can't leave. If we do, the guards will follow us."

The rules were the same everywhere. Everyone had to attend Gifting and Taking ceremonies with unless they had a written exception.

"I can't go. The king's guards are looking for me."

Oh gods. This was it. They were going to drag me away from this place, throw me in the back of a barred carriage, and take me to the city to burn.

"Look at me." He waited until I met his eyes once more. "They know there are two people in this room. The innkeeper recorded it. And thanks to your little game last night, the entire inn knows we have a woman traveling with us."

He was right. This was my fault.

Lorian seemed to regret his words, because his hands tightened around my arms and his expression softened. "We'll go to the Taking, and we'll be ready to leave as soon as it's done."

"They're going to notice me, Lorian. This is it."

A stupid way to die. This felt like a waste. I hadn't even gotten close to the city. Hadn't had the chance to see my brother one last time.

"I won't let them hurt you." Lorian's words seemed to be coming from somewhere far away. I could practically smell the smoke.

"Enough. You're stronger than this. And you don't have the luxury of falling apart. Do you understand me?"

I nodded.

"Good." He let me go. "Now put on your cloak, and let's all pretend to be pious."

"I'll use my magic on the innkeeper so we can sneak past him. He won't know if we've left the room already. It can buy us some time."

Lorian shook his head. "The innkeeper is a null."

"What's a null?"

He was already dragging me toward the door. "Someone who repels magic. It's unlikely your magic will work on him, and if it did, it would cost you so much power, you'd be useless for the rest of the day."

Fear had gripped my throat and was squeezing. My only choice was to rely on Lorian and the others.

Lorian swung the door open. Galon was already waiting outside our room. "Marth has the horses ready," he muttered. "They're tied at the edge of the town, near the road to Lesdryn. As soon as the ceremony is over, we'll leave."

"What if the guards follow us?" I asked, my lips numb. Sometime over the past few days, my concerns had changed. I was no longer worried that Lorian would hand me over to the guards. No, I was more concerned that the mercenaries would die in an attempt to protect me.

"I asked the innkeeper, and they'll be traveling south from here. As long as we don't give them any reason to suspect you."

I followed the men downstairs, noting the innkeeper crossing something off his list as we walked past. Lorian was right. He would have informed the guards if I'd stayed behind.

More guards lined the streets outside. My stomach

twisted. I ruthlessly clamped down on the nausea and pulled up the hood of my cloak. Thankfully, it was cold enough that many of the townspeople had done the same. Lorian strode next to me, his huge body shielding me from the crowd. I could practically feel the warmth emanating from him. I could definitely sense the icy rage. Galon strode on my other side, shoulders back, expression unconcerned. His confidence helped with the worst of my terror, and I squared my shoulders.

Cavis and Rythos were waiting at the edge of the crowd, as far from the guards as they could get.

Rythos reached out and grabbed my hand, giving it a squeeze. My stomach settled a little, and I squeezed back. Almost immediately, I was surrounded by hard male bodies. They formed a circle around me, and I knew for sure that if they had to, they'd slaughter anyone who took me. Not just because I was pretty sure at least Rythos and Cavis liked me, but because if I went down, they'd go down with me.

Not to mention, they were all territorial brutes who were currently eyeing the guards like they were imagining their heads on pikes. My own gaze slid to the king's assessor and got stuck there.

King Sabium had several assessors he liked to use. I hadn't seen this one before, but they were all the same with their black robes, silver brooches and beady-eyed stares. All of them seemed to enjoy finding the corrupt and ordering their deaths.

Hunching under my cloak, I had to fight the urge to

battle my way through this crowd and sprint as far from the assessor as I could. Yet my legs had turned rubbery. Lorian seemed to sense it, wrapping his hand around my arm. I forced my gaze away and turned to Galon, who was glowering at the king's assessor with a kind of malevolence I'd never seen from him before. I elbowed him, and he scowled at me, dropping his gaze as the town's priestess walked past.

She was younger than the priestess from our village. But her expression held the same peaceful piety I'd seen so many times before.

The wooden platform she climbed was similar to the one I'd stared at so many times in my town. Next to the platform, a man and woman both stood, their baby clutched in her mother's arms. The woman was pale, but she strode up the stairs beneath the king's guards' watchful gaze.

"Such a sweet little girl," a woman said to one of her friends, her voice carrying over the wall of muscle next to me.

A girl. The baby wouldn't be named until after the Taking ceremony, as was tradition.

"Where's Marth?" I whispered.

Rythos jerked his head toward the other side of the crowd. "We'll meet him after."

The priestess began to speak. I'd practically memorized the story of our history, but as always, I focused closely, hoping for some hint about why I still had my power.

"Centuries ago, our people went to war with the fae," the priestess said. Several townspeople spat on the ground at the mention of the creatures who'd caused such heartache. The priestess allowed it, closing her eyes.

"Not content with their incredible power, indescribable wealth, and fertile lands, the fae decided they wanted more. They wanted humans," she said in a hushed tone. My skin crawled at the thought of being stolen in the middle of the night.

"They wanted women to be their brides to make up for their low fertility. They wanted human servants to manage their households and work in their mines. They wanted more power. More wealth. More, more, more. Finally, the king's great-great-grandfather, a strong, wise king called Regner said 'enough.' He was tired of his people being preyed upon. Tired of the fae taking whatever they wanted. And so, they went to war."

Statues of Regner stood in most northern villages. I remembered climbing on top of one of them as a child. The king had been practically a myth while alive, and once dead, he'd become almost godlike himself.

The priestess ran her gaze over the crowd, clearly in her element.

"The fae may have been outnumbered by us, but they had the kind of power that could flood valleys. The kind of power that could burn entire cities to the ground. Our people had fae iron. And they used it to fight back however they could."

I'd spent many hours mumbling prayers during

various ceremonies in my village, and many of those prayers had involved thanking the gods for risplite—the strange mineral they'd gifted us. When added to iron while it was in the furnace, it turned previously normal iron into a true weapon against the fae.

The priestess continued talking. "The slaughter continued for weeks. And then months. Our people—on the brink of being destroyed completely—were losing hope. And so, King Regner went to the gods and begged them to intervene. If they helped us defeat the fae, we would give the gods back our power while it was young and potent. Because that power would grow as it aged, and the gods could sip on it, staying strong themselves in a time where few were worshipping as they should."

Next to me, Rythos let out a soft snort. Lorian glanced at him, and Rythos's expression turned blank.

"For the gods had been losing power themselves," the priestess said. "As fewer people prayed to them. As fewer people sacrificed to the deities. The gods—on the verge of fading—agreed to the king's deal. And so, the bargain was struck.

"Every year, we celebrate the first Taking—on a day known forever as Gods Day—to respect the sacrifice our people made that day. They were willing to give up their power, to lose their magic until they reached maturity at the age of twenty-five winters. They screamed as they gave the king everything they had. Some of them died. But it was enough. The gods accepted the sacrifice and helped King Regner drive the fae back behind their borders. And now, that sacrifice protects those borders from the monsters who would avenge their fallen friends and family members. Because the fae are much longer-lived than us mere mortals. And while this may be history to us, that time is a *memory* for most of the fae. And they will not forget."

The priestess turned her smile onto the couple standing below her. "Come, and help your daughter sacrifice to keep all of us safe."

The man followed his wife up the stairs, and the priestess held up her hands, the wide sleeves of her impeccable gray robes falling down her arms.

"Just as the gods gift, they also take."

The town priestess waved her hand at one of her novices, and the priestess-in-training walked toward the platform, the basket of dark, empty blue stones in her hands. The blood rushed in my ears as I stared at the stones I'd imagined would be the answer to my problems.

The novice bowed her head, offering up the oceartus stones.

The priestess plucked one at random. She lifted her hand, held the stone high in the air, and began to chant. Slowly, she lowered the stone, until it was poised just above the baby's head.

"Heed our sacrifice and see our piety. Have mercy on our weakest, bolster our strongest, and protect all who live here. For our power will always belong to the gods from whom it came."

We all began to speak the words we'd memorized

when we were children. "Faric, see our sacrifice. Tronin, see our sacrifice. Bretis, see our sacrifice," I chanted along, hearing Galon's and Lorian's low rumbles next to me as they spoke the same words. Faric was the god of knowledge, Tronin, the god of strength, and Bretis, the god of protection.

If those gods had any mercy, this would finish soon, and we could flee.

The priestess spoke a few more sentences in the old language. A language never to be spoken by those who hadn't taken the holy vows.

I tensed. I hated this part.

The baby began to scream. Her parents kept their expressions blank, but any who cared to look could see the pain in her mother's eyes. Could see the way her father's hands fisted as the priestess took his daughter's magic, sucking it into the oceartus stone, which glowed so brightly, it hurt to look at it.

I shifted my attention to the guards. They were watching too, their gazes intent as they witnessed the Taking. Occasionally, parents would attempt to protect their babies. It wasn't common, but it happened.

My heart began to thunder in my chest.

The Taking was over. The baby continued to scream as if she were being tortured, and her mother lifted her, pressing her to her chest.

The priestesses insisted that the Taking was painless. But no one who had ever seen a newborn lose their magic could ever believe that lie.

Everyone climbed off the platform. They would have a quiet service at their home and announce their baby's name. My legs had gone weak again—this time with relief. We'd survived this long. Now we just had to find our horses.

The crowd began to disperse. We slowly began to move toward the road leading out of the town. I wanted to shove my way through these people. To beg them to *move*. But that would only draw attention.

Lorian's grip changed on my arm, and I looked up. Marth was standing in front of us, his face pale.

"We have a problem."

He handed us a piece of parchment. Someone had drawn my likeness and described my features. It wasn't exact, but it was close enough that I was sure to be questioned if we attempted to leave. Everything receded until all I could see was my own face. My lungs seized, and a line of cold sweat slid down my spine.

Beneath the picture were the names of the corrupt who had been taken to the city. This wasn't uncommon. I'd seen this list before, hung in our village square.

My gaze got stuck on a name halfway down the list.

"No. No, no, no."

Asinia. My *best friend* Asinia.

Asinia had been in hiding too. And I'd never known. Just as she'd never known about my own magic. When the corrupt were found, all their friends and family members were assessed. Asinia likely wouldn't have been caught if not for me. She wouldn't be in some dank dungeon awaiting her death while I laughed and ate and learned how to fight.

"We need to go," Marth murmured.

I stared at the parchment.

I couldn't cry. I was too numb. My whole body shook, my teeth chattering as I pictured Asinia alone on a stone floor, with nothing to eat, counting down the moments until she—

I leaned over and vomited. Lorian sighed, pulled my hair away from my face, and shifted us both a few footspans to the side.

Strangely, it was his nonchalance that blew the worst of the fog from my mind.

He handed me water, and I rinsed my mouth.

Then we were moving. Lorian tucked me beneath his shoulder, steering me toward the outskirts of the city. Dimly, I was aware of the mercenaries discussing our situation. Their voices sounded like they were standing at the other end of a tunnel.

"The innkeeper paid attention to her face. So did the barmaid. It's possible they've already spoken to the guards." Rythos reached out and squeezed my hand. I squeezed back.

"There's only one road out of the city, unless we cut through the forest. But that will seem suspicious," Cavis said.

My heart was frozen. It was stuck to the walls of my chest, to my lungs, all of it just a big clump of ice.

There was no question I was still going to the city.

But I wouldn't be finding a ship.

I was never meant to live a full life. The gods had determined that when they'd rejected my power when I was just days old.

But if I could save Asinia's life, it would all be worth it. And I would. Somehow, I would.

"Prisca."

Someone was gently shaking me. I looked up into Lorian's eyes. "What?"

"You can mourn later. For now, we need to get past the guards at the town gates."

Mourn. Because if Asinia was in the king's dungeon, she was as good as dead.

Fury burned in my belly. But I nodded, and a hint of what might've been relief flickered over Lorian's face.

"Listen to me. You need to use your power. Remember what you learned," he said, and the breath froze in my lungs.

I was the one who was supposed to save us?

He gave me a warning look as I shook my head. "I can't." I'd only ever managed to hold it for a few seconds of time. We would need much longer than that if we were all to get past the guards on the road out of this town.

Lorian's eyes narrowed, and the warning turned to disgust. "Every time I think you're about to stop being a scared little mouse and actually reveal the woman I believe you are, you prove me wrong. Well, sweetheart, we don't have time for your insecurity and self-doubt."

"I hate you."

He just shook his head. "Either you freeze those guards long enough for us to get past them, or we all die here. Rythos goes first, and his death is the hardest. The king has been looking for him for some time."

My face was numb, but I turned my head until I could see Rythos. His gaze was on the guards standing at the town gates. He watched them the way I might watch a poisonous snake slithering through the grass toward me.

I looked at the king's guards, and all I could see were flames. All I could smell was the scent of burning hair. All I could see was my skin, slowly turning to ash.

"Prisca."

I would have been better off dying in the river. It would have been an easier death.

Strong fingers dug into my arms, squeezing until I came back to myself. I stared at Lorian. His eyes blazed into mine, and a muscle jumped in his cheek.

Beneath the terror, my fury burned bright. So bright, I didn't have to reach for my power. No, instead, the threads seemed to reach for me, my skin heating.

"There it is," Lorian breathed. "Now, use it."

The guards were standing at the gates, paying careful attention to each person who walked toward them. As we watched, one of the guards snagged a woman's cloak, throwing the hood off her head. Her hair was a fiery red, and the guard nodded at her to continue walking.

"You need to freeze time before the guards see us," Lorian said. "Or it will appear that we have disappeared in front of their eyes, and they will come after us with everything they have."

It was difficult, freezing time for everyone except our group. Staring at the guard in the middle, I watched as he began to strut toward another woman who went still. Her shoulders hunched, and I could practically feel her terror from here.

I took a slow, deep breath. Then I reached for the tangled thread of time and *pulled*. It took every drop of my will. But time froze.

"Hold it," Lorian instructed. "Don't let go."

It was already slipping. Immediately. Panic roared through me. Something wet dripped from my nose. Blood.

"Hold it!" Lorian roared at me, dragging me toward the guards. My vision began to dim at the edges.

"Focus, Prisca," he snarled. "Dig deep."

I pushed everything I had into it, stretching time, molding it.

This was my only hope if I was going to save Asinia.

My head felt as if a giant had trapped it between his hands and was squeezing. I let out a whimper that would mortify me later.

Asinia.

"Don't let go," Lorian growled, hauling me into his arms and running for the horses.

My vision had gone dark.

I couldn't fail. If I let go, we were all dead.

But it was so difficult. The thread was slipping like sand through my fingers, the seconds of time fighting to resume.

Lorian handed me to someone else briefly. Then I was lifted up, into his arms, and held tight to his chest once more.

"Almost there," he ground out.

I could feel the horse galloping beneath me. Its movements shook me, distracting me further.

"Can't. Hold. It."

Speaking split my concentration, and I lost my grip on the thread. I caught it an instant later, but I was holding on to the very end.

"Let go," Lorian said.

I slumped against him. My vision hadn't returned. A dull panic spread through my chest, and I buried my hands in Lorian's shirt, almost desperate for something to hold on to.

"Good girl," Lorian purred in my ear.

"Can't see," I choked out, panic battling the exhaustion that had swept through my body.

I felt him take a deep breath. "Flameout. That shouldn't be happening. You have much more power than you're using."

It didn't *feel* like I had more power available to me. But his unconcerned tone helped dull the edges of my terror. My hearing seemed to sharpen, and I focused on the sound of the horses, on the low murmurs of the other men, and the thumping of my own heart.

We rode in silence as my vision gradually returned. First, sunlight appeared around the edges, and then blurry shapes began to take form. I let out a shuddering breath.

"I'd thought it was fear that would help you unlock your power," Lorian said eventually. I wished he wouldn't murmur in my ear like that. It was far too intimate. Not to mention, my head was pounding.

"It wasn't, though, was it?" he asked when I didn't reply. "It was anger. The reason you were flaming out at the end was because you allowed the fear in."

I considered that, but my brain was still foggy, my thoughts distant. When I'd let myself channel my fury, my power had been easy to grasp. But the longer I'd held time, the more my mind had focused on what would happen if I failed. If I lost hold of that thread and we were caught.

"You're saying I should use my rage?"

Mama had always said I needed to control my anger. That focusing on the way the gods had messed with my life would only make that life harder.

"I'm saying your emotions may help you find your power, but they won't help you keep it. You need to dig deeper. Follow the thread into the center of that power and memorize it, until you can pull it free with just a thought."

I considered that as we rode for the rest of the day. The notion that I'd be able to reach for my power that easily was thrilling. The possibility burrowed into my mind and stayed there, as I imagined myself freezing time easily, without a thought.

The mercenaries had left the main road at the first opportunity, and we were once more traveling through the forest. Around me, a thousand shades of green and brown blurred together.

Despite the danger, a dull pride wormed its way through my chest. We'd escaped certain death in that town. *I* had done that. If I could do that, I could get us through the city gates. And from there, I could find a way to free Asinia.

Asinia.

When Papa died, I'd lain next to him for hours. When his body was taken away, I'd crawled into my bed and stayed there for days, unable to move. Asinia lay with me, her arms wrapped around me. She didn't say a word, just let me know she was there. When I cried, it was in her arms. When my stomach growled, she made me eat.

The hole inside me—the one that had been created when I'd fled my village, when I'd left my family behind…

That hole had deepened with the realization that my mother was dead. And now, knowing Asinia would die on Gods Day—all because of *me*…

That hole turned into an abyss that could never be filled.

Gods Day happened on the full moon closest to the anniversary of the first Taking. If you were unlucky enough to be arrested just days after the prison was emptied, you'd have an entire year to rot in the king's dungeon and picture yourself burning.

The next full moon was just days away. The full moon after that… I had a little over a month to come up with a way to free Asinia before she was burned.

"I'm sorry about your friend," Lorian rumbled

behind me. He said it as if she were already dead, and I tensed.

"She's going to be okay."

He went silent, his disbelief evident.

That was fine. He didn't know Asinia. And he also didn't know me. *I* barely knew me. But I knew there was no way I was allowing Asinia to be burned alive. Even if it meant the gods punished us both when we died.

Finally, Lorian found a clearing that pleased him, and we stopped for the day. The mercenaries seemed to realize I needed to think, because they let me sit in silence.

I'd used my power today. For longer than I could've imagined. Lorian had said it was like a muscle that needed to be trained. In that case, I would train every day, as often as I could. Because with that power, I had a chance I could save Asinia's life.

Eventually, I got up to wash. Marth and Lorian were sitting by the river.

"Why didn't we take the back gate?" Marth complained.

My gaze snapped to Lorian's. I let him see just how badly I wanted to hurt him.

Marth seemed to realize he'd said something he shouldn't have, because he winced, glancing away.

"You knew another way out of that village?" My voice was hoarse.

Lorian gave me an indolent shrug. "You weren't progressing with your power. I hope you remember how it felt, because we're going to practice all night until you can be trusted tomorrow."

One moment, I was standing, staring at him, and the next, I was flying through the air.

He blinked, but my hands were already wrapped around his throat. I'd launched myself at him, and he just sighed, prying my fingers off him.

"Save it for your training with Galon," he said disinterestedly.

I'd thought I hated the king's assessors. I hadn't known what hate was.

Rythos hauled me away. "There now. Probably better not to annoy Lorian when he's in this mood." He petted me on the shoulder, and I shrugged him off. Yet another thing these men had lied about. How often did they need to prove they couldn't be trusted before I finally understood it?

I narrowed my eyes at him. "You knew too, didn't you?"

"I didn't know all of his plan until I was caught up in it."

I just watched him silently until he sighed. "He *may* have asked me to play up my fear for you."

"You have magic," I got out. "You could have befriended those guards, and they would have allowed us out of the town."

For the first time, fury burned in Rythos's eyes. "Once, I could have. Once, I could have charmed the entire town into doing my bidding. Now?" He let out a bitter laugh.

Lorian's warning snarl cut through the air. I wasn't surprised. He was determined to keep me as ignorant as possible.

"Keep your secrets." I gave Lorian my best bored look. "Tomorrow, we'll be done with each other."

His eyes narrowed on my face. With a stiff nod, he turned and stalked away.

12
PRISCA

practiced stopping time for most of the night. Even after the others had gone to bed, I continued to practice, stopping and starting Marth's snores until my own eyelids grew too heavy to keep open.

I was the first to wake, a chill shuddering through me that had nothing to do with the cold morning. My stomach spiraled, and I sat up, hugging my knees to my chest.

"It's going to be okay," a gruff voice said.

Lorian's eyes met mine. His eyes were still a little hazy with sleep, his jaw dark with stubble. And his hair was ruffled in a way that made me drop my gaze.

"You don't know that."

"You get to believe anything you want. Why would you choose to believe you will fail?"

"It seems so simple when you put it that way."

He stretched, and I got to my knees, pulling Galon's cloak tighter around me. Soon, we would be separated—likely forever. At some points in our journey, I'd longed for this day more than anything else. Now that it was here, I didn't know how to feel.

I took a deep breath. "You said once I mastered my power, you'd tell me why I still have it. Why people like me are hunted."

Lorian cocked his eyebrow in a way that told me in no way had I *mastered* my power.

I glowered at him. "Please."

He gave me a slow smile. "Since you asked so nicely. Come closer, and I'll tell you exactly how your lives have been altered, your destinies stolen."

Given that I was desperate to hear his explanation, I complied.

"You believe the gods favor the king? Believe he is powerful because he has been blessed?" He shook his head. "Every time a mother hands over her child's precious gift, Sabium takes most of it for himself. The gods play no part in your people's suffering. What need do they have for more power?"

It was as if his words had stolen the air from my lungs. My lips were so numb, my mouth so dry, it took several moments before I could form words.

Maybe…maybe it was the king's only option. He'd needed our power to protect us from the fae…

"He uses that magic to protect our borders," I said.

Lorian gave me a pitying look. "Yes. But he still gives power to his councillors to keep them loyal. He gives it to the priestesses to ensure they continue the Takings. He gives it to his guards so they can hunt those whom he considers corrupt. And he keeps much of it himself."

I couldn't breathe.

"My father…" I licked my lips. I didn't want to ask. Didn't want to know. Because I might not be able to handle the answer.

Lorian was watching me with those inscrutable eyes of his. "What is it?"

I forced myself to swallow around the lump in my throat. "My brother is a healer. If he'd kept all of his power, would he have been able to…"

"To save your father?" He gave an elegant shrug. "Perhaps. At least for a time."

I had no words for this feeling. It was worse than betrayal. Greater than rage. It burned through me with no end.

"How…how do I still have my power, then? How does Asinia?"

Lorian stretched out his legs. "Eons ago, this world was divided into four kingdoms. Two human kingdoms called Eprotha and Gromalia. The fae kingdom in the south. And to the west—across the Sleeping Sea—was a kingdom filled with people who had once been wholly fae but had split from their people during the Long War. They became hybrids, mating with humans and producing offspring with unique powers of their own."

When I could speak again, I sucked in deep breath. "The hybrid kingdom was on the Barren Continent?" There was a reason no one traveled to the Barren Continent.

Nothing grew there. And any ships that attempted the journey never returned.

Lorian smiled. "That continent was never barren. No, the hybrid kingdom was beautiful." His smile faded. "When the hybrid kingdom was invaded, many of its people traveled north, to the mountains. Some fled across the Sleeping Sea on merchant ships or winged creatures, landing on this continent where they crossed the Asric Pass. Hundreds of thousands died. Those who lived made it to cities and villages on this continent. And they've remained hidden ever since."

All I could hear was a dull ringing in my ears. My instinct was to refute him. To believe he was playing with me. But it made a sick kind of sense.

"How come the...hybrids... How come we're not discovered during the Taking?"

"Your power does not belong to this kingdom. It's not Sabium's to give away to the *gods*, and it's certainly not his to keep and share among his court." Lorian's eyes had turned icy, and his voice was tight with banked fury. I almost shivered. But he seemed to regain control, his voice evening once more. "The oceartus stones may take all *human* magic. But that's not how they work for hybrids."

"Why?"

"Because you're more powerful than humans and your magic is very different. At a hybrid Taking ceremony, the magic is taken, the stone glows, and the priestesses warble their prayers, but the seed of hybrid power remains deep within you. And it replenishes and grows as you age."

I stared at Lorian. Did I trust him? He'd lied to me over and over again. But at least those lies had been for a reason. I had no illusions about my ability to withstand torture. If I found out just what the mercenaries were planning when they murmured to each other out of my earshot, those plans would be at great risk.

And while he'd lied to me…even terrified me so I would use my power, his strategy had worked—regardless of how awful it had been.

He had no true reason to lie to me now. At least, none that I could see.

If he was telling the truth, I wasn't corrupt at all. My power was different because *I* was different. Part fae. *A hybrid.*

I swallowed. "I know you know more. Things you're not telling me."

"An understatement. You want to learn more about the history of these lands? About the king? See if you can find a narminoi."

"What's a narminoi?"

"Their power is the power of knowledge. Unlike Marth, who can look back a few days, perhaps a few years if he is at full strength, narminoi can look back centuries if they choose. And they are unable to lie. Not about the past. The king has hunted them all these years, until only a few of them remain."

The more I understood about my power, the history

of this kingdom, and the royal family, the greater the chance I could free Asinia and find my brother.

"How will I find a narminoi?"

One dark eyebrow kicked up in that infuriating way that made me want to slap him. "I'm sure you'll manage."

Rythos yawned and sat up. "Some of us were trying to sleep."

Galon was already getting to his feet. "We don't have time to sleep." He eyed me. "One last lesson before we leave. The others can ready the horses."

Lorian pushed his blanket off himself and slowly stood. "Today, you need to wield your magic the way you were born to use it."

My chest constricted at the thought of what was to come. If I'd been alone, I might've leaned over and hyperventilated.

Lorian just gave me that look he gave me when he'd set an impossible task and was expecting me to complete it. "It's up to you to coax it out. To make it do what you need. Your problem isn't a lack of power. It's a lack of control. You're terrified of your power, and a part of you doesn't truly believe you have what I'm saying you have."

I opened my mouth, but he was already walking away.

I wanted to sit with my thoughts for a few hours. To come to terms with the fact that King Sabium had been lying to us. All of us. Even worse, his father, his father's father...all of them were liars, all of them stealing from their people in the worst way. The blood was pounding so loudly in my ears, I almost missed Galon's next words.

He was standing in front of me, holding out his hand.

"You can think about what Lorian just told you later," he said. "Time to stretch."

PRISCA

Galon pinned me to the ground. I struggled, but it was no use.

He glowered down at me, clearly impatient. "You know what to do here."

I *did* know. Wiggling one leg out from under us, I shoved my knee against his chest and and *pushed*.

"Take your hands off me." A familiar voice cut through the clearing.

I froze. My eyes flooded, my throat tightened, and then I went wild, scratching and clawing for my freedom.

Galon cursed and rolled off me, but I was already sitting up. Across the clearing, Marth held Tibris in a headlock—my brother's face already swollen and bruised.

"Found him spying on us," Marth announced.

Was Tibris truly in front of me? Or was I imagining it? I glanced around at the mercenaries. All of them had gone quiet, and all of them were watching my brother closely.

"Let him go, Marth," I demanded. Marth just looked at Lorian, who was already getting to his feet.

Lorian nodded and Tibris straightened.

My brother looked like he'd aged five years. He wore a rough beard, his clothes dirty and unkempt. He stalked toward me, dropped a small pack at my feet, and positioned his body in front of mine, a long knife held ready in his hand.

"Run, Prisca," Tibris ordered.

"Friend of yours, wildcat?" Lorian crooned.

"Don't talk to her," Tibris snarled. "Pris, go."

Lorian slowly stood. He moved like a predatory cat, his gaze now solely on my brother.

I unfroze and shot to my own feet, darting in front of Tibris. My brother cursed as Lorian's gaze dropped to me.

"A lover come to rescue you from our...embrace?"

Was *that* why he was acting so strangely? "No, you idiot. This is my brother."

Some of the malice left Lorian's expression, and I threw my arms around Tibris. My eyes slid closed, and I just basked in the feel of him. Alive.

I took a deep breath and opened my eyes. "They're not hurting me, Tibris. If anything, they've protected me. That one—" I stepped back and pointed to Galon "—fished me out of the river after Mama threw me in."

I didn't mention Lorian had abandoned me directly after that. But I squinted my eyes at him so he'd know I hadn't forgotten that part.

The corner of his mouth twitched.

Tibris gave a small bow of his head. "In that case, thank you for keeping my sister alive. But we're leaving now."

Lorian went still, and I watched as he pondered my brother, clearly deciding how much of a threat he was to his plan to sneak into the city.

I knew what Lorian did to people who got in his way. I shot him what I hoped was a threatening look. "We need to talk," I told Tibris. "Come with me."

Tibris allowed it, and I led him over to the huge boulder by the river. Hopefully the noise of the water would drown out our conversation.

Tibris stared at me for a long moment. I stared back. It was as if we were memorizing each other's features. And then I was in his arms, tears rolling down my face.

"Mama?"

He tensed, and I felt him shake his head. "I'm sorry."

I shook with fresh sobs. I'd known. But some tiny part of me had hoped anyway.

"I thought you were dead," I admitted against his chest. "I told myself you'd make it—that you were smart, prepared. But…"

"I know exactly how you felt," Tibris said. "I told myself the same. But I didn't see how you could've survived. Mercenaries? Really?"

I laughed. And then I cried some more.

When I had no tears left, Tibris slowly released me. "I have so much to tell you, I barely know where to start, although I know you suspect some of it. Those notes from

Vicer weren't just a way to keep in touch." He gave me a faint smile.

I rolled my eyes. "I had a feeling that was the case."

"Vicer always knew you still had your magic."

My mouth went dry. "He did?"

Tibris sighed. "If there's one thing Vicer does well, it's observe. He noted how tense we both were at the ceremonies. How protective I was of you. And how I insisted you learn to fight. You'd get this...hunted look in your eyes whenever anyone talked about the Gifting ceremony. Vicer watched closely over the years, and he figured it out."

"Did he blackmail you somehow?"

"No. Vicer's ruthless, but he would never..." Tibris glanced away. "Shortly after he got to the city, he began to send those notes you were so curious about." He nudged me, and I attempted a smile. "In the villages, we've always been told that the gods favored many of the city residents because they were more pious. Vicer learned that wasn't true at all. Councillors and courtiers favored by King Sabium have the most power, followed by families who've shown loyalty over the years."

I took a deep, steadying breath. "Lorian told me some of this. If you'd had your power...if we'd been *favored*, Papa might still be alive."

Tibris swallowed. "Yes."

"How did you escape? What happened in the village? And how did you find me?"

"One of my friends told me what had happened. His

warning gave me enough time to run, and my contacts helped me stay hidden. I went from inn to inn, searching for rumors of a woman traveling alone. One who might look desperate. Then I heard a barmaid laughing about a woman who'd been traveling with five men, servicing them all. She'd overheard one of the men say your name."

My cheeks flamed, and I winced. "It's definitely not what it sounds like."

"Good. I didn't even like the thought of you with Thol. Five *mercenaries*…"

I squinted at him and he laughed, but the amusement instantly disappeared. His considering look told me he was wondering if I could handle whatever he was about to tell me.

Finally, he took a deep breath. "Prisca, it's bad."

"Tell me. Quickly."

"After you disappeared, and after Mama was… After she died…" His voice turned hoarse, and he paused for a long moment before continuing. "They began to question anyone close to us. The king's assessor performed Testings on all of our friends. All of our neighbors."

My face turned numb. "I know it was Asinia. I saw her on the list."

Tibris closed his eyes, as if he couldn't look at me, couldn't stand to watch me while he broke my heart.

"She tried to run, but they caught her. They killed her mother and took Asinia to the city."

My knees hit the dirt. Asinia's mother. The woman who'd always had a kind word, an extra plate of food.

Of course she was dead. I'd seen what had happened to Lina's grandparents. And I'd chosen denial over reality once again.

Asinia and I were both motherless now. Only, I'd been free this entire time, and she'd been grieving in a dank, dark cell, waiting to die herself.

"Prisca. Please." Tibris's voice was pained.

"What did you do?" Lorian sounded livid.

"Don't touch her," Tibris snapped.

I was vaguely aware of being lifted, of huge arms wrapping around me. I could hear my brother shouting obscenities, could hear Galon's sharp voice, but all I could see was Asinia's laughing face as she teased her mother in their kitchen.

When my vision cleared, I was being held several inches above the ground, the side of my face pressed to a huge, familiar male chest.

Tibris was standing a few feet away, his expression incredulous as his gaze flicked between Lorian and me.

I patted Lorian's arm. "I'm okay," I said. "You can let me go."

Lorian slowly released me, and a small part of me mourned the loss as he stepped back. "We need to move soon, while there are fewer guards on the gate."

In other words, I needed to pull myself together. I nodded.

The mercenaries resumed packing up the camp. Tibris wrapped his arm around my shoulders. "I'm sorry. I wish I didn't have to tell you. Wish it could be different."

I looked up at him. "I'm getting Asinia out. Will you help me?" I asked.

My brother sighed. But he'd obviously known this was coming, because the hint of a smile curved his mouth. "Of course I will. But we have to be smart about this. You think no one's tried to free their friend or family member before?"

"I know. But she's all alone. Her mother is dead, and she's all alone. Oh gods, Tibris."

"Shh." He held me and rocked. "We'll go to the city. Vicer will help us."

I pulled away. "And *what* exactly is Vicer doing?"

He lowered his voice. "He's a rebel, Pris. The people in our kingdom shouldn't have to live this way. So he's fighting back."

"And you are too. That's how you managed to find me."

"Yes."

A rebel. My kindhearted, healer brother. Now *that* explained how he'd managed to stay on the run long enough to find me. Those contacts of his weren't just friends he'd trained with.

It also meant Tibris knew what I was. Mama had never mentioned kidnapping Tibris, and he wasn't a hybrid, which meant we likely weren't truly related.

"What are you thinking, Pris?"

"Do you still love me?"

He burst out laughing. "Now that I know you're a hybrid?"

"That…and the fact that we're not technically siblings."

His smile dropped. "Don't be ridiculous," he snapped. "I don't care who you are or what you can do. You're my sister. Even when you're being strangely insecure."

It was my turn to laugh. But Tibris's expression was still serious. "I've known you were a hybrid for years. And I've been planning your escape. Vicer agreed to help me get you out." He rubbed a hand over his jaw. "I should've talked to you about it. It's your life after all. But I wanted you to enjoy being normal for as long as you could. When you started trying to read Vicer's notes, I knew it was time to tell you everything."

He *knew?*

All this time, when I'd thought I just wasn't pious enough for the gods, when I'd created and discarded plan after plan, Tibris had been making plans of his own?

It felt like a punch to the face. Betrayal and misery lay like a stone in my gut.

"You should've told me. I was planning to try to steal an oceartus stone. I was going to follow Kreilor."

The blood drained from his face. "You were *what?*"

"I was desperate, Tibris. I'd just seen Lina's grandparents slaughtered. Do you think I wanted to watch that happen to you?"

He just frowned at me, obviously still wrestling with my plan.

I was so fucking happy to see him, and yet I wanted to punch him in the gut. Siblings.

I put my hands on my hips. "I barely slept, Tibris. Sometimes, I couldn't keep my food down. I started losing my hair. Occasionally, I'd do everything I could to *not* think about what would happen to us, and I'd fantasize about staying in the village. But most of the time, I could barely get out of bed because I was so fucking afraid." My throat ached, and I fought to get the rest of it out. "And you were making plans. Plans that could've given me hope."

Tibris's eyes gleamed bright. He was quiet for so long, all I could hear were the low murmurs of the mercenaries as they saddled the horses.

Finally, he took my hand. "I don't know what to say. Sorry isn't enough, Pris. You…you seemed to be doing okay. I didn't know you were struggling that much. But I should've asked. And I should've told you I was working on a way for us to get out."

"Don't lie to me again."

"I won't. I promise."

I blew out a breath. I needed to let it go. We had to focus on what was important. Asinia. "You truly think Vicer will help?"

"Yes. But Pris, I don't think we should tell your mercenary friends what we're planning." He said it carefully, like he was expecting me to protest.

I rolled my shoulders. I trusted the mercenaries in this, at least. They were cagey and secretive and would lie to me whenever they felt the need. But they didn't want me dead. Still, we were about to separate. There was no need to tell them.

"I agree."

Lorian gestured imperiously from across the clearing. I nodded at him.

"We need to go."

Tibris eyed me. "Go where?"

"Lorian's been teaching me to use my powers. We made a deal—he got me this far and now it's my turn."

"Your turn to do what?"

"I'm going to freeze time for everyone but us at the city gate. I need you to listen to everything Lorian says and move as quickly as you can."

Tibris's mouth dropped open.

"We're ready," Galon called.

"Pris. Are you sure about this?"

"I am. It's going to be okay."

If only I believed that. My mouth had turned watery, my hands shook, and I was suddenly ice-cold. This was it. Everything now relied on my tenuous grasp on my power.

Tibris reached out and squeezed my shoulder. "My horse is tied just off the trail."

Lorian had already mounted, and he held his hand out for me when I approached. My hand slid into his, and he helped pull me up into the saddle. I tensed. I hadn't even considered riding with my brother. I'd grown so used to Lorian's huge body surrounding my own, to the strange comfort I found in his arms, I'd automatically turned to him for that comfort.

"I'm glad you found your brother," he said as we all

filed out of the clearing and toward the road. "You'll be able to start a new life together."

"Mm-hmm." I wasn't quite as used to lying as Lorian was, so I kept my tone noncommittal.

"Prisca."

Lorian held the reins in one hand and caught my chin in the other. "Whatever you do, make sure you get on a ship. Soon."

"I will." I met his eyes as I said it, and he searched my face. With a brisk nod, he let me go, spurring his horse on.

I *would* be on a ship soon. Just as soon as I freed Asinia.

Tibris was already waiting on the road. He gave me a nod, but his eyebrows had lowered. "How exactly is this going to work?"

"You'll soon see," Lorian said. He squeezed his thighs, and then we were galloping toward the city.

We rounded the bend, and the gates appeared in the distance. My stomach swam, a metallic taste flooded my mouth, and my heart kicked in my chest.

"Harness your fear," Lorian reminded me. "*Now*."

I reached for my power and tugged with everything in me.

All movement at the gate stopped. It was suddenly eerily silent.

Except for Tibris, who was cursing, his eyes wide as he gazed over his shoulder at me.

"Go!" Lorian roared.

We hurtled past the line of people, stretching hundreds deep. Past the thicket of trees on the right, where beggars held out their tins and enterprising merchants sold fruit and water. Past the guards, who'd surrounded an unkept man with blond hair, their hands on their weapons.

My power wanted to slip from my grip. I held tighter, refusing to panic.

Lorian's words ran through my head as he pushed his horse faster.

"It's up to you to coax it out. To make it do what you need. Your problem isn't a lack of power. It's a lack of control. You're terrified of your power, and a part of you doesn't truly believe you have what I'm saying you have."

I loosened my grip on my power. And then I reached for more.

You're mine, I told it.

It was heady. All these people, the birds in the trees, the horses, all of them were frozen because I *willed* it.

Wait.

Not everyone was frozen.

The blond man who was surrounded by guards had turned his head. I jolted, almost losing my grip on the thread of time.

I'd never seen that before. Lorian had occasionally managed to shake off my power earlier than most, but even he had been caught when I'd aimed that power at him.

The man was watching us. Likely, he would be able to give an excellent description to the guards. My heart attempted to thump right out of my chest.

"Who is that man?"

Lorian said nothing. Likely, he couldn't hear me over the sound of hooves on stone. "Hold on!" he yelled.

I looked over my shoulder. The man winked at me. And then we were in the city.

"Who was that man?" I gasped out as we rounded a corner, and time resumed.

I wasn't bleeding from my nose this time. And I wasn't blind. Progress.

"Who?" Lorian slowed the horse.

"The man at the gates. Time stopped for everyone but him. He *winked* at me."

Rythos must've overheard, because he smiled. "Sounds like you have some relatives in the city."

"What do you mean?"

"Time magic is in the blood."

My heart pounded in my chest. My mother had said I had family here. Was that man truly related to me?

Tibris gave me a look that said this would be yet another thing we would discuss later, but he was already eyeing the mercenaries. "Time to say goodbye," he said.

Something twisted in my chest.

"We'll escort you to the docks." Galon's voice was gruff.

"No need." Tibris shook his head. "We need to sell my horse and buy supplies. Thank you for everything you did for Prisca."

That was my brother. Unfailingly polite, even when

he'd likely been daydreaming about stabbing Lorian since the moment he'd met him. Fondness made me beam at him. I'd thought I'd never see him again. And now, he'd help me save Asinia, and then we'd find a new life in a new land.

What about the others like you? Will you leave them here to die?

I buried that thought beneath the reality I was actually living. I was just a village girl with a bounty on her head. One who could stop time for mere moments.

We all dismounted, and I reached for Marth. We couldn't afford to spend too much time here. But I needed to say goodbye. "Good luck," I told him. He wrapped me in a hug, one hand a little *too* low on my back. I'd miss this lech.

"To you also." For the first time since I'd met him, Marth's expression was grave. He pulled away and nodded at me, moving over for Cavis.

"Wherever you go, I know you'll have a good life," the quiet man said.

"Thank you. I hope you get to see your wife and daughter soon."

"So do I." He gave me a faint smile, and then it was Rythos's turn.

"Get over here."

My eyes burned as he embraced me. A sob left my throat.

"None of that, darlin'. My people believe there are those we are meant to have in our lives. We'll see each other again."

"P-promise?"

"I promise."

Galon cleared his throat. I wiped my eyes with the back of my hand and laughed at his pained expression. I'd seen men with broken limbs look more comfortable.

Surprisingly, Galon's discomfort with my tears helped. I gave him a shaky smile, and he reached out and ruffled my hair.

I brushed more tears off my face. "You want your cloak back?"

We both looked at the cloak, which was filthy. Since it was far too long for me, the hem had been dragged across the ground all this time, and it was riddled with holes.

Galon's mouth twitched. "You keep it," he said.

"Thanks." More tears welled.

Fresh discomfort darted over his face. "You're welcome." He stepped back and gestured rather desperately for Lorian to take his place.

It was strange, given that a large part of me knew I couldn't trust this group of mercenaries, but they'd still kept me safe. They'd taught me to use my magic, trained me to better defend myself, and—in their own ways—kept me from falling apart.

Despite their closed-mouthed insistence on secrets, I'd miss them.

Even Lorian.

He'd taken Galon's place. And he was staring down

at me like he was memorizing my features.

"In another life," he said, his eyes dark. It sounded like a promise. I sucked in a shaky breath. I felt it too. That maybe in another life, we were meant to be different people. And we would have been those people together.

"In another life." I forced a smile.

His gaze dropped to my lips.

And then he buried his hand in my hair and crushed his mouth to mine.

13
PRISCA

Lorian's lips were firm, warm, tender. They caressed mine like we had all the time in the world. Like this kiss could last forever. I sighed against his mouth, and his tongue slipped between my lips to tangle with mine.

His body was so hard. So large. Warmth spread from my stomach into my core. My knees went weak.

This was not at all like kissing the village boys. Lorian's huge hand held me in place for him while he kissed me expertly. Thoroughly. He slipped his other hand to my lower back, pressing me close to him, and I shivered with *want*.

Tibris's voice reached my ears. My usually mild-mannered brother was yelling all kinds of threats, Rythos and Marth holding him back.

Lorian pulled away and tucked my hair behind my ear.

"Goodbye, Prisca."

"Goodbye, Lorian."

Tibris reached for my arm, practically dragging me away. Which was a good thing since I was still a little dazed.

"Are you crazy?" he hissed at me, leading his horse with his other hand. "The mercenary? Really?"

"*He* kissed *me*," I snarled back. And that argument was weak. The moment Lorian's mouth met mine, I'd participated wholeheartedly.

Tibris's lips trembled in an almost-smile before he ruthlessly firmed them. "Fine. For now, how about you put your hood up and attempt to walk in a straight line?"

My cheeks flamed. Yes, I was walking unsteadily, as if I were drunk. After a single *kiss*. I was glad Lorian couldn't see me now. His ego didn't need the stroking.

What had he been thinking?

Oh, I knew what he'd been thinking. He wanted to make me think about him. It was yet another way to mess with my mind.

Well, I wouldn't give him the satisfaction. As far as I was concerned, that part of my life was over. We were in the city now, which meant we needed to focus on rescuing Asinia and getting on a ship before the full moon. But gods, I'd miss the mercenaries.

"Where'd you get the horse?"

"Stole it," Tibris said, his voice carefully neutral.

I sighed. My brother was *good* to his core. And because of me, he was now a wanted criminal. A thief. Of course, he was also a rebel.

I nodded, but my attention had caught on the scene in front of us. Next to me, Tibris went still.

The carriage was white and gold. But that wasn't

why my breath had stuck in my throat.

There was no horse attached to the carriage. And yet…it moved of its own accord.

"What magic is this?" I breathed.

"Stolen magic." Bitterness seeped from each of my brother's words.

"Move!" someone roared, and Tibris led his horse to the side of the road. Another carriage barreled past us, this one with a horse. Perhaps only the most powerful people in the city were using horseless carriages.

Lorian hadn't warned me about this. From the way he'd talked about the king, it was clear he loathed him. And yet he hadn't told me the people in the city would walk around using so much magic, it was clear they had received much, much more back than anyone living in the northern villages.

He'd wanted me to see it for myself. He'd known it would shock and enrage me, and he didn't want to dampen that shock and rage by telling me about it.

"Where's Vicer?" I asked, my gaze on a woman who used her magic to levitate a satchel as she walked down the street.

"He gave me an address." Tibris pulled a note from his pocket, and I recognized our code.

"Did you know about this?" I nodded toward the woman casually using her power.

Tibris shrugged. "Vicer told me some of it. But he said I'd need to see the worst of it for myself in order to truly believe it."

We'd turned left when we entered the city gates, and now we were standing in the southwest corner of the city. Tibris pulled out a rough map—likely also from Vicer—and began frowning down at it.

"We need a stable for my horse," he muttered. "There should be one a few streets north of here."

I nodded, and we set off, both of us with the hoods of our cloaks up. I would have worried about looking suspicious, but the people here...

Merchants strolled by in clothes similar to ours—tunics and breeches and cloaks. Among them, the nobles wandered, men in tailored waistcoats and women in the kinds of dresses that would get them killed if they needed to fight.

But why would they need to fight? The people here obviously lived a charmed life, ducking into the bookstores and teahouses, the taverns and dressmakers. For one wild moment, I wanted to burn the city to the ground, if only to watch these privileged, ignorant people run for their lives.

"Prisca," Tibris hissed, and I jolted. I'd pushed my cloak back off my face at some point, and I was glowering at the people going about their lives.

This was *not* how I would keep us alive.

"Sorry."

"I feel it too. But..."

"We have to be smart. I know."

Tibris found the stables and instructed the boy who took his horse to tell him if anyone was in need of a mare.

Regret flashed across his face, and my chest tightened. At some point, Tibris had obviously become fond of his stolen horse.

I followed Tibris north. Within a few minutes, clothing stores gave way to taverns. The stone beneath our feet became cracked, and we dodged pickpockets, prostitutes, and puddles of piss.

The difference between the wealthier parts of the city and the slums was staggering.

A drunk stumbled toward me, hands sweeping under my cloak in an attempt to find my purse. The feel of strange hands on me... Bile climbed up my throat. Elbowing the drunk in the face, I slid to the side and neatly tripped him. His face hit the wall, and he crumpled with a groan.

Guilt twisted my stomach. He was just a drunk. Not the hunter from the forest. Not the bearded giant from the inn. Just a harmless drunk.

Tibris stared at me. "I see you continued your lessons."

"The mercenaries fight dirty." I forced myself to keep walking. "They taught me a few things."

He just nodded, his brow creasing. "There's something I've been meaning to tell you."

Surely it couldn't get any worse. I waited, watching as Tibris stepped around a puddle, swallowed, took a deep breath, rolled his shoulders.

"The person who suggested Asinia be assessed... it was Frinik."

I closed my eyes. When I thought of Frinik, I thought

of sneaking into the forest, creeping out my window, whispers, hushed laughter, rough kisses. He was my first. We'd known even then that we weren't forever, but for a few months, before his parents arranged his marriage to their friend's daughter, we'd both had *someone.*

Now, if I ever saw him again, I would slit his throat.

Oh, how I'd changed since the day I'd fled my village.

"Pris?"

"I'm okay." Neighbors turned on each other. It was how it worked. And the only reason there was no loyalty among us was because the king had stamped out that loyalty and replaced it with terror.

Tibris gave me a look that said he didn't quite believe me, but he wasn't going to press the subject. "We're here."

I examined the wooden door in front of us. Tibris reached out and knocked, and I sucked in a breath as we waited. Had the city changed Vicer? Was this a trap?

A woman answered the door. She wore an apron, her curly brown hair touched with gray. Deep frown lines had settled between her brows.

"Code," she demanded.

Tibris rattled off a series of numbers.

Sweeping her gaze over both of us, the woman wordlessly stepped aside and allowed us in.

My eyes took a moment to adjust to the dim light. The air was warm, and the scent of cinnamon wound toward me.

"Tibris." Vicer appeared out of the gloom. He'd let

his dark hair grow, and it was in a low ponytail against his neck. He was wearing a clean gray overcoat that matched his eyes, and he was also clean-shaven—something I'd rarely seen from him before he left.

Tibris had gone still, but he relaxed when Vicer grinned and slapped him on the back. I pushed the hood of my cloak down, and Vicer's grin fell as he pondered me. He flicked a glance at Tibris.

"You didn't say you were bringing your sister."

Tibris cleared his throat. "After Pris…after everything that happened, I was even more careful than usual with the notes I sent. I had enough contacts at my end to help me find her, but I knew we needed to come here."

Vicer just nodded, some of the tightness leaving his expression. His eyes laughed at me. "You always did follow us around like a lost puppy."

"This lost puppy is rabid," I told him.

Tibris sighed. "She's right about that. Can we sit somewhere and talk?"

The woman who'd answered the door had wandered away. But at our question, she poked her head around a door. "Come and eat," she said.

I'd been far too nervous to break my fast this morning, and now my stomach grumbled at the thought of food. I felt…safe here. Well, as safe as we could be in the capital.

Vicer shook his head at her. "Always eavesdropping." But it was clear from his fond expression that he didn't blame her for it. "Margie here cooks the best chicken in the city."

She waved that off, but her cheeks had flushed. "Wash your hands before you sit at my table," she said. "All of you."

The way she'd taken charge reminded me of my own mother. And of Asinia's. My chest ached, but I followed Vicer as he led us into a small washroom.

"I didn't think you'd have easy access to water," Tibris said as I washed up.

"We're based in the slums for a reason. This was once an orphanage, and no one notices when people are coming and going at all hours of the day and night," Vicer said. "But there are enough of us living here and contributing that we can enjoy some comforts."

Tibris washed his hands, and Vicer led us into a large kitchen. Margie had already set three plates of chicken on the table, along with hunks of fresh bread.

"Thank you," I told her. "You're not hungry?"

She looked at me, and her expression softened slightly. "I've already eaten. And you're welcome."

"Sit with us, Margie," Vicer said.

She brought over three cups of water, and Vicer took them from her.

"You can speak freely in front of Margie," he said softly.

I'd become more than a little suspicious and paranoid myself since leaving our village. But for some reason, Margie had immediately put me at ease. That was likely a good reason *not* to trust her.

"I lost my daughter to the king's lies," Margie said softly, interrupting my thoughts. "They tore her from my arms and took her to the castle. She was burned last year on Gods Day."

Margie opened the top of her dress, revealing a gnarled scar that wound from one side of her throat down her chest. "Then they tried to kill me. But I survived."

I stared at the scar. Was that how my mother had been killed? Tibris still refused to tell me, and I'd stopped asking.

"I'm sorry," I said.

I'd heard what Margie hadn't said. Everything she did was in her daughter's name.

"I was told King Sabium has been lying all this time," I said. "Our magic doesn't go to the gods at all."

Margie sighed. "No."

"How has he gotten away with it? And his father? And his father before him?"

"I asked this question of a narminoi, soon after my daughter was taken from me. It took months for Vicer to locate her." She slid Vicer a fond look. He picked up her hand and squeezed it.

Lorian had mentioned a narminoi. "Would it be possible for me to talk to her?"

Vicer shrugged. "If she's feeling sane that day."

It seemed as if narminoi succumbed to the same insanity seers eventually did.

Tibris frowned. I knew what he was thinking. Was

that how people would have eventually spoken about Mama?

Vicer seemed to have realized what he'd said, because he gave us an apologetic look and gestured for Margie to speak.

She took a sip of water. "According to the narminoi, this all began when the gods were arguing among themselves. They were anticipating the time when alliances between the kingdoms would snap and they would turn on one another—as creatures with sentience eventually do. Each of the gods had a theory about which kingdom would survive such a war. The gods argued about this for centuries until, finally, they agreed to a test."

Tibris grimaced at me, and I nodded back. What were we but entertainment for the gods?

Margie gave us a faint smile. "Faric, god of knowledge, gave an artifact to the humans. Tronin, god of strength, gave the fae *three* artifacts. And Bretis, god of protection, had become reluctantly intrigued by the hybrid kingdom to the west. The people who had somehow thrived—even after separating from the fae. Bretis donated something that held such power, Tronin and Faric immediately grew jealous."

"What did the gods give each kingdom?" I asked.

"The narminoi couldn't tell me." She nodded at my plate. "Eat."

I took a bite. Margie's chicken was tender and flavorful. But I could barely taste it. "What happened next?"

"The humans used their power not to look into their own lands and determine the health and wellness of their subjects. No, they began to look to their neighbors. And they grew envious. Why had the fae been given so much more magic than the humans? Why were the hybrids more powerful *and* longer-lived? Eventually, the human king became obsessed with these questions. His name was Regner.

"King Regner ignored the faes' weaknesses—such as their ancient grudges and low fertility—and focused only on their great power and long lives. The jealous king decided he would take what he hadn't been given, ensuring that his kingdom prospered."

Tibris made a small noise. Obviously, he'd never heard this story either. Margie sighed, and she turned toward me.

"During this time, Regner's son Crotopos died. Died from an injury that no healer in his kingdom could fix. Any fae visitors had already fled the human kingdom, their seers warning them of the king's evil heart. The hybrids were already wary of both fae and humans—and had closed their borders decades before. And so, the prince died—while his wife was pregnant with their unborn child—and King Regner knew that if his son had been fae or hybrid, he would have lived."

I couldn't imagine what it had been like for Regner to watch his son die, knowing he could have been saved. Knowing the wound would have healed if he were anything but human.

It must have been torture.

"It was enough to drive the king to madness," Margie said, nodding at whatever she saw on my face. "And yet Regner *wasn't* mad when he ordered his people to invade the fae lands. He was sane when he ordered the slaughter of a peaceful group of fae nymphs in the forest close to his border. He was sane when he planned how he would make the fae king pay. And he was sane when he turned his attention to the hybrids, because they had something he wanted."

No matter what had happened to his son, it didn't excuse Regner from what he'd done to the hybrids. I wanted to weep for my people. To rage. I wanted *vengeance*.

Tibris reached out and peeled my hand off the side of the table. I'd been clenching it, white-knuckled, as Margie told her story. "What did the hybrids have that Regner wanted?"

She sighed. "The narminoi couldn't tell me. It was only after several visits that I put this much together."

"Why do people believe Sabium's lies and those of his line? How have they gotten away with it for so long?"

Margie shrugged, but her expression was bleak. "How do you control a population? You keep the people poor and uneducated. Tell them the same lie for centuries, and tie that lie to religion. Those people will believe you even when the truth is dancing naked in front of them. Because to believe otherwise would mean their entire world has always been a lie. And *that* realization is too difficult for most people to take."

I could understand that. Sometimes—even if only for a few seconds—I wished I could turn back time and never know just how Sabium deceived us.

Vicer had already finished his plate, and he leaned back in his seat.

"You've seen the people here," he said. "Seen how much magic they have. Most villagers like us will never visit the city. They'll live their whole lives firmly believing that the gods only gave them back a tiny sliver of magic. And those who do visit? They're told the gods gave the city people back more magic for a reason. The people here are simply more *worthy.*"

If I'd thought I was bitter, it was nothing compared to Vicer's acerbic tone. And I could understand why. I'd only been here for a few hours. What must it be like for people like Vicer? I didn't know what kind of power he had, only that it was the kind considered useful. Hundreds, maybe thousands, of villagers had been brought here to be of use to the crown, and I couldn't imagine what it must be like to continually see just how well people in the city lived. The wealth and power here would be inconceivable to those who had never left our village. If Vicer had tried to tell them about the horseless carriages, most would have laughed.

I took a deep breath. "If hybrids are so powerful, how does the king kill us so easily?"

Vicer leveled me with his hard stare. "It takes three things for magic to grow. Use, time, and training. Raw power is one thing, but hybrids must learn to wield that power."

A dull fury made my hands shake. We never had a *chance* to grow our power because wielding it was a death sentence. The king's great-great-grandfather had ravaged our kingdom. And now Sabium continued the slaughter to cover his crimes.

Vicer's eyes met mine. "I know you still have your power."

He hadn't changed. He still enjoyed keeping people off-balance. I just nodded. "Tibris told me you knew."

"And yet, even trusting us as he does, your brother refused to ever tell us what power you had. I must admit I'm curious."

I forced a smile. "Maybe I'll tell you. But...I need to know if you can help me."

"You want to get on a ship."

"No. Well, yes. But not yet. Asinia is a hybrid too. And she was taken."

Vicer's expression turned mournful. And that was true grief in his eyes. He'd known Asinia even longer than I had. "I'm sorry to hear that. If she's been scooped up by the king's guards, she'll be in his dungeon."

I forced my voice to stay steady, even as desperation clawed at me. "I'm getting her out." And I was counting on Vicer and whatever connections he had to help make that happen.

"We're getting her out," my brother said mildly.

"And how do you think you'll do that?" Vicer's

words dripped with sarcasm.

"My power allows me to stop time for a few moments."

Margie dropped her cup, staring at me. Then she startled, seeming to come back to herself, and her face reddened. "I'm sorry." She stepped away to find a cloth, and Vicer studied me.

"You can stop time?"

This was the moment when I had to pretend to be much, much more confident than I really was. Vicer wouldn't involve himself in my plans if he thought my power was undeveloped. "You want a demonstration?"

His eyes lit up. "Of course."

I reached for my power, and it jumped into my grasp. Time stopped, and I held it just long enough to get to my feet and take a few steps closer to Vicer.

I released the thread, and everyone else unfroze. Vicer shot to his feet, the blood draining from his face.

"You— I— We—"

Tibris grinned at me. "You've done the unthinkable. You've managed to make *Vicer* speechless."

"Well," Vicer said, and his entire body bristled with energy, color returning to his cheeks. "This changes some things. I have someone who can get you false work papers. We currently have two people in the castle. They're attempting to update our intel, help us map the castle, and undermine the king when they can. But none of our people has ever been able to get into the dungeon. You would be the first."

For the first time since I'd vowed to get Asinia out of the dungeon, hope fluttered its wings in my chest. My body felt oddly light.

"Just how big is this...rebellion?" I asked.

Vicer gave me a cool look. "If you're serious about getting into the castle, you know I can't tell you that."

Because if we were captured, we would be tortured. The less we knew, the better.

"But what I can tell you is that all the rebellion members we had in the castle were caught up in a random sweep. The king has an assessor search his servants occasionally to ensure they're not hybrids. The final two rebels I've sent in are volunteers and they refuse to be pulled out, but we won't send anyone else in again. It's too dangerous."

My heartbeat quickened, but I nodded. I knew what we were risking. The question was whether I could convince Tibris to stay behind.

One look at his stubborn expression and I knew the answer. He glowered at me, daring me to make the suggestion. I sighed. At least he wasn't a hybrid.

Margie returned, her face still a little flushed as she avoided my eyes. Was my power that horrifying?

I cut that thought off at the knees. My power *was* horrifying. And dangerous. And incredibly useful. My power was going to allow me to free Asinia. My power was going to help us *escape*.

"It'll take a day or two for us to get you papers," Vicer said. "There are a few other things you'll need to do in the meantime, along with information you'll need to memorize."

I studied him. Vicer liked Asinia, but he certainly wasn't doing this out of benevolence. "And what is it that you want in exchange?"

Vicer smiled. "We have someone in the dungeons too. You get him out when you get Asinia out, and we'll help you with everything you need."

"Why is this prisoner more valuable than the others?"

"Because he was the one who organized many of the rebels in this city. Who ensured the splinter groups began to work together. And who learned our enemies' weaknesses. His mind is a wealth of knowledge. Knowledge we need."

I studied Vicer's face. The man I'd known had changed. He was sterner now. And when he laughed, he often cut his laughter off suddenly, as if he'd remembered he shouldn't feel joy.

"Why are you doing this? You're not one of the hybrids."

"We've all lost those we love to the king's greed."

Vicer's expression had turned cold. Obviously, he wasn't going to say anything more.

"There's another problem," I said. Reaching into my back pocket, I pulled out the piece of parchment with my face sketched onto it.

Vicer studied the parchment. "Says here you have blond hair. We can fix that. I also know someone who can take care of those eyes," he said. "Maids are invisible, and no one would expect a wanted criminal to be in the castle. Keep your head down, use that terrifying power of yours when you have to, and you'll be fine."

His confidence eased the worst of my own worries. It was easy to see just why Vicer had stepped into his role here.

Margie took our plates from us and walked away to wash them.

Vicer got to his feet. "I'll show you to your rooms."

I nodded. I was more than ready for a moment alone.

We trailed after him, back into the gloomy entrance. Clearly, it was *supposed* to be gloomy—another way for it to blend in with the other homes in the slum. Vicer led us upstairs to a long hall. "All these rooms are being used," he said, and one of the doors opened. A tall, thin man stepped out, nodding at us.

I tensed, still instinctively wary about being recognized. But neither Vicer nor Tibris seemed worried.

"This is Jeronth," Vicer said. "Jeronth, this is Prisca and Tibris. They'll be staying here for a few days."

"Nice to meet you," he said. His eyes met mine and darted away. But not before I caught the hopelessness in them.

Vicer glanced at me. "Most of the people here have experienced incredible loss. The kind of loss that breaks you. Working with the rebellion…it's the only reason some of them have to keep breathing."

I could understand that.

We climbed another set of stairs, which led to a large

common room. A few people were reading, and a couple of women talked softly in one corner. But my gaze landed on the group of men eating a snack.

It felt like years ago that I'd eaten with Tibris and Mama in our home. For a moment, I wished with everything in me that I could go back to that time once more. That instead of trying everything I could to find a way to hide my power, I'd been appreciating my family and friends. That I'd looked for the signs that Asinia had power too. That I'd spent more time with Mama.

My regrets were piling so high, it felt as if they would bury me alive.

"Prisca?"

"Hmm?"

"Through here." Vicer nodded toward a slight, dark-haired girl with brilliant blue eyes. "This is Ameri. She'll take you to the narminoi. She'll charge you for it, though."

Ameri nodded at me.

I still carried the hunter's purse. I hadn't even counted how many coins he had, but hopefully it would be enough.

I had much more to learn, and if my plan was going to have the best chance of success, I needed to know the truth. Not just a few tidbits. All of it.

LORIAN

Dear L,

The man I have sent you is the best at what he does. Do try not to scream too loudly when the spell takes.

My sources tell me the woman you were traveling with stoked more passion than they'd seen from you for years. I find myself intrigued by the kind of woman who could distract you from your brooding.

Her power must be impressive for you to be able to get into the city. Describe that power for me, please.

Emara sends her regards. And also wishes to know about this woman you refuse to discuss.

In the meantime, try not to get killed. I'd hate to have to plan your funeral when I'm already so busy.

Your older, wiser brother,
C

"Lorian?"

I pulled my attention away from the letter and swept my gaze over the men standing in the cramped room. I knew who my brother's sources were, and their expressions ranged from guilty—Marth, to belligerent—Rythos, to grave—Galon. Cavis was staring out the window.

It was no use telling them not to message my brother about Prisca. If I told them not to advise him about something we encountered on the road, or a plan I created without his approval, all of them would take that information to their graves. And yet, when it came to gossiping about women in my life…

I shook my head at them and scrawled my reply.

Dear C,

No, the girl did not stoke more passion in me than anything else has in years. But your interest is noted. Tell your wife I don't need her meddling in my life. Although, the moment she's ready to leave you for me, I'll be waiting.

Our mutual friend has been spotted in Thobirea. I have various thoughts about the subject, but will wait for yours.

Your younger, stronger, and infinitely better-looking brother,
L

Raucous laughter sounded from outside our door as a group of men walked past. The inn we were staying in was more comfortable than anything we'd used while traveling, but still noisy, and I missed the comforts of my room. Missed my own space.

The wildcat would say I missed having time to brood.

That kiss…her body had *melted* for me. There was something incredibly arousing about a woman who loathed and wanted me in equal measure. I couldn't help but imagine what that passion would be like in bed.

"Lorian?" Rythos gave me a knowing look. I ignored it.

"Has our contact arrived?"

"He's downstairs. I have to ask… Are you sure this will work?"

"No," I growled. "But I *am* sure that this is our only chance. Our families are relying on us to get into the castle. This is the closest we've been to such an opportunity in years."

Rythos nodded, his gaze flicking to the vials we'd collected on our travels—from both the stone hags and the fae at the Gromalian border. The vials waited, ready to be used—the most valuable items any of us owned in this moment.

"Do you think Prisca is on a ship already?" Cavis asked. It was rare for him to care about anything other than his wife and baby, and I turned my head. He was staring down at the street below us, eyebrows lowered.

"Her brother would have insisted," Rythos said.

I just shook my head. No one could drag that little wildcat on to a ship if she didn't want to go. But if there was one thing she did have, it was a healthy sense of self-preservation. She wasn't a fool, and she wanted to stay alive.

Even when she wasn't here, she was distracting me.

Rolling to my feet, I glanced at Galon. He nodded, his own gaze thoughtful as he picked up the vial.

"Bring him up here," I said, and Rythos strode out the door.

Soon, we'd be in the castle, ready to complete our task and finally return *home*.

A few minutes later, the door opened, and the fae pushed his heavy cloak off his head, revealing his pointed ears. It was dangerous for him to be here, so close to the city, but all of us were in agreement about this plan.

The fae bowed his head in greeting. "Are you sure about this?"

"Yes."

He didn't bother asking me again, just held out his hand for the first vial. Galon handed it over, his gaze still on each precious drop.

"This will hurt," the fae said.

"I understand."

"Sit on the bed, please."

I gave him a look, and he just shrugged. "Your legs will fail you. I've seen it time and time again. Everyone downstairs will be alerted when you fall like a tree in the forest."

I could imagine the way Prisca would laugh if she'd heard that.

And thinking about the little wildcat did nothing to improve my mood. I pushed her out of my head and nodded at the fae.

"Fine."

I sat. He opened the vial and dipped his thumb into the crimson liquid. He painted runes on my face, runes that *burned.*

Then he began to chant.

I threw back my head as agony erupted throughout my body. Magic ignited, and I bit my fist, smothering the urge to roar. It felt as if my body were being burned alive. If I didn't know this fae, didn't know just how closely our goals aligned, I would have slit his throat.

I almost laughed at the thought. My vision had darkened, and I was likely too weak to stand. I wouldn't be slitting anyone's throat.

The taste of copper filled my mouth. Galon began a steady stream of curses. I smiled despite the pain. It wasn't often that he reacted to anything these days.

The fae reached for the second vial and chanted some more. If I'd been able to take a full breath, I likely would have screamed—a fact that darkened my mood even further.

Finally, it was done. And I was left as weak as a newborn. Galon leaned over me, brow creased.

"He should rest," the fae said.

I managed to turn my head, finding the fae swaying on his feet.

"Get him a room," I ordered. My voice was hoarse, weak. The sound of it annoyed me.

"Thank you, but I should go." He bowed his head. "May the gods be with you during your task."

PRISCA

Tibris's low laugh sounded, and I glanced up from where I'd been sitting in the corner while he talked with some of the other rebels. On my lap, a few pieces of parchment summed up my new life and background. Later today, Vicer would be testing both Tibris and me to ensure we could answer any question he threw at us without hesitation.

I didn't have it in me to socialize right now. I was too busy staring into space, going over everything I'd learned during the past two days.

I missed the mercenaries. Which was ridiculous, because they'd probably already completed whatever nefarious task had brought them to the city, and now they'd be moving on to whatever came next for people with no allegiance to anything but coin.

That wasn't fair. They had allegiance to one another too.

The truth was, I'd studied them enough that I was relatively sure they were planning something big. And there was none of the excitement or anticipation I would've expected if it was something that would make them wealthy beyond their wildest dreams. No, they'd mostly radiated a grim determination.

Vicer appeared, and the room went quiet. He just nodded his hello, strolling over to me and gesturing to Tibris.

"Come with me."

He led us into an office off the common room and leaned against the large wooden desk.

"Your work papers are finished. A carriage will pick you up tomorrow afternoon," Vicer said. "Pris, you'll go by the name of Setella. It's your job to map the castle as much as you can. I'll help you with your plans, but I have to remind you again. We have never gotten anyone out."

Tibris nodded grimly. "We know."

I didn't like the look Vicer gave my brother. As if he was already mourning his friend. I glowered at him, and he seemed to snap out of it, returning to business once more.

"Tibris, you're going to be in the wine cellar. We had to work hard to ensure you'd be placed there, and it's an excellent opportunity for us. We have an idea about where the entrance to the dungeon is, but you'll need to confirm."

I swallowed, my pulse tripping at the danger my brother would face. "And the guards?"

"The guards' schedules haven't changed at all over the last few years. We had one of our people befriend two of those guards last year before he had to flee to avoid a random check. According to him, the guards are rarely in the dungeon itself unless they're feeding the prisoners or bringing in someone new. There are always two guards posted on the dungeon door, which, until now—" he smirked at me "—has been more than enough security. The posted guards always have an active combat power."

I forced my voice to stay steady. "So we just have to find a way to get all the prisoners past those guards."

Vicer's gaze turned distant. "According to numerous sources, there's a tunnel leading into the castle, and the entrance is somewhere in the dungeon. If we can find the entrance and the tunnel is still clear, we can use it."

My mouth dropped open. "A tunnel? Why would Sabium leave such a vulnerability?"

"One of his ancestors built it a couple of centuries ago, and it hasn't been used since. Sabium prefers to have his corrupt marched through the city on their way to their deaths. Likely the only reason the tunnel still exists is because the king keeps his prisoners so weak and docile, even if there were a prison break, there's no way they would be able to make it to the end of that tunnel before the guards caught them—not unless they were being carried." Distaste flashed across Vicer's face. "If you can get into the dungeon, your job will be to find the tunnel and figure out where it ends."

The tiniest spark of hope ignited in my chest. We could do this.

"I don't need to remind you to be careful with your words," Vicer said.

"We will."

"All messages should be in code. And burned immediately. Make sure you're not followed back here—"

"Vicer," Tibris said. "We know. We'd never do anything to risk you or the others. You know that."

Vicer looked back at him for a long moment. Finally, he nodded.

"Ameri is waiting to take you to the narminoi. Tomorrow, we'll make sure you're disguised appropriately, check your papers, and you'll be in."

I took a deep breath. "Thank you, Vicer."

"Thank me when you get out of there. Alive."

I nodded, walking out and giving Tibris a couple of minutes with his friend.

Ameri leaned against the wall. "I spoke to my contact. We need to go now."

Tibris stepped through the door. Obviously, he hadn't known what to say to Vicer. "I'm coming with you."

We followed Ameri down the stairs. She was a quiet woman, and I'd only been with the rebels for an afternoon, but already I'd noticed her slipping in and out of rooms unnoticed. She just seemed to fade into the background.

"What magic do you have?" I asked when we opened the front door.

She shot me a look. "Guess."

"Something to do with the way you never seem to be where we're expecting you to be?" Tibris asked dryly, and she smirked.

"Maybe. Our contact is a few streets over. But just so you know, narminoi have a tendency to stay in the past. They sometimes forget to live in the present. Even before the king ordered them to be wiped out, they wrestled with insanity. She may not be able to respond to your questions."

"Margie warned me. She said she had to put things together after she'd talked to the narminoi multiple times."

There was a high chance this visit would be a waste of time. Still…if I could get even one scrap of helpful information, it would be worth it.

By the time we'd traveled deeper into the slums, I was breathing through my mouth. Beggars huddled on every corner, although most of the people walking past them looked too poor to spare even a single copper themselves. Children ran barefoot on the cold ground, and each person we passed carried with them an air of hopelessness.

All the magic in this city, and yet the poorest citizens would likely have had better lives in the villages.

Ameri turned into a small potions shop. I glanced at the labels on some of the bottles, and my stomach roiled. Even the most powerful people in our villages could never hope to have enough magic left over to create potions. The merchants who came to our village brought with them brightly colored water and fake charms.

But here, the people had so much magic, they were selling potions to grow back thinning hair, to find a lost heirloom, to increase luck.

"Are these real?" I croaked.

"Of course they're real," a high-pitched voice said, and I turned to find a short woman with her hands on her hips. The blue mark on her temple would have made it clear she had her magic back, even if I hadn't seen the lines next to her eyes.

"Ignore her," Ameri told the woman, shooting me an exasperated look. "We're here for Lanos."

"Out the back." The woman gave me another dark look before turning and stalking away.

Ameri led us to blue door, which opened into a room filled with wooden crates. A weathered man sat on one of those crates. He wore a filthy, ripped cloak and scuffed boots, and he launched to his feet when we walked in. I clamped my hand around the hilt of my knife, and he went still.

"I mean you no harm," he said carefully. "I was expecting one person."

Ameri sighed. "This is Prisca and her brother Tibris."

Lanos just nodded. Leaning down, he pushed a crate aside, revealing a hidden door in the floor. "We need to go through here," he said. "You'll have to crawl. It's narrow."

Just looking at the small space made my chest tight. Already, it felt as if the walls around me were closing in, ready to suffocate me.

"I'll bring the narminoi back here," Tibris murmured to me.

Ameri's gaze hardened as she watched me, silently judging. "If you truly want to work in the castle, you better get used to this. Rebels are the rats creeping in tunnels beneath the city, in secret passages within the castle. If you're going to stay alive, you'll need to master that fear. Besides, you'll need to use the tunnels tomorrow with Vicer."

I swallowed, humiliation making my cheeks heat. "I can do it."

Tibris hesitated. Ignoring him, I stalked to the open door.

"Wait," Tibris said. "He goes first." He pointed at Lanos. "Then you." He nodded at Ameri.

She just sent him a shrug and a placid smile. "Fine."

Within a few moments, I was staring down at the ladder and beneath it to where Ameri's feet had just slipped out of sight.

People were buried in graves this narrow.

Tibris had decided he'd follow me to "guard my back." Part of me wondered if it was so he could soothe me if I lost my mind halfway.

Lorian's voice played through my mind.

"Every time I think you're about to stop being a scared little mouse and actually reveal the woman I believe you are, you prove me wrong. Well, sweetheart, we don't have time for your insecurity or self-doubt."

I loathed that I'd let the cold mercenary into my head. But he was right. We didn't have time for my insecurity. Or my self-doubt.

Sucking in a deep breath, I forced myself to think about anything except the tiny space below us.

Asinia. Think of Asinia.

That helped. If she could suffer in the king's dungeon, I could do *this*.

I began counting off the seconds as I lowered myself down the ladder. Prickles of dread traveled from the back of my neck down my spine. My eyes met Tibris's, and he gave me a reassuring smile.

Why couldn't I have been afraid of *anything* except small spaces?

I made it to the bottom of the ladder, moving aside so Tibris could come down too. My heart tripped over its next beat until it was racing fast enough, it was as if I were sprinting, fleeing for my life.

Dropping to my knees, I peered into the tunnel. Ameri's feet were barely visible in the gloom, but the fact that I could see them meant the tunnel couldn't be as long as I'd imagined.

Tibris landed behind me. "We don't have to do this."

"Don't coddle me." If I was going to be the kind of person who could break Asinia out of the king's dungeon, I could no longer afford weaknesses. I needed to conquer my fears. Needed to become hardened to such things.

Tibris turned silent.

I sighed. "I've…come to realize that in these kinds of situations, I respond better to impatience and the implication that I'm a coward than I do to soft words and encouragement."

"Well, that's not entirely healthy, but if it's what you need…"

More silence. Tibris cleared his throat, obviously searching for an insult.

I hadn't thought I'd have it in me to laugh at a time like this, but giggles burst from me. Even when asked to treat me with disdain, my brother couldn't do it.

"We're losing sight of them," he said finally, and I huffed out another laugh. If that was all Tibris had, I'd take it.

The dirt floor was rough beneath my hands and knees. The walls around me were so close, my head brushed against them a few times. My pulse galloped. Exactly how long would it take to die down here if the exit was blocked?

"You're doing great, Pris. Ah, I mean, move faster, you weakling."

His voice had turned miserable by the last word, and I awkwardly reached behind me, squeezing his hand. "It's okay. You don't have to be mean to me. It's enough that you're here."

Besides, I was suspecting I only responded to taunts from a certain gruff, endlessly amused mercenary. And that was just depressing.

"I'll always be with you," Tibris said.

Because we were all each other had. Because of me. Sometimes, the grief and guilt expanded inside me until I could barely breathe.

"We're here." Ameri's voice echoed down the tunnel.

Echoed because the tunnel *was* longer than I'd thought. I shuddered, and for an awful moment, bile burned up my throat.

No. I could do this. This was *nothing* compared to what Asinia was going through right now. I kept crawling, attempting to ignore the feel of dirt beneath my hands and knees.

Eventually, the tunnel opened into a small hollow carved out of the dirt. We were still underground, but we could stand if we bent almost in two. An old woman sat on a rickety-looking crate against one wall. Several tunnels branched from the hollow, and in the corner, another ladder led back up to what was likely another store or someone's house. That was our best escape route if the tunnel were to collapse.

Lanos leaned against one of those ladders and nodded at me. I turned and studied the old woman. She was blind, her lips were cracked and dry, and her clothes dirty and torn. Fury poured through me at her condition.

Ameri cleared her throat, and I glanced at her. She stiffened at whatever she saw on my face. "We've tried," was all she said.

I crouched in front of the woman. "My name is Prisca," I said softly.

"Hello, Prisca." The woman's voice was soft, almost childlike. She smiled, and despite her cracked teeth, it was a sweet smile. "My name is Ivene."

"Hello, Ivene."

"You've come to learn about the past."

"Yes. If you wouldn't mind telling me."

She reached her hands up, and I held myself still as she used them to trace my face. "You're a beautiful woman." She smiled, and it was sadder. "It won't make your life any easier, you know."

I smiled back, keeping my voice gentle. "I thought you saw the past, not the future."

"You don't have to be a seer to know life is kind to no woman, even those who are blessed with beauty."

"Can't argue with that," Ameri said. My lips twitched. We shared a look, and for the first time, I felt her thaw a little toward me.

"Will you tell me of the king? And the hybrids?" I asked, but Ivene was already turning away, her head angled as if she was listening to someone.

"I told you not to talk to me while I am speaking to others."

Ameri sighed but gestured for me to wait. Eventually, Ivene turned back toward me.

"The king. The king, the king, the king." She cackled, and the sound seemed to rip through the air. "Siiiit. You should make yourselves comfortable."

We sat at her feet, and she tipped her head back. When she spoke, her voice was *different*. No longer childlike, now it was deeper, as if someone else were speaking through her. I shivered.

"Get to the prince, your mother said. But you ignored her. When will you focus on your task, Prissss-caaaa?"

I opened my mouth, but she'd already turned away again, speaking gibberish. Her hands slammed to her ears. "Be quiet," she roared.

I looked at my brother. He stared steadily back. Those who looked both forward and backward were destined to lose their minds to their gifts. Ivene was likely somewhere between ten and twenty winters older than Mama. Had she lived, this would have been her future.

Was Tibris right, and that was why she'd let herself die by that river?

Ivene was sitting back on her crate. She waited until we were all looking at her once more—I still couldn't understand how she knew such a thing—and then she smiled that sweet smile once more. "Ask your questions."

I had so many, I didn't know where to start. But I focused on Asinia. "What do you know of the castle? The royal family? What's the best way for us to get someone out of the dungeon?"

"Shhhh." Ivene hushed whatever voice she could hear. "This is important." She faced me again. "In order to understand the elite, you must become like them. The queen has long been lonely, afraid, *weak*."

I folded my legs under me. "What do you mean?"

"Shhhh," she said again. But whatever she could hear obviously refused to quiet, because she turned and screamed, high and long. Her face flushed red, and Tibris gave me an unhappy look.

I couldn't just give up. If she could see the past, maybe she could see what decisions the royals had made. The security the king had in place. And potential weaknesses in that security.

"When we leave the castle, which route will give us the highest chance of survival? Where can we go?"

Ivene sighed, obviously weary. But her mouth curled into a gentle smile. "I can't see the future."

"I know. But...given what you *can* see...is there anything you can tell us?"

"The gods are *very* interested in what you do next."

Fuck the gods. I took a deep breath. "Thank you for your time."

"Wait," Tibris said. "I just have a couple of questions. If it's okay."

Ivene turned, shushing whomever she could hear once more. But this time, she laughed playfully, waving her hand at the empty air. When her attention returned to us, Tibris cleared his throat. "The people who raised us… was I taken by them too?"

Something that might have been sympathy creased Ivene's brows. "No, child. You were born of the people you called Mama and Papa."

Tibris kept his expression neutral. All those games of King's Web had paid off. I couldn't tell how he felt about that.

"And Prisca? Why did my mother take her from her birth parents?"

She gave him a sweet smile, as if he'd finally asked the right question. And then she turned to me.

"There are some things I can't tell you yet. Things you must learn when the time is right. But I can tell you this… You were just three winters old. If you had been in your bed that night, you would have died. The man you called your papa did everything he could to take those memories from you, but eventually, you will begin to remember."

A dull betrayal slipped beneath my skin. My papa—who I'd thought could do no wrong—had been using his power on me for my entire life.

"Where are my birth parents now?"

"I can't see that. I can only see what has been." Ivene held out her hand to me. I took it. Her skin felt as fragile as paper in mine. "But occasionally, the gods whisper warnings in my ear." She laughed at me. "And I know just what you think of those gods."

I opened my mouth, but she just shook her head.

"One day soon, you will have to make a choice. Be a torch for just one soul in the dark…or burn like the sun for all of them."

14
PRISCA

Jolted awake as someone slammed a fist on my door. "Hurry up, Pris."

Vicer.

I groaned, wanting nothing more than to roll back over. Hauling myself out of bed, I dressed, splashed water on my face, and met Tibris and Vicer downstairs.

The sun had barely risen, and Tibris looked as bleary-eyed as I felt. Vicer seemed to have been up for hours.

"Where are we going?" I asked.

"You'll see."

I scowled. Vicer ignored me and turned to the door, stepping out into the cool air. I lifted Galon's cloak off the hook by the door and followed him. If Tibris was tired of Vicer's cryptic behavior, I couldn't tell. His expression was placid as we strolled through the slums, back toward the potions shop we'd visited yesterday.

I was more prepared for the tunnel this time—not that it helped. Still, I refused to let Vicer see how much I struggled, so I kept my head down, counting off the approximate foot-spans once we passed the nook where we'd met Ivene.

Vicer continued down to a four-way intersection of tunnels and turned right. It felt like several years later when the low hum of voices reached my ears.

A lot of voices.

Vicer didn't seem concerned. He just continued his slow, methodical crawl, ducked his head, and disappeared around a corner.

I followed and found him standing in a huge cavern, holding out his hand for me.

Grabbing it, I stepped past him so Tibris could join us. The noise was even louder here, but it still had a hushed quality to it.

The space was larger than it should be. The part of me that continually worried about such things wondered how the roof didn't fall in on the hundreds of people who were wandering from stall to stall.

The walls were dirt, but every few foot-spans, a large blue-green crystal had been sunk *into* the wall, illuminating the merchants' faces and casting everything in a blue glow.

Tibris reached me, and we both stared, taking in the tiny tables straining beneath weapons, scrolls, books, charms, precious stones, potions... My head spun. The light was dim enough that it took me moment to realize some of the cave walls had been cut out—large swaths of cloth hanging in front of them to ensure privacy.

Whatever happened behind those curtains, the merchants wanted kept private.

I glanced at Vicer, who was surveying the market with a satisfied gleam in his eye.

"Explain," I said. "Please."

Vicer shrugged one shoulder. *"This* is how most of the hybrids in this city stay alive until they're old enough to pass for twenty-five winters." He led us to the closest table, which held a variety of charms and stones. "Depending on the kind of power a hybrid has, how strong it is, if it's passive or active, these can sometimes help keep them hidden—even from an assessor."

The merchant, an older man with a black-and-white speckled beard, nodded at Vicer, then turned as a girl who was likely no more than sixteen winters approached.

I'd expected Vicer to continue walking down the aisle between the stalls, but instead, he jerked his head, leading me to one of the nooks hidden by a dull gray sheet.

"Charms are better for small changes, like your eyes. I'll show you where to find the necklace you need after this. But your hair can easily be dyed."

A woman poked her head out of the smaller cave, grinning up at Vicer.

Her skin was a creamy white, so light I imagined she must constantly have to hide from the sun, yet there wasn't a single freckle to be seen. She looked my age, but there was something about her eyes that told me she was much older.

"This is Chava," Vicer said.

"I'm Setella," I introduced myself with my new name.

Vicer nodded approvingly at me. "We'll come back for you."

He disappeared, leaving me with Chava, who waved at me to take a seat on one of the overturned crates in her tiny space. I wasn't surprised to see several huge bowls of water—one of them clearly recently used. But Chava waved her hand over it, and the water cleared, clean once more.

"That's a helpful power."

"Indeed."

I sat in front of the mirror, and Chava got started on my hair. When I attempted conversation, she replied with one-word answers until I gave up and got lost in my own thoughts.

Eventually, she instructed me to wash my hair, and when the water ran clear, my hair was a dark brown. I stared. It was as if I was looking at a stranger.

"You suit both," she said with a satisfied hum. "Most women don't."

"Thank you."

A hand shifted the curtain, and Tibris met my eyes. "Wow. It'll take some getting used to."

Vicer looked over his shoulder and nodded. "Good. Let's get your eyes altered." He held out his hand, dumping several coins into Chava's palm, and I got to my feet. She nodded at me.

"Nice to meet you."

"You too."

Vicer led us to another table—this one closer to the back of the large space. My skin was prickling with the knowledge of just how deep we were—and how little it would take for the cave to collapse around us.

"You okay?"

"Fine."

Tibris gave me a look that told me he didn't believe me, but he stayed silent while Vicer murmured to another merchant, this one a beautiful woman with dark skin and eyes.

Those eyes met mine, crinkling around the corners.

"I can see why you need some help with those. They're pretty, but they're an unusual color that makes people look twice. I have a charm that will work, but you'll need to have it replenished. I'll talk to Vicer about getting you a new one every few days."

The thought of relying on someone else to help with my disguise made me nervous. But with no other choice, I took the necklace she handed me.

"Try it on," she instructed.

I pulled it over my head, and she held up a mirror. With my dark hair and brown eyes, I looked nothing like my description on the parchment, and my stomach settled as I examined my reflection.

"This is perfect. Thank you."

"Good luck to you," she said.

I nodded. She didn't know who I was, but clearly the fact that I'd arrived with Vicer gave her some idea of what

I was up to. He led us toward the tunnel we'd crawled through, but the cloth to my left parted, just enough for me to see what was happening beyond.

As I watched, a man held his hand to a woman's temple. A moment later, she stood, wearing the blue mark that marked her as twenty-five winters.

I let out a strangled sound, and the man's eyes met mine. He raised an eyebrow, his eyes a cool gray as he watched me. Tibris grabbed my arm, pulling me away.

"There are people who can do that?" I hissed.

Vicer gave us a warning look over his shoulder, continuing toward the tunnel. Tibris continued pulling until I fell into step with him.

I glanced over my shoulder at the line that was forming outside the gray-eyed man's cave. If hybrids were lucky enough to be born in the city, they at least had a scrap of hope.

"Vicer's people smuggle as many hybrids as they can—usually down to Gromalia. Areas still exist there where hybrids can live quiet lives. But that mark…for those who can afford it, it is freedom."

"For those who can *afford it*," I said. "The king's guards keep records. What happens when the hybrids don't appear on the day of their Gifting ceremony?"

Vicer glanced over his shoulder at us. For a moment, I wondered if he was about to tell us to shut our mouths. I glanced around us, at the people who were purchasing all kinds of highly illegal goods and services, and almost laughed. No one cared what we were up to. Several of the people here had already slapped Vicer on the back, leaned close to have a murmured conversation, or introduced family members.

Vicer waited for us to catch up to him. "They flee long before the ceremony," he said. "Whole families disappear in the middle of the night—along with anyone loyal to them. Sometimes, they fake their own deaths. There are hybrids with a gift for illusion who can help there."

"And those without the coin they need are eventually caught using their power or found attempting to flee, or worse."

Vicer just nodded, turning away.

I glanced back at my brother. Tibris's face was hidden in shadows. When he took his next step into the blue-green light, he looked older than his twenty-seven winters. "There are only a few with the ability to mimic the priestess's mark, and most get discovered, slaughtered by the king," he murmured. "This…this was my plan for you. I wanted to get you to the city, get you marked, and then we would find somewhere new. As a family."

"How could *we* have afforded it?"

"I was working on it. Hiding money away. Vicer has someone who owed him a favor. And…I had a few ideas."

I gave him a gentle elbow in the side. "I'm still mad at you for not sharing those plans with me. But I love you."

He sighed. "I know. I'm sorry. And I love you too."

"Tibris?"

All three of us froze. It was Vicer who relaxed first,

and Tibris's mouth curved in a wide grin.

"Gudram?" Tibris released my arm and turned to slap his friend on the back. Vicer just sighed.

"One of his contacts. They've only met once but worked together for years. This will take a while."

Someone bumped into me, mumbling an apology, and Vicer jerked his head, gesturing for me to follow him to lean against the cave wall.

"Do you think we can do this?" I asked.

Vicer kept his gaze on the market. "I've been a part of the rebellion since shortly after I arrived in the city. This is the first time many of us have felt hope. If we can get both Asinia and Demos free... I don't have to tell you that it will strike a blow to the king's reputation. It will bolster those who doubt the rebellion and allow us to strike where the king thinks he has no weaknesses."

"This Demos...how well do you know him?"

Vicer sighed. "He's a hard man but a fair one, and he has done more for your people than anyone else I can think of. I worked under him until he was arrested—it was pure luck I wasn't there when the king's guards raided our headquarters that night."

Pure luck? I had to know I could trust Vicer. He'd been in the city for years now. How could I be certain he wasn't sending me to my death? "Who did you lose, Vicer?"

He turned and gave me a faint smile. "I understand. You need to know I won't betray you. You always were the calculating type. Smarter than you were given credit for."

I winced and he laughed. "It's not an insult."

But he'd said it like it was.

Vicer heaved a sigh. "When I first moved to the city, I thought my life was finally beginning. The gods had given me back more power than most, and it was the kind that would be *useful*."

"What can you do?"

He glanced away. "I don't like to talk about it. I… can't. Not yet."

"It's okay." I'd only recently been able to talk about my own power myself. And I hadn't been forced to use that power for the crown every day.

Vicer seemed to steady himself. "I arrived, eager to do the king's bidding. For those who have a *purpose*, we're blindfolded and taken somewhere outside the city. There, we have a separate ceremony. They said it was to thank the gods for our power. But directly after, I noticed I had more power, and that power seemed to grow each day."

"Because that power was useful to the king."

"Yes. At the time, I thought the gods had blessed me more than most. I embraced life here. I went to the best parties, wore the most fashionable clothes, drank the most expensive wines. Then one day, at one of those parties, I met a woman."

His eyes held such desolation, a lump formed in my throat. "You don't have to tell me."

"No, it's okay. I…I should talk about her more. For a

while, I couldn't even say her name. But everything I do is for her."

Dread rippled through me. "She was a hybrid, wasn't she?"

He closed his eyes. "Yes. I didn't find out until months later. Guards stormed our home. One moment, she was in my arms, and the next, she wasn't. I was taken to be interrogated by one of their truth-seekers. When they found I had no knowledge of what she was, I was freed." He opened his eyes once more, and they blazed with fury. "Because my power was still *useful*. But the love of my life had been taken. By the time they let me go, Gods Day had passed. I never saw her again."

The color had disappeared from Vicer's cheeks, and he looked drained. Almost lifeless.

I took a shaky breath. "What was her name?"

"Rosin. She was Margie's daughter."

That explained why they'd become so close. And why he trusted her so deeply. Reaching out, I grabbed Vicer's hand.

"I'll do whatever I have to. For Rosin."

He squeezed my hand. "For Rosin."

PRISCA

Just a few hours later, Vicer stood waiting outside the

rebels' headquarters. He handed me a piece of parchment, and I stared at the royal seal. I'd known Vicer had contacts in the castle, but this looked so…official.

"How?"

"We have someone with replication magic."

I'd heard of replication magic, even in my small village. Not only was it incredibly rare—and therefore valuable—but those with the power of replication were almost always taken to the city to work for the king. It was an open secret that some people with this magic were able not just to replicate, but to make small changes when necessary. That meant my identification was legal—at least as far as the guards would be able to tell.

Such magic would be incredibly useful. Weapons, food, clothes…where did that power end?

"Are you ready?" Vicer asked, jolting me from my thoughts. He hadn't seemed nervous until this very moment, but the tension on his face rekindled my own.

Tibris slapped him on the back. "We're ready."

Nerves fluttered in my stomach.

We don't have time for your insecurity and self-doubt.

How Lorian would laugh if he knew just how much I was relying on those words.

In another life.

My chest tightened, and I shoved the memory out of my mind.

Vicer nodded at us. "A carriage will take you to the servants' entrance. Your identification will be checked at every stop. Keep your eyes down, your attitude meek,"

Vicer addressed the last to me. "No matter what the guards say to you."

I sighed. For Asinia, I could be *meek*. After all, I'd had plenty of practice at every Gifting and Taking ceremony in our village as I'd fought not to draw attention to myself. "I will."

He opened the door, and I surveyed the carriage. Thankfully, it had a horse. The driver leaned against the carriage and waited, a scowl on his face.

Margie had followed us out. "Good luck," she said.

I met her eyes. Hope gleamed at me, and I wanted to hunch my shoulders under the weight of it. But I held her gaze. "Thank you."

Within a few moments, we were sitting in the carriage, watching as the slums gave way to townhouses and green parks.

"You know, with your dark hair, we look more alike now than we ever have," Tibris said casually.

"Are you…angry about Papa?"

We both knew what I meant. If Papa had been working on my memories…

When he didn't speak, I took a deep breath and kept talking, unable to leave it alone. "I'm younger than you by almost five winters. Ivene said I was three winters when Mama took me."

Our eyes met, and this time, Tibris's eyes were hollow. "I had seen eight winters. And yet I have no recollection of suddenly having a new sister. As far as my memories are concerned, you were just always…there."

It was bitterness I tasted now. Both our parents were dead. We couldn't turn back time and ask Papa why he'd gone along with whatever reason Mama had given him for taking me from my true parents.

She had said it was to save my life. But to keep it hidden for so many years, to never *tell* those parents that I was okay?

Unless she didn't need to tell them. Because they were dead. The thought made me want to howl.

"Papa must have been working on me constantly." Tibris's voice was as bitter as the taste in my mouth.

I couldn't blame him. As far as we'd known, Papa had only ever used his magic for good. Like most people, he'd only had enough power to help temporarily, so he'd gone from village to village, softening the kinds of memories that ruined lives. Mothers who'd lost their children, husbands who'd lost their wives. Usually, those memories were hardest due to self-blame. My father had been the last hope for those who couldn't live with the guilt.

But he'd always told me there were few things worse than altering the memories of someone who hadn't given their permission.

If he'd been working on Tibris and me for all those years, the guilt would have been eating him alive.

"I can't forgive him for it," Tibris said hoarsely. "I don't know if I'll ever be able to forgive him."

My chest clenched. My brother was known among his friends for his inability to hold a grudge.

"I think…I think he was trying to protect you."

He lowered his brows. "I don't want to talk about it anymore."

"Understood. Uh, just so you know…one day I want to try to find my birth parents. At first, I thought it would be a kind of betrayal. But they had a daughter taken from them, and they deserve to know what happened. If they're still alive. But that doesn't mean I don't still consider you to be my brother."

"I know. You don't have to worry about me."

I'd always worry about him. It was my job as his sister. But from the frown on Tibris's face, it was clear he was ready to change the subject.

"So…how much do you know about wine and ale?"

Tibris let out a laugh. "Less than you know about cleaning."

"My work at Herica's bakery must have been good for *something*," I said.

I hoped she was okay. Hoped she hadn't been punished by the village for having hired one of the corrupt. She was old enough that she hadn't needed to be assessed, but…

How much trouble had I caused for her?

We rounded a corner, and the castle came into view. It looked like a fortress that had been built to defend against some ancient enemy, with stone walls so dark they appeared almost black—each brick cut into perfect rectangles. Several towers loomed over us, stretching into the sky with tiny windows dotted at what seemed like random intervals.

I reached for my brother's hand. "I'm scared," I admitted. There were very few people I would admit such weakness to.

"I am too."

Tibris looked at me and shook his head at whatever he saw on my face. "I've been scared since I got home and found you gone. Since I heard you'd fled and Asinia had been taken. Since Mama…" A muscle ticked in his jaw. "But every time I think about it, about how part of me wondered if you were dead too, the fear gives way to rage. Focus on that, Prisca. Focus on everything they took from us. Focus on Asinia."

Vengeance burned in my belly. Tibris was right. Fury was better than fear. Lorian had said the same when it came to using my power.

Our carriage continued past the castle and the long line of horseless carriages, most of them white and gold. Likely nobles arriving for some party. We continued straight, taking the next right, and the carriage slowed for the gatehouse. Several guards stood outside the servants' gate, and I forced myself to slow my breathing.

"Halt," a voice said, and the carriage stopped.

I pulled out my papers and buried my other hand in the folds of my dress to hide the shaking. The guards would expect some nerves—after all, we were peasants about to begin working in the castle. But blind terror would make them take a closer look.

One of the guards leaned in the window of the

carriage, his gaze sweeping over both of us. "Papers."

We handed them over. He scanned them and nodded, holding them back out for us to take. The gates opened, and the carriage continued to the next checkpoint. Now that we'd passed the first test, my limbs went weak.

This guard took longer, reading each word and comparing the descriptions to our faces. I lowered my gaze, as would be expected.

"Where are you coming from?" he asked.

My skin tightened at his hard stare. "Mistrun," I said without hesitation.

Silence stretched as he continued to study our papers. A line of sweat slid down my spine, and I fought to keep my expression neutral, a little bored. Finally, he nodded, holding out our papers. The carriage continued, and I let out a shuddery breath.

"I thought I was going to vomit all over myself," I muttered.

Tibris shook with laughter, and it was easy to see the relief that had set in. "We did it," he said. "The hardest part is over."

I shook my head as the carriage stopped once more, directly outside the servants' entrance.

"Somehow I doubt that."

We got out of the carriage, each carrying a satchel that held our few belongings. A stern-faced woman appeared in the doorway.

"You're the new recruits from Mistrun."

"That's right." Tibris smiled at her.

Her eyes softened slightly. "Well, get moving, then."

We both jumped into action, following her into the castle. The servants' entrance opened into a narrow room, where several delivery boys were waiting. One of them leered at me, and I gave him a killing look.

Tibris elbowed me, and I forced my gaze down once more.

"Names," the woman barked.

"I'm Setella, and this is Loukas," I said.

"My name is Nelia. I run an organized castle. Loukas, you will go into the next room, where one of the other cellar servants will give you a uniform and show you your bed. Setella, follow me."

Tibris gave me a reassuring smile and disappeared. I followed Nelia, taking mental notes of every turn. Directions weren't something I was typically good at, but by the time I left this castle, I would know every inch of it.

Nelia led me through the kitchen, which was so hot and steamy, I was instantly grateful to Vicer that my position had nothing to do with cooking. By the time we walked past the roaring fire—and the cook who was screaming at a maid—I was sweating in my cloak.

We exited the kitchen into a long corridor. "These are the servant hallways." Nelia nodded at varying doors, which must have opened to more corridors. "They allow us to travel through the castle without disturbing the nobility."

Because reminding the nobility that there were people catering to their every whim would be the height of bad manners.

Nelia seemed to be waiting for a response, so I gave her a nod.

"Tell me you're not another empty-headed, slow-moving fool," she growled, striding down the hall.

I trotted after her. "No, not at all," I protested. "Merely taking everything in."

"Move faster." At the next intersection, she turned left and led me up a flight of stairs. Glancing down at the paper in her hand, she nodded. "We have an empty bed in the third room to our right."

Opening the door, she gestured to the bed farthest from the fire. "That's yours. Put your things away and follow me."

I counted eleven other beds.

Sleeping in a room with that many women would make sneaking around this place even more challenging.

"Dress, and meet me in the corridor. I'll return for you."

I nodded, and she just rolled her eyes at me, stalking away. A few minutes later, I was wearing a maroon woolen dress that fell to my ankles. The dress had a row of tiny gold buttons down the front—even the maids had to wear the king's colors.

With nowhere else to store my satchel, I shoved it beneath the bed, meeting Nelia in the hallway once more.

Where were the dungeons?

That question played in my mind over and over. Obviously, they were below us. But who kept the keys?

Where was the entrance? How well was it guarded? Was Asinia still alive?

"In here," Nelia said, opening another door. The room was large, shelved, and stuffed full of cleaning supplies.

"You will be in charge of cleaning the floors," she said. "We have a woman who uses her magic on each floor once a day, but so many people walk through this castle that many of them are filthy again by lunch."

My pulse stuttered, and I fought to keep the eagerness off my face. It was easy to see why Vicer had worked to get me this position. I would have a legitimate reason to be in different areas of the castle. *Lingering* in those areas as I learned everything I needed to know.

"You'll get started now," Nelia said. "You can mop the servant hallways until I'm satisfied that you're a good worker."

"Thank you," I said when she handed me the bucket.

Within a few minutes, I was swiping water over the floor outside the servant bedrooms. I got to work, replaying every turn I'd taken, every door I'd seen so far.

"Hello," a voice said.

I turned to find a woman standing in front of me. Her skin was flawless, her blue eyes large and curious, and she was wearing a dress that matched mine, several blankets piled in her arms.

"I'm Auria," she said. "I heard we had someone new and thought you might need some extra blankets. I was given that bed farthest from the fire when I first got here, and it was freezing. I work in the laundry," she explained.

"I'm...Setella. Thank you, that's truly kind."

She beamed at me. "You're welcome. Where are you from?"

"Mistrun."

"I have a cousin from Mistrun," she started, and I prepared myself for my lies to crack. Footsteps sounded down the hall, and I turned, grateful for the interruption.

A woman was stalking down the hall, her face almost as red as her hair. She was incredibly beautiful, with sharp cheekbones, plush lips, and slightly uptilted eyes. But it was the color of her eyes that was truly remarkable—a blue so deep, it reminded me of the first and only time I'd seen the ocean.

The woman was wearing a dark blue dress which perfectly matched her eyes, with intricate beading emphasizing the hourglass shape of her figure. She looked like a noble, yet she was in the servants' quarters.

She strode over my newly cleaned floors without sparing us a single glance. I raised my eyebrow at Auria.

"Who is that?" I mouthed.

Auria waited until the woman turned a corner and sighed. "Your clean floors. She could have taken another route."

"Never mind that. She looks like she should be dining with the nobility."

"That's because she *is* the nobility. She's one of the queen's ladies."

My face must have looked as confused as I felt, because Auria smiled. "Madinia works directly with the queen. Providing her with entertainment, walking with her, going to all the lovely balls and dinners," she sighed.

"And…she has quarters here?"

"The ladies' quarters are the floor above us. They're still technically within the servants' quarters, but they're much, much nicer. I had to clean them once, and you would've thought *they* were royalty."

"That sounds like a great position."

She nodded, her eyes wide. "They get to go almost anywhere. They can leave the castle when they have an afternoon free—as long as the queen approves, of course. Not all of them are nobility either. And two of them are having trysts with the king's guards." She flushed. "I shouldn't gossip. My friends say it's my worst quality."

As far as I was concerned, it was her *best*. "Nonsense, you're merely telling me how the castle works. I just arrived today." I hunched my shoulders a little. "It's… different here."

"It is." Sympathy creased her face. "I better get back to the laundry, but I'll come get you when it's time for dinner."

"I'd like that."

15
PRISCA

Once I'd cleaned the floors to Nelia's satisfaction, Auria came and found me. She was friendly with one of the cooks, and we sat in front of the fire, shoes off, aching feet close to the warmth of the flames.

I'd met some of the maids as they came and went, finishing their work and readying themselves for dinner. Most of them had been kind, although they seemed to keep to themselves. A woman named Yirus had winced when she'd learned which bed I had, then offered to show me the quickest routes around the castle.

Auria would have made an excellent spy herself. Over a bowl of thick stew and fresh bread, she chatted relentlessly about the castle, the king, the queen, the queen's ladies, the king's guards—she found one of them exceptionally good-looking—and I attempted to memorize all of it.

"I'm sorry," she laughed. "I've done it again. My mother always said I talked like it was a competition."

"It's fine. Truly. I can be a little…shy."

She smiled, and I reached for my wine. "Uh, earlier you said not all of the queen's ladies were nobility?"

Auria nodded, using her bread to mop up the last of her stew. "Yes, while most of them are, the queen has always been a little…eccentric. I think sometimes she grows bored with court life. Caraceli was once the girl in charge of lighting her fire each night and keeping it burning. They became close, and when she was old enough, the queen offered her the position. And Katina was born in one of the northern villages. Close to the mountains." Auria gave a mock shiver. "The queen was traveling, and Katina was at the market, selling her father's wares. They began talking, and before anyone realized what had happened, Katina had been plucked from her village and was living here."

"So, each of them either showed loyalty to the queen or amused her in some way." There was potential there. I tucked that information away to think about later.

"I guess you could say that." Auria shrugged. "One of my friends says it's the queen's way of undermining the king." She flushed. "But you didn't hear that from me."

My head felt stuffed with all the information I needed to consider, and I finished the rest of my stew in silence while Auria told me a story about one of the kitchen maids.

"You must be exhausted," she said finally, when I was stifling a yawn. "Let me show you to the bathing rooms. You'll need to clean up before the ceremony."

I swallowed, my mouth suddenly dry. "What

ceremony?"

"Oh, I forgot, villagers don't pay homage to the gods as often as we do." Auria smiled and took my arm. "I suppose that's why most people living in the city are given back more magic than the villagers."

I stiffened. "Most of the villagers I know were too busy to worship every day. They were trying to eke out a living to take care of their families."

"I would argue that if they had worshipped more, perhaps they wouldn't have needed to work so hard. Perhaps the gods would have rewarded them. Oh, listen to me," Auria said. "Going on when you need to bathe. It's just…the gods were here for me when my mother died. Without their blessings, I don't know how I would have gotten through that time."

I tamped down my instinct to defend my neighbors. Instead, I offered her a smile. "I understand."

And I did understand. Many people used faith to cope with the worst parts of their lives. As something greater than themselves to turn to when they had lost their way. But some people used it to justify why others had less than they did–and why *they* were deserving of more. As much as I burned to tell Auria exactly why people in the city—especially the courtiers—were so much more powerful than us villagers, I bit my tongue until it almost bled.

One day, Auria would learn just how many lies she had believed.

She smiled at me somewhat awkwardly as we

approached the bathing rooms. Thankfully, she was ready to launch into an explanation about how the servants' bathing rooms were divided based on rank. Usually, one had to put their name down to use a bathing room, hoping it became available before you had to return to your duties. If you missed your turn, you went to the back of the line.

Thankfully, Auria was friends with the servant in charge of the bathing rooms. As she seemed to be friends with everyone.

"I can give you ten minutes," the woman said, handing me the key.

"Oh, here's a fresh dress." Auria opened a closet and handed me a maroon dress identical to the one I had on. "I'll get this one back to you once it's cleaned."

"Thank you."

The bath was better than the rivers and streams I'd been bathing in while traveling with the mercenaries. But my mind returned me to the bath I'd taken that night at the inn, right after I'd heard Lorian laugh properly for the first time.

He'd seemed bemused by himself, as if unused to laughing.

We don't think about him, Prisca.

I lounged in the bath, stopping and starting time to stretch out the bath while also getting some practice in. It gave me time to go over everything I'd heard so far.

I'd seen a variety of people in the castle. Some of them had already reached their Gifting, the blue on their temples marking them as safe. But plenty of younger servants were here as well. According to Auria, several of the queen's ladies hadn't yet reached twenty-five winters.

Auria knew more than I could've hoped, but she wasn't an idiot. She'd made a few comments that told me just how closely she paid attention to everyone around her. Hopefully, she could also tell me where the dungeon was. The sooner I could see Asinia, the sooner I could begin working on a plan to get her out.

Finally, the water was cold, and my eyes were heavy with the strain of holding my power. Slipping out of the bath, I pulled on the dress, braided my hair, and opened the door to find Auria waiting for me.

"We can go to the sanctuary together," she said, taking my arm once more. "This service is just for people who work in the castle. The royal family and the courtiers have their own service available to them in the mornings, although few of the nobles worship as they should." She frowned.

The sanctuary turned out to be in a separate building behind the castle. The stone was so light it was almost white, and the walls inside were draped with swaths of light-blue cloth. Hundreds of servants dressed in maroon were making their way from the castle toward the sanctuary, and Auria and I joined the crowd shuffling inside.

The ceiling of the sanctuary towered over our heads, adorned with gold etchings. Huge windows on either side spilled the last of the daylight onto the wooden floors, and I followed Auria to a chair a few rows from the front.

Glancing behind me, I looked for Tibris but couldn't see him anywhere. The skin on the back of my neck tingled, and I turned back around to find one of the king's assessors sweeping his gaze over the crowd. His black robes swished around his feet as he turned to the priestess.

I sucked in a breath. The *High* Priestess. She wore a long blue-and-gold gown, a plain gold diadem on her head. I wanted to rip it off her and slam it into her face.

"Are you well, Setella?" Auria asked.

"Yes. Merely excited to worship." Did the assessors know what the king did with our stolen magic? Did the priestesses know?

The crowd quieted, and the High Priestess launched into her prayers. Most of them were the same as those that were said during Giftings and Takings in the villages, and I followed along automatically.

I turned my attention to the assessor, watching him beneath my lashes. Even disguised as I was, I had to fight the urge to duck lower, hiding myself within the crowd. This assessor was an older man, tall and lean. A permanent frown line was etched between his brows, and his mouth turned down with displeasure. He angled his head, revealing a long scar across his neck.

I drew in a slow breath as nausea swept through my body.

I was eight winters, and we were preparing to move once more. I would miss my friends, but Papa said it was an adventure, and Tibris had promised he would make enough friends for both of us.

One of our neighbors had insisted we attend a party at her house. Ovida was one of the wealthiest women in our village and had become friends with my mother. Her son Ardaric was Tibris's age. He and Tibris would sometimes let me play by the river with them.

"Come, Prisca. Have something to eat." Ovida smiled down at me.

The door crashed open. Ovida whirled, her smile disappearing. My father grabbed my hand and pulled me away, holding me close. "Tibris," he called, and I'd never heard his voice sound like that before.

Papa was scared.

Tibris stood next to Ardaric, both of them staring at the doorway.

I turned my head, dread rippling through my body.

A man dressed in black robes stalked into the room, guards behind him. "Ardaric Narayon," he called, and Tibris went rigid, shoving his friend behind him. Papa let out a desperate, choked sound that made my chest hurt.

The assessor strolled toward Tibris, and all I could see was my brother's face, so pale, his lower lip trembling. But he stood his ground.

I launched myself toward him. Papa scooped me up, holding me against his chest and covering my mouth with his huge hand. I twisted in his arms until I could see the assessor looming over Tibris, his hand inches away from his chest. The assessor angled his head and then pushed Tibris away. Mama darted forward and grabbed Tibris's arm, pulling him toward us.

Ardaric faced the assessor. His chin stuck out, but his eyes were wide and glassy. I kept my gaze on his face as Mama took me from Papa's arms. Ovida was struggling in the arms of one of the guards.

"Please, please don't hurt him. Please!" Ovida screamed. "He's just a little boy."

Why would Ardaric be hurt? He'd never hurt anyone in this village. He always shared his toys.

Mama leaned close until her lips were pressed against my ear.

"Watch, Prisca. Watch closely. See what happens when a child is caught using forbidden magic."

The assessor was smiling now, his hand hovering above Ovida's chest.

"One of the corrupt, here in this very village," he announced.

"Ardaric!" a voice roared. Matous was here. Ardaric's father was a bear of a man, and he carried his sword. He sliced through one of the guards holding his wife. The assessor ducked, but Matous caught his neck with the edge of his sword. Blood sprayed.

Black spots danced in front of me, and the world suddenly seemed far away. Voices had turned to echoes, but I could hear my father.

"Cover her eyes," Papa hissed, holding Tibris back. Mama ignored him.

Matous fought like a man possessed, but more guards were streaming into the house, the crowd of villagers pressed against the walls with nowhere to go.

One of the guards ran Matous through. The big man fell to his knees, the light already dimming in his eyes. The eyes that had crinkled each time he smiled at us, handing out sweet treats whenever we visited.

Ardaric's scream was haunting. Ovida echoed that scream, falling to her knees.

A healer had already arrived and was holding one hand over the assessor's neck. He pushed her away.

"Without proper healing, it will scar," she said.

"Silence," the assessor hissed.

The room was quiet but for Ovida's sobs as the assessor stood once more.

"Oh, how the corrupt have been allowed to flourish in this village," the assessor said. "We must keep a closer eye on the peasants. Take the corrupt to the city," he ordered. Ardaric struggled, but he was no match for the guard, who cuffed him about the head. He reached for his mother, arms wild, his mouth open in a silent scream.

"Please don't take him. Please. Burn me instead. Please! My baby!"

The assessor ignored her, stalking toward the door. Ovida's eyes met mine, and then she gazed past me to my mother.

"You're a seer! How could you not see this?"

The guard swung his sword.

I cried out. My father's hand clamped over my eyes. Ovida's scream cut off with a thud.

I shuddered. A cold sweat broke out on the back of my neck, and the assessor's face swam in front of my eyes. The High Priestess was still chanting, so I bowed my head in an attempt to pull myself together.

Had my mother allowed that family to die so I would be forever haunted by the knowledge of what would happen if I were caught? So I would stifle the flame of my magic until the day it burst free, too strong for me to control without training?

She couldn't have done something so *evil*. Surely…

Yet this was the same woman who had stolen me from my real family. And never returned me. I had parents out there somewhere who had mourned me. Who had likely assumed I was dead.

I felt eyes on me and glanced over my shoulder. A woman with pale blond hair was staring at me, her gray eyes burning into mine. I turned around and leaned close to Auria.

"Who is that woman behind me? The one who looks like she wants to slit my throat."

Auria turned. "Oh, that's Wila," she whispered. "Don't worry about her. She hates *everyone*."

The High Priestess flicked us a glance, and I bowed my head. When I was sure she was no longer looking, I watched the assessor.

The child-killer.

I mouthed the prayers and made my own vow.

Before I left this castle—whether it was out the front gates, through the tunnel in the dungeon, or through that same tunnel to the stake—the king's assessor would be dead.

LORIAN

Finally, we were ready. Time and time again, spies had been sent into Sabium's castle. And always, he had found them, killing them in new and inventive ways.

So now, it was my turn. Our new plan was bold— bordering on reckless. But Sabium had taken so much from us, our revenge was well overdue.

I pulled on my boots. We were in some no-name inn, and I'd had little sleep on the sagging mattress the night before. I would have preferred sleeping on the ground, but my men had once again demanded better food.

"You think he'll issue the invite?" Rythos asked.

Sabium wouldn't be able to help himself. "Oh yes. If I act suitably chastened and desperate for an alliance, he'll invite me into the castle."

"Hunting with him? How will you refrain from killing him?" Marth muttered.

"Simple. Lorian kills him, and we never get into that castle." Galon glowered at Marth, then turned the same look on me. "This is risky, and you know it."

"It's the only option. I'll meet him to hunt a few beasts, let him best me with his magicked arrows, and tell him I've rethought Gromalia's insistence on staying out of his little issue with the fae."

As far as the king was concerned, I'd taken the first step, tucking my tail between my legs and agreeing to meet in his kingdom. Sabium's hunting cabin was close to the town where I had forced Prisca to use her magic.

Amber eyes flashed in front of my face, filled with accusation. I shoved the image away and reached for my bow.

The thought of butchering an animal without the need to eat it was distasteful.

But not as distasteful as the thought of a conversation with Sabium. Of standing that close to him and not ripping out his throat.

"You kill him, and we have no way to find—"

"I know. I won't kill him. Have our friends arrived?"

"See for yourself."

Pushing the curtain aside, I looked down into the courtyard, where several men waited, all dressed in dark green overcoats.

"Good." I glanced at Marth, who was waiting by the door, dressed in the same color. He was the only one of us the king would not be looking for. He nodded to me, and I slung my bow over my shoulder, taking the quiver Galon handed me.

Everything we had done so far—all our plans, years of waiting, and each endless minute of travel—all of it had led to this. I would control my temper, curb my instincts, and secure my invite to the castle.

And then, Sabium would pay.

PRISCA

I spent the next several days cleaning the floors in the servants' quarters, until Nelia was finally pleased and I was allowed to clean the rest of the castle—although she'd insisted I had to prove myself once more by cleaning the lower levels.

On my fourth day in the castle, I caught sight of Tibris. Something in my chest relaxed. If anything had happened to him, Vicer would've found a way to get a message to me. But that hadn't stopped me from imagining the worst. My brother winked at me as he walked past with several other men, all of them carrying large crates. He was wearing tight breeches that fell to his knees, a maroon waistcoat embroidered in gold, and a shirt with… frills. I gave him a smirk.

When he returned, he nodded to the other men. "I just need a word with my sister."

"Don't be too long," an older, bearded man said.

"Are you okay?" Tibris asked.

I nodded. "You?"

"Yes. Prisca…" He lowered his voice to a whisper. "I know where the entrance to the dungeon is."

My heart stopped. "Truly?"

"Yes. I set everything up for tonight." His mouth

twisted. "But I've just learned that the king is traveling overnight and I may be sent as part of his entourage."

"I'll go," I said. "Just tell me where it is."

"I don't like the idea of you going alone."

"Tibris," I said warningly, and he sighed, handing me a few pieces of parchment—all of it in our code. I studied the map on top of the pile, and my heart beat faster in my chest. This was the key to our plans. With this, I could find Asinia.

"I've been working on the guards." He nodded to the parchment—and the instructions I'd have to decipher later. "But I need you to promise me you'll be careful."

"I promise."

"Loukas. Let's go."

"I'm coming." Tibris squeezed my hand. "Good luck."

That night, I studied the parchment. As usual, my brother had done his research. The guards were replaced at midnight, which meant the best time to get near the dungeon was right before the change, when they would already be tired.

Vicer had said the prisoners were fed once a day—in the morning. I'd still need to watch out for the guards adding new prisoners. Each shift had one guard who was in charge of the dungeon keys. Those keys hung on a large ring from their belt.

I would need to freeze time before they noticed me, take those keys, and sneak into the dungeon. I couldn't risk getting locked in, which meant I needed to keep the keys. The most dangerous part would be the time I was in the dungeon. If the king's guard noticed the keys were missing, I was dead.

But Tibris had helped there too. According to his note, he'd made friends with those guards, offering them several of the many bottles of wine that didn't meet the standards for the king's table. By the time I arrived, the guards should be deep into their cups.

It was risky. But I needed to see Asinia. Needed to give her hope. There was no point being in the castle if I wasn't actively finding a way to get her out.

The other women were already in bed when the clocktower struck eleven. Most of them were sound asleep, although Auria was tossing and turning. Wila had sneered at me when she'd walked in, making it clear she wasn't interested in friendship.

With a deep breath, I pulled my power to me, jumping out of bed to drag Galon's cloak over my nightgown. Stuffing a pillow under my blankets, I bolted for the door.

This would be the most I'd used my power in days. And while I'd practiced on the mercenaries while we were riding, this was much, much more important. I dropped the thread of magic and tiptoed down the hall. If only I could freeze time for longer.

I lost myself in fantasies of freezing the entire castle for hours at a time, free to do whatever I needed to do.

Scuffing sounded, and I froze, peering around the corner. Nelia was walking down the corridor, a lamp in her hand. I sucked in a breath, freezing time once more. I wanted to conserve my power, but at this point, I had no choice.

Breaking into a sprint, I careened past Nelia and down the stairs, feeling the thread slowly slipping through my fingers.

By the time I'd reached the lowest level of the castle, that thread had fallen from my grasp. Time resumed, and I was sweating with the effort of holding it as long as I had.

Urgency crawled through me. I needed to move faster.

Tibris had said the entrance to the dungeon was next to the wine cellar. I crept toward it, my heart pounding in my throat. The door looked like it opened to some kind of storage room or closet. It was only the muffled sounds of the guards' voices that made me pause.

"You hear something?" one of the guards asked, and I scowled down at my traitorous foot. *Weeks* of traveling with the mercenaries, and I was still no better at sneaking.

"Sure. I heard the sound of me opening another bottle of this wine," the second guard laughed.

Thank you, Tibris.

Closing my eyes, I reached down, down, down into the place where my power resided. I needed more than a few seconds. I needed enough time to steal the keys and open the door. I needed to get far enough down the stairs that the guards wouldn't hear me.

I visualized each move I'd make while the guards gossiped about the queen's ladies. Apparently, one of them was particularly inventive in bed.

Asinia was on the other side of that door. Asinia, who

probably assumed she'd been left to die. I didn't have time for fear. Didn't have time to second-guess myself.

I opened my eyes.

And time stopped.

I knew before I was moving that this time was different. Usually, the thread of my power immediately began slipping from my grasp. Now, I held it tighter than ever before.

Launching myself into motion, I opened the door. This was an antechamber that allowed for the dungeon itself to be guarded without the guards needing to be posted down with the prisoners. Across the room, the door I needed looked like steel, heavy and secure. The guards were sitting down, leaning against the wall next to the door, a bottle of wine on the floor between them. Three other empty bottles were lying next to them.

My brother had done everything he could to make this easier.

The keys hung from the guard's belt, and I crouched in front of him. It took me several seconds to unhitch them from his belt, but then I was standing, hands shaking as I shoved one of the keys into the door.

Time had begun to slip once more. As tightly as I grasped the thread, it was sliding from me.

Wrong key.

My hands shook harder. The thread slipped even more. My eyes burned. This was *not* how it ended.

The next key went all the way in. The lock clicked, the door opening to dark steps. Shoving the keys into the pocket of my cloak, I darted through the door, closing it behind me.

My eyes were still adjusting to the dim light, but I only had moments to get as far as I could from the door. My hand found the smooth wall of the dungeon, and I used it to steady myself, wincing as my palm touched moss and mold. My lungs ached, my mouth was bone-dry, but I picked up my pace, stretching my power until black spots appeared in the edges of my vision.

I dropped the thread and time resumed. A surge of victory flooded through me. I'd made it this far. Ahead, a torch cast an orange glow on the stone wall. I wiggled the torch free and took it with me.

The stairs felt never-ending. The scent of rusty metal and human waste slid up my nostrils before I heard the groans. Dread rose, quickening my pulse and making my head swim. I forced myself to take several deep breaths, but by the time I reached the bottom of the stairs, I was trembling. The stench was sickening, but it was the cold that made me shudder.

I pulled my cloak up over my head, just in case I found Lina here. She would be desperate for the king's pardon, and there was a good chance she would recognize me.

Tightening my hand around the torch, I stepped forward.

This was an ageless, evil place. Cells stretched out on either side of me for as far as I could see. I splashed through stagnant puddles of water, peering into each cell, my heart breaking.

Would Asinia even still be alive?

All the prisoners were lying on the floor. Many of them seemed half dead. I crouched outside the closest cell and pressed my face next to the bars.

"Hello? Can you hear me?"

The man opened his eyes to slits, but that seemed to take all of his energy. A moment later, those eyes were closed again.

Vicer had warned that the prisoners were kept docile. But this wasn't just docile. This was much, much worse.

If only I could break them all out. Could lead them straight out the front door of the castle and set them free. Back to their families.

My eyes burning, I stumbled to my feet and kept moving, passing prisoner after prisoner. I kept my voice low, but none of them responded, and I didn't see Lina.

It felt as if years had passed by the time I found Asinia. She was on my left, curled into a ball on the stone floor, without even a blanket.

My heart cracked into pieces.

"Asinia?"

She didn't reply. My hands shook as I shoved the key into the lock, swinging her cell door open. Crouching next to her, I leaned down.

"Asinia. Please be okay. Asinia, open your eyes."

She cracked them open. "Pris?" she whispered, her voice so quiet I could barely make out her words. "Dreaming?"

"No, you're not dreaming." I pushed Asinia's hair

off her face, and my blood froze in my veins. "You're burning up."

"Miss you."

I had to get her some medicine.

Her eyes met mine, blurry and lost. "My mother is dead." They sharpened. "So is yours."

My breath hitched. "I know."

And then her head was lolling once more.

"She's not going to last," a weary voice said, and I turned my head.

The man in the cell to the right of Asinia's looked about Tibris's age, although he was little more than skin and bones. I could barely make out his face in this light, but a beard covered most of the lower half of it.

"She *will* last," I snarled.

He smiled. "Perhaps she will, with a friend as fierce as you."

I glanced around us. The cell to the left of Asinia's was empty. Across the narrow corridor, most of the cells were occupied by more prisoners who lay as if already dead.

Turning my attention back to the prisoner, I surveyed him. The light was too dim to see much, but I could tell his hair was dark and his clothes were in even worse condition than most of the other prisoners I'd seen so far.

"How can you hold a conversation and no one else can?"

He twisted his lips. "I've built up somewhat of a tolerance to the guards' poison."

I swallowed around the lump in my throat. "What's your name?"

"Demos."

I closed my eyes. *This* was the man Vicer had ordered me to get out when I freed Asinia.

"I'm—"

"Don't tell me."

Because if he was tortured for that information, he would be forced to give it up.

I blew out a breath. "How long have you been here?"

"Almost two years." He must have seen the surprise on my face. "I was caught days after Gods Day. For some unknown reason, I was spared during the next Gods Day. I doubt I'll be as lucky this time."

He didn't look all that concerned about it. I had a feeling he was ready to end his existence in this cell.

"Why can't any of you use your powers?"

"Iron poisoning."

I frowned, peeking at his ears, which were most definitely *not* pointed. "We're not fae. We can tolerate fae iron."

He nodded. "We can *tolerate* it. But the first thing they do when we're brought here is slice at our skin and push fae iron into our wounds. Then they crush it into dust and feed it to us in what little food they give us."

I stored that information away, attempting to distance myself from the sickening reality of it. If I was going to get them both out of here, I needed them to be able to walk.

"Is the iron still in your body?"

He shifted closer, and for a moment, he seemed so

familiar I had to blink. Then he was holding up his arm once more, the rags he wore shifting back to show me his shoulder.

The world dimmed around me. Demos was cursing, covering up the wound, but I could still see it in my mind. Could still see the infection that had spread through his entire shoulder. Could still see the pus that wept from it.

I leaned over Asinia, pushing her tunic off her shoulder. She had a wound in the same place, although it was nowhere near as infected as Demos's.

Blowing out a breath, I met his gaze. "Why is yours so much worse?"

"I may have decided to dig the fae iron out myself. Turns out, that wasn't a good idea. Still, dying of infection is a better way to go than burning alive." He gave me a grim smile.

I couldn't disagree. "The guards still only feed you once a day, in the mornings?"

Surprise flickered across his face. "Yes. Keeps us hungry for the next bellyful of iron."

"Don't eat for the next few days. Try to make sure Asinia doesn't either." It was risky, given that she didn't have any weight left on her to lose. But a few bites of food tainted with fae iron would likely do more harm than good.

He canted his head. "You have some kind of plan. Usually, I would laugh at you. But the fact that you managed to get down here tells me you might be my only hope in this place."

"Just don't eat the food. I'll be back as soon as I can."

16
PRISCA

*R*ough, warm hands on my skin, unerringly finding the spots that made me moan. One hand slid to my breast, flicking my nipple, and I arched my back, desperate for more.

"Patience," a low, infinitely amused voice said.

I shook my head, reaching into the darkness, pulling the man closer, until our lips met in a filthy mimicry of a kiss. His mouth teased mine, his tongue thrusting deep, and I clawed at him, pulling him even closer.

He let out a rough growl that made me shiver, and I swept my hands along the muscles of his back. When he raised his head, dark green eyes burned into mine.

My eyes popped open and met amused brown. "Who is Lorian?" the woman asked.

I groaned, mortification making my cheeks burn.

She just laughed, jumping out of bed. I hadn't caught her name, and she was already hurrying away.

Sitting up, I ran my hands over my face in an attempt to clear my head.

Getting out of the dungeon had been easier than getting in. My power had felt strong, likely fed by my rage. But every time I'd closed my eyes last night, I'd seen Demos's shoulder, the other prisoners who couldn't even lift their heads, and Asinia, shivering on that stone floor.

Dreaming of Lorian was the final twist of the knife.

No matter how many times he'd featured in my dreams over the years—and one day I'd figure out exactly why *that* had happened—they'd never turned into *those* kinds of dreams.

It was the kiss at the city walls that had caused this. Swinging my legs out of bed, I silently cursed the man who, even now, was messing with my mind.

"You should hurry, or you'll be late," a maid named Kryana told me.

"I will. Thanks."

I wouldn't have time to meet Auria for breakfast, so I went straight to Nelia.

"Ah, Setella. Today, I'm trusting you with the floors in the queen's wing."

My heart tripped. The distraction was welcome, but more importantly, it was a chance to start *doing* something.

"You are never to speak to anyone above your station unless they ask you a direct question. Do you understand?"

"Yes, Nelia."

"Good. Work quickly."

"I will."

And so I spent the next several hours in the queen's wing. First, I swept the nonexistent dirt—whoever used their magic to clean had likely been here just hours before I arrived—and then I got to work mopping the already spotless floors.

At least it gave me time to think. Time to remember everything I'd seen last night.

I kept my head down, but my body shook.

Rage burned through me, so brightly, I felt as if I might explode with it.

Seeing Asinia in such a state, coming face-to-face with the condition of the prisoners...not to mention Demos's wound...

Bile burned up my throat at the thought.

It wasn't enough to kill us. The king had to bring us so low, we *longed* for death.

All so he could keep our magic.

Could I really free two of the prisoners and leave the rest to rot?

I lifted my head and caught sight of my reflection in one of the mirrors. Apparently, the queen liked to be able to gaze at herself wherever she went.

I looked nothing like myself with my dark hair and brown eyes. I also looked pale, shell-shocked. But my eyes burned with vengeance.

Ivene's voice had been playing in my head over and over again since I'd seen the dungeons.

"One day soon, you will have to make a choice. Be

a torch for just one soul in the dark...or burn like the sun for all of them."

The thought of leaving the others here made me sick to my stomach. I couldn't do it. I didn't know how, but I was going to free *all* the prisoners the king considered corrupt. And I was going to do it before Gods Day.

A door opened, and the swish of long skirts warned me to step out of the way.

I froze. The queen. It was the first time I'd seen her, and I stood with my head bowed, hands behind my back as I'd been instructed.

She ignored me, and I dared to glance at her face as she swept past.

She was beautiful, as I'd expected. What I hadn't expected was the smattering of freckles over her nose, which gave her an almost childlike appearance. Her eyes were dark gray, wide and solemn.

Her ladies trailed behind her silently. Six of them, walking in pairs. I recognized the one with the flame-colored hair, and she sneered at me as she met my eyes.

The beginnings of a plan started to form in my mind. A dangerous plan. But a plan that could change everything.

The queen continued her stroll, and I got back to work, my mind whirring.

"Prisca," a voice hissed.

I jolted. Tibris was standing in the closest room, the door cracked open. I gaped at him.

"How—"

"Servants' hall. Did you see Asinia?"

"Yes. She's sick. Burning up with fever."

He lowered his brows. "I need to heal her."

I nodded. I'd planned to make the same suggestion. My brother could at least buy us time. "Tonight. There's something else. I need you to get a message to Vicer."

Voices reached us, and Tibris closed the door. I lowered my head once more, sweeping my mop over the stone. Eventually, the voices quieted, and Tibris cracked the door open again.

"What are you thinking, Pris?"

I handed him the note I'd written earlier. His eyes widened as he read it. He'd been using our code for much longer than me, and he instantly understood what I was asking for.

He lifted his head, eyes incredulous. "It will never work."

I felt my chin jut out—my usual reaction to being told I couldn't do something by my brother. But this time, I *knew* it could work. "Let's wait for Vicer's reply."

LORIAN

Dear L,

Our mutual friend should be allowed his freedom for now. Let us keep a close eye on him so we can see who he is talking to. Congratulations on securing the invite to the castle. The temptation to let an arrow pierce Sabium's heart must have been...great.

While I cannot begin to understand how difficult it will be to interact with those loathsome creatures, I beg you to leash your temper.

One day, we will have our revenge. We will watch Sabium's head roll free and know he has paid for everything he has done to our family.

That time is not now. As much as both of us would wish it otherwise.

Your appreciative brother,
C

PRISCA

"Shh," Tibris soothed Asinia that night. The devastation had been clear on his face when I'd opened her cell door. Now, he was crouching next to her, attempting to heal the worst of her sickness, while I handed some of the smuggled food through the cell bars to Demos.

His mouth had fallen open when he'd seen me again. Obviously, he hadn't truly believed I would return. Now, he was shoving bread and cheese into his mouth.

"Don't eat too much," Tibris warned. "Or it'll come

straight back up.

Demos nodded, taking smaller bites. My chest clenched.

"I'll try to bring some meat tomorrow," I told him.

I turned to Tibris. His expression was grim. I'd told him about the iron, and he was studying the slice along Asinia's shoulder.

"We need to get this out. I can't heal her with the fae iron in her body."

Slipping into the cell, I knelt next to Asinia. She'd gotten worse overnight, and now she was so pale, it seemed as if she was moments from death. A chill slid over me. We couldn't have gotten here just in time to watch Asinia die. We *had* to be able to save her.

"What do you need me to do?"

"Hold her down and keep her from alerting every guard in the castle."

Asinia was completely unresponsive. Was she dying? Had she already slipped into an unconsciousness from which she could never be woken? The backs of my eyes burned as I waited for Tibris to ready himself, and when he nodded, I placed one hand over her mouth, leaning on her other arm to keep her still.

"Go."

The wound had healed enough that Tibris had to open it once more. Asinia remained unconscious for that. But when it came time to dig out the iron, she screamed against my hand, bucking weakly as we held her down.

Her screams, the sight of her writhing... Tears dripped down my cheeks. But she was alive. Alive and awake.

Her eyes met mine, clear for the first time.

I leaned down. "We're saving you. I'm sorry, but it has to be done."

She nodded, but whatever Tibris was doing made her let out another weak scream. At Tibris's order, I poured water over the wound, flushing out the tiny iron pieces he hadn't been able to remove.

It went on for what seemed like forever. By the time Asinia's eyes rolled back in her head, I was covered in sweat. Tibris met my eyes and gave me a nod. He'd brought a tiny healer's kit with him into the castle, and as soon as he'd cleaned the wound enough, he'd sewn it shut once more.

"If they examine her, they'll know someone was in here," Tibris said.

Hopelessness squeezed my lungs tight. After what we'd just had to do to Asinia, the thought of someone doing it to her again…

Demos cleared his throat. "They won't examine her," he said. "I've been here almost two years, and no one has checked mine. It had to be done."

I turned and surveyed him. "I'm glad you feel that way. Because you're next."

He sucked in a breath but nodded. If Asinia's wound had been bad, Demos's was horrifying. Tibris stepped into his cell and handed him a piece of wood from his pocket kit.

"What's that for?" I asked.

"For him to bite down on."

I stayed next to Asinia while Tibris cleaned out Demos's wound. Demos's low groans made my stomach churn, and I glanced over my shoulder to find him clutching on to the bars between the cells, his knuckles white.

I couldn't just let him suffer, even if it meant leaving Asinia for a few moments.

Getting to my feet, I wrapped my hand around one of his. "You're doing great," I murmured. "Just think about all the ways we're going to make these bastards pay."

Demos nodded.

"I'm sorry. I'm so sorry."

He spat out the wood from between his teeth. "It's not your fault. Fuuuck." He clutched at the bars, and I squeezed his hand tighter.

"Think about something you love," I said desperately. "Tell me about it."

He let out a choked sound, and for a long moment, it seemed as if he couldn't manage a single word. I hoped Tibris was almost done.

"I love watching the clouds," Demos murmured. "I used to lie on the grass and watch them for hours. Especially when the sun was right about to set."

"Beautiful."

He opened his mouth, but a muffled yelp came out.

"It's okay if you need to cry."

I peered at his shoulder. Tibris had began sewing up the wound.

"First rule of being a prisoner," Demos told me, "you cry, and you're done."

This was a man who refused to be victimized by life. Even after everything he'd obviously gone through in these dungeons. "I'll keep that in mind."

He smiled, his teeth flashing in the low light. "I've only known you for a day, but something tells me you probably should."

"My sister will *never* end up in one of these cells," Tibris growled.

I rolled my eyes. "How's his shoulder?"

"I'll need to keep working on it, but my magic is almost completely drained."

I fisted my hands. How many more prisoners could Tibris be healing if the king hadn't stolen his magic?

"We'll come back tomorrow," I said, turning to press a kiss to Asinia's brow. I wished I could bring her a blanket, but we couldn't risk a guard walking past and noticing.

"The next guards will be on shift soon," Tibris said. "We need to go."

We snuck back up to the servants' quarters. When it was time for Tibris to turn left to the men's rooms, he slumped against the wall instead. His eyes were bleak when they met mine.

"She would have died tonight," he said. "I have no doubt. It was that close, Pris."

Nausea swept through me until I had to pant a few breaths to clear my head. "I'm so glad you're here."

"So am I. We need to get her out, but for the life of me, I can't figure out how. We take her and run, and we may get out of the castle, but we'll never get out of the city."

Oh yes, we would. "I'm going to figure something out."

He opened his mouth to argue, rolled his eyes, and closed it with a snap. Likely, he didn't have enough energy to verbally spar with me tonight. Instead, he slipped his hand into his pocket and pulled out a note. "From Vicer."

"Thanks."

By the time I made it back to my room, I was almost shaking with fatigue. It took everything in me to still time long enough to crawl into my bed.

The bed was freezing, given that it was next to the window. But I pushed the curtain back and read Vicer's coded note by the light of the moon.

Pris,

I don't have to tell you how risky such a strategy would be. For the first part of your plan, I need a day to organize the note.

For the second part, I have two people who could potentially help you, but I won't order them to do it. If one of them volunteers, you'll have your distraction.

Vicer

I blew out a shaky breath. It might be too much to hope for a volunteer. It was dangerous. But if there was one thing I knew about the rebels, it was that most of them were living solely for revenge.

Could I use that need to get one step closer to the queen?

Asinia's face flashed in front of my eyes. It was followed by every prisoner I'd walked past in that dank, dark dungeon.

Yes. Yes, I could.

17
PRISCA

The next time the queen strolled past, ladies in tow, the pretty blond woman with the deep brown eyes was gone. Katina had received a note from her village about a death in the family, and the queen had given her permission to travel home.

The queen's ladies usually walked in pairs. The solitary woman at the back was a glaring difference.

Hopefully enough of a difference to play in the queen's mind.

For the next two nights, I stole food from the kitchen and escorted Tibris into the dungeon so he could work on Asinia. And each day, I chewed my nails until they bled, conscious of Gods Day looming. I had a little over three weeks left, and I still didn't have a clear plan.

Finally, I received the answer I needed.

One of Vicer's rebels had agreed to volunteer for my plan. If this worked, I could be one step closer to freeing Asinia and Demos. My stomach churned. If it *didn't* work, I could get someone punished and still end up in the same position I was now.

With nothing.

Right now, Asinia was still far too weak to travel. Tibris had said the attempt would kill her. While I'd been keeping an eye out for the hidden entrance to the tunnel each time I was in the dungeon, I hadn't yet found anything hopeful.

Frustration tightened my muscles. Everything was taking too long. I knew I needed patience—knew if we moved without careful preparation, we were dead. But it seemed as if time was crawling, even as each second that passed was another second closer to Gods Day.

I burned Vicer's note and made sure I was in position, mopping the castle entrance. It took at least an hour for the queen to appear, ready to get into the large horseless carriage waiting outside. According to Auria, she was going to the market with her ladies.

I slid out of the way when I heard her appear. My head was down, arms behind my back when she strolled past, the train of her long silver dress trailing behind her.

The back of my neck turned slick with sweat. Vicer hadn't told me who to look out for. I could admit it was much safer that way. The maid walked toward the queen with her lamp in her hands, and I went still as I recognized her light-blond hair.

Wila.

Her eyes held nothing but cold retribution. And the lamp she carried held a flame that burned purple at the center.

A flame that only I could put out.

Wila stumbled once, seemed to catch herself, then tripped over her feet once more.

The queen passed Wila right as the lamp landed on the train of her dress.

The queen kept walking.

And her dress burst into flames.

The queen whirled, the flames shooting higher. A desperate scream left her throat, and for a moment, I was tempted to let her burn to death right there.

But that wasn't part of the plan.

Yanking on the thread of my magic, I froze everyone but myself and the queen.

She let out another choked scream, and I launched forward, pouring my bucket of water—carefully mixed with the damask weed powder Vicer had sourced—onto her dress, making sure to douse the lamp.

Time unfroze, and the guards were suddenly standing in front of me, swords out.

"What in the gods…"

The queen attempted to turn, but I was standing on the long train of her dress. I jumped off it, and her eyes met mine, cool and surprisingly clear. Then she was staring down at the scorched ruin of her dress. The fire had spread high enough that it would have engulfed her within seconds.

One of the guards called for a healer. The queen ignored him.

"Name, girl."

"Setella, Your Majesty."

The queen's eyes turned ice-cold as she swept her gaze over everyone else surrounding her. The people I'd frozen while the queen panicked. In her mind, the guards had been too slow to move, her ladies had gawked, and any onlookers had likely secretly hoped she burned to death, the way her husband ordered for so many people in this kingdom.

I saw the moment she realized she was achingly alone.

And my blood thrilled at it.

"What were all of you doing while this servant was helping?"

Stuttering, helpless looks, blood draining from terror-stricken faces.

The queen held up her hand. Everyone went silent.

"You," she said, pointing at me. "You will come to my quarters after lunch."

I bowed my head, my heart slamming against my ribs. "Yes, Your Majesty."

Her attention turned to Wila. "And *what* exactly were you doing?"

"I tripped, Your Majesty. The floor is uneven—"

The queen slapped her across the face. I flinched. Wila's expression turned blank.

"Perhaps some time in my husband's dungeon will improve your agility."

The guard closest to Wila stalked toward her. Wila's

eyes met mine for a single moment, and then she was dragged away, her eyes burning even brighter.

My fault. The dungeons were an overreaction—the queen lashing out. I hadn't anticipated it, and now Wila would suffer the consequences.

I turned to the queen. Her eyes were darkly satisfied as she watched the guards take Wila away.

I wished I could have let the bitch burn.

The queen turned and stalked back toward her rooms. Obviously, there would be no trip to the market today. Her ladies followed her, whispering among themselves.

I finished mopping the floors, conscious of the eyes on me. Minutes ago, I'd been just another maid. One only trusted with cleaning the floors. Now, I had the queen's attention, which meant I also had everyone else's too.

Auria ate lunch with me in the kitchen. She'd charmed the cook into giving us a piece of cake to share, and we sat in one corner, away from the worst of the noise.

"Wila never seemed clumsy before," Auria said, her expression solemn. Our eyes met, and she angled her head. "I hope she's okay."

My memory provided me with Wila's face and the banked rage in her eyes. "I hope so too."

Auria took a neat bite. "What do you think the queen wants?"

"I have no idea. But I should go."

Gods, I hoped it was worth it.

"Let me fix your hair first. And your apron is filthy. Take mine."

Auria shoved pins into my hair, rolling it up into a neat bun. Whipping off her apron, she switched it for mine before pronouncing me ready. My chest clenched. I didn't know what I'd do without Auria. She was one of the kindest people I'd ever met.

"Thank you."

"Good luck."

The queen's guards had obviously been told to expect me, because they stepped aside when I approached her chambers. My stomach roiled with nerves as I knocked on her door.

"Enter."

I stepped inside, my gaze immediately finding the queen, who was now dressed in gold, sitting next to the window. Her chambers were in the eastern wing of the castle, overlooking a lush garden. The scents of rose and mint teased my nostrils.

Unlike the maroon and gold of the rest of the castle, the queen's chambers were all silver and blue. Silver mirrors lined the opposite wall, reflecting the light and making the room look even bigger.

My gaze caught on one of those mirrors. It hung in the center of the wall, the bottom edge almost hitting the floor, while the top brushed the ceiling, at least two foot-spans above my head.

The silver edges surrounded a glass so clear, it felt as if I could walk through it and into a new world.

But it was the blue jewel in the silver setting at the top of the mirror that made me suck in a sharp breath.

"A gift from my husband," the queen said, and I blushed. I'd been staring. She turned away, murmuring to one of her ladies, and I gawked at the remaining walls and the high ceiling, all painted in fine, detailed patterns.

The fire was so large, both Tibris and I could have stood inside it, and the room was almost stiflingly warm as the flames roared.

"Come closer," the queen ordered.

I buried my shaking hands in the folds of my dress and complied, ignoring the ladies as they filed in, sitting on the long sofa and plush armchairs near the queen. She looked older up close, with deep lines etched between her brows. But she was incredibly beautiful with her glossy hair and dewy skin.

"Where did you say you were from?"

"Mistrun, Your Majesty."

She nodded dismissively, her gaze thoughtful. "You were quick to act today."

"It's my nature, Your Majesty."

"So it seems. Oh, do sit down. I keep informal chambers."

It felt like a trick, but I sat on the closest chair.

"Tell me about yourself."

If I lived through the next few days, I would kiss Vicer on the mouth. His insistence on us memorizing even the smallest details was the only reason I was able to instantly respond to the queen's questions.

So I smiled and told her everything I'd learned. My father was a woodworker, originally from the city. He'd met my mother while trading and moved to Mistrun to live since she'd refused to leave her aging parents. I had one brother, who was also working in the castle, and our parents missed us very much, but they understood the opportunity we'd been given.

It wasn't unusual for me to be still living at home since I hadn't completed the Gifting. But the queen frowned when I mentioned *Loukas* hadn't yet married.

A line of sweat dripped down my neck, along my spine, and settled in the hollow of my lower back. I didn't dare show any signs of discomfort.

"My brother was engaged, but it wasn't a good fit. The ending of that engagement was a mutual decision."

I had to give Vicer credit. He really had covered everything. If the queen cared to investigate, her people would find a woman from Mistrun who would swear she had been engaged to a man named Loukas.

Finally, the queen waved her hand for more tea. One of the servants jumped forward, handing her a cup.

"Can you read?" the queen asked.

"Yes, Your Majesty."

"Sew?"

I barely hid a wince. "I can, although my stitches need some work."

One of the ladies snorted. I ignored her.

"Can you sing?"

I couldn't carry a tune to save my life. The fine edge of panic sliced at me like a blade.

The queen sighed at my silence. "Well, your hair is

certainly drab, but you have remarkably delicate features for a peasant."

Gods, I hated this woman.

"Thank you, Your Majesty."

"One of my ladies was recently called home. A death in the family. She won't be back for weeks. There is a reason I have six ladies. Six is a number that is blessed by the gods. Five?" Her expression darkened. "Five is nothing but bad luck. You will step into Katina's place until she returns."

I let my mouth fall open. "This is…incredibly kind of you, Your Majesty."

"Yes, well, many will say I tend toward unusual decisions when it comes to those around me. But I value loyalty and character above all. A peasant with good character may be turned into a lady, but it is much more difficult to take a lady and embed good character. Is that not so, Madinia?"

Madinia lifted her head, red hair gleaming in the light, her eyes bored. "Quite, Your Majesty."

The queen pulled a bell next to her, and several maids appeared. I didn't recognize them, but it was likely they slept in a room near me.

"Have her cleaned up and dressed appropriately. We'll start lessons later today. I do *so* love a project."

That was something I'd counted on. And yet rage coursed through me as I slowly stood. I didn't yet know if the queen was aware of just how her husband had kept most of their people almost powerless. But I did know that she knew he had hundreds—if not thousands—of his subjects executed each year. And yet, she needed a *project*.

I beamed at the queen in an attempt to convey shocked awe and gratitude, but she was already turning away.

Ivene's voice played through my head. *"In order to understand the elite, you must become like them. The queen has long been lonely, afraid, weak."*

"Come with me," one of the maids murmured, and I followed her out of the queen's chambers. She led me back toward the servants' quarters, but instead of heading downstairs, we continued walking.

"Her Majesty likes her ladies to be within reach," the maid said coolly, pushing a strand of blond hair off her face.

"My name is Setella," I said.

"I know."

I winced. I couldn't blame her for being upset. I'd been here for mere days, and in her eyes, I'd gained one of the most coveted positions in the castle through sheer luck.

I would hate me too.

Another maid had followed me in. "I'm Erea," she told me. She had curly dark hair and a chipped tooth that showed when she smiled. "This is Daselis." She gestured to the other woman.

Daselis ignored her and pushed open the door.

"Well?" Daselis snapped. "In."

I stepped inside. A bed took up most of the room, several times larger than the one I'd been sleeping in each night. It was piled with pillows and furs, while a fire crackled on the other side of the room.

"This is your new room," Erea sighed. "Isn't it lovely?"

"I'm to…sleep here?" It *was* lovely. Beautiful, in fact. And Wila was in the dungeon, thanks to *my* plan.

"Not before you wash the filth from your skin," Daselis muttered, stalking into the attached bathing room.

The sound of running water almost made me sigh. I was covered in grime at this point, with barely enough time each night to hand-wash in the small bathing room all the maids shared. I hadn't been lucky enough to take another bath in the servants' bathing rooms.

"I'll pick your dress," Erea whispered. "You better go clean up. Daselis can be…difficult."

Even though I'd planned this for a larger reason, guilt burrowed into my gut when I walked in to find Daselis casting a longing look at my bath.

"Remove your jewelry," she said.

My hand immediately clutched at the charmed necklace. "I'd rather not. It's okay, I can get it wet."

"Suit yourself. In," she said, and I began to strip. She stalked away, returning with several scented oils, which she poured into the water. "Take the pins out of your hair," she instructed, and I began to slide them out.

"Wet your hair," she barked when I'd let it down.

Leaning back, I complied. The water turned murky

around me, and my cheeks heated.

She just sighed, but some of the rancor had left her expression. "I'll help you wash it."

It would be the first time my hair had been washed since I'd dyed it. But I'd been assured the color wouldn't wash out. "Thank you." I met her eyes. "I really appreciate it."

She just nodded, pouring soap into my hair.

In the end, she washed it three times, until it was as clean as it had ever been. The water left in the tub was gray with dirt when I stood up, and Daselis insisted on sending Erea for a bucket of clean water to rinse me off while I attempted to cover myself and shivered.

Finally, she allowed me to dry myself. But if I'd hoped to dress alone, those hopes were quickly crushed.

The dress was a dark gray, embroidered with intricate silver swirls. It was cut in such a way that it would cling to my body.

I stared at it. I'd thought the wool of my maroon dress had been fine. It had certainly been the warmest material I'd ever worn—other than Galon's cloak. For a moment, his put-upon expression danced across my mind, and my heart twisted.

Where were they now?

"We don't have time for your daydreaming," Daselis snapped.

I jolted. She'd been waiting for me to lift my arms, and I threw them into the air, almost hitting her in the face.

Erea muffled a laugh, which was quickly quashed at a glare from Daselis. I slid Erea a tiny smile, and she flashed that crooked tooth at me.

"Ouch," I winced as Daselis began lacing the dress.

"You have a tiny waist," she muttered. "The dress was cut to show it off."

I had a tiny waist because we hadn't had enough food in my village, and then I'd barely eaten before I'd found the mercenaries in the forest. While Rythos's cooking had helped me put on some of the weight I'd lost, as soon as I'd heard about Asinia, my stomach had twisted most of the time when I'd attempted to eat.

Daselis went silent, and I realized I'd been scowling. "I didn't mean to offend," she said carefully. The closest I'd get to an apology.

"No, it's okay. It's just… We didn't have much food where I grew up."

Understanding flickered in her eyes. "I know what that is like."

"How did you come to work in the castle?"

Her mouth clamped shut, her expression turning blank. "We need to get you back to the queen. Erea, you can do her hair while I find shoes that will fit."

Erea smiled at me. "Come sit down."

I met my eyes in the mirror. Likely, the charmed necklace would begin to fail soon, and with maids paying close attention to how I looked, that could be a fatal mistake. I'd need to reach out to Vicer. If he couldn't help, I'd find a way to source my own necklace.

We were both quiet as Erea wound my hair into a complicated, braided updo. Finally, she stepped back, a pleased smile on her face.

I'd gotten used to not recognizing myself, with my hair and eyes being so different. But I took a moment to smile at Erea, grateful for freshly washed hair and my clean dress. "You did a wonderful job," I murmured.

She flushed. "I enjoy it."

"Time to go," Daselis said, dropping the heels to the floor in front of me. I slipped them on and stood while she cast a critical look over my form. With a nod, she turned and stalked out the door.

I followed her unsteadily in the heels, my palms sweating.

Being close to the queen would mean I was watched more closely, but I would also have many more opportunities to figure out how to get Asinia out of the dungeon.

Three of the queen's ladies were daughters of nobles. And two of their fathers were trusted advisers to the king. It was likely the men would often speak of important matters in front of women, assuming they were either too stupid to understand or bored by political talk. Those same women would gossip about it later.

From the way most of the ladies had sneered at me, befriending them was unlikely. But I could stay quiet and listen, soaking up any information that could help. Besides, the queen's ladies could go almost anywhere in this castle. They sat at royal dinners and danced with the nobility closest to the king.

Just the thought made my stomach swim, but I clenched my fists and trailed after Daselis.

The queen raised her eyebrow, taking me in when I stepped into her room.

"You do good work, Daselis," she said, and Daselis smiled for the first time since I'd met her.

"We must attend one of my husband's dinners within the hour, but I do hope you will interest me, Setella. I grow bored with the same topics." She glanced at her ladies, who hunched their shoulders. "While I would prefer to eat elsewhere, we must join my husband and the rest of the court. The king has a guest and has insisted I attend."

From the way her mouth twisted, she wasn't exactly in love with her husband. I noted that information.

The other ladies had been quiet, most of them appearing bored, but they all stood when the queen did. I winced as I realized I was at the head of their line since I'd stupidly positioned myself directly behind the queen.

The woman who stood next to me was slight, with curly blond hair several shades darker than my natural color.

"I'm Lisveth." She smiled. I smiled back. I'd imagined it would be impossible to befriend any of the queen's ladies, but Lisveth, at least, seemed welcoming.

"Setella," I murmured back.

"I remember my first dinner. I was *so* nervous. I'll show you where to sit."

One of the other women snorted, and I glanced over

my shoulder at Madinia. According to Auria, her father was currently the closest to the king. We filed out of the room, and Madinia walked so close, she was stepping on my heels.

I ground my teeth, refusing to give her the satisfaction of a reaction. By the time we reached the dining hall, any nerves I'd felt had been stifled by irritation.

Until the guards opened the doors and the queen stepped into the dining hall. Everyone jumped to their feet and bowed low.

I hesitated, but the other ladies were still moving, so I followed Lisveth, keeping my head down.

I was well aware that I had enemies on all sides. The servants would be incredulous and jealous. The courtiers and nobility would see me as an interesting amusement and a way for the queen to put them in their place.

Look at how little I value you. How much power I have. I can even pluck a servant from obscurity and force you to interact with her.

The queen slowed her steps, until all eyes were on her. Finally, she walked to the table and sat. With a wave of her hand, she gestured for us to sit at the table nearby.

I scanned the royal table. And my eyes met amused green.

I stopped so suddenly, Madinia slammed into my back. She hissed a curse at me, but I was too busy staring at Lorian.

His gaze turned predatory.

What?

How?

Why?

"Setella?" Lisveth was glancing between me and the king's table.

"Sorry. First time seeing so many nobles. I'm a little nervous."

Madinia snorted again, and I moved automatically, sliding myself into the only empty chair. Unfortunately, that put my back to Lorian, and I refused to give him the satisfaction—or draw attention to either one of us—by turning around to glower at him.

How was a mercenary dining with the royal family?

Everyone stood once more, and I scrambled to my feet. The king was walking in. It was the first time I'd seen him, and I swept my gaze over him as I bowed.

Tall and broad-shouldered, Sabium looked like he was at the peak of health. Which he likely *was* since his healers no doubt used stolen magic from people like my brother. His cheeks were ruddy, though, his eyes so dark they were almost black.

The king gestured for us to lift our heads. We all stayed standing, and the room went silent.

"Today, I would like to welcome Prince Rekja from Gromalia to our court. May this visit pave the way for greater cooperation between our kingdoms for centuries to come."

"Thank you, Your Majesty." Lorian's voice seemed to caress every inch of my skin. For a moment, all I could think about was the way his mouth had felt when he'd kissed me, right before we parted inside the city gates.

Back when I thought he was in the city to find his next client.

I almost laughed at how stupid I'd been. I'd thought Tibris and I were cunning for managing to get into the castle. Of course, Lorian had walked in the front door while pretending to be a *prince.*

"Be seated," the king said, and I fumbled for my chair.

One of the other women let out a quiet snort. "As if the king wants to work with those cowardly Gromalian dogs long-term."

I didn't look up. If I showed any interest, she would immediately clamp her mouth shut. Luckily, Lisveth lifted her head.

"What do you mean, Alcandre?"

Alcandre heaved a sigh. I didn't need to look at her to know she was rolling her eyes. "I *mean* Gromalia turned its back on us during the fae wars. They refused to get involved. They didn't want to risk losing and the fae turning their attention their way. Luckily, *we* had the gods on our side. But if there's one thing I know about our king, it's that he values our history. King Regner was the one to seek an alliance with Gromalia. King Sabium may need Gromalia to help us shore up our borders, but he'll make them pay for siding with the fae last time."

18
PRISCA

Dinner was a buffet of breads, cheeses, fruits, vegetables, and meat. So much meat. The wine flowed freely, and the servants brought out sweet pastries, candied fruits... It was the kind of meal I'd dreamed of in my village.

I didn't taste any of it.

The queen's ladies ignored me. Lisveth attempted to start a conversation a few times, but I was distracted, and she quickly gave up, likely tired of my one-word answers.

When my mind slowed enough, I listened to the ladies' conversation, mentally taking notes of everything they were saying—even as I felt Lorian's eyes on me.

The five other ladies had been accompanying the queen for years. Lisveth's mother had been one of the queen's close friends, and she'd died from fever shortly after Lisveth was born when the healer hadn't arrived in time to save her life. Lisveth was the youngest of us all at just sixteen winters, and the queen treated her almost like a daughter at times.

Caraceli was the woman who'd once been in charge of the queen's fire and was closest to Katina—the woman the queen had found at the market. The woman I'd arranged to return to her village.

When Katina arrived home, she would find her parents in excellent health. Caraceli seemed to hate me even more than Madinia, likely because I'd taken her friend's place.

Caraceli and Madinia also hated each other. Madinia seemed to hate everyone, but occasionally when the queen wasn't looking, she'd call Caraceli *fire girl* with a smug smile.

There was a reason no one seemed to like Madinia. And it wasn't just because her father was apparently so close to the king.

Pelopia and Alcandre were sitting at the other end of the table, murmuring quietly to each other. I hadn't yet learned how they'd come to be in the queen's employ— likely Auria could tell me later. Both had nodded to me, but other than Alcandre's comments about Gromalia, they'd stayed quiet. Likely because neither of them wanted to attract Madinia's ire.

I could still feel Lorian watching me. How exactly had he ended up here? My heart thumped faster at the memory of the fae he'd met with near the Gromalian border. I needed to know what Lorian was planning and how his plans would affect my own.

I risked a glance over my shoulder when the room went quiet. The queen had gotten to her feet. With a few murmured words to the king, she walked toward the door.

"Do we need to follow her?" I asked.

Lisveth shook her head. "The queen likes privacy after one of the king's dinners. And she *especially* enjoys being alone after the castle balls. We're allowed to leave whenever we like."

I studied the others at the king's table, ignoring Lorian, who was deep in conversation with King Sabium. "Who are the other people sitting with the king?" I asked quietly.

Lisveth smiled. "They're the king's patriarchs. They own huge swaths of land, depending on how much of the king's favor they've courted over the years. Down the end of the table is Patriarch Kofod." She nodded toward a man with a mournful expression who looked drunk already. "Next to him is Patriarch Farrow—Madinia's father."

I studied the man. Madinia's mother must have been a beauty, because other than their red hair, the two had no other similarities that I could see. I glanced at Madinia. She raised one eyebrow at me.

Patriarch Farrow was sitting next to the king. A powerful man, indeed. The Gromalian prince sat on his other side. "And next to the...prince?"

"Patriarch Thueson." She smiled. Thueson had wiry white hair that stood out from his head as if he couldn't help but run his hands through it. He looked deep in contemplation as he studied his plate. "He's a nice man,"

Lisveth said. "My father was rarely at court when I was young, and Patriarch Thueson always had a piece of honeyed fruit for me." She leaned close and lowered her voice to a whisper. "He hates court. He'd much rather be managing his lands with his husband, but the king enjoys his company and often insists he stay here. Next to him is Patriarch Greve." She nodded toward a man with a thin, sharp nose and a sallow complexion. Something like fear darted across her face, and I opened my mouth, but Lisveth turned back to face the table. Clearly, she didn't want to talk about it.

I waited a few more minutes, but none of the other ladies showed any signs of retiring. Finally, I pushed back my chair.

"I'm tired," I said.

Lisveth smiled at me. The others ignored me.

"Good night."

I practically ran from the dining hall. I hadn't seen Rythos or the rest of the group, but if Lorian was here, I had little doubt they were around somewhere.

Someone took my arm, and I stumbled. Then I was being swept into an empty room.

Lorian glowered down at me. My stupid body wanted to arch against him. Clearly, all the stress was impacting my mind.

"You were supposed to get on a ship," he growled.

I took a deep breath, and his enticing scent wound toward me. He smelled wild, like the forest, and it reminded me of sleeping outdoors beneath the stars. "I'm going nowhere until Asinia is safe."

He went still in that strange way he so often did. "You're risking everything for a woman who is probably dead already?"

I sniffed. "I don't know how to explain friendship and loyalty to you. You either know what those things are, or you don't."

The ghost of a smile crossed his face. We both knew he was intensely loyal to his friends. "Tell me."

"It's simple. She's my best friend. More like a sister than a friend. And I know, without a doubt, that if I were the one who'd been taken, she'd do the same for me."

"Yet neither of you knew the other had power."

Something I'd avoided thinking about until I could talk to Asinia.

"Our friendship had secrets. But none of that matters now. The question is, what the hell are *you* doing here?" I hissed.

He just raised one dark brow. "How about you tell me how a villager gets a position as one of the queen's ladies?"

"As soon as you tell me how a mercenary has a seat at the king's table."

He gave me a slow smile. "I never said I was a mercenary."

Of all the— "You're not from Gromalia either!"

"According to whom?" He had the audacity to look affronted.

"The idea of *you* being a prince is ludicrous."

"Almost as ludicrous as a villager being a queen's lady?"

I sneered at him.

"Although, for a savage villager, you certainly manage to outshine the other ladies," he purred.

"Don't try to distract me."

He grinned down at me. "But you make it so easy." He reached a hand up to play with the curl that had been left free over my forehead. "I like your real hair better. And I miss those strange eyes."

"Strange?"

"Strangely beautiful."

Something had sparked in Lorian since I'd seen him last. He was almost…charming. Was it because he was close to getting whatever it was he'd come here for?

His hand slid to my chin. "I missed the rest of you too. The way you scowl at me when I say something you disagree with. And that face you make when you're wondering what I'd look like naked."

My heart thundered, an entirely unwelcome awareness flooding my body. "*I don't wonder what you'd look like naked!*"

"Ah, you wouldn't need to wonder, would you? Because you watched me bathing at the inn, you wicked thing."

My cheeks blazed. I thought back to the way he'd stretched, as if on display. Because he had been. This man was a predator at his core. Had I really thought he hadn't felt my eyes on him?

This conversation had quickly slipped out of my control.

Lorian shifted closer to me, leaning down to sniff at my neck. I pulled my head back and planted my hands on my hips. "Whatever you're doing here, stay out of my way."

His expression turned serious. "Only if you restrain yourself from spying on me."

"Fine."

He stepped back, his eyes still intent in that strange way.

He cursed, and then he was kissing me. His lips caressed mine achingly slowly. As if I'd stopped time for us. Warmth traveled through my body, my limbs strangely languid. One of his hands slid to my ribs, right beneath my breast, and I wanted to arch my body, wanted to writhe until he was touching me higher.

He slowly lifted his head. His expression was cold, but his eyes...blazed. "Unless you want to end up in my bed, stay away from me."

Of all the—

I shoved against his chest, and he took his time stepping back. "That will *never* happen," I hissed, ignoring his low laugh. I stalked out of the room.

Tibris was waiting for me in the servants' hall near my chambers.

"Is everything okay?"

I leaned close, keeping my voice to the barest whisper. "Lorian is here."

His face twisted into a deep scowl. "The *mercenary*?" he whispered back. "Did you know about this?"

"Of course not. I don't know what he's up to. I swear."

I could see Tibris mentally calculating what Lorian's presence meant for our own plans.

"How did he get in here?"

"You'll love this. He's pretending to be the Gromalian prince."

Tibris let out a choked laugh. When he realized I was serious, he sighed. "Stay away from him, Pris."

"Oh, I will."

"The dungeon guards are already drunk. It seems they took advantage of the distraction in the castle. We should go see Asinia now."

Shame stabbed into my gut. I'd been busy kissing Lorian, while Asinia and Demos were waiting for us. "I need to get some food for her and Demos."

He held up a sack. "The cook likes me."

"Why am I not surprised?"

"You look good, Pris. Royal."

While I hated the thought of looking *royal*, it was exactly what we needed. "Thank Vicer for me. I need to check on Wila." If she would even be willing to speak to me. "She's the reason the plan worked."

Tibris was right. Both guards were slumped against the wall, one of them with his eyes at half-mast. It was difficult to pull the thread of my magic to me today, maybe because my mind was circling through so much information. But I managed to pause time long enough for us to sneak past the guards and make our way down the stone steps.

After experiencing a royal dinner, the dungeon seemed even worse. The scent of excrement and hopelessness was heavy in the air.

"Setella," a voice whispered, and I whirled. Wila was in one of the cells closest to the stairs. She had a black eye and a split lip.

"Go work on Asinia," I told Tibris. His gaze flicked between Wila and me, and I just nodded at him. "It's okay. Go."

Fury burned through me as I knelt outside her cage.

"Thank you."

"You're welcome."

"My real name is Prisca," I whispered. It was the least I could give her.

Wila studied me. Her eyes were strangely clear, and she seemed older than her years. "Prisca. I like it. Vicer may not have told me who you were, but I figured it out. I hated you at first, you know."

"I know."

"I thought you were just another girl playing at being a rebel. We've been fighting back for years, and you thought you could stroll in here and change the world. It made me want to hit you."

I smiled. "I can't blame you."

Wila smiled too. It must have hurt her lip. "But I was watching every move you made. You know, all this time, none of us ever tried to get that close to the queen?" She waved her hand over my new dress. "You've been here mere days, and today, we could have killed her if we'd wanted."

"I wanted to." It was terrifying how much I wanted to. I'd changed so much since I'd left my village, I barely recognized myself.

"I know. So did I. I would have listened to her screams and laughed and laughed." Wila smirked. "But you're thinking bigger. And that's why I agreed to do this. Because you're going to make them pay."

Her confidence both strengthened and terrified me. Gods, I hoped I could be the person she thought I was.

"I will. How long did the queen say you have to stay down here?"

"I'm not getting out."

"What?"

She just ran a hand over her face.

Fury blazed through me. "I'll get you out of here with the others."

She slowly shook her head. "No, you won't. The king intervened. He wasn't pleased with his *beloved* coming so close to harm. I've been sentenced to die two days from today."

The dungeon did one slow spin around me. Wila was still talking, but all I could hear was my blood rushing in my ears.

"Then I'm getting you out tonight," I said through numb lips. "Now."

"You know you can't." Tears glistened in her eyes now. "It's okay. I've been in this castle for over a year, and I haven't done anything greater than passing on information to Vicer. And not one scrap of information has saved a single life. This was something I could do that *mattered*."

I clutched the bars between us, staring at her. "You can't *give up*."

Tears dripped down her cheeks. "They took my brother," she told me. "We were born minutes apart. I was away from the village that day, and I ran. By the time I got to the city, he'd already burned. I never got to say goodbye. Never got to thank him for being the best brother I could have hoped for. The king took him from me without a thought. Because if his people found out just how many of us have magic, and why, all his lies would begin to fall apart. You have a brother." Her gaze drifted behind me in the direction Tibris had gone.

"I do. And my brother wouldn't want me to throw your life away. Neither would yours."

"I'm not. You're going to free them, I know it. Promise me, Prisca. Promise me you'll free them. And one day, you'll come back and burn this fucking place to the ground."

There was only one thing I could say. "I promise."

LORIAN

A scuff sounded to my left.

My hand instantly went to my dagger, and I turned. Prisca stood in my room, her face pale.

"Using your power to sneak into my rooms, wildcat? How very *scandalous.*"

"I don't have time to play."

Her eyes met mine, and I experienced another jolt at the color. I loathed the change. But more importantly, those eyes were desperate. Desperate in a way that filled me with a strange disquiet.

"What is it?"

"You asked how I ended up as one of the queen's ladies. I worked with a woman named Wila. She dropped a lamp on the queen's dress. A lamp with fae fire. I froze time long enough for it to catch and for the queen to assume the people surrounding her did nothing."

Her face had gone even paler, as if admitting to her deeds was sucking the life from her.

"And then you put the fire out, drawing the queen's attention for your bravery and fast instincts."

"Yes."

I studied her. She'd glanced away with that word, shifting on her feet. "You're not telling me all of it. From what I've learned of the queen, she usually keeps no more than six ladies at any one time."

She stuck her chin out in that stubborn way she had, and I raised one eyebrow.

"You arranged for one of those ladies to disappear, didn't you, wildcat?"

"I didn't kill her," she said quickly. "She's traveling back to her village."

"You're a better schemer than I'd anticipated. Congratulations. That doesn't explain why you've come to me so distraught, directly after we agreed to pretend the other doesn't exist."

"Wila...I'd thought she would be embarrassed. Maybe demoted. But they took her to the dungeon." Her voice broke, and something in my chest wrenched.

I sighed. "They're putting her to death, and you want me to intervene."

"The king heard what happened and decided to use it as proof of his *love*," she spat. "He sentenced Wila to death. She dies at sunrise, two days from now."

"What exactly is it you think I can do?"

"Anything. *Please,* Lorian. I'm begging you. If I take her now, they'll start an investigation and increase security. Then I won't be able to get Asinia out. She's still too weak to travel."

My jaw clenched. She was asking for my help. *Begging.* And I couldn't give her what she wanted. What she needed. A strange kind of powerlessness punched into me. "I can't."

"Lorian—"

I held up a hand. At some point in the past few

weeks, dulling the hope in Prisca's eyes had turned from an absolute necessity to a living hell.

"Let me tell you how executions happen here. The prisoner is led out the back entrance of the castle while blindfolded. Denied even the sight of one last sunrise. They're surrounded by guards at all times, dragged to one of the many squares in the city that were designed exactly for this purpose. Even if I could create a big enough distraction to get her free, the city gates would immediately be shut. Every man, woman, and child who attempted to leave would be searched. The violence would become inescapable until she was found. Many other innocent people would die."

I knew all about the prisoners in this castle. Knew what happened to them. Every excruciating detail. And at some point, this vexing woman had become too important to me. Important enough that the thought of her going ahead with such plans—and taking that long, lonely walk to her execution…

I would do whatever it took to make sure that didn't happen. Even if it meant I had to tie her up and hide her in a closet.

Prisca swayed on her feet. Her face had turned ashen. I took a step toward her, attempting to steady her. She flinched.

I forced my hands back to my sides. "Coming here was a mistake," I said. "You're not the only one with people you need to protect. I can't help you."

She stumbled back toward the door. Her eyes met

mine, and for a single moment, the amber shone through whatever charm she had in place.

"Of course you can't. You've proven you have no concerns about leaving women to die. I don't know why I expected anything more of you." She turned and stalked out.

I pinched the bridge of my nose and let out a low laugh.

Because despite everything I'd just said, I was going to try to get the maid out.

PRISCA

My door opened shortly after sunrise the next morning. Daselis swept in, throwing open the curtains.

"The queen expects her ladies to eat breakfast with her this morning," she said.

"I can get myself ready." My voice was hoarse. After I'd begged Lorian for help, I'd cried myself to sleep.

Daselis just stalked into the bathing room. Water began running directly after, and I forced myself to get out of bed.

"Are you okay?" Erea whispered. "Your eyes are all swollen, your face blotchy."

"It must be difficult landing such a coveted position,"

Daselis said, stepping back into the room, her voice heavy with sarcasm. "Bathe."

I didn't have it in me to argue. I made my way to the bathing room, stripped, and slipped into the bath, my mind whirling.

I *hated* that Lorian had sounded so assured. That every word he'd said had made perfect sense. I'd known since I'd seen Asinia in the dungeon that I'd need a better strategy than "use my power to freeze time and sneak her out of the castle." But the thought of Wila dying because of my stupid plan…

I couldn't let her lose her life that way.

I *wouldn't*.

Someone knocked on the bedroom door. Either Erea or Daselis must have opened it, because I heard murmuring. Erea poked her head into the bathing room.

"That was a messenger. Instead of eating in the queen's rooms, you'll be eating at a formal breakfast with the king. He has an announcement."

A headache had begun to pound behind my right eye. But I nodded, stepping out of the bath.

"You need to hurry," Daselis said.

I was barely present as they helped me dress. My mind returned to Wila in that cell again and again. The bruises on her face. The freezing air. And the thought of her being taken from that cell, only to die. There had to be a way to get her out. If Lorian wouldn't help, I'd try something else.

I just needed a big enough distraction that I could

buy Wila a day or two.

"Time to go," Daselis said grimly.

Erea's hands fluttered from where she'd been fixing my hair.

"It looks perfect," I told her.

Getting to my feet, I made my way down to the royal dining hall. The last people I wanted to see were the king and queen. Although today, the thought of seeing Lorian was just as distasteful. The other ladies were already waiting, the same seat empty. I sat in it and glanced at Lisveth.

"Is this something that happens often?"

She shook her head. "Usually, the king doesn't rise for another few hours."

Obviously being an evil bastard took it out of him.

"Do you know what's going on?"

"Nope. Want some breakfast?"

My stomach was churning too much to eat. I shook my head, and she sighed. "You barely ate anything last night either. Are you feeling okay?"

"I'm fine. I just don't like big meals in the morning." A man I didn't recognize was sitting at the king's table. A man with sharp features and cold gray eyes. "Who is that?"

"Rothnic Boria. He's the one who used his magic to create the horseless carriages. He's one of the king's favorites, and everyone at court is desperate to see what he does next with his magic and genius mind."

"And the man beside him?"

"His son Davis. He's *obsessed* with Madinia, but she has been ignoring him for years."

Davis was handsome, although he had a weak jaw. But his eyes were even colder than his father's, and something about him made me shiver. Maybe he was the perfect match for Madinia. Although I wouldn't wish someone with eyes that lifeless on anyone, even her.

We all stood as the king and queen walked in together. Behind them, Lorian strolled, his lithe movements making him seem less of the giant brute I knew him to be and more…elegant. He'd disappointed me. Not only because he'd refused to help, but because I'd gone to him when I should have known better.

Lorian was surrounded by men dressed in Gromalian green. His gaze slid to mine, and a muscle twitched in his cheek. His eyes were empty, his expression…apologetic.

Dread swept through my body in a wave.

The king stayed on his feet, so everyone else did too.

"You're probably wondering why we're eating together this morning. Some of you may be aware that my queen was almost gravely injured yesterday. I'm pleased to announce that the woman responsible was executed this morning."

My vision narrowed. I clutched at the top of my chair.

No. No, no, no, no, no.

Lorian was staring intently at me. I knew that look. It was the same look he'd given me every time he was about to berate me, about to order me to hold it together. I sucked in a deep breath, the backs of my eyes burning.

Don't fall apart here.

"While she was put to death, she screamed a name that one of my guards recognized."

The thought of Wila screaming as she died… My knees went weak, and I was instantly covered in a greasy sweat.

The king was sweeping his gaze over the entire room. "That name belonged to her brother. One of the *corrupt*." His voice lowered to a hiss. "The corrupt had infiltrated this castle."

Murmurs sounded as the nobles processed this news.

I stayed very still, ignoring the instinct to make myself as small as possible. That would only draw attention.

"Due to this event, my assessor will be examining every servant in this castle and the grounds."

Lisveth leaned close. "I'm glad we don't count as *servants*. The king's assessor is scary."

I gave her a nod. Tibris would be okay. He wasn't a hybrid. But he needed to get a message to Vicer. He still had another rebel in the castle, and they needed to get out.

The king was still talking, his cold gaze moving to our table. Lisveth straightened.

"Thankfully, another maid was nearby and saved my queen," he boomed. "One loyal to the crown. I have learned she has been rewarded with a temporary position as one of the queen's ladies."

The king's eyes met mine.

Smile like your life depends on it. Because it does.

I beamed, lowering my head in a bow. I could feel

the court's eyes on me. All of them judging, weighing.

"Now, eat," the king said. "And let us celebrate the burning of yet another of the corrupt."

"Promise me, Prisca. Promise me you'll free them. And one day, you'll come back and burn this fucking place to the ground."

I looked over my shoulder at the king, who was smiling at Lorian.

Burn this fucking place to the ground.

I sucked in a steadying breath. Just a few minutes, and I could fall apart.

"I don't feel well," I murmured to Lisveth. "I'll meet you in the queen's quarters."

Pelopia's eyes widened. "The queen won't like that."

"She won't like it if I disgrace myself here either." I smiled to soften my words, and after a moment, she smiled back.

I could feel eyes on me as I walked out of the hall. I made it as far as the closest storage room before I fell apart.

Slumping to my knees, I stuffed my fist in my mouth, sobs choking me.

My fault. I'd thought I could do this. Thought I could stroll into this castle and free the king's prisoners. Instead, I'd gotten a good woman killed.

Strong arms surrounded me, and I lashed out. The guards—

But I recognized that scent. I stilled, and then I swung my fist.

"You'll have to do better than that, wildcat."

How *dare* he? "Don't fucking touch me."

"I'm sorry, Prisca." His voice was grim. "Would you believe me if I told you I tried?"

"No."

I was fighting him, rage burning through me as I hit and clawed. I made contact, and he cursed, catching my hands in his.

"Let go," he growled. "Just fucking let go."

I bowed my head.

Lorian pulled me close. I lashed out at him again, and he ignored it, his arms tightening around me. I sobbed, great big gulping sobs that choked me until I could barely breathe. Lorian was silent, but one of his hands gently stroked my back.

This place was worse than I could have ever imagined.

Lorian began humming, his hand still slowly stroking my back. I kept crying.

Eventually, I wore myself out. Sniffling, I wiped my face on his shirt.

He let that go.

The song was a tune I'd never heard before. Something strange and different. I finally lifted my head to find him gazing at the ceiling. His eyes met mine, and they blazed with barely suppressed wrath as he peeled me off him as if I were a kitten, his hand on the back of my neck. A tiny white line had appeared on his cheek. He was clenching his jaw. Lorian wasn't unaffected at all. He was just as furious as I was.

"I tried," he said. "The king's spies learned that I had asked about the woman who'd tripped near the queen, and they reported back to him. If anything, I hastened her death."

Fresh tears flooded my eyes, and Lorian sighed. "I'd tell you not to blame yourself, but both of us know it wouldn't help. If you want to blame anyone, blame me."

A group of women walked past the door, laughing and gossiping. How could they act like nothing had happened when an innocent woman had lost her life?

Because she was *corrupt*. Just like me.

"Why are you really here, Lorian?"

His face closed off. In a swift movement, he clutched me to him once more so he could stand, dragging me to my feet. "Because the king took everything from my family. And now I'm going to take everything from him."

19
PRISCA

I didn't see Lorian at all for the next two days. The queen insisted on taking her meals in her chambers, and I was still staying quiet in an attempt to learn everything I could.

I became very good at slipping around the castle unseen. I'd learned just why the servants' halls were so important. Not only did they allow them to be mostly unseen…

But they also allowed them to spy.

Tiny holes had been carved into various parts of the hall. Small enough that most wouldn't notice. No one mentioned it, but I'd spotted a maid leaning against a door just yesterday. She'd cast me an unconcerned look when I strolled past.

Each night, we visited Asinia. And each night, she looked worse. Tonight, the dungeon seemed even colder than it had been. I was sitting next to Asinia, who was still mostly unconscious. Tibris's expression was grim.

"What is it?"

The corners of his eyes tightened. "She needs medicine. I can keep healing the worst of it, but each time I go back, she's just as bad. If we don't get her help, she'll be dead within days."

I felt the blood drain from my face. I'd already let one person die. The thought of Wila's screams would haunt me for the rest of my life. Pushing Asinia's hair off her head, I leaned down.

"I won't let that happen," I whispered in her ear. "I *promise*."

In the cage next to us, Demos watched quietly. Since we'd been bringing him food and he was no longer eating the slop contaminated with fae iron, he seemed more alert. Tibris had been slowly healing his wound each night.

"There must be healers in this castle," I said. "For the king. Tell me what you need, and I'll find it."

Tibris described a blue liquid that would likely be in a small jar. It would help Asinia fight off the sickness and allow her body to rest and recover.

"I'll find it." I no longer cared what I would need to do to get what we needed. This was war. And so far, we were losing.

"I need to work on her some more," Tibris murmured. He was already ashen, but I nodded, stepping out of the cage.

I drifted from cage to cage, taking in the slumped forms in each. Most of the prisoners could do little more than blink at me. But there were some who hadn't been here as long. While they were weakened, they could still communicate. And they told me their stories in voices hoarse from disuse.

Many of the tales were similar, and yet all were heartbreaking.

A man named Dashiel told me of the day his brother Thayer had used his magic.

The power of nightmares.

At just eleven winters, Thayer had been suppressing his power his whole life. But when the king's assessor appeared in the village with no warning, Thayer had *erupted*.

Half of the village had turned crazed.

The assessor had been traveling with a shield-guard, who'd raised a magical buffer around him.

"He didn't mean to do it," Dashiel said, his eyes wet as he slumped against the bars of his cage. "He was just scared. I should have taught him. But I was terrified someone would learn of what we were doing. Instead, I got him killed."

My own eyes burned at the hopelessness on his face. "It wasn't your fault."

Dashiel just shook his head and continued talking in that low, grief-stricken voice. Like most of us hybrids, Thayer had been actively fighting his power. So he didn't know how to tamp down his power once he started using it. Half of his village was turned into little more than ghosts, unable to work.

"When…when he saw what he had done to our

family, our friends… I couldn't get to him. I couldn't get to my brother. He took the knife on his belt and slit his own throat."

Tears streamed down my cheeks, and I crouched in front of his cell. "We're going to make them pay."

Dashiel's breath hitched, his pale blue eyes finding mine. "It was a better end for him than any he would have had at the king's hand. Sabium doesn't just burn those of us with the most *helpful* powers, you know. Some of us, he puts to *work*."

I shivered at the thought of being used to hunt the king's enemies.

"He used Thayer as an example of what happened to villages that hid the corrupt. His guards went from village to village, town to town, with the story of how Thayer had turned half of his village mad. But they made it sound like he meant to do it. Like my gentle brother lashed out because he *could*."

"The king's assessor who came to your village… Did he have a scar on the side of his neck?"

Dashiel nodded. "You know him?"

"He's here at the castle now."

Dashiel went still, and some of the life returned to those pale eyes. Life and *vengeance*. "I want him dead."

"Then stop eating the food they give you. I'll try to bring more down in the next day or two."

He was quiet for a long moment. "I do this, and you'll help me kill the assessor?"

"I will." I'd already planned to kill him anyway. If

this was what Dashiel needed…

He let out a long breath. "Very well."

I'd figured out which cell Lina was in by process of elimination. I made to scuttle past her, and she let out a low laugh.

"I know it's you, Prisca."

I turned. Unsurprisingly, she looked terrible. Her blond hair was dark with dirt, hanging limp in front of her face, which was covered in bruises.

"It's okay," Lina said. "I won't say anything. I know you're here for Asinia."

And no one had come for her.

Her lower lip trembled, but she bit down on it.

"I'm sorry about your grandparents."

"Thank you. The worst part is…they didn't know. Or I think they would have tried to get me out. But *I* didn't know either. I thought I was just a lucky person. I thought the gods were smiling down at me. That I was *blessed*." She let out a hollow laugh.

"I'm getting you out."

A flash of hope sparked in her eyes, quickly suppressed. "You'll never be able to do it. If you're smart, you'll take Asinia and run far from this kingdom."

"Stop eating the food. And start exercising as much as you can."

She stared at me.

I crouched down and leaned close. "I know you don't want to hope. But if you can't do it for yourself, do it for your grandparents."

She let out a long breath, but her mouth had firmed. "Get me out of here, Pris. And I'll owe you my life."

"You won't owe me anything."

I spent the next hour searching for the tunnel entrance. But that search was futile. We had to be careful how long we spent down here, and when Tibris finally insisted we leave, I allowed him to take my arm.

Walking past Wila's empty cell felt like being stabbed in the chest. I stalked past the frozen guards, holding the thread of my magic without a thought. I barely restrained myself from slitting their throats as Tibris tucked the keys back into the older guard's belt.

"Are you okay?" Tibris murmured when we were back in the servants' hall.

"No. But I will be." I reached out and hugged him. Wila's face flashed through my mind, the sorrow and rage as she'd talked about her brother. And I squeezed Tibris a little tighter. "I'll see you tomorrow."

By the time I made it the hall outside my chambers, I was more than ready to crawl under my covers.

"And just *what* are you up to?" a low voice purred.

I whirled, finding Lorian leaning against a wall.

"What are you doing here?"

He gave me a slow, feline grin. It was as if this morning had never happened. Good. Shockingly, I didn't enjoy being reminded that I'd sobbed in his arms.

"All this sneaking around the castle. Have you found a way to get your friend out yet?"

My heart twisted. "No."

The smile left his face. "What's wrong?"

I stared at him in disbelief. Everything was wrong. A good woman had just been put to death because of *my* stupid plan. Asinia was imprisoned because I'd been caught using my power. Both of our mothers were dead.

He leveled me with a hard stare. "Prisca. What's wrong with your friend?"

I ground my teeth. Lorian had always seen more than I'd wanted.

"Asinia is sick. Tibris is healing her each night, but he's barely keeping her alive. She needs medicine." The servants gossiped enough that it wouldn't be difficult to find where that medicine was kept.

"And I expect you're planning to steal it from the king's healers."

I narrowed my eyes at him and stayed silent.

"The king's healers have underlings who keep count of all of their supplies." Lorian's voice was surprisingly gentle. "If you do this thing, the castle will be searched. Guards will be alerted, and it will be even more difficult for you to get your friend out."

"And I suppose you have an alternative?" The bastard was always ready for a bargain. Except when it mattered. Wila's face flashed in front of my eyes, and I took a step back.

Lorian merely followed me until, once again, my back was against the wall.

"I have the ability to source this medicine," he said, and my heart rate tripled.

"And I suppose you want me to do something for you in return." The fact was, I'd do anything at this point— something I was sure Lorian knew.

His body practically radiated heat, and I'd been cold for days.

No, Prisca.

"I have many capabilities. Stopping time is not one of them. That makes you infinitely valuable to me."

I ignored the warmth that spread in my chest at his words. He was literally talking about using me as a tool to get what he wanted.

That was fine. I could use him too.

"Just say it," I snapped.

"The king has a hidden room. The door is in his chambers. I need to get inside and find the entrance." I didn't bother asking just how he knew about the hidden room. It didn't surprise me at all that he'd already learned of such a thing.

"When?" I asked.

"Now."

I licked my lips. "I've been using my power all night."

Lorian's gaze dropped to my mouth, and he shrugged one shoulder. As usual, he was unconcerned about my perceived limitations.

"As I've told you, you're much more powerful than you think. This will be a good training session for you."

He grabbed my hand and pulled me down the hall.

I dragged my feet. If this went wrong, Asinia was

dead. I couldn't afford any missteps. "What guarantee do I have that you'll help Asinia?"

He cast me an affronted look over his shoulder. "You believe I would lie?"

I waved a hand, taking in his *princely* wardrobe. His eyes lit with amusement, and he turned, placing his hands on his hips.

"I vow it," he said solemnly. "I will have the medicine for you by midnight tomorrow."

We stared at each other. Footsteps sounded on the stone. "I suggest you use your power," Lorian said.

I hoped he was right about how much I had left. I pulled the thread to me, my skin heating as I froze everyone except us.

"Good," he murmured. "Now, move."

We ran. Well, Lorian sprinted, dragging me along with him. Within minutes, we were standing outside the king's chambers, the guards frozen in front of us. I attempted to swallow, but my throat wasn't working properly. My breath was coming too fast, and I couldn't seem to slow it.

"What if the king is in there?"

"He's not. I made sure of it. But I suggest you take a firm grasp on your power."

I glowered at him, but he was already pushing the door open and hauling me inside with him.

Thankfully, no one was inside the huge entry area. The room had been decorated in maroon and gold. The king was nowhere to be seen, and the rest of the room was a blur, my eyes darting too quickly for me to take in the details.

"Which way?" I whispered.

"In the next room."

I followed him into a lavish sitting room, also dripping gold. "Hold tight to your power," he said.

"I am." Tight enough that my head was beginning to ache.

Lorian was searching the walls for the entrance to the chamber, running his hand along each smooth surface, his eyes intent. I scanned the room for anything out of place.

One wall contained shelves that held ancient-looking weapons, scrolls, even a jeweled crown, which looked to have been tossed absently onto a shelf.

Just a few of those jewels could feed my village for months.

I took a step closer, peering at it.

"You help me find what I'm looking for, and I'll give you jewels of your very own," Lorian said, starting on the next wall.

I surveyed the shelves. They weren't completely flush against the wall. One side jutted out slightly, drawing my attention.

I squinted into the gap.

"Those jewels better be *big*," I muttered. "Because I've found it."

Lorian's hard body was caging mine before I finished my sentence. I went still, but he merely shifted me aside, then leaned against the shelves. Blood dripped from my nose, and I wiped at it. Panic returned with a vengeance. If my power slipped in front of a guard, we were both dead.

"I'm almost out."

He sent me an unconcerned look. "No, you're not. Work harder."

He was facing the wall. I could pick up that decorative knife and stab him straight in the back.

"An attack from behind isn't your style, wildcat," Lorian murmured, still pushing the shelves aside.

"You know nothing about me."

He just snorted at that, stepping back to survey the door. With a glance at me, he tore the bottom of his shirt, handing the material to me. "Let's go."

"If someone walks into this room, they'll know we're in here." I could picture it. The guards drawing their weapons and either killing us immediately or hauling us down to the dungeon. They'd torture us down there. They'd need to know just how we'd gotten this close to the king. Iron would be shoved into my body, and they'd likely execute me the next day—just like Wila.

"Then you better ensure no one walks in here."

Bastard. Smug, glib bastard.

He was already grabbing my hand and pulling me after him. "I can wait here," I insisted, pressing his shirt to my nose to stanch the bleeding. Now I was breathing in his wild scent. For some inexplicable reason, my heart rate slowed and I could take a full breath. I scowled.

"I don't think so," he said.

Grinding my teeth, I stepped into the space. The stone was clean and dry, although the air smelled stale.

It wasn't a *room*. Lorian was walking down a set of stairs. The walls were so narrow, if I held out my arms, I couldn't straighten them. My breath came faster. The walls seemed to press in on me, the roof inches from my head. My power slipped, and I caught it once more, a metallic taste flooding my mouth.

"I'm not doing this."

"Oh yes, you are."

"I, uh, don't do well in small spaces."

"It will be over soon."

"Did no one ever teach you empathy?"

He chuckled. "Empathy is useless in this world. Besides, my *empathy* won't make you strong."

Was that why he was like this with me? Because he wanted to *make me strong?*

My heart was already galloping in my chest. I stumbled on a step, hitting Lorian in the back, and he sent me an exasperated look over his shoulder.

"Almost there."

He was right. The stairs expanded, and so did my lungs as I could finally take a full breath. We were in a tunnel. Torches were positioned every few foot-spans, and while it was still far too narrow, I focused on holding time. This was much longer than I'd ever attempted to hold it, and blood dripped freely from my nose. The scrap of Lorian's shirt was soaked.

"Ah," he murmured, satisfaction dripping from his

voice.

The tunnel ended. I looked up. And up.

The stairs suddenly made sense. The cavern was expansive, the ceiling so high it loomed above our heads.

Marble pillars stood several foot-spans apart, encircling the room like silent sentries. But my gaze snagged on the middle of the huge space, where an altar was surrounded by tall, unlit candles.

And on the altar? Basket after basket of oceartus stones. Not one of them was glowing. Empty.

Lorian prowled across the cavern, headed for a collection of wooden chests.

I gazed around the cavern. Surrounding the pillars, walls of bookshelves were stuffed with thousands of books. I wandered closer, intrigued despite myself.

Hunting the Fae. The Human's Guide to Fae Magic. The Fae Wars. Gods: A Complete History.

My fingers tingled at the thought of having access to these books. Oh, the things I could learn. Maybe I'd discover some way out for us hybrids. Perhaps one day, I could even have that future I'd always dreamed of.

A quiet life. A life without killing.

Small dots appeared in front of my eyes. Pain erupted inside me, as if I were being ripped in two.

The world had gone white, and then the white turned dark once more. My grip on the thread of my power was slipping, slipping…

I dropped the thread and leaned over, almost vomiting.

Oh gods. We were dead.

Lorian turned. Somehow, he knew, and he opened his mouth—likely for some cutting remark that would, in his mind, motivate me to do better.

Scuffing on the stairs.

Footsteps.

My lungs forgot how to breathe.

Lorian moved faster than I'd ever seen. He leaped across the cavern and pulled me behind the closest pillar, his eyes glittering with banked fury.

My heart thundered, and I trembled. Behind me, Lorian was so still it was as if he'd stopped breathing.

The High Priestess stepped into the cavern. She didn't bother glancing around, her gaze on the blue stones. My eyes met Lorian's, and he gave me a warning look.

I peered around the pillar, just in time to see the High Priestess pluck one of the stones and shove it into the pocket of her robe.

She glanced around the cavern and then whirled, striding toward the stairs.

Relief crashed through me, my knees turning to water. If not for Lorian pressing me against the pillar, I would have slumped to the floor.

Neither of us moved for several long moments.

Finally, Lorian let me go.

I swallowed. "What do we do?"

"We don't need to do anything. Except you. *You* need to—"

"Work harder. I know. But why wouldn't we need to

do something?" My voice was very small. "Should we… kill her?" She would have seen the door cracked so we could get back out. Unless she was an idiot, she either knew someone had been here or knew she was being watched.

Lorian's eyes gleamed in amusement. "My, how things change. Just weeks away from your village, and you're already turning into a little savage."

I stared at him. He turned and strolled away, back toward the chests he'd been inspecting.

"She must have noticed we'd unblocked the entrance," I said, reaching for patience.

Lorian just shrugged. "She was clearly busy with her own sordid deeds. What do you think she'll do? Tell the king she noticed the door was ajar when she snuck down here to steal from him?"

He had a point. But… "You're not worried?"

He glowered over his shoulder at me, obviously tired of my inane questions.

"Of course I'm worried. If it had been a guard—or worse, Sabium himself—the entire castle would have been searched. Likely, truth-seekers and assessors would have been involved. Let this be a warning. Distractions will get you *killed*." He studied my face, and I saw curiosity in his eyes. A curious Lorian had never boded well for me. "Just what were you thinking about enough that you dropped the thread?"

My face flamed. If I told him I was imagining a future back in my village, he'd likely snarl at me.

"Nothing. I'm tired, that's all."

He just shook his head at my obvious lie. "You have a few minutes to rest. The priestess wouldn't have sauntered down here if there were a chance of discovery."

I turned my attention to the empty oceartus stones, my own curiosity like an itch I couldn't scratch. "Why do you think she took the stone?"

He shrugged absently, throwing open another chest. "We're not the only ones in this castle with plans of our own."

I let him work, wandering toward the stones. Not long ago, I'd daydreamed about having one for myself. I'd thought if I could just drain my magic until the Gifting, everything would be fine.

The worst part? I *still* had to actively prevent myself from darting forward and swiping one of those stones. Even knowing I needed my power to survive, I wanted to listen to the little voice inside me that said if I could just be *normal*, everything would go back to the way it was.

I turned away, disgusted with myself.

Something caught my eye, and I took a step closer to the marble pillar. The carvings weren't just decorative. They showed strange creatures I'd never seen before. Creatures with wings and claws, tentacles and talons. Furred beasts that stood on two legs and tiny men with misshapen faces.

"What are these?"

"Did you truly think we were the only creatures on this continent?"

"Well, yes."

Silence. I turned.

Lorian had finished his search. And from his empty hands and emptier eyes, he hadn't found what he was looking for.

The mercenary practically vibrated with rage as he stared at the chests—in fact, I'd never seen him this angry before. While he was a master of hiding his expressions from me, I'd gotten used to studying his face while I attempted to figure out what he was thinking. And if I wasn't wrong, buried beneath the rage was...desolation.

For some stupid reason, I hated the thought of this man feeling despair. "Do you want to tell me what you're looking for? Maybe I can help you find it."

Lorian slowly lifted his head, his gaze pinning me in place. He showed me his teeth, taking a single step closer. Cold fury poured off him in waves.

I froze, and my mind flashed me back to Kreilor in the bakery, trapping me with his bulk and his threats. To the hunter, approaching me slowly, ready to cut me down.

Lorian wasn't either of those men. But my fear had already slithered through every muscle of my body, settled in my chest, tightened my throat.

I took a deep breath. If Lorian's search wasn't successful, at least we could leave this place.

Forcing my expression to go blank, I yanked on the thread of my magic, stalking out of the cavern and up the stairs. Lorian shadowed my every step. His rage felt as if it was sucking up all the oxygen in an already tiny space, and my breaths turned shallow as the walls seemed to squeeze closer and closer with my every step.

Trust him to make this even more awful.

Halfway up, I yanked that thread tighter, focusing on the brute lumbering behind me.

He froze. Now that I knew he couldn't chide me for my terror, I scampered up the remaining stairs. As soon as I got to the top, I allowed time to resume for him once more. My head pounded until it took everything in me not to vomit.

Lorian let out a low hiss that made me want to slam the door and shove the bookcase in front of it. Within moments, he was standing behind me, pushing me through the open door.

"You dare to use your powers on me without permission?" he crooned.

I shivered at his tone. At the strange way he angled his head. Something told me I was closer to death than I'd ever been, even in the river.

Whatever it was that Lorian had been looking for, he'd expected to find it in the king's hidden rooms. And not finding it had pushed him over the edge. I'd wanted to see beyond the expressionless mask he so often wore.

Now I was. And it was terrifying.

But I refused to be cowed by him.

Leaning close, I gave him a nasty little smile. "I suggest you get yourself back to your room yourself, impostor prince."

"Don't you *dare*—"

I froze time for him once more. Then I sprinted past the guards and down the hall, back toward the servants' quarters, my nose dripping blood.

I didn't have long. My power seemed to be tied to my fury, and while I was angry, it was *hurt* that bubbled beneath that anger.

Thankfully, the fact that I even felt hurt was so distasteful, I managed to get back to my room before time resumed once more.

I pictured Lorian attempting to move the bookcase back into place without drawing the attention of the guards. A hint of regret slid through me, and I ruthlessly shoved it away.

I fell asleep with a frown on my face and vengeance in my heart.

20
PRISCA

woke with my stomach churning with regret, my chest heavy. I needed Lorian to help Asinia, and yet I'd left him in danger. Technically, he'd only asked me to help him get *into* the king's chambers, but he'd been furious enough that a part of me wondered if he'd choose not to help her out of spite.

If Asinia died because of him... because of *me*...

No. Somehow, I'd find the medicine Asinia needed. If not through Vicer, then somewhere else. I'd beg and borrow and steal if I had to.

An hour later, I followed the queen on her walk among the castle grounds. The other ladies spoke quietly, conscious of the queen's bad mood. Hopefully she would decide she needed rest later this afternoon.

I'd taken to wandering the servants' halls while the queen was napping each day. They stretched through almost every inch of the castle, allowing servants to appear in sitting rooms and bedrooms without disturbing the nobility with their existence. The amount of court gossip I'd learned was incredible. Unfortunately, none of it had given me anything I needed.

"Is something wrong, Your Majesty?" I asked. I couldn't have cared less. But I needed to know everything about my enemies.

Everyone went quiet. Perhaps I wasn't supposed to address her when she was so clearly upset.

She frowned at me. After a long moment, she heaved a sigh. "The king insists I attend another dinner tonight." Turning away, she continued her stroll.

Dinner meant feeling Lorian's venomous gaze on the back of my neck. But it also meant it was less risky for Tibris and me to get down to Asinia since the guards would be drinking and enjoying the distraction.

Since I hadn't heard any whispers about the Gromalian *prince* being arrested, he'd obviously managed to get himself back to his room last night.

That was *not* a prickle of guilt I felt.

"I wish to go out," the queen announced. "We will go to the market."

Anticipation slid through me, and I had to fight not to shift restlessly on my feet. I'd wanted to see the market for some time. Knowing the layout of the city would be helpful as we made our plans.

Madinia nodded. "I will tell the servants." She hurried away, clearly delighted.

The queen decided she needed to change her dress. Finally, we all followed her out of the castle.

"You look wide-eyed," the queen smirked, and I bowed my head.

"I had never seen a carriage like this before I arrived in the city," I admitted.

Madinia snorted. Caraceli sent her a poisonous look. But Caraceli and I obviously weren't going to bond over the fact that she also wasn't from the city since the look she sent me was worse.

I slid into the carriage, eager to get away from the castle for a few hours, even if it meant doing it in the company of the queen. We had more than enough room—the carriage likely designed specifically for the queen to travel with her ladies.

The seats were long benches, high enough that my feet barely touched the bottom of the carriage as it began to bump along. Not only were there no horses, but the carriage seemed to *know* where it was going.

I wanted to ask how the magic worked, but the queen was scowling out the window. She rolled her shoulders and gazed around the carriage at us.

"For the first time, the king has decided to call representatives from each town and village to the city to discuss the corrupt and ensure we are taking every possible step to remove their presence from our kingdom. They will begin arriving four days from now, and we will have a welcome ball to mark the occasion. Some of them will also likely be invited to stay for the Gods Day ball two weeks later."

I lowered my gaze, my mind whirling. Which

representatives would come from my village? Our village was small. We all knew each other. What if my different eyes and hair weren't enough? How would I ensure they didn't recognize me?

I'd need to stay far away from the representatives.

Most importantly, there would be a lot of new people in the castle. The king would likely bring in more guards, but they would probably still be stretched thin. Perhaps either the welcome ball or the Gods Day ball would present us with an opportunity.

The queen's mouth twisted, and it was clear she saw nothing to celebrate. I'd expected the queen to enjoy any chance to dress in her most ostentatious gowns and wear her most lavish jewels, but that didn't seem to be the case. If anything, she seemed to wish to avoid both the king and any occasions that called for her to be around large numbers of people.

"You will all need new dresses." The queen's gaze lingered on me. I wished I could conjure up a blush. Instead, I just nodded, smiling back at her.

Yesterday, I'd learned that the dresses I'd been given were Katina's castoffs, three seasons out of date. Madinia had enjoyed letting me know, as if I cared about the latest fashions at court.

Vicer had already arranged for my necklace to be replaced once more, but I would need another one before the villagers arrived. A thin line of my blond hair was also beginning to show, and soon people would begin to notice. I needed it to be darkened again before someone realized I had changed my original hair.

According to Lisveth, the queen wasn't unopposed to us taking the occasional afternoon to ourselves. The key was to ask when she was in the right mood. I needed to pay a visit to Vicer. And it needed to be soon. Especially with representatives from our village in the castle.

The market was just a few minutes from the castle. The moment we arrived, our carriage was encircled by guards who'd followed on horseback. The queen took one of the guard's hands, and he helped her out of the carriage.

We all clambered out behind her, and I surveyed the market. It was many times bigger than my village square, with long lines of stalls stretching out in neat rows. That was where any organization ended, the market a flurry of colors and life, of laughter and wails. The air was filled with the scents of spices, cooking meat, sweat, animal hides, wood, and metal.

"It's the queen," someone called out, and everyone around us went silent. The queen ignored them all, and we fell into our usual two-by-two formation, following her into the market.

I ignored Madinia's snort at my wide-eyed gaze, focusing instead on the food stalls and children's games and jugglers performing for coin and vendors hawking their wares.

Lisveth took my arm, hauling me along with her, and I realized I'd stopped and was staring at the stalls, the people, all of it.

"Sorry."

"I did the same thing the first time I came here."

I raised an eyebrow. "And how old were you?"

She burst out laughing. "Ten winters."

The queen stopped to inspect some jewelry, allowing us to catch up. The merchant seemed surprisingly calm, considering she was speaking to royalty. When I murmured exactly that to Lisveth, she just shrugged.

"The queen likes to come to the market often. I think she's...bored in the castle."

It must be difficult, indeed, for the queen to spend her days being waited on and entertained while her subjects suffered.

The queen moved on, and we spent the rest of the afternoon trailing after her. By the time we left, the queen was in a much better mood. This was my opportunity. She would likely just become annoyed once more as soon as we arrived back at the castle.

I took a deep breath as she was helped into the carriage, stepping forward so I could sit next to her. My heart tripped in my chest.

"Your Majesty?"

She glanced at me. "Yes, Setella?"

"I was wondering—if it's not too much trouble—if I could take a few hours tomorrow. My brother works in the castle, and I haven't had a chance to see him."

The queen studied my face for an endless moment. Finally, she sighed. "I, too, remember what it was to be young. You may have your afternoon tomorrow." She glanced around at the others, who had all filed in. "You all may. I am quite capable of entertaining myself for a few hours."

So said the woman who had six of us trailing after her every day.

The other ladies whispered, clearly planning their time off. Lisveth grinned at me.

I smiled at her but addressed the queen. "Thank you, Your Majesty."

We arrived at the castle grounds, and the queen dismissed us. By the time I'd returned to my room, my head was pounding.

Daselis was in her usual grim mood as she arrived to dress me for dinner. Why I had to change out of a perfectly fine dress and into another one was beyond me, but she'd snarled at me when I made that little comment.

When she finally let me make my way down to dinner, my stomach was grumbling, adding to the discomfort of my throbbing head. I scanned the royal table as I walked in.

Madinia's father was sitting next to the king. Patriarch Farrow was a fit, muscular man with that red hair and hard blue eyes. His gaze was constantly sweeping the room, as if looking for enemies.

And he was one of the king's most ardent supporters when it came to the corrupt.

Farrow nodded at something the king said, and I took my seat. Madinia was watching them both, her eyes narrowed.

Lorian sat a few seats away, a bored expression on

his face. Obviously, he'd had no problem getting back to his rooms last night. He was gazing at a group of courtiers, but I had no doubt he was also listening to every word the king said.

King Sabium raised his hand, and everyone went silent.

"Today marks the start of a new alliance with Gromalia," the king announced. "Patriarch Farrow?"

Farrow stood, his eyes alight.

"No longer will the corrupt be able to flee Eprotha, hiding among the pious. Now, the Gromalians will return those who would run from the flames of fate back to our lands, where they will be dealt with. Soon, both of our kingdoms will be cleansed of those who would deny the gods their due."

My stomach churned. That alliance wouldn't really be happening since Lorian wasn't the Gromalian prince. But if that was the king's plan, it was only a matter of time. We needed to make our way to Gromalia and get hidden before that deal went into place.

Cheers sounded. I glanced at Madinia, who sneered at me. "What?"

"You must be proud of your father."

She just ignored me, reaching for her wine.

As usual, I felt Lorian's eyes on me throughout dinner. I focused on my food and rehearsed the apology I would make myself give him. At this point, I would get down on my knees and beg if he agreed to help Asinia.

Auria had sent me a message inviting me for a cup

of tea after dinner. It was too early to sneak down to the dungeon anyway, so the moment the queen left, I nodded to the others and made my way out the door.

Unlike most of the other servants, Auria didn't seem to despise me for my new role. When they sneered at me, she instructed me to ignore it. "Jealousy is normal," she'd murmured to me once. "But you did nothing except help the queen. The fact that you were rewarded for it was entirely out of your control."

I'd just nodded.

"Ah," Auria said, stretching her feet out in front of the fire. "It feels good to be off my feet." We were in the servants' quarters—sitting in my old room. Guilt twisted in my stomach as I glanced at my old bed—and the rumpled blankets that told me some other unfortunate girl had been given the spot beneath the window.

Everyone else was still working, but Auria had finished her duties early.

"You know a lot about the people here," I murmured, and Auria laughed.

"Well, I've worked here my whole life. My mother was born in this very castle to a servant who'd been raped by a guard."

I gaped at her, and she just shrugged. "It happens. Even now. To this day, I don't know who my father is. I was put to work as soon as I was old enough to scrub a pot."

And yet, she was still a servant, while I'd walked in and become one of the queen's ladies.

"Oh, don't look so guilty, Setella. I would be miserable in such a position." She sipped her tea, and I finally relaxed.

"What do you know about Madinia?"

Auria smiled. "She'll be making your life difficult."

"She tries. But I was raised in a village, and she was raised at court. She has no idea what true difficulty is."

Auria nodded. "She must be annoyed that she can't shake you. Madinia's mother was from a village like yours."

"You're not…jesting?"

Auria laughed. "It was a rather large scandal at the time. Patriarch Farrow was supposed to marry the king's cousin, but he fell in love." She sighed. "A *love* match. Can you imagine?"

Could I imagine the cold, devout Farrow caring about anything except wiping out the corrupt? Absolutely not.

"But then Madinia's mother died." Auria's voice dropped to a whisper. "She'd insisted on traveling back to her village, and along the way, her carriage was attacked by a group of corrupt who'd escaped from the king. They robbed them of all food and water and killed her guards. There was so much blood in her carriage, there was no way she could have survived. And yet they didn't even leave her body for a decent burial."

So that was why Farrow was obsessed with wiping out the corrupt. I knew what it was like to hate the people who'd hurt your family. To loathe them with every beat of your heart.

My eyes were growing heavy, and the other maids were slowly drifting in, sneering when they caught sight of me.

"I'd better head to bed," I told Auria. "Thanks for the tea."

"You're welcome."

"Shouldn't you be in your luxurious room with your bath and furs?" one of the women asked. I didn't recognize her, but she'd obviously heard of me. I just sighed and walked out the door. The castle was becoming quieter, but it was still a dangerous time to risk sneaking down to Asinia, the guards likely still alert.

But I couldn't seem to help myself. The thought of her burning with fever…

I didn't have the medicine yet. I had the beginnings of a plan for that, but it would require Tibris's help. But I needed to see Asinia. Needed to tell her I was coming back. To urge her to hold on.

I snuck down to the dungeons, my power coming to me quicker than it ever had before.

I kept my gaze on the stone floor in front of me, still unable to look at the empty cell where Wila had spent her final hours.

"Promise me you'll free them. And one day, you'll come back and burn this fucking place to the ground."

Wila had spent her final hours thinking of the others in here. I'd arrived planning to free only Asinia.

Sometimes I thought I'd suffocate on my own guilt and self-loathing.

I sucked in a breath, terrified of what I was about to see.

My body froze. My eyes flooded. I let out a sound that might have been a choked sob.

Asinia sat up in her cage, her face no longer pale, her eyes clear as she gazed back at me.

21

PRISCA

"You're...better."

She attempted a smile. "A man came down with a healer last night. They gave me medicine, and the healer looked half dead by the time he was finished with me."

I handed her the bread and cheese I'd stolen from the kitchen, nodding at Demos as I pressed his bundle through the bars.

He nodded back, falling on the food. Ever since Tibris had worked on his arm, Demos had gained weight, his appetite returning.

Letting myself into Asinia's cell, I sat in front of her. She looked much, much healthier than I'd ever hoped for. Her eyes were bright, and even as thin as she was, she was sitting up by herself, tearing off a hunk of bread.

"I'm sorry," we both said, and she laughed. The sound was incredibly out of place down here, but it felt good to hear it from her.

"I thought you were bad at lying." I attempted a smile. And yet, she'd kept the same secret I had. And neither of us had ever known.

"I never let myself think about it," she admitted. "It didn't feel like lying, because in my mind, my power didn't exist. I'd buried it so deep, I never dared think about it unless I was alone in my bed at night."

I'd done the same until recently, when I'd finally realized nothing was going to change and I needed to prepare to run.

"What was your plan, Asinia? For the Gifting?"

She gave me a shaky smile. "I figured I'd be executed then. But some part of me thought I could escape to the city, maybe pay someone to replicate the blue mark and disappear. Or get on a ship to someplace new. There are places where we would be safe. I know there are. What were you going to do?"

"I think some part of me always knew I'd run. I'd hoped for a miracle, but I'd known one day I'd have to flee the village. Once they found me, my plan was the same as yours. I was going to get to the city and get on a ship."

"But you came here instead."

"The moment I learned you'd been taken, my plans changed."

"Even if...even if I don't get out, it means everything that you tried."

"You're getting out."

She attempted a smile, but her expression crumpled. "They killed my mother," she whispered.

I pulled her into my arms. "I know," I said. "And I swear to you, they'll pay."

"And your mother."

"Yes." I hadn't allowed myself to mourn her properly, because I knew if I thought about her too much, if I considered her last moments…

"Pris?"

Her voice was barely a whisper, but I shook my head. "Call me Setella. Tibris is Loukas," I murmured into her ear. "Don't say Vicer's name at all."

She pulled away, her mouth falling open. "Ti… Loukas is here?"

"Oh yes. He's the reason you're alive. He was healing you a little each day, but you kept getting worse. It was…"

"Like your father. Gods, it must have reminded him of…"

Of trying desperately to keep our father alive. Only now he knew it wasn't because our magic had been sacrificed to the gods. It was all for the king's greed.

I wanted Sabium dead more than I'd ever wanted anything before. In my quiet moments, I fantasized about it.

"Who was the man who helped me last night?"

I had a feeling I knew. I lowered my voice until it was nothing but a whisper. "What did he look like?"

"I didn't see him. He stayed hidden, but I could hear the healer murmuring to him."

My throat tightened, and I took a deep breath. He'd

come through for me. Even after I'd left him alone in the king's chamber.

"His name is Lorian. He's a mercenary. Don't worry about him."

Asinia's eyes were already growing heavy. "Eat a little more before you sleep." I pushed the bread toward her.

She took it, absently shoving it into her mouth. Something in my chest relaxed at the sight of her eating. She'd lost so much weight, her dress was gaping on her.

"What day is it?" she asked around her next mouthful.

I knew what she was asking. My heart was being squeezed in my chest. "You're not going to burn, Asinia. I'm going to get you out of here."

"Don't forget about me," Demos muttered, and I turned to look at him.

He'd pressed himself up against the bars, still listening to our every word. When I frowned at him, he shrugged unrepentantly. He looked better too. Even with the scant amount of food we'd been able to bring him.

"I won't forget about you," I said seriously. He stared at me for a long moment, and then he smiled. I had that vague feeling of recognition again.

"I have to get back," I whispered. "I'll see you tomorrow night."

Asinia hugged me, and it was a long time before she finally let go.

Leaving her in that cell when she'd been out of her mind with fever had been the hardest thing I'd ever done. Leaving her there when she was alert, her lower lip trembling…

"I'll keep an eye on her," Demos said gruffly.

Asinia firmed her mouth. "I don't need you to *keep an eye on me*."

He ignored her. I nodded my thanks, and she gave me a betrayed look. I didn't know what exactly had happened between them, but obviously Asinia wasn't pleased by her neighbor.

I froze time and opened the dungeon door.

The guards were *standing*, one of them gesturing to the spot on his belt where the keys should be hanging. The other was frowning at him from his place against the wall. I sucked in a sharp breath.

I dropped the keys on the floor behind the guard. Then I memorized the standing guard's face. He was likely to keep a close eye on those keys now. I could no longer risk visiting Asinia when he was one of the guards on duty. I cursed myself as I walked back toward my rooms. I'd taken too long in the dungeon. And I couldn't afford to make mistakes like that.

At the last moment, I headed left instead of right, moving toward Lorian's rooms. Since he was already irritated with me, I knocked.

He opened the door, grabbed my arm, and hauled me into his room.

"Not sneaking in tonight, wildcat?"

Gods, this man annoyed me.

"I came to thank you. For what you did for Asinia.

And, ah, sorry for leaving you last night."

He slowly shook his head. "You're not sorry."

"You don't know that," I said sullenly. Of course I wasn't sorry. But I was grateful he'd followed through on his promise.

He just smiled. My lower lip stuck out. "You deserved it."

His smile widened. And then I was in his arms, pressed against the door. His mouth was so close to mine, tingles of anticipation swept through my body. I watched him, wide-eyed, enraptured, desperate to see what he would do next.

Lorian raised one hand, leaning close and tucking a lock of my hair behind my ear. His finger brushed the shell of my ear, and I shivered.

His eyes heated. And he did it again.

I sighed, and he captured the sound with his mouth, his tongue thrusting deep.

His growl was so low, it was more of a rumble, and my nipples hardened. My tongue twined with his until I was clawing at him, dragging him closer. He lifted me in his arms, and I wrapped my legs around him, holding him close. He was hard and thick as he settled between my thighs, rocking against me.

My mind went blank.

And I moaned.

He pulled away long enough to curse, and then his huge hand was cradling my head, his lips were pressed against my throat, and his warm breath danced along my skin. He nuzzled a spot on the side of my neck, and I arched.

"You taste so sweet. Will you taste this sweet everywhere?"

The thought of him tasting me *there* made me groan, and he cursed again, his mouth dragging up my neck until he found my lips once more.

I wanted him. No, I *needed* him. Now, now, now, now—

The door vibrated against my back. Lorian pulled away, and I buried my hand in his hair in an attempt to pull him back.

Amusement flickered through his eyes. Amusement, and something darker.

"The next time you're in my arms like this, you're mine," he whispered.

More knocking thumped on the door behind me. That was what the sound had been.

I pulled my magic to me, and the knocking instantly cut off.

"Prepare yourself, Prisca," Lorian said. "Because I'm out of patience."

I wriggled in Lorian's arms, ignoring the way my heart thundered at the thought. "Down," I demanded.

He complied, and I peered up at him. "This was a mistake."

If I'd thought he'd be annoyed by my declaration, I was wrong. He just gave me a faint smile, opened the door, and pushed me out. I slid past the messenger, who had a piece of parchment in one hand. Rising on tiptoes, I attempted to see just what that parchment said.

"*Prisca.*"

I sighed and stalked down the hall toward my rooms. And a cold bath.

PRISCA

The next morning, I woke to a valeo next to my bed. I had no idea how Tibris had smuggled the fruit in to me, but I appreciated it just the same.

I spent the morning by the queen's side, boredom tugging at me as I counted down the hours until I could escape. Thankfully, breakfast was taken in her chambers, and the other ladies gossiped quietly while the queen looked on. Finally, she dismissed us.

Tibris met me outside, taking my arm. Just two siblings out for a stroll. He'd been granted permission for a single hour of freedom, and only because he was seen as such a hard worker. My stomach churned at the thought of the long hours he was working while I ate pastries with the queen.

We'd decided to take a roundabout route to Vicer's, just in case anyone followed us. It was unlikely, but we were taking no chances.

He squeezed my arm gently as we walked out the

castle gates.

"What's wrong?"

I sighed. "It's just… You're working so hard."

Tibris gave me an incredulous look. "Pris, I'm working with people like *us*. People who came from villages to work in the castle. People who'd never imagined how much magic there was here. People who think the gods *favor* the king's court and we villagers suffer because we're simply not worthy."

I threw up my hands as we rounded a corner. Above us, a woman hung clothes to dry on her balcony while a drunk lay below her in the alley. We were getting closer to the slums.

"You're making my point."

Tibris shook his head. "You deal with people who believe—down to their bones—that the gods find them worthier than us. The people who mock us villagers. The people who would stab one another in the back just to get closer to the king. So don't feel sorry for me, Pris. I'd take a hundred more days of stacking wine bottles cheerfully if it meant I could avoid dealing with the courtiers."

We both kept our heads down as we walked past a group of guards stationed on the street. According to Vicer, the city guards rotated through various locations each day. But the worst were the random searches. I glanced over at the man who had his arms out while the guards mocked him, searching for anything that could give them an excuse to lock him up.

My body went hot, and I itched to freeze all of the

guards and teach them a lesson. "I hate this place."

Tibris sighed. "I know."

Even more access to magic couldn't dull the fact that life in the city was even worse than life in the villages for many people here. I understood now–why Rythos had told me there were those in this city using fae fire right under the king's nose. It was a small way to rebel, but a rebellion just the same. Sometimes, you had to take your victories where you could find them.

Then I was stumbling as Tibris shoved me into an alley. I opened my mouth, and he held his finger to his lips.

I went still. "What is it?" I mouthed.

He turned his head, and I watched as a group of merchants walked by, likely heading toward the market. Behind them, Madinia followed, a scowl on her face as she squinted into the distance.

Why had she been following us?

After a few moments, we crept out of the alley.

"We have to move quickly in case she circles back around," Tibris said, his expression hard. We trotted down the street and took the next left. Ahead of us, Madinia continued to walk, clearly scanning the street for us. Was she just curious? Did she want to find something to pass on to the queen? Or had I said something to make her suspicious?

Tibris knocked, and Vicer immediately opened the door, obviously expecting us. He waved us inside, and we followed him into the kitchen. Unfortunately, Margie was nowhere to be seen. Vicer leaned against the wall, hands on his hips.

His expression was serious, his eyes solemn. So different from the village boy I'd once known.

"How's Asinia?"

I smiled. "She's doing better."

Tibris's mouth twisted. "With a little help from Prisca's mercenary friend. But she's still not healthy enough to travel."

Vicer crossed his arms at the *mercenary friend* part. "Explain."

I chafed at the order. Telling Vicer everything I knew about Lorian would only make him more curious. And if Lorian found out, there was no way he would help me.

"I traveled with him. He needed my powers at the city gates, so he kept me alive and then we went our separate ways. I don't know why he's at the castle."

Vicer opened his mouth, but I'd already moved on.

"The man responsible for the carriages," I said. "Rothnic Boria. Is there any chance he could be bribed?"

Vicer shook his head. "He is one of the king's most ardent supporters. His magic has made him one of the richest men in the kingdom. He could live anywhere, and yet he stays at court."

"How do the carriages work?"

"All of the horseless carriages are on loan from the king. While noble families are given permission to borrow them, each month they must be returned to the king and the magic renewed. It's seen as a status symbol to be allowed to borrow them. A sign of the king's favor. According to our spies, the royal carriages are all spelled from a single map in the carriage-maker's study. Another way for the king to keep track of who the courtiers are visiting."

The carriages wouldn't work. But I'd figure out another way. I had to. A feral kind of determination settled in my chest.

Vicer was studying my face. "What is it, Pris?"

"It's not enough to get Asinia and Demos out. I'm going to free them all."

Vicer gaped at me. Tibris just clenched his teeth. He'd known this was coming. Our discussion about it had been in low, hissed voices, both of us brimming with frustration.

"You can't," Vicer said. For the first time, he seemed vaguely shocked.

But something in me had awakened now. Something that needed to see all those prisoners free. Something that screamed for retribution. "Think about it. If I'm getting two people out, we can expand the plan and get them all out."

"You say it like it's easy. Like we haven't been trying for *years.*"

"Two weeks before Gods Day, the king is holding another ball. According to the queen, some of the village representatives will be staying until Gods Day. Think of the blow it would be for them to witness his entire dungeon escaping. Think of the representatives who would carry that news back to their villages. And think of the people just like us who would have hope for the first time."

Vicer's mouth twisted. "You make it sound so simple. What are those people supposed to do when we get them out? Where are they going to go?"

I lifted my chin. "I've been watching the prisoners. Talking to some of them. The younger children…they mostly don't survive the dungeon. Most of those who are still alive can pass for twenty-five winters. They get a blue mark, and they're free."

Vicer burst out laughing, holding up his hands. "Well then, in that case, it should all be fine." The laughter faded from his voice. "Did you miss the part where Tibris told you he was saving for *years* just to get a blue mark for you?"

I glanced at Tibris. He winced.

"You said there are other options. Now's the time to start asking around. I know it's dangerous. Tibris and I will do anything we can. But there has to be someone who can help."

Vicer's expression was stony. "*If* I could achieve such a miracle, that person wouldn't be able to handle three hundred prisoners in one night."

He wasn't saying it couldn't be done. A tiny flame of hope lit inside me, glowing like one of those blue-green stones in the hybrid market. "We get them out of the city. The prisoners will separate, travel in groups. They'll know where to go and when, so your contact can get through them all."

Tibris's voice was quiet. "And the ones who are too young to pass as twenty-five winters?"

"They get the mark anyway. And they get some kind of charm to make it invisible." I threw up my hands. "They grow their hair long. They hide for a few years until they could pass. But once they *can* pass, they're free. They can settle somewhere and start a new life."

Vicer closed his eyes. He wanted it. I knew he did. And yet, Vicer lived here. He knew what could be done. And what couldn't.

But maybe...maybe we all needed to be pushed. Just once. Maybe saving these people was worth everything. I could justify it with the embarrassment it would cause the king, the hope it would give other hybrids...but three hundred lives was enough. That was all the justification I needed.

"I can't leave those people there to die, Vicer. I don't have it in me."

Not Lina, with her solemn eyes. Not Dashiel, who deserved his vengeance. Not Demos, Asinia, or any other prisoner would be left behind. Not while I still drew breath.

He pinched the bridge of his nose. "The moment I saw you again, I knew you were going to complicate everything." Finally, he heaved a sigh. "I'm not agreeing to anything except helping you set it up. If I think it's too dangerous, I have the right to say no. At any time."

Victory flashed through me, and I fought to keep my expression blank. "Fine."

Some of the tension left his shoulders, and he leaned

against the wall. "If we could do this…"

I grinned. "Who is in charge of the guards on the city walls?"

"The king."

Tibris nodded, picking up my thought. "Surely there's someone beneath him who oversees the guards."

"Patriarch Farrow."

One of the men most loyal to the king. I sighed. "Who works beneath him?"

Vicer shrugged. "I'll look into it. But you're right. If we're going to get our people out, we need to get them as far from the city as possible and have anyone who agrees to help with the marks meet them elsewhere. I'll find out who oversees the guards at the city walls."

I nodded. "One more thing. I need another charm for my eyes. They're lightening more each day."

Vicer winced. "The woman we usually buy the charms from had to flee the city. Another was just killed."

My chest tightened until it was difficult to take a full breath. Without a charm, my eyes were noticeable. It was a risk we couldn't afford to take.

Tibris went still. "So, we'll find someone else."

"The charms are becoming difficult to find. Changing your eye color is the latest trend. Charms are being fixed on to bracelets, rings, earrings…"

"I'm trusting you with my sister," Tibris hissed. I reached out and squeezed his arm, unused to such a tone from him.

Vicer held up a hand. "I know. Just keep your head down,

Pris, and I'll have a new necklace for you in a few days."

Not for the first time, I hated the strange color of my eyes.

"We need to go. One of the queen's other ladies followed us here," I said. Who knew if she was wandering around, hoping to glimpse us again?

The walk back to the castle was long, but it gave me time to think.

"I know you want to get them out, Pris," Tibris said when the castle came into view. "But…just think before you do anything that could get you arrested. I…I can't lose you too."

Something in my chest wrenched. "I know. I will. We'll figure it out. Together."

He nodded, and I headed to my room, my mind replaying the curiosity in Vicer's eyes when he learned about Lorian.

I couldn't blame him. I was curious too.

I knew Lorian wasn't the Gromalian Prince. He'd slept on the ground next to me. He'd stayed in the kinds of inns only villagers could afford. And he fought like someone who enjoyed it. Not just because he was trained.

And sometimes when he fought, he moved faster than the eye could see.

Maybe *that* was his power.

It would certainly explain a lot.

Lorian must look similar to the real Gromalian prince. But the moment the Gromalian royals learned what was happening, the ruse was up. Lorian and the others were dead. My body turned cold at the thought.

Unless the Gromalian prince was incapacitated. I'd traveled with the mercenaries to the Gromalian border. The fae handed Lorian a vial. It was possible the fae either kidnapped or killed the real prince and Lorian took his place.

In that case, the Gromalians wouldn't even know their prince was gone, unless someone who knew the prince interacted with Lorian.

I swallowed at the thought of that much brutality. But the fact remained that without Lorian's help, Asinia could be dead now. I owed him.

And still, I needed to be careful. I didn't know what his power was…or much of anything about him.

But I knew when he touched me, as he did last night, I felt like I was flying. Guilt coiled in my stomach, and I pushed open the door to my chambers.

Daselis was waiting. "The seamstress will be here soon."

Hello to you too. "The seamstress?"

"The queen said you need a few new dresses. Something fashionable for the balls. You may as well undress now."

A few minutes later, I was wrapped in a bath sheet, the seamstress casting a critical eye over me. She was an older woman with a slightly hunched back and deep frown lines.

"Drop the sheet."

Thankfully, Daselis and Erea had made themselves scarce. The seamstress began her measurements. And I turned my attention on the mirror in front of me.

My heart pounded as I met my own eyes. The charm on my necklace was no longer working at all.

"One of the queen's other ladies had to leave town suddenly before picking up her dresses. I can tailor them for you. I'll work on hers in the coming weeks."

I barely hid a wince. Guilt stabbed into me at the thought of the woman who'd rushed back to her village.

"Thank you. What's your name?"

The seamstress angled her head from where she was measuring my waist. "Telean."

"I'm Setella."

She just nodded. When she stepped back, our eyes met.

And the blood slowly drained from her face. "Your eyes are beautiful."

I cleared my throat, glancing away. "Thank you."

My heart skipped several beats and then began to race. Had she seen one of the pieces of parchment that were likely circulating with my face and description on them. I opened my mouth, but the words wouldn't come.

Any minute now, she would run from the room and alert the guards.

I forced myself to meet her gaze. "Please," I got out.

She just shook her head, leaning over and handing me the bath sheet.

"I'm finished."

Her expression twisted in something that might've been grief, and then she was walking out the door.

I did nothing to stop her.

22
LORIAN

I'd known Prisca was up to something. And yet when she knocked on my door, a part of me was convinced she was here to finish what she'd started yesterday.

One look at her, and it was evident that was not going to happen. Her face was bone-white, and she seemed oddly fragile.

"I need to talk to you."

I opened the door wider, and she walked in. It had been a terrible day, and I'd spent most of it at Sabium's side. My head pounded with a rare headache. And yet, the moment the wildcat walked in, my cock hardened in anticipation.

I scowled, and Prisca raised one eyebrow. "What is your problem?"

Sometimes I longed to be able to talk to her about my life. "My problems are my own."

Her expression turned cool. "Perhaps that needs to change."

I waved my hand in the way I knew she loathed, gesturing for her to talk.

She glowered at me but took a deep breath. "You need something in this castle, and I could use some help. I think we should work together."

"You want me to help get your friend out."

She studied me as if wondering if I could be trusted. I ground my teeth. This woman.

But you can't *be trusted.*

I pushed that thought away and focused on Prisca as she began to pace. She had dark circles beneath her eyes. I considered everything I knew about her, and my blood turned to ice.

"You're planning to get them all out. Are you mad?"

She sighed. "I have a plan."

I watched her, and she shrugged. "Fine. I have the beginnings of a plan."

Of course. Prisca wouldn't be content breaking one prisoner out of the king's dungeon—a feat that had never been done before. No, she somehow imagined she could get them *all* out. And with that power of hers, she likely could. But there was no way she could transport them all out of the city.

And yet...

Even if she *couldn't* get them out, the chaos that would ensue when the king learned his prisoners were missing? It would be the perfect distraction for my own plans. Perhaps fate would step in and both of us could get what we needed. Hope was almost a foreign sensation at this point in my life, but I felt the dull edge of it.

"How many prisoners are down there?"

"Three hundred and nine."

I winced. Prisca stuck out her chin. Stubborn as a mule.

"Are you sure all of them are—"

"Hybrids? Yes. Thieves and murderers are taken to the city jail. I learned something else today too. Those oceartus stones? They're here for a reason. The king doesn't just burn the hybrids. He drains them first."

It made sense.

She put her hands on her hips. "So, if you're hoping to weaken the king…"

I smiled. "Is that what I'm doing?"

She looked down her pert little nose at me, and I couldn't help but smile. Surprise flashed across her face, but she recovered quickly. "The king will be even more powerful after Gods Day. Something tells me you would prefer for that not to happen."

It was a situation I'd known we would potentially have to deal with. A sudden influx of magic for a king who was already rivaling the fae for power. And I would, indeed, prefer that he didn't receive that power.

Prisca gave me that knowing smile that made me want to strangle her. Or kiss her. Or both.

I lost myself in a fantasy of my hand circling her throat while I thrust inside her, making it clear that I was still in charge.

"Lorian?"

A blush tinged her cheekbones. She'd guessed where my mind had gone. This distraction had to stop.

"When I took my healer to your friend, we used a tunnel. It has existed for years, and thanks to the fae iron the guards shove down the prisoner's throats, even if they could somehow get out of their cells and locate the hidden entrance, they'd be too weak to get all the way to the end of the tunnel."

Surprise and victory gleamed in her eyes. "I know about the tunnel. I've been searching the dungeon for that entrance. Will you tell me where it is?"

"Yes."

I could see her mind processing that information instantly as she readjusted whatever plans she'd been making. Fascinating creature.

"Where does the tunnel end?"

"The central market. Decades ago, the market didn't exist. It was solely an execution square. The tunnel allowed the guards to take prisoners out directly to their death." On Gods Day, the streets would run red with blood. Even someone like me—who cared little for the agony of others—could feel the waste of it.

Prisca shivered and turned to pace some more. Each time I watched her scheme, I grew more reluctantly intrigued despite myself. She'd always thought quickly— the fact that she had survived after we'd left her that day was proof of that.

My mind provided me with the memory of her lying next to Galon, her skin pale—so pale it had seemed as if she were already dead. The way she'd pleaded with me and then her eyes had burned, silently vowing vengeance.

That spark had almost been doused like one of Rythos's fires. My hands fisted at the thought. For the first time, I felt something that might have been…regret.

She turned and peered up at me.

"Your eyes are reverting," I said. It was dangerous to her. And yet, it was as if something inside me unlocked when I could see the gold flecks in her eyes.

"I know," she sighed. "The charms are difficult to find right now."

I was beginning to learn that I hated it, knowing she skulked around the castle using magic that, if I was honest, she should have had years to train with and not days. I loathed that she was often down in the dungeons, where all it would take was one wrong move, one moment of inattention, and she was dead.

The fact that she'd somehow made me *care* about her like this—to the extent that I was unfocused while on my own task… I glowered at her.

"You take too many risks."

She gave me that wary look that told me she had something to tell me and I wasn't going to like it.

"Out with it."

She spoke casually, but it was easy to see the fear darting across her face. "The seamstress saw my eyes. She remarked on the color. Her face turned white, and she rushed out of the room."

Then the seamstress was dead.

"You've got your murder face on," she murmured. "I don't want her to die, Lorian."

The fact that the seamstress hadn't said anything yet likely meant she was hoping to wait for the perfect chance to wield that information. At any second, Prisca could be arrested. My instincts roared at me to remove the threat.

"Then convince her not to say a word. And quickly."

"Tell me something," she said suddenly. Almost desperately. "One of the secrets you're hiding. Please."

I studied her face. Her eyes were intent on mine, her teeth biting into her lower lip. This seemed like some kind of test. And for some reason, I wanted to pass it.

Unfortunately, I couldn't tell her my own secrets. If she learned exactly why I was here…

For some reason, the thought of her looking at me with fear and revulsion made my stomach twist.

"The king," I said, my voice hoarse. "What do you know of him?"

She frowned, clearly not expecting that subject. "He has a son, Jamic, who is away at one of the king's estates. Jamic has seen nineteen winters," she said. "And he'll likely return for the Gods Day ball. According to the rumors, he rarely sees the king."

Her frown deepened, and I angled my head. "What is it?"

"Just something my mother said. She insisted I find the prince."

She looked tired. Wrung-out. And yet, it was time for her to know just some of what made Sabium so dangerous. "You may want to sit down."

Her eyes narrowed on my face, but she sat on the

long sofa.

I took a deep breath. "It was the king's great-great-grandfather who started warring with the fae."

She nodded.

"And what do you know of Regner's son?"

"His name was Crotopos. Crotopos died, but his wife was pregnant and his son Aybrias—Regner's grandson—took the throne. Aybrias's son was named Hiarnus—Sabium's father."

I wasn't surprised Prisca knew this. Most villagers were taught more about the royal family than they were languages or basic mathematics.

It felt foreign to talk to someone other than my men about the king. But I forced myself to continue speaking. "And what if I told you they were all the same man?"

Her frown deepened, followed immediately by disbelief. Prisca jumped to her feet. "That's not possible. That's not how magic works." Something that might've been betrayal had tightened her shoulders. I caught her arm as she moved toward the door.

In a rare moment of vulnerability, she'd asked for a secret. And now, she thought I was lying to her.

No, I realized. She *hoped* I was lying to her. After everything she'd learned, this was the realization that would sting the most. Her own father had died because her brother had only a scant amount of power left. And yet the king was almost immortal.

"I'm not playing a game. Regner was the king who began taking his subjects' power. You don't think it's possible he could find a way to mimic fae and hybrid long lives?"

She swallowed, her gaze searching my face. "But that would mean... Does he kill the boys he says are his sons?"

"Likely."

"But how does he step into the younger boys' shoes?"

"Changing one's appearance is easy if you have access to the right kind of magic." I lifted her necklace with a raised eyebrow.

"A small charm is one thing. You're talking about changing his appearance completely."

"Easy enough to do with stolen power. Often the boys are sent away for a time when they're growing from boys into men. That way, he doesn't need to be exact with their features."

She shook off my hand, turning to pace once more. How the woman didn't grow dizzy, I would never understand.

"Sabium is getting old," she murmured. "At least on the outside. It's only a matter of time before he fakes his death again. And then secretly kills the boy he raised as his son." She turned and met my eyes. "He's truly that evil?"

I cupped her cheek. Her skin was softer than it had any right to be. "He's worse. He's evil with the conviction that his actions are for the greater good."

PRISCA

There were no more quiet evenings after dinner. Representatives from the villages had begun to arrive, and each night, dancing would commence and extend until the early hours of the morning.

The queen was expected to attend, which meant so were her ladies. Each night after the dancing, I took Tibris down to the dungeons. He'd also begun visiting the other prisoners and working on the wounds in their shoulders. Each time we walked up those dungeon stairs, he looked more tired.

I'd warned him that I might be arrested at any moment. I had to trust that Lorian wouldn't risk killing the queen's favorite seamstress. And yet, she hadn't said a word. I'd caught a glimpse of her yesterday, which meant Lorian was keeping his word. So far.

When I'd told Tibris the woman had recognized my eyes, he'd gotten a look on his face I'd never seen before. "If you get arrested, I'm going to kill Vicer."

He wasn't joking. I swallowed. "Maybe you should take a break from healing for a night."

He just shook his head. "The more prisoners who can access their magic, the better."

I needed to talk to Lorian. Needed to convince him that if the seamstress changed her mind and I was arrested and executed, he had to work with Tibris to get the prisoners out.

Tonight, I was sitting at our table, listening to the other women as they gossiped. Lisveth rose to dance with one of the king's advisers—a lecherous old man who insisted on dancing with each of us at least once every night.

Davis Boria had already asked Madinia to dance once, and she'd refused him, claiming her feet were sore. Now, he sat next to his father, his dark gaze continually drifting to her. I would have felt sorry for him, but according to rumors, he didn't bother asking other women before he touched them. Women whose fathers weren't close to the king. Women whom he caught in servants' halls and stables.

Caraceli slid into Lisveth's empty seat. From the malevolent look on her face, it wasn't because she wanted to be friends.

"Katina would have *loved* this." She leaned close, her eyes cold. "There's nothing she enjoys more than dancing."

I kept my expression bored with a hint of confusion. "Is that right?"

She gave me a slow smile, and my hands began to sweat.

"I know you had something to do with her removal from court," she hissed.

I forced my mouth to fall open. "What are you talking about?"

"Unlike the rest of these idiots, I know how things work. No one *stumbles* into this position like you have.

All you needed for your plans to work was for Katina to disappear. And when I find out what you did, I'm going to make you pay."

I dropped my gaze. Hoping she would think I was intimidated. In reality, I needed to make sure she didn't pay close attention to my eyes. The other ladies had gone quiet, and Madinia cleared her throat.

I opened my mouth, but a deep voice made me snap it closed once more.

"Setella?"

I took a long, deep breath and forced a smile on to my face, glancing up at the courtier standing in front of me.

Peiter was remarkably handsome, I could admit that much. He was also one of the few courtiers I didn't want to stab with my dinner knife. With his sparkling blue eyes and blond curls, he had a boyish kind of charm. Almost innocent, which was something I hadn't seen much of in this place.

But talking to him occasionally felt like walking a tightrope as he asked questions about my village. I knew enough about Mistrun to get the basics right, but I was terrified I would stir his curiosity—and that curiosity would mean he would look closer at who I was pretending to be.

"Will you dance with me?" If he felt the tension at our table, he politely ignored it.

I blushed. "I'm not a very skilled dancer, I'm afraid."

Across the table, Madinia snorted her agreement. I

turned my head, and she raised one eyebrow at me.

I scowled back at her. "Yes, I'll dance with you," I said, and Peiter held out his hand.

Sliding my hand into his, I followed him into the smaller ballroom attached to the dining hall. The musicians were playing a lively tune.

"Will you teach me the steps?"

Delight danced across Peiter's face. "Of course."

He raised our joined hands, sliding his other hand to my waist.

He led me through the steps, never wincing when I turned the wrong way or stepped on his toes. When he twirled me, I laughed.

The sound shocked me. I couldn't remember the last time I'd laughed.

My stomach twisted. Asinia was huddled in a freezing cell, and I was dancing just floors above her.

"You're beautiful," Peiter said.

I attempted a smile, and he slowed our steps. "What's wrong?"

"Nothing," I said.

Couples whirled behind us, and I froze. Was that... Marth?

Peiter followed my gaze. "Are you sure nothing is wrong?"

I beamed at him with everything I had. "I'm sure."

I glanced over Peiter's shoulder. My gaze met Lorian's. He wore a dark scowl as he watched me, and I raised one eyebrow.

He couldn't possibly be...jealous?

After the next dance, I thanked Peiter and laughingly begged for relief, insisting my feet were aching. He gave a mock sigh but let me go, leading me to the side of the room and gesturing to a servant for a cup of wine.

"Promise me one more dance after you've rested, and I'll leave you to recover." I nodded, and Peiter grinned at me, turning to stride away.

More and more village representatives had begun arriving today. The queen was sitting at the royal table, speaking to one of the courtiers as she watched some of the villagers make fools of themselves with her husband's wine. She'd declared all the dancing a waste of time, and today, she had finally decreed that her ladies didn't need to suffer just because she was and we could go to bed when we were tired. I could count on one hand the number of decent things she had done since I had met her, but that was one of them.

"Enjoying yourself?"

I whirled. "Marth." I *had* seen him.

He sidled up next to me, a cup of wine in his own hand as he watched the dancing. His hair had been darkened as well, and he looked tired.

"What are you doing here?" I'd missed him ridiculously. In fact, I was struggling not to beam at him.

He grinned at me, but his eyes turned to ice when Sabium walked past. It was strange seeing malevolence on Marth's face. He was the lewd one. The one who never took anything seriously. Except bedding women.

"Serving my prince. What else?"

"Mm-hmm. Well, I—" My heart stopped.

Marth followed my gaze. "Who is that?"

I stared at the handsome man with the wide shoulders and the grin that invited you to grin right back. My mouth had gone so dry, I could barely get the words out.

"Prisca?"

"His name is Thol. I'd thought maybe I'd see his father here, but not…"

My heart cracked as I watched Thol dance. Watched him laugh. Watched him lift another woman's hand—just as he'd once done to me.

"What's wrong?" Marth asked.

"Nothing."

He followed my gaze to where Thol was now dancing, the light from the chandeliers flitting across his handsome face.

"Ah," he said. "So that's the way of things. He's from your village."

"Yes."

Homesickness struck me like a backhanded slap as I watched Thol. Visiting the city would be the highlight of his life. When he told people back home that he'd danced in the same room as the king?

My stomach swam.

Lorian sauntered past, looking exactly like the spoiled prince he was playing. His gaze met mine, and he changed course, slipping through the crowd to stand next to Marth.

"What are you doing?" I hissed. "We shouldn't be seen together."

He gave a languid shrug. "I'm a prince. You're a pretty courtier. I'm expected to have…dalliances."

I chewed on that while he murmured something to Marth. Then Lorian was standing next to me.

"What's wrong?"

If one more man asked me that tonight…

I opened my mouth, but Marth jumped in. As usual.

"Prisca's watching the handsome boy from her village."

My cheeks burned. Marth was likely only a few years older than Thol, but he spoke of him as if he were a child.

Lorian followed my gaze. "Let me guess. You're desperately wishing you could walk into his arms and pretend you're just a normal woman."

I hated that he'd figured me out so quickly.

"Fuck you."

"Perhaps, if I ever get through those who are already waiting." He turned toward Pelopia and winked at her. She actually fluttered her eyelashes.

I smirked. "Looks like she has something stuck in her eyes. Must be why she's blind enough to entertain the thought of you in her bed."

"Jealousy is a most unattractive trait."

Smiling, I turned my gaze to where Peiter was waiting for me. Lorian stiffened, and I gave him a haughty look I knew would make him want to strangle me.

"It is, isn't it?"

Lorian bared his teeth in a mockery of a smile. Whatever came out of his hateful mouth next would be vicious.

He leaned close, his breath warm on my ear. I shivered, glancing at Pelopia, who was frowning at me from across the room.

"You talk about saving the hybrids in the dungeon beneath us, but you're still that scared little girl who is waiting to wake up from a nightmare. You better find a way to stop running away from your fate, because the kinds of people who refuse to accept the realities of their lives are not the same people who free the helpless and enslaved."

Numbness swept through my body. I stared at Lorian for a long moment. Something flickered in his eyes, but I was already turning away, stalking toward the door.

I was done with this night.

I sucked in a deep breath of fresh air when I reached the hall. My shoes echoed on the stone, the space empty, with everyone either watching or partaking in the dancing.

A huge hand came down on my shoulder. Lorian spun me, pressing me up against the wall.

I glanced down the corridor. This would draw attention from anyone who happened to walk past. "What are you doing?"

He frowned down at me. Something that might have been concern flickered in his eyes. "Why are you so upset?"

I threw my hands in the air. "You just called me a scared little girl."

"And you've called me worse." He leaned even closer, studying my face.

I shoved his chest. "Are you crazy? Someone will see." The last thing either of us needed was the court gossiping about us. Gossip would make people look closer.

Lorian sighed. My head spun as he opened the closest door and shoved me inside.

I snarled. "This is going to surprise you, so prepare yourself—Not everything is your business."

"Everything that concerns you is my business. This is not a game." His words were flat, but his eyes blazed into mine.

My laugh was so bitter I barely recognized it. "No one knows that more than me!"

He studied my face for a long, uncomfortable moment.

"Ah."

"Ah?"

"The village boy means something to you."

The air between us grew dangerously hot. I swallowed. "Like I said, none of your business."

"Did he tell you pretty lies?" Lorian asked softly. "Oh no. You would have told *him* pretty lies. Because you were never going to stay in that village and have his babies. No matter how much you wanted to. No matter how much you ignored reality and pretended you wouldn't be burned alive for having the audacity to keep what was yours."

Something sharp was stabbing into my stomach.

"Stop."

He leaned close. "When you're crying into your pillow tonight, remember one thing. It would never have worked between you two."

Sorrow stole the air from my lungs. Rage gave it back. I shoved at Lorian's chest. Predictably, he caught my hands. "You know *nothing*."

"I know *that*. You wanted him because he was handsome, but most importantly, he was *safe*. You weren't meant for a life of safety. A life of kisses on your cheek and mediocre fucking. A life of gossiping with *villagers*."

My cheeks burned. "Those villagers are good people."

"Those villagers would have watched you burn, and you know it."

I flinched. Lorian cursed and released my hands.

Then his mouth was on mine, and I could taste his frustration and fury. The air left my lungs, but breathing was secondary to the feel of him hard and enraged against me.

"Your Thol would never have given you *this*," he whispered against my mouth. "And you know that too." He took a step back. "Until you face up to the reality of your life, you will forever be a victim to it."

Then he was stalking out of the room. He didn't look back.

I *hated* him.

Making my way back to my chambers, I threw myself onto my bed. But I didn't cry.

I was too angry.

23
PRISCA

I was in a black mood the next morning when Erea and Daselis woke me. As usual, so was Daselis, while Erea beamed at me. The maids bustled around, opening curtains and murmuring to each other.

I swung my legs out of bed, and my gaze caught on the new necklace next to the fresh valeo on my nightstand. I smiled. Vicer had come through, and Tibris had likely helped. How had they managed to smuggle this in while I was sleeping, though? These days, I woke easily and often.

I picked up the necklace and almost choked on my next breath. Unlike the cheap trinket currently around my neck, this necklace was... gorgeous.

The chain was so fine, I fumbled with it when I attempted to put it on. Swinging my legs out of bed, I made my way to my long mirror and studied the gem.

The center stone was the same brown-gold as my real eyes, only it gleamed in the light. The stones surrounding it would be fake, but they glimmered like real diamonds.

Obviously, Vicer felt bad about how close I'd come to walking around with no charm at all. Either that, or my brother had terrified him.

As a maid, wearing this necklace would have drawn too much attention. As one of the queen's ladies, I was *expected* to wear jewels. Something Madinia had reminded me of just a few nights ago.

"Telean will be here soon." Erea smiled at me as she turned from tying back the heavy curtains. "You'll see to the queen later."

My blood froze. The seamstress was coming back? Was this a trick? Maybe she was really returning with the king's guards.

Daselis emerged from the bathing room. "In," she said.

"You look tired," Erea murmured. "Bad sleep?"

My mind had refused to allow me to rest. Instead, it had helpfully provided me with images of Caraceli's hate-filled eyes, Thol's handsome face, and Lorian snarling down at me. Not to mention the fear that, at any point, Telean could tell others just what she'd noticed about my eyes.

"It wasn't the best."

"Must be difficult sleeping in such a large bed in such a warm room," Daselis muttered.

I sighed and walked into the bathing room. Behind me, Erea and Daselis had a hissed conversation.

Erea slipped into the room and chatted to me, likely attempting to make up for Daselis's grim mood. I nodded occasionally, although she didn't seem to require a response. My attention was caught when she discussed Lorian.

"I heard Prince Rekja has gone hunting with the king today. He's so handsome," she sighed.

I stored that information away. It was always a good idea to know what Lorian was up to.

"Bathe quickly," Daselis muttered when she leaned her head in.

"I will."

Erea left me to finish, and I ran the stone she'd given me over my legs. It somehow removed the hair, making my legs smooth. Although it couldn't remove the scars and bruises that decorated my shins.

My finger brushed against the scar on my knee, and Thol's face flashed in my mind. Asinia still teased me about the day Thol had been training with Tibris. And Thol had taken off his shirt.

I'd been just eighteen winters at the time, walking past the clearing where the boys trained.

That was the moment I'd realized that Thol was no longer a *boy*.

I'd tripped, falling flat on my face, and almost every boy in our village had seen. My eyes had burned, my cheeks had blazed, but it had been Thol who'd stopped training and helped me up. Thol who'd grinned down at me, all that smooth, pale skin on display.

The moment I'd seen him yesterday, I'd wanted nothing more than to step in front of him until he recognized me.

I'd wanted to tell him that, yes, I was corrupt, but it wasn't my fault and the king was a filthy liar and there was more to life than training for the king's armies and handing over our power like puppets.

"Let me guess. You're desperately wishing you could walk into his arms and pretend you're just a normal woman."

I was. The moment I'd seen Thol, with his wide grin and those dimples, I'd longed for just a single moment to pretend.

"You wanted him because he was handsome, but most importantly, he was safe. You weren't meant for a life of safety. A life of kisses on your cheek and mediocre fucking. A life of gossiping with villagers."

My eyes burned. Lorian didn't know what he was talking about. And what was the alternative? A life of hiding? Of fighting and killing and scheming?

The worst part was…he was right. At least about the way I'd felt— No. The way my *body* had *reacted* when Lorian claimed my mouth like it was made for him.

The touch of Thol's hand had made me sigh.

Lorian's kisses made me *burn*.

And I loathed that fact just as much as I craved him.

It was all a game for Lorian. A fun way for him to mess with me. To make my thighs clench, my core ache. Another way for him to make me hard and mean, just like him.

"Until you face up to the reality of your life, you will forever be a victim to it."

I got out of the bath, and a knock sounded on the door. My heart pounded, but I couldn't hear any male voices. And the guards wouldn't have knocked.

Wrapping the bath sheet around myself, I stepped into the room. Daselis and Erea were speaking to Telean. Behind her, two more maids were carrying dresses, which they placed on my bed. Telean's eyes met mine.

Within seconds, we were alone.

We watched each other for a long, awkward moment.

"You didn't go to the guards," I murmured. Was this the part where she demanded something from me in return for her silence?

Her brow creased. "You thought I would?"

"Well…yes."

"I'm sorry. My reaction was to go somewhere quiet, where I could cry."

I angled my head. "Cry? Why?"

She let out a shaky breath. "Because, you see, I knew your mother."

For a wild moment, I thought she meant Mama. And then I understood. She meant my real mother. My skin turned clammy. "And how do you know who my mother is? We just met."

"Those eyes, child. I once looked into eyes that exact color. And you look just like your mother—even with the dark hair." She took a deep breath and met my gaze once more. "Your mother was my best friend. You called me aunt. She met me years before she knew your father, when she was looking for a seamstress she could trust to be honest with her. We became close, until we shared everything. And when it was time for children, she begged me stay on as your nanny." She smiled, but her eyes were glistening. "Your real name is Nelayra."

My stomach spiraled. Was this woman being truthful? What did she have to gain by lying? She already knew I wasn't who I'd claimed to be, and she could have taken that information to the guards at any moment.

Someone my birth mother had considered close enough to call sister. Someone I'd called aunt. A member of my family who was still alive. Maybe she could even tell me about my mother. About my father. Had I had siblings? I forced myself to dampen the hope that had sparked in my chest.

I couldn't afford to make a mistake here. Couldn't afford to trust blindly. As much as I longed for her to be telling me the truth, I needed *more*.

"How do I know you're not lying?"

The hint of a smile curved her mouth. "So suspicious. I bet you have time magic, just like your mother." I jolted, and she merely sighed, picking up one of the dresses. "We may as well get this done while I tell you what you need to know."

I didn't pay attention to anything about the dress as she helped me slip it on. A member of my family. Would she remember what my father sounded like when he laughed? Had my parents been happy together? Where did we live? I was so lost in my thoughts, I almost missed when she began speaking.

"Long before you were born, our people lived in Crawyth."

I went still. "Crawyth?" That was the city Vicer had mentioned in one of his notes to Tibris. The city that had once been a famed place of learning, until the fae king's brutal brother had destroyed it, killing hundreds of thousands of people.

"We had a community there. Unlike in the rest of Eprotha, our people were welcome." Her voice had turned wistful, her eyes distant.

I couldn't even imagine it. "The…hybrids?"

She nodded, walking around me to tighten my dress. "The king rarely sent his own assessors, and ours had been paid off. Even our priestess was a hybrid. We lived in peace."

"I lived there too?"

Telean took a step back, and our eyes met in the mirror. "That looks beautiful."

I glanced at the lavender dress without much interest. "I lived in Crawyth?"

"Yes. With your parents. And your brother."

I had another brother. My throat constricted until I had to fight to get my words out. "Where are they?"

"The night the fae came—the night the Bloodthirsty Prince destroyed our city, your mother walked into your room and found you gone, your brother lying unconscious on the floor of his room. You'd seen just three winters. At first, we assumed you had wandered away. You were a curious, precocious child." Telean took a deep breath, her eyes haunted. "I can still hear your mother's screams."

The woman I'd thought was my real mother had caused that pain. It was difficult to imagine the woman whom I loved—the woman who'd died just weeks ago—hurting someone like that. Even if she insisted she had done it to save my life.

"Everyone began searching for you. I remember your brother and the way he cried, begging your father to find you. He'd seen just six winters himself, and he swore someone had come in and taken you. Eventually, one of the neighbors said she had seen Vuena entering through the side door. She was a seer, and most trusted her with access to their homes." Telean's expression tightened, her eyes glittering. To her, to my real family, Mama was the villain who had betrayed their trust, taking me from the people who'd loved me.

"Then what happened?" My lips were numb. Telean helped me remove the dress and reached for another one.

"Then the Bloodthirsty Prince burned our city to the ground. No one knows why. We were close to the fae border, but they knew we were hybrids. Often, they would return our children to us when they accidentally crossed the border." She shook her head. "I never saw your parents again."

No. No, I was going to meet them. I was going to tell them I was still alive, and we were going to make up for all the years we'd lost. I was going to hug my mother and laugh with my father and introduce my brother to Tibris.

I sucked in a steadying breath, heat searing the backs of my eyes. "They…died?"

"I don't know. I fell while I was fleeing and hit my head. When I woke up, I was half buried in ash, and our city was gone. The king's people came and rounded up any survivors. Most assumed we were saved. But somehow, he knew many of us were hybrids. I was supposed to burn with the others, but the queen learned of my skill as a seamstress, and the king spared me as a wedding gift to her. This fits you perfectly," she marveled. I gaped at her. How was she thinking about a *dress*?

She gave me a sad smile. "I have lived with this loss for years, child. Now, there is something else I must tell you. And you must take this news with courage."

"Oh gods."

"It will be okay."

She took my hands in hers. "Your brother is alive. And he is here, in the castle."

PRISCA

The queen wished to be left alone for most of the morning, leaving me with my thoughts. I paced in my room, attempting to talk myself out of what I really wanted to do.

It was stupid, going anywhere near the dungeon in the morning, when the guards were neither drunk nor tired.

But my *brother* was down there.

What would Tibris say when he learned I had another brother—who was still alive? The last thing I wanted to do was hurt him. And yet, I pictured that boy of just six winters screaming for his sister. He would assume I was dead.

It suddenly seemed intolerable. I might have missed the chance to ever know my real parents. But the reality was, I could be arrested and executed any day. I felt a deep need for him to know who I was.

I chewed on my lower lip. Would telling him I was alive be ripping his wounds open?

I would want to know if it were me. And…my parents could be alive too. He could tell me where they were. Maybe…maybe they'd found a safe place to live. Somewhere we could all go after we escaped this castle.

I slipped out of my room and strolled down to the lower level of the castle. Already, servants were decorating for Gods Day. The thought made bile sting the back of my throat.

Only one guard was on duty, the steel door open. They must be bringing a prisoner in.

A cold sweat broke out on my forehead, and I backed out, into the hall. If I'd been a little earlier, I would have been trapped in the dungeon. What if my power had faltered? What if…

No. It didn't happen. Shuddering, I released my hold on my power and snuck into the closest storage closet, waiting for what felt like an eternity.

When I returned, both guards were sitting on the floor. Thankfully, the guard who'd noticed his keys missing wasn't on duty. I slipped them into my pocket and took the stairs down to the dungeon, my heart tripping in my chest.

"Pris?" Asinia murmured. She still looked alert, although being clearheaded in this place only meant she was aware of what would happen to her if I failed.

"Hey."

"It's cold."

"I know." It did feel even colder, and yet I was sleeping with a roaring fire each night. "I'll bring you a blanket. We can find a way to hide it—"

"No." She shook her head. "The guards checked us today. Likely ensuring we were all capable of walking to be burned." Her face drained of color. "They'll notice."

"I'm not going to let you burn." Each day, I became more and more certain of that one fact. I would do whatever it took to free her.

She attempted a smile, but her eyes were turning alarmingly blank. "I know."

I gave her some of the food I'd stolen, but anticipation was making me shiver. "I need to hand this out. I'll be back."

Tibris had convinced the other prisoners to stop eating

the food the guards gave them. They'd had to find ways to hide their slop, ensuring the guards didn't notice, but many of them were already more alert as I handed them bread and meat. It was easy to see which prisoners Tibris had been working on, their shoulders finally healing, their eyes no longer dazed.

When I was done, I made my way to Demos's cell.

"Please tell me you left some of that for me." He gave me a half grin.

I unlocked his cell and slipped inside, sitting in front of him. He tensed. "What is it?"

I glanced at Asinia, who'd scooted closer, wrapping her hands around the bars between us. A silent support.

"I have a few things to tell you." I held up the lamp, and his face came into view.

And there were those eyes, the same strange color as mine. I'd never paid attention—never seen his eyes in the light. A tear slipped down my cheek.

Demos scowled. "No crying in the dungeon. It's a rule. You know that."

I let out a choked laugh, placing the lantern on the ground between us.

"That's better."

"I met a woman today. She told me...she told me we're related."

He stiffened. "You and me?"

"She said she was my nanny. When I was small." I hadn't realized I was so afraid of his rejection, but I forced myself to keep talking. "I guess she was yours too."

The blood slowly drained from his face, until it was as if I was staring at a corpse. "You have time magic, don't you? That's how you get down here. That makes you…"

"Your sister." The words came out strangled, my hands shaking as I removed my necklace. Demos was already picking up the lantern and bringing it close to my face.

"Nelayra. Oh gods."

My throat tightened, and I attempted a smile. "Um. I think I'll still use Prisca, if it's all the same—"

He placed the lantern down, and then I was in his arms. More tears welled, but his body shook in a way that told me he'd broken his own rule about crying.

When he let me go, both of our faces were wet. "You really stink," I mumbled, and he laughed.

"Wait, so you have *two* brothers now?" Asinia let out a choked sound that might've been a laugh.

Demos went still, his eyes turning cold. "She has *one*. Those people *stole* her."

I took a deep breath. "Tibris had nothing to do with that. He's my brother too."

Demos's jaw tightened, but he let it go. "How is this possible?"

I filled him in. When I reached the part where Mama had pushed me into the river, he got to his feet to pace.

"She said she was saving my life. She died that day, Demos." My loyalty to Mama remained, even as I ached to ease his pain.

He whirled on me with a snarl. I held up a hand. "Be

careful what you say about her. She's still my mother."

"No, she's not. Our mother *died* because we were looking for you that night instead of paying attention to the people who warned the fae prince had been spotted outside our city walls. Instead of preparing to flee, our parents were searching every foot-span of that city, desperate to find you."

The words echoed between us. A deep ache spread through me, settling behind my ribs. "Our mother is... dead?"

A small flame of hope—one I hadn't wanted to admit that I'd felt—went out.

"Nice work," Asinia muttered. "What a kind way to tell a woman both of her mothers are dead."

"The woman who stole her wasn't her mother," Demos hissed.

I got to my feet. Even after everything Mama had done, I couldn't bear to hear her disparaged. Not when I knew she'd died protecting me.

I was allowed to rail against her for what she'd done. But I couldn't bear to hear anyone else do the same. Not yet. Not while her death was so fresh.

"Wait. Don't leave. I'm sorry." Demos caught my hand. "I'm just... Fuck, I never expected to meet you. I'd convinced myself you were dead. Hoped for it sometimes, because there is rarely a happy ending when tiny girl children are stolen. And now you're here, and you're alive, and..."

"I understand." Taking a deep breath, I attempted to

prepare myself for the answer to my next question. "Um, our father. Is he…?"

Demos's mouth thinned. "I don't know. I watched our mother die that day. She'd refused to leave, certain she would find you. And she'd run back into our house when it collapsed. She didn't even use her power—I think she was out of her mind with terror and grief. She pushed me toward Father and insisted she needed to check the cupboards one last time. That maybe you were scared and hiding."

My eyes filled with tears. In reality, I'd been out of the city. Why couldn't Mama have left them a note, letting them know I was safe? Would they be alive then?

"And…Father?"

He swallowed, glancing down at his hands. "When the house collapsed, he fell to his knees. It was like he was unable to move. They loved each other so much, Nelayra—uh, Prisca. So much that if not for me, I think he would have climbed into that burning pile of rubble and lay down beside her." Demos looked away. "One of the neighbors pulled him to his feet. I remember her screaming that he still had one child to keep safe. She died moments later. A block of stone fell on her."

Gods, the things he had seen at just six winters old.

"We were almost at the city walls when Father went down. I don't know what happened. Someone said the fae were shooting arrows. We were separated, and one of our neighbors grabbed me. She raised me with some of the other orphan children, until I was old enough to fall in with the rebellion. Two years ago, our headquarters were raided. Everyone who was arrested was burned months later. Everyone but me. I don't understand why."

"Telean works for the queen. She was spared because the queen had heard of her skill with fabric. When she learned you'd been arrested, she begged the queen to allow you to live. That's why you're still here."

"Telean." Demos went quiet.

We both sat in silence for a while.

Eventually, I sighed. "I better get back."

Demos looked at me some more. "I just... I can't believe it. Be patient with me...please."

"I will. And I'll ask the same of you."

My mind whirled as I made my way out of the dungeon. I needed to talk to Tibris. And then, unfortunately, I would need to find Lorian.

Thankfully, Lorian's hunting trip with the king had taken him away from both the castle and Telean. But I'd recognized that cold expression he'd worn when he'd learned of the threat to me, and I needed to make sure he didn't get any ideas about killing her. My stomach tightened at the thought of seeing the bane of my existence. After the way we'd lashed out at each other last night, I'd prefer to avoid him until I absolutely had to deal with him.

Tibris met me on my way to my room. He raised his eyebrow at whatever he saw on my face.

"You look...strange."

I linked my arm through his. "Strange?"

"Your eyes are all swollen, but you also look happy.

What's going on, Pris?"

Yanking on the thread of time, I pulled Tibris into my room.

"You may want to sit down," I told him, pacing to the window.

"You're making me nervous."

"It's nothing bad. It's good. At least, I hope you think so…"

"Pris."

"My other brother. My birth brother. He's alive."

I turned back just in time to catch Tibris's mouth fall open. "How do you know this?"

I told him about Telean. And when I got to the part about Demos, Tibris launched to his feet.

"*He's* your brother? Are you sure?"

I let out a strained laugh. "Yes. I'm positive. Are you…are you okay?"

Tibris sighed, stalked over to me, and wrapped me in a hug. "Of course I'm okay. I'd rather your brother was alive than dead, even if it means I'll have to deal with Demos for the rest of my life."

I squeezed him back. "Thank you. I know this has been…difficult."

"Stop worrying about me."

"That would be impossible."

"I have to get back to work." He stepped back. "I guess I need to talk to your other brother at some point. And that's a sentence I'd never imagined I'd say." He grinned, and if there was a hint of strain in it, I ignored it since he clearly wanted me to.

Tibris strolled out, and I sat on the edge of my bed for a long moment. Finally, I couldn't put it off any longer, and I took the servants' halls toward Lorian's room, nodding to the maids—most of whom ignored me. Auria grinned at me, a load of laundry in her arms. "Tea tonight?"

I nodded. "After the dancing." Just the thought of pretending everything was normal made me exhausted. All I wanted to do was curl up in bed with the blankets over my head.

She smiled and strolled away.

Just a few moments later, I realized I'd gotten myself lost in the servants' hall.

Usually when I snuck into Lorian's rooms, I wandered through the main hall, stopped time for a few moments, and let myself in.

Grinding my teeth, I leaned close to the door on the left. I was relatively sure the *prince* was in one of these rooms—some of the most ostentatious in the castle.

I glanced over my shoulder, but no one else was walking down the hall. Someone was talking. No, ranting. Pressing my eye to the tiny hole, I went still.

Patriarch Farrow was pacing, spittle flying from his face as he ranted.

I caught the words "corrupt" and "burn." So, it was his usual topic of choice. But it was Madinia I paid the most attention to. She sat on a sofa facing me.

Her face was as white as death.

"Father…what if the corrupt could be…reintegrated

into society? We could give them a chance to give back their magic and appease the gods."

I sucked in a breath, almost choking on it. Now *that* hadn't been something I'd expected to hear from her.

Someone was coming. I stalked across the hall and held my hand to the closest door, as if about to knock.

The maid ignored me and continued walking. I shifted on my feet until she was out of sight.

Launching myself back across the hall, I pressed myself to the door once more.

Farrow was losing control.

"How could you say such a thing? Did you forget those demons killed *your mother?*" He threw his cup of wine across the room, and Madinia flinched.

For the first time, I felt almost…sorry for her.

It didn't excuse her awful behavior, but—

Her hand lit up. With fire.

A ringing sounded in my ears. She wasn't yet twenty-five winters. Which meant…

Madinia was a hybrid.

Her father whirled, a choked sound escaping his throat.

Oh gods.

Madinia looked at her father.

And then she looked at her hand.

Something that might have been resignation flickered in her eyes.

She pressed her hand to her dress.

I'd frozen time before I realized I'd pulled the magic

to me. Shoving wildly at the door, I slammed it behind me, launching myself across the room to a vase of flowers.

I began pouring, but I hadn't grabbed enough of the thread of my magic. I'd acted purely on fear.

Time resumed.

Madinia let out a scream. Farrow roared.

I dumped the entire vase on Madinia's dress, flowers included.

The fire went out. Our eyes met, and hers were bleak.

I'd just killed us both.

My throat tightened. Madinia had decided to burn on her own terms. And I'd saved her life just in time to end up caught in her father's net myself. I'd sacrificed three hundred lives for this impulsive decision.

Turning, I watched Farrow. He was gasping for breath, his face red.

I had nothing left to lose. "Get a hold of yourself before you drop dead," I snapped.

He gaped at me, clearly unused to anyone speaking to him with anything less than fawning respect.

"Corrupt," he said.

"That's right."

I flicked a glance at Madinia. She was staring at me like she'd never seen me before. I paid close attention to her, just in case she got any interesting ideas about burning herself alive again.

Farrow turned his gaze on Madinia, and this time, his eyes filled with tears.

"How? Gods, how? How did I miss such a thing?"

I stared at him. Was he seriously asking that? "Maybe because of your determination to wipe out anyone you considered unclean."

"Silence," he snarled. He stared at Madinia as if he was already mourning her. "I don't…understand."

Since Madinia didn't seem able to speak, I shook my head. "It's simple. The woman you claimed to love? Madinia's mother? The one whose name you insist on throwing around when you burn hybrids? *She* was one of the so-called corrupt."

Madinia stiffened, and I shook my head at her. "Surely it must have occurred to you."

"I… The gods…"

"The gods have nothing to do with this." I didn't have time to make the truth easier to swallow. "The king takes our magic because he wants it for himself. And because he thinks it will allow him to kill all the fae."

Madinia took a step closer to her father. And her eyes burned with retribution.

"Is this true?"

Farrow swallowed. "The king's intentions were good at the beginning."

So, he *had* known the truth. I smiled a nasty smile. "At the beginning? Four hundred years ago, when he started a war with the fae?"

Farrow narrowed his eyes at me. "And just how do you know *that* information, hmm?"

If I hadn't known what his power was, I would have stopped time at the vicious look in his eyes. But Farrow had no combat magic. No, his magic allowed him to strategize much better than the average person. It was why he was in charge of the guards at the city walls. And why it was so difficult to sneak in—or out—of the city.

"You're saying the king is immortal?" Madinia gave me her usual haughty expression. I simply raised my eyebrow.

"Just one of the reasons he takes his subjects' power. To keep himself alive." My voice was bitter.

Madinia stared at me. Then her gaze was on her father. "Tell me she's lying."

Farrow couldn't.

"Who else knows this?" I asked. I wanted to know just how many people were aware of the truth—how many the king had convinced to lie for him. How many people were not just dangerous, but were hypocrites too.

He was silent. Madinia's hand lit up with fire once more. From the horror in her eyes, she hadn't meant for that to happen. Farrow stared at her, his expression tight.

"You would hurt me?"

"You would see me *burn*," Madinia hissed, and the fire burned brighter.

If she burned him here, we would both be arrested and executed immediately after. "Pull yourself together," I advised her.

"Only the king's inner circle know," Farrow said finally. "Five other men."

"Does his queen know as well?" I asked.

"I don't know."

Madinia was crying silently, tears dripping down her face. Unsurprisingly, she still looked beautiful. For the first time, I pitied her.

"We'll get you out somehow," Farrow said.

Madinia's breath hitched. She hadn't expected that. Neither had I. But I should've.

"Ah," I said, my mouth curving. "What was it you said just yesterday about the corrupt and how you were looking forward to seeing them all imprisoned and burned?"

His mouth twisted, but he was wise enough to stay quiet. Next to me, Madinia's silent tears turned to sobs.

I couldn't help but continue. I was so sick of these royals and these courtiers, with their evil and their hypocrisy. "It's different, though, isn't it—when it's your own? People like you are so quick to steal the freedoms—even the lives—of others, according to their own morality. But also so, so quick to change your minds when those same laws apply to the ones *you* love. Why is that, do you think?"

"Please," he said, and my brow lifted. No, I hadn't expected him to beg either. "You are close to the queen, and I've seen you talking to the Gromalian prince. You can get her out."

"And why would I do that?"

"I would owe you a life debt. To be used whenever you like."

Was I dreaming? This man whom I'd fantasized about murdering was going to be in my debt. Perhaps this was why Lorian made so many deals. It was heady, having the upper hand in one of those bargains for once.

"One condition."

Hope sparked in his eyes. For all his contempt, he still had a weakness.

"Anything."

"Repeat after me. I am weak. And I am also a hypocrite."

"Enough, Setella," Madinia said.

I ignored that. Farrow swallowed, some of the color coming back to his face. But he dutifully repeated my words.

Grim satisfaction swept through me.

"Fine," I said. "Let's talk about how you're going to help me get your daughter, and all of the other hybrids, out of this castle."

He sighed and sat, waving his hand for me to tell him what we needed. In the end, there was only one way he could help—we would be getting prisoners out through the tunnel, and they would need transportation from the market out of the city. Farrow would order the guards to allow the carriages, horses, and wagons through the city gates. And while those guards were loyal to him, we would likely have just a few minutes at most before at least one of them would question the order.

"I'll be in touch." My eyes met Madinia's. She looked drained, but for the first time, she wasn't looking at me with vitriol. "Why did you follow me that day in the slums?"

Her eyes widened. "No wonder you disappeared. You knew I was there. I've been watching you since you arrived. I knew you were up to something."

"And what were you planning to do with that information?"

"I'm corrupt," she said hoarsely. "If you knew a way out, I would have blackmailed you until you got me out too."

I couldn't blame her. I would have done the exact same thing. I got to my feet.

"I want to help," Madinia said. "With whatever plan you're making."

Even knowing her life was at risk, I still didn't trust her. "I'll think about it."

It turned out Lorian's door was two down on the left. I took a moment to lean against the wall outside his room. If I hadn't gotten hopelessly lost, Madinia would be little more than a pile of ash right now. And if Farrow hadn't loved his daughter more than the king, we'd both be in the dungeon, waiting to burn.

The thought made me sway on my feet.

I knocked on Lorian's door, and he instantly opened it. Had he known I was here?

He stepped aside, allowing me into his rooms, and I paced to the window.

If I didn't know Lorian as well as I did now, I would have thought that was wariness in his gaze.

"What is it?" he asked, turning to pour himself a drink.

I opened my mouth, and it all came spilling out. The seamstress—my aunt, Demos, and of course, everything that had just happened with Patriarch Farrow.

"What happened with your magic?"

"I don't know. I reacted too fast or something."

He raised his eyebrow at me. "That's not how it works."

Whatever I had done, I'd nearly gotten myself killed. I shuddered. I needed to figure out what had gone wrong. So I never did it again.

Lorian stared down into his drink, obviously coming to terms with all that I told him.

"Your nanny."

"Apparently we called her 'aunt.'"

I could see him weighing what that would mean. I didn't think I needed to be clear on this part, but with murderous mercenaries, it was best to be safe. "Don't kill her."

Lorian rolled his eyes. It was such a strange gesture from him, I almost laughed.

Instead, I leveled him with my best hard stare. "I want your word."

"I give you my word I won't kill your aunt. Unless she actively gets in my way."

I opened my mouth at that, but he was already moving on to the next topic.

"The queen's lady tried to set herself on fire?"

"Yes."

He sipped at his drink. Then he gave me a brooding

look. "The coward's way out."

I blinked. "She was going to die on her terms. And prevent her death from being a spectacle."

"What would you have done if she were sent to burn?"

"I would've attempted to get her out," I admitted.

He nodded, his gaze steady on mine. "And she didn't know that."

"Of course not. We're not exactly friends." I knew he had a point somewhere, but I just couldn't see it.

"Precisely. Even when things look as hopeless as they've ever been, you never give up. No matter how much pain you're in. You never remove any chance at *life*. Because you never know when something could change. Something you never even expected."

Madinia's distraught expression flashed in front of my eyes. "Sometimes you do whatever you can to stop the pain."

"Sometimes you just need to hold on a little longer and the pain will be over. And you'll be alive." He put his drink down and took a step closer. "Don't you *ever* make that choice."

"Lorian—"

"Promise me." His expression was intent.

This seemed to matter to him. I took a deep breath. "I promise."

Thankfully, he appeared ready to change the subject. He turned and paced away. "You're sure Farrow will help us?"

The fact that he said *us* made me feel slightly better about the situation. Especially after last night.

"Yes. He loves his daughter. He'll betray the king to keep her alive."

Lorian paused, clearly thinking over our options. Finally, he sighed.

"I'm looking for an amulet. It's a blue stone set in silver with ancient writing etched into the back. That's why I'm here."

"You thought it would be in the king's chamber."

"Yes. I'm positive it's in this castle somewhere. I've searched the libraries, Sabium's chambers, and anywhere else it's rumored to be."

"Why can't you kill the king?"

He raised one eyebrow. "Vicious thing."

I scowled at him, and he flicked his gaze over me, lingering on my mouth. "It wasn't an insult. I *like* it." My stomach flipped, and I attempted to keep my expression bored. Thankfully, he continued his thought. "I can't kill the king yet because I have other plans in motion, and if he were to die early, I wouldn't be able to finish my tasks."

"Because that's not mysterious at all. Are you ever going to tell me who you are?" He wasn't a prince. I knew that much. What I didn't know was how he'd managed to convince the royals that he was.

One side of his mouth kicked up. "Yes. But not today."

"Why not?"

Silence.

I sighed. "I'll help you look for your amulet. If you help me with the prisoners."

He studied me. "What's your plan, Prisca?"

"Vicer said if we can get the prisoners out through the tunnel from the dungeon, he can have rebels meet us at the market. Vicer has been finding any mode of transportation that he can, so we can get the prisoners from the market to the city walls. If Farrow is serious about saving his daughter's life, the guards will receive an order to stand down—just long enough for the rebels to get out. Farrow is respected enough that they'll do what he says—at least for the few minutes we need."

"The hybrids will be hunted." His expression was blank, giving me no hint of what he thought about that strategy.

"Yes. But at least they'll have a chance. They're weakened, but they'll travel in groups. Those who can't make a long journey will be smuggled into various parts of the city—Vicer will help there. We're hoping to find someone who can help with the blue marks. Besides, once they've been free for a few days, many of them will be able to use their powers again. They'll fight to stay free."

"And you?" His voice was quieter. Almost intimate.

I hadn't yet thought about my next move. "I don't know. We have to tell people that Sabium is the one who started the war with the fae. And that he's the reason it continues."

"No one will believe you until you have irrefutable

proof. Even then, many will choose to ignore the facts."

"Why?"

A languid shrug. "Their ancestors sent their sons to that war. Their brothers. Their cousins. All for them to die for the king's greed. To believe it was all for nothing... Most people would prefer to never know the truth."

Bitterness flooded my mouth. Because he was right. "How is Sabium storing the power? The chamber we saw only had a few stones in it, compared to how large this kingdom is. He must have a way to leach the power from those stones and use it himself."

"He does. But it's not in this castle. We've had those stones followed time and time again when they're moved from the villages. Each time, the priestess disappears in various places."

"He can't be siphoning the power stone by stone." It would take too long. This was a large kingdom.

Lorian nodded. "He's using some kind of magical artifact or device."

"If we were to destroy it, would the power return to the people it belongs to?"

"I don't know." Lorian frowned. "I would like to think so, but it could be that the power goes to the person closest to it."

My dreams of breaking open the king's hidden cache of power, while knowing all the villagers in this kingdom would be getting what was rightfully theirs...

Those dreams turned to dust.

I nodded, moving toward the door.

Obviously, we weren't going to talk about the vicious words we'd said to each other last night. Suddenly, I felt bone-tired. A deep exhaustion that was all-encompassing.

"Prisca."

I glanced over my shoulder. Lorian watched me out of those dark green eyes. He snapped his mouth closed.

With a sigh, I opened the door and walked out.

24
PRISCA

The queen insisted on eating lunch outside. We would have been freezing if not for one of her servants who had the power of flame. He used his magic to create large fireballs that surrounded our table, radiating heat.

I carefully kept my gaze away from Madinia, who sat across from me, miserable and pale. Lisveth had been forced to sit next to her when Caraceli insisted on sitting next to me. Dread lay in my stomach like a heavy stone.

Lisveth had given me a wide-eyed look as Caraceli hissed insults at me. The woman had taken to drinking more each night, until even the queen had noticed. Today, Caraceli had already had several cups of wine at lunch.

The queen ate quietly, murmuring to Alcandre. A few minutes into the meal, she got to her feet, ignoring the servant who used his power to pull her chair aside. "I have a headache," she murmured. "I will see you all tonight at the ball."

She walked away, and I focused on the stew, bread, fruit, and pastries in front of me. I wished I could haul all of this food down to the dungeons.

"I received a messenger from Katina last night," Caraceli slurred. "Do you know what she said?"

The table had gone quiet. "What did she say?" Pelopia asked disinterestedly, poking at her meat.

"She said there was no illness, no death in her family. Her father never sent the message that made her return home. And yet the handwriting is identical to his own." Something cold wormed through my chest.

That was exactly how I'd arranged to lure Katina home.

I wasn't sure exactly how Vicer had done it–I didn't think replication magic would work since the note hadn't existed before we created it. But Caraceli was getting far too close to the truth.

"Her father is sure he didn't send it?" Lisveth had a puzzled look on her face.

"Yes. You know what I think?" Caraceli raised her cup, drinking deep. "I think someone lured Katina back to her village so there would be a spot for *Setella*."

I forced myself to raise my eyebrows, my tone mildly amused. "You think I somehow arranged for a woman I've never met to be lured home so I could save the queen's life and spend my days dealing with you?"

Alcandre burst out laughing. Caraceli flushed. A part of me felt bad for making her doubt what her intuition and evidence had put together. But lives depended on my having access to the entire castle. Caraceli was close to becoming a threat.

Stumbling across Patriarch Farrow and Madinia had proven that.

"I *know* you can't be trusted," Caraceli snarled.

Across the table, Madinia let out a mocking laugh. "Obviously, when Katina left, she took your ability to reason with her. You're disgracing yourself, and don't think the queen hasn't noticed. If you're not careful, you'll be her *fire girl* once more."

Caraceli went stark-white. Madinia kept her gaze on her until she lowered her head, focusing on her food. My relief was tinged with disquiet. It was only a matter of time before Caraceli began taking her suspicions elsewhere.

I swallowed. Madinia met my eyes with a tiny nod. It was strange colluding with her.

"We need to get ready for the ball," Madinia said.

I frowned. "It doesn't begin for hours."

She gave me a disdainful look. "Unless you want to have half the court gossiping because you look like you belong in one of the northern villages, you'll need every second of those hours."

I *did* belong in one of the northern villages.

Madinia's gaze slid over my shoulder. "And look, your maids are here to collect you. Obviously, they feel the same." She nodded at Daselis, who bowed her head.

I'd rather be in my room being ordered about by Daselis than dealing with Caraceli. Getting to my feet,

I nodded to the others and followed Daselis back to my rooms.

As usual, she was silent. Erea smiled at me, gesturing at the lavender dress lying on my bed. "The seamstress was right. It's a risky color, but it will draw attention."

"I don't want to draw attention." My current circumstances felt as fragile as fine crystal. All it would take was the wrong kind of attention from the wrong person, and that crystal would shatter.

"The good kind of attention," she said hurriedly.

I felt like I'd kicked a kitten. "Thank you."

"Bath," Daselis said. "Do you need help washing your hair?"

"No. I can do it."

I got in and began washing. Daselis stuck her head in and glowered at me when I didn't move fast enough for her liking.

As soon as I'd washed my hair, I got out of the tub and dried off, squeezing my hair with the bath sheet. Erea handed me a robe and gestured for me to sit at the vanity. If she noticed the tiny line of light hair at my scalp, she didn't comment.

She chattered about the ball while I nodded occasionally, my mind on Thol. I'd been careful to stay away from him, as the color had been slowly fading from my hair. In his mind, I was one of the corrupt. And no matter how much he'd liked the village girl he'd known, I was his enemy now.

If we had married one day, and my corrupt status had

become known, would Thol have turned on me?

My stomach churned. I knew that answer. More importantly, if we'd had children who were hybrids, would he have allowed them to be taken to the city? Or would he have fought for them?

Lorian's dark scowl drifted into my mind. The mercenary didn't get involved unnecessarily. But now, I suspected it wasn't because he was cold and unfeeling like I'd once assumed. Now, I wondered if it was because he felt *too* much. If it was because he knew that once someone was under his protection, he would die for them.

I knew Lorian well enough to know that if such a thing ever happened to his family, he would slaughter every guard who attempted to take his wife from him. And he would *never* allow anyone to harm his children.

The idea of him with children should be almost amusing—but instead, it made me…sad. Because it was unlikely Lorian would ever accept the weakness that children would represent. The hole in his defenses. It was possible to keep a spouse at arm's length, but children had a way of burrowing into your heart.

"You're quiet," Erea said cheerfully.

"Sorry. Just thinking." I glanced up to find my hair almost finished. She'd used one of the many magical tools the courtiers had access to, drying my curls while ensuring they kept their shape. She'd left some of them free to tumble over my shoulders, braiding the rest back from my face.

Daselis nodded at Erea. "Nice work. I'll finish here."

Erea smiled at the compliment and stepped aside, moving toward the dress lying on the bed.

"Close your eyes," Daselis ordered.

I complied, keeping them closed as she swept brushes over my face. By the time she was finished, I'd almost been lulled into a doze.

"There," she said, and I heard satisfaction in her voice.

I opened my eyes. Wow.

With the curls falling over my shoulders, I could have looked almost innocent. But Daselis had darkened and lengthened my lashes, adding something shadowy and purple to my eyes so they looked bigger. She'd also applied some color to my cheeks, and my lips were poutier, shimmering in the light.

I was losing track of the different versions of myself I'd discovered so far. But I was no longer that girl stuck in her village, desperate for an answer to her problems.

Now, I found those answers myself.

"Thank you," I said. She merely nodded, gesturing for Erea to bring the dress to me.

They held it for me while I stepped into it, and Daselis handled the row of lavender buttons at the back.

"You look beautiful," Erea sighed.

"Would you…would you like this dress?"

She gaped at me. Even Daselis went still.

"I'm not— What—"

"You said the queen's ladies weren't supposed to wear the same dress to more than one formal occasion." *A stupid rule.* "That means it's unlikely I'll wear it again."

"It was a gift from the queen."

"And now it's a gift from me. Please. It would make me happy for you to take it."

Erea's eyes met mine. That crooked tooth glinted as she smiled. "Thank you, Setella."

I just gazed at myself in the mirror, at the armor these women had helped me don. Armor that would ensure I could pass unnoticed as I listened to drunken conversations and plotted just how I would make these people pay.

"No," I said. "Thank *you.*"

LORIAN

I was in a dark mood that night when I watched Prisca walk into the ballroom. The seamstress...her aunt—and wasn't that a strange thought?—had dressed her in lavender. The gown fell to her feet in layers, each panel almost translucent, offering teasing glimpses of her legs when those layers parted as she walked.

It was daring and different, most of the court wearing dark colors and their best jewels.

Thol watched her, a puzzled look on his face. Did he recognize her? With a frown, he looked away, clearly dismissing the resemblance.

Idiot.

What did it say about me that I'd recognized her across a dining hall the moment I'd seen her again?

She nodded at something one of the other women said, and then she was turning to that fucking blond courtier. *Peiter*.

He took her into his arms, and she smiled up at him.

She looked beautiful—even with her darkened hair and eyes. She also looked tired, almost fragile, and I clamped down on the urge to haul her over my shoulder, dump her on my bed, and order her to sleep.

She would likely attempt to gut me.

My mouth curved.

"I've been thinking," Marth said.

He was watching Prisca in a way that made me want to tear out his throat. I somehow managed not to snarl at him.

"You've been thinking?" I prompted.

His face paled at whatever he saw in my eyes, but he stuck out his chin, turning his attention back to Prisca.

"I think you're afraid."

Insult flashed through me, but I kept my voice neutral. "Afraid?"

His skin was almost bloodless now, but he continued talking. "She's the first woman you've felt anything for since—"

"Careful."

He took a deep breath. "*And* she's the same woman you left to die. Now you're pushing her away because, deep down, you know it will be worse when she eventually sees who you really are. And hates you still."

I angled my head. "You're becoming surprisingly perceptive, Marth."

He shivered and took a step away from me.

I had many reasons I'd attempted to stay away from the little wildcat. Among those was the fact that I was as different from these courtiers—and from her village boy—as night was from day. My affections were dark, possessive, all-consuming.

Sabium began his speech, spewing his usual poison. Thankfully, it was shorter than usual, and I politely clapped with everyone else as the music began once more.

Rythos appeared at my shoulder. He'd been staying out of sight, but he leaned close. "There's something wrong with Prisca."

I went still. Wrath rose inside me, a beast that howled for vengeance.

The world narrowed, until all I could see was Prisca, weaving across the dance floor toward the wall. Fear flickered in her eyes, and she stumbled.

"Lorian," Rythos hissed, but I was already moving.

My arms came around her as her knees almost buckled. "Too much wine?"

I knew the answer before she managed to lift her head, her gaze clouded. "You. I know you."

A chill began in my stomach and radiated outward. "Prisca. You've been poisoned. I need you to do exactly what I say."

She tugged weakly at my grip. "Let go."

"No. You're going to walk toward that door over there. Can you do that?"

"Gold door."

"That's right. The gold door."

"Pretty."

My pulse thudded as the color began to drain from her face. She stumbled, and fear plunged into my chest, as sharp as my sword. Whatever she had been given was fast-acting. I had to get a healer to her before she collapsed.

"Prisca, listen." I was trembling, I realized. Shaking more than the woman in my arms. My every instinct told me to carry her away from here. But Sabium was already frowning at me, clearly wondering why I was taking the time to dance with a woman so far below my station.

Sending him a wicked smile, I waited until realization crossed his face. Let him think I'd decided to bed one of the queen's women. A woman who was clearly incapacitated.

The king smirked, his gaze drifting away, and I let out a long breath. There was no way Prisca could walk alone. She could barely stand. We would both have to deal with the rumors and interest.

Wrapping my arm around her shoulders, I turned and escorted her off the dance floor, ensuring my expression showed nothing more than bored amusement.

Not a single person stepped in front of me to ask what I was doing steering a clearly drunk woman away from the ball. Most of them smirked, turning to whisper to their friends—already creating vicious gossip.

Rythos fell into step next to me, his expression serious, eyes hard. Courtiers glanced at his face and away, and we suddenly had a clear path to the door.

"You're being remarkably well controlled," he murmured.

I glanced at him, and he stiffened. "Fuck. Keep your head down."

Turning my attention back to Prisca, I allowed Rythos to lead the way.

"What happened to her?" a feminine voice asked.

I recognized this woman. This was Farrow's daughter. The hybrid who was now beholden to Prisca. Our first piece of luck.

"We need to get her to her room," Rythos said.

She gave me a cool look. "I'll take her."

I showed her my teeth. Rythos elbowed me.

"She's unwell," he said carefully. "We will escort her."

"I'm not letting you take her alone."

"Come with us, then," Rythos gritted out.

I was already turning, guiding Prisca up the steps. She stumbled again, almost going down, and Rythos took her other arm, until we were practically carrying her between us.

As soon as we were far enough from the ballroom to avoid most of the curious eyes, I hauled Prisca into my arms, striding faster.

"Get a healer," I ordered Rythos. "One of ours."

Our eyes met and he nodded. He knew exactly who to find.

"Why would she need a healer?" The woman puffed behind us, her shorter legs and heavy gown making it difficult for her to keep up.

Ignoring her, I glanced down the corridor. "Which room is hers?"

No one could know just how much I knew about this woman.

"That one," the woman pointed. She opened the door, and I strode inside, laying Prisca on the bed. Her breathing had turned thready, her skin almost gray. She shivered occasionally, and her lips had already taken on a blue tinge. Dread expanded through my veins, tinged with a kind of brutal helplessness I hadn't felt in a long, long time.

"You can leave now," the woman said.

My gaze met hers, and she flinched at whatever she saw in my eyes. "Get away from her," she hissed.

"What is your name?"

"Madinia."

"Madinia, look at her."

The woman complied, and her eyes widened.

"Poison."

"Yes. You need to leave."

She immediately shook her head. "I'll inform the queen."

My dagger was nestled against her throat before I was aware I'd moved. "Say anything of this, and you'll *wish* for a death as kind as poison."

She shuddered, but to her credit, she met my gaze. "You're not the prince. Who are you?"

I just smiled. She stared at me. "I won't say anything."

"Good. Leave."

Her breath hitched, and I reached for patience I didn't have. "You'll be noticed missing. We'll take good care of her."

She frowned. "Please don't let her die."

The thought was intolerable. Ridiculous. Prisca wouldn't die. I wouldn't allow it.

Whatever the woman saw on my face convinced her. She nodded at me. Stepping close to Prisca, she reached for her hand, giving it a squeeze. "Fight. Please."

Whirling, she strode from the room.

Rythos was immediately there, pushing open the door and gesturing for the healer to approach the bed.

He stepped inside and stalked toward the bed, dark eyes narrowed. I'd known the hybrid for years, and yet his existence—and incredible power—was such a secret, no one knew his true name. He was known only as "the healer."

I watched closely, waiting for him to start his work. But he took one look at Prisca and sighed. "Viperbane," he said. "A terrible death."

"Fix her."

He bowed his head. "Impossible. There are some poisons without an antidote. This is one of them. Most people live mere minutes after ingestion. All you can do at this point is gather her family to say their goodbyes."

Fog filled the edges of my vision. I couldn't hear over the sound of the blood thundering in my ears. Someone was hitting my arm, and I slowly turned my head.

"Let him go, Lorian."

I snarled. Rythos's eyes had gone wider than I'd ever seen them. "You're killing him, Lorian. He can't help her if he's dead."

Slowly turning my head, I found my hand wrapped around the healer's throat. It took everything in me to slowly unwrap my fingers until he slumped to the floor, still choking.

I was vaguely aware that I was speaking, and that each word made the healer turn paler. Rythos bowed his head, and even my friend refused to look into my eyes.

The healer turned and hurried to Prisca's side. The room was silent.

"Find her brother," I rasped.

PRISCA

I was in hell. The flames burned me alive until I cried out desperately, begging for it to stop.

Someone was talking in a low, gravelly murmur that both hurt my ears and made me long for the voice to come closer.

There were no words for this kind of agony. Darkness called to me, and I wanted nothing more than to be done with this pain. Done with all of it.

The voice paused, and I ached for it to continue. Somehow, I managed to crack my eyes open to slits. I was on my bed, surrounded by people. Lorian's eyes met mine.

"Dying."

"You're not dying. Don't be dramatic," he snarled.

But the deep line between his eyes told me he lied. I attempted a smile, but my eyes were drifting shut once more.

"Tell my brother...*brothers*..."

"I'll tell them nothing. You die here, Prisca, and I won't tell anyone a single fucking thing."

His hand was cool as it brushed my forehead. What had happened? One minute, I'd been dancing, and the next...

"Poison."

"Yes. But you will fight it."

"So tired."

"I know you're tired. I *know*. But they need you." He leaned closer until his mouth was pressed against my neck, right below my ear. "I need you."

Was I imagining his words? My eyes were shut, but Lorian was close enough that his scent drifted toward me, and I basked in it.

He lifted his head slightly, and I mourned the loss

of his heat. "Those prisoners in the king's dungeon? If you die, they're all dead too. *All* of them. Including your friend and your brother."

My heart twisted. "Save them."

"Never. You hear me? You fight, or *everyone* dies."

My eyes burned. I opened my mouth to beg, to *plead*...

Unconsciousness beckoned.

I opened Demos's door. He was so young, his cheeks rounded. His eyes had a mischievous glint in them, and he gave me a very adult, put-upon look.

"What are you doing?"

"I'm scared."

He sighed. "Come here."

He held out his hand and helped me climb onto his bed.

"What are you scared of?"

"I don't know." Everything. I was scared of the dark, of the sound the tree made when the branches hit my window. Of the shadow that tree cast on my bedroom wall.

"I think Mama and Papa are scared too," Demos said.

They couldn't be scared. They were big.

"They keep whispering." Demos scowled. "And Mama was crying yesterday."

"Crying? Truly?" The thought of Mama crying made my stomach hurt.

Something tapped on the window. The tree.

Demos stiffened. He didn't have a tree outside his

window.

"Nelayra, go get Papa."

I heard fear in Demos's voice. My feet got tangled in my nightgown as I hit the floor. I ran for the door.

Strong arms came around me. I cried out for my parents, for Demos.

"Shh, it's okay, little one. Come with me."

My eyes met Demos's. He was bound to the wall with dark threads of magic. Papa's servant had magic just like that. I'd seen him show Papa one day when I'd been hiding in the crawl space near his office.

Demos was roaring, but the black thread across his mouth muffled the sound. I sucked in a breath to scream for our parents, but something was pressed against my face, and I was suddenly so drowsy...

My eyes were sliding closed. I reached for Demos, but the woman was dragging me toward the window.

The next time I opened my eyes, I was in total darkness. I kicked and writhed, punching out at the fabric. A horse snorted beneath me, and in the distance, I could hear my mother's screams.

"Is she going to be okay?"

I shuddered, still half in my dream where Demos waited for me. The fear and sorrow mixed with the pain in my body until I wished I had the energy to howl.

Was that...Madinia?

"She's strong." That was definitely Tibris. His voice was hoarse, filled with pain, and I attempted to open my eyes, but they were far too heavy.

"Why are you here?" Tibris asked. "You made Prisca's life hell."

"Prisca? Oh, *that's* her real name."

Lorian let out a low, warning growl. "Forget you ever heard it."

There was no "or else." Likely, the dark expression on his face was all the warning Madinia needed.

"I won't tell anyone," Madinia whispered.

"And why should we trust you?" Tibris asked.

"I'm on your side."

"That's likely." Sarcasm dripped from Tibris's voice.

"I'm...corrupt."

"You mean you're a hybrid."

"Yes. That."

"Enough chatter," Lorian said. "You're disturbing her."

"Tyrant," I muttered.

A large hand squeezed my own. "Just stay alive."

ear L,

According to my sources, you recently became quite unhinged when the woman you claim is the bane of your existence almost died. It was said that you threatened a healer with a "long, excruciatingly painful death" and declared that you would kill everyone in the castle until you found whoever had poisoned her.

This kind of behavior is not what we agreed to.

C

Dear C,

Go fuck yourself.

L

PRISCA

I opened my eyes. Lorian's gaze met mine, and then he was standing next to me, shoving pillows under my head until I was sitting up. His eyes were shuttered, but I caught a glimpse of relief.

I could relate. I was alive. My body ached, but the pain had dulled enough that I could think.

Lorian handed me a cup of water. "Drink."

I gulped at it, but my hand trembled so violently, I spilled water over the side. Lorian's expression darkened, and he held the cup for me.

"What happened?"

"You were poisoned."

"I know that much. How long have I been…"

"Fighting death? Two days."

My blood turned to ice. "That means it's only nine days until the Gods Day ball." How could I have lost two whole days? I needed every second. "Who—"

"Poisoned you? One of the queen's ladies. Her name is Caraceli."

I closed my eyes. Lorian took my hand, and I opened my eyes once more, startled by the feel of him. "Don't sleep again. Not yet. Please."

A lump formed in my throat. Despite our complicated relationship, I'd obviously scared him. I didn't know how to feel about that.

"I think that might be the first time I've ever heard you say please. How do you know it was Caraceli?"

He scowled. "She was stupid enough to *brag* about it to one of the other ladies. It got back to the queen."

She'd finally snapped. I'd feel guilty if she hadn't almost killed me. "She has suspicions about me. Correct suspicions."

"She hasn't been interrogated yet. I'll take care of it."

"I don't want her dead."

He dropped my hand. "Your soft heart will be the death of you. It almost was. Did you take a cup from her?"

"I didn't think she would poison me!"

He just shook his head.

"Surely there must be some way to silence her temporarily until this is all over. Please."

He sighed. "I'll think about it."

I raised my hand to his jaw, wanting to feel the scruff along his chin. "You stayed here the whole time?"

He shrugged, glancing away. "Whenever I could. The entire castle is gossiping about our so-called relationship."

I rolled my eyes. "The queen's lady and the handsome prince. Of course they're gossiping."

His gaze returned to my face. "You enjoy the way I look?" His eyes glittered, and for a wild moment, I wanted to pluck them from his face.

My cheeks burned. "Yes, yes, your face is very symmetrical. An incredible achievement."

He stared at me. Then he threw back his head with a

laugh. The sound was the best thing I'd ever heard.

"You could convince the gods they were little more than peasants with that sharp tongue of yours."

"You stayed here with me all that time? What about Pelopia?"

He sent me an affronted look. "You were dying."

"I suppose I should feel flattered."

"Oh, how you wound me. I would rather be holding your head over a bucket than whispering sweet nothings to any of the ladies in this court."

The visual was so disgusting, I curled my lip. Lorian and I stared at each other. His mouth twitched.

I couldn't help it. I dissolved into laughter. Lorian chuckled.

"I'm glad you're having so much fun," Rythos's voice came from the doorway. He grinned at me. "You look much better than you did two nights ago."

I grinned back at him, delighted. "From what I hear, it would've been difficult to look worse."

"You made Lorian laugh," Rythos said. "That's a greater miracle than surviving viperbane."

"What are you doing here?"

All amusement had left Lorian's face. I reached out and took his hand. He stiffened but allowed it.

"I'm not supposed to be here, which is why Lorian looks like he's ready to gut me. But I wanted to see for myself that you were okay."

"I missed you."

Rythos grinned. "Missed you too, darlin'."

"Out," Lorian rumbled.

Rythos winked at me and disappeared.

Lorian and I looked at each other. Something had changed between us. But I couldn't put that change into words.

"I really need to, um…"

He raised one eyebrow, clearly delighted with my mortification. "Say it, Prisca. You need to what?"

"Forget it."

I swung my legs over the bed and immediately regretted it. My head felt like it was about to explode.

"You need to rest." Lorian didn't look amused anymore. He plucked me from the bed, carried me to the bathing room, and insisted on standing outside the door.

"Shouldn't the maids be in here helping me?" I muttered when he hauled me back to the bed.

"They scattered when I roared at them," Lorian said. "They haven't been back since."

I sighed. Since I had him alone and we had a few minutes, perhaps it was a good time to clear the air. "We should talk about the other night. About…Thol."

His face went blank, and he placed me on the bed and then drew away.

"Don't do that. You can't be by my side when I almost die and then push me away again."

"You want to know what happened?" Lorian caught my chin in his hand. "You looked so fucking beautiful, dancing with that piece-of-shit courtier. And all I wanted to do was rip your dress off you and press you up against the closest wall. I thought I knew what jealousy was, and then you saw *him*. The man you've always wanted. The man you'd choose if you had your way. And I almost slaughtered him right there."

My heart tripped, fluttering in my chest, and awareness burst through me. I'd mocked Lorian about being jealous, but here he was, in the light of day, admitting to it.

That muscle ticked in his cheek. I should probably say something. I managed to close my mouth. "I wanted to rip Pelopia's hair out," I admitted.

He gave me a slow, feline grin. And then his mouth was on mine, and all thought fled.

"I want to make you scream for me." His mouth traveled up my neck, and he caught my lobe between his teeth. "But you're too weak right now."

"I disagree."

He pulled back and gave me a look. "When you can walk to the bathing room by yourself, then we'll talk. But, wildcat..." He leaned close once more. "When I finally get you in my bed, I'm not stopping until you forget your own name."

I was speechless for long enough that his mouth curved in a faint smile, and he turned away to pick up something from my nightstand.

I gaped at the sweet fruit. "*You're* the one who has been leaving me valeo?"

He gave a sharp nod. If I didn't know better, I'd think Lorian looked...uncomfortable.

"But how did you— Marth."

He nodded. He was already backing away. Marth had likely informed him about my reaction to the valeo I'd found in the hunter's belongings. When he looked into my past.

"Lorian. Thank you."

His nostrils flared, and laughter bubbled in my chest. This man could take any insult I hissed at him, but the moment I showed gratitude, he looked like I'd run him through with his own sword.

"I need to go before anyone begins to question what I'm doing here." His gaze dropped to my mouth. "Get some rest."

My core clenched at the promise in his eyes.

And then he was gone.

Dear L,

I do hope you're feeling more yourself after your last letter. Please update me on the current situation. Is it true that the woman has the power of time?

C

Dear C,

I'm taking the wildcat with me when we leave. She

won't be pleased by this, so I'm afraid you're unlikely to meet her at her best—although, you've always enjoyed seeing me with my hands full.

And I have no doubt that she will make me pay.

Yes, she has the power of time. And has even kept me frozen for several moments.

Everything else is going according to plan. Apart from the fact that I still can't find what we're looking for.

L

PRISCA

I spent most of the next two days in bed through no choice of my own. The one bright spot was that Tibris had told me Thol and his father had left the castle. I wouldn't need to focus on avoiding them. Each night, I stumbled down to the kitchen, loaded up a sack of food, and hauled it down the dungeon stairs, my limbs shaking. The poison hadn't just impacted my body. It had also made it more difficult to use my magic. It felt as if I was swimming through mud instead of water.

Demos had glowered at me when he'd seen how I trembled.

"What are you doing down here?"

"You all need to eat."

"Where's… Ah, you didn't tell Tibris you were coming down here, because he would have told you no."

I scowled. "Tibris isn't in charge here."

"And he would have been right," Demos continued, ignoring me, "because you almost *died*."

I wasn't surprised he'd heard about that.

"While it's nice to see you and Tibris finally agreeing on something, I'm okay."

I turned to Asinia, who'd been quiet so far. I let myself into her cell, and she wrapped her arms around me. "I would've been really annoyed if you'd died."

I let out a choked laugh. "Same."

"Poison?"

"Yes. This court…" I shook my head. "Vicer warned me, but I think Caraceli couldn't handle the idea that I'd replaced Katina."

"Do you think they're lovers?"

I shrugged. That was an angle I hadn't considered. "I don't know. At the very least, they're best friends."

And I knew just how much a woman would fight for her best friend.

"How come she's not down here?"

"The queen is having her confined to her rooms. Which means she won't be a threat for at least a few days. Lorian also paid her a visit."

Asinia raised her eyebrow. I sighed. "I don't know what he did. He wouldn't tell me. But he convinced her not to speak a word of her suspicions about me. She told the queen she lashed out because she missed Katina. And she thought she might be having some problems with her mind. The queen said she will miss the Gods Day ball as punishment."

"She almost kills you, and her punishment is she misses a *ball*?"

"The queen summoned me to her chambers today. Formally. She said I had the right to ask for Caraceli's death, but she would appreciate if I spared her."

I'd stood in her sitting room, gazing at my reflection in her silver mirror. And I'd agreed. The queen had been elated. She was incredibly fond of Caraceli, although puzzled by her actions.

"And why would you do that?"

"Because if Caraceli knew she was going to die, she would have nothing to lose. There's a chance people would listen to some of her accusations and pay closer attention to my background. And my papers. Besides, all her accusations are correct."

"That doesn't give her the right to poison you!"

"I know. Believe me, I know."

Asinia let it go, taking the bread I handed her. She was still thin but had gained a little weight. So had Demos. According to Tibris, he'd ordered the prisoners down here to eat as much as they could, hounding the hybrids until many of them were pacing their cells for hours each day.

We needed as many of them able to walk as possible.

Demos studied me as I let myself back into his cell.

"You should be—"

"If another male tells me to rest, I'll scream."

He gave me a faint smile. I sat next to him.

"What's wrong?"

Our gazes met, and I almost sucked in a breath at the hopeless rage in his eyes.

"You were dying, and I was stuck down here. Tibris…he let me know."

"He shouldn't have worried you."

"I'm your brother. I have the right to know. I deserve that much."

"You do. I'm sorry."

"It was hell, knowing I might lose you. When I've just found you."

I took his hand. "I had a dream when I was battling the fever. It was about the day I was taken."

He tensed, and my throat thickened. "I want you to know that I remember how you fought for me that day. You were so young. But I know if you could've, you would have gotten to me."

He swallowed, and it was a long moment before he could speak once more. "She took you from us. The woman you called your mother."

"I know." And I was struggling to understand why. Struggling to understand how I could forgive her myself.

My birth father's servant had betrayed him, allowing me to be taken. Using his power to hold Demos back. And then I'd woken in a huge satchel, in the dark.

Now I knew where my fear of small spaces had come from.

"I have a question for you."

"Ask it."

"When we snuck into the city, I used my power. But there was a man who didn't freeze. A man with blond hair. He turned and looked at me…and winked."

Demos closed his eyes briefly with a sigh. "A cousin. Now's not the time to go into *that* family history." He gave my hand a squeeze. "You're not going to be able to help any of us if you don't recover. Go to bed, Prisca. We'll talk soon."

It must be difficult for him to call me Prisca. And yet he did it. For me. I squeezed his hand back. "Look after yourself."

With a whispered "good night" to Asinia, I went in search of Lorian.

He'd been writing something at his desk and didn't look surprised to see me. But he frowned as he took in my shaky legs.

"Sit."

I didn't have it in me to argue, and I slumped on his sofa.

"I know where your amulet is."

Lorian cocked his head in that strange way of his, and his eyes narrowed on my face. "Where?" His voice held no inflection. It was as if he'd turned cold. Emotionless.

"I can get to it. With my power. But you have to help the prisoners get out in return."

He shook his head. "If you think I have the ability to trust *anyone* else with my task, you obviously don't know me at all."

Frustration rose, sharp and swift. It was what I'd expected from him, and yet it was still disappointing. "Yes, yes, you're a tyrant who believes he must always be in control. That's not exactly a secret."

"I could get that information out of you," he said softly.

I raised an eyebrow, although my heart thumped harder in my chest.

"I thought we'd moved past threats of torture," I muttered.

He took a single step closer, and my skin tingled at the look he gave me. Dark, hopelessly amused, dripping with lust. "I wouldn't need to torture you. A few hours in my bed and you'd answer any question I asked."

"How do you bear the weight of such an ego?"

He just smiled. "Not ego. Fact."

My toes curled, even as I fought the urge to growl. "You just ensured I'll never be in your bed."

He gave a low chuckle that made me want to slam my fist into his face. "We both know *that's* not true."

"Take the deal, Lorian. We can do this together."

"You've come a long way with your power, but I swore not to leave this castle until I found what I came for."

"You can trust me."

He was already shaking his head. I let out a low, slow breath and fought for patience. "I would be trusting *you* with everyone I love, Lorian. *Everyone.*"

"I'll consider it."

I blew out a breath. That was all I could hope for. Getting to my feet, I eyed him. He watched me back.

"What is it?"

"You've been in the dungeons." Disapproval dripped from the words.

Spare me from overprotective males. "I…I had a memory when I was sick."

Something feral flickered in his eyes. "When you were *dying*."

"I'm still here. It was from when I was taken. When Mama took me. From my real parents. I needed to see Demos. I can't lose him, Lorian. I can't lose any of them."

My lungs seized, and for a long moment, I couldn't breathe. So many people. And if I made one wrong move, they were all dead.

Lorian grabbed my hand and pulled me close. "If anyone can get them out, it's you."

I blinked. "You really believe that?"

He cocked his eyebrow. "The better question is, why don't you?"

"There are so many things that could go wrong."

"You'll prepare for them."

The way he looked at me sometimes, it made my knees weak. I still didn't understand what was happening between us. I'd imagined I'd always loathe him, but the more I glimpsed the man behind the mercenary, the more I wanted to see.

He was brutal, yes. His solution to most problems was murder. And yet, despite his obvious reluctance, he'd slept next to me that night at the inn when I'd killed the bearded man. He'd worked with me until I could use my magic to defend myself—and I knew it wasn't all just so he could get past the city walls. He was there for me when Wila died. And without his quick thinking and the healer he'd summoned, I would have died from that poison.

"What are you thinking?" His voice was low, intimate.

"Nothing," I said, too quickly.

His lips curved in a slow grin. "Were you thinking about me?"

I squirmed under that look, backing toward the wall. He followed me, until his huge body was caging mine. And I *liked* it.

"Tell me you want me, wildcat."

"Why? So you can mock me for it?"

"Is that what you think I'd do?"

"Maybe."

He leaned closer. "Tell me you want me, so I can tell you how badly I want you too." His gaze dropped to my mouth, and his eyes darkened.

Always with the power games with this man. "Why do I have to say it first?"

He laughed, and my stomach tightened.

"Fine. I want you so badly that I wake up in the middle of the night, a single stroke away from coming. I dream of your face. Especially your mouth. Gods, that smart mouth. You don't want to know the things I've dreamed about doing with your mouth."

My toes curled, my knees weakened, and I fisted his shirt in my hand. "What kinds of things?"

He just gave me a smug, male smile. "Tell me all the ways you want me to touch you, Prisca." His eyes glittered, and I knew if I let him take me to bed, I'd be ruined for any other man.

The trouble was, it would likely be worth it.

I peered up at him. "I'm not good at this kind of thing."

He cocked an eyebrow. "At what kind of thing? Telling men what you want?"

My cheeks heated, and his expression turned oddly... tender. "You've been fucking the wrong men. Those village boys would never have satisfied you."

He cupped my face, and then his mouth was on mine, my back against the wall, and I was moaning, my body saying *more, more, more*. He slid his other hand to my breast, his thumb caressing my nipple, and my thighs clenched.

My hands were scrabbling at him, pulling him closer, *needing* him closer. He slid his hands to my ass, and a desperate groan left my throat as he was suddenly pressed against my stomach, so thick and hard and long.

He ground into me, and I writhed against him, even as his lips swallowed all the tiny noises I was making. Then he was carrying me to the sofa, pressing me into the cushion and pushing my dress up, until he was staring down at me, eyes dark.

"These are...interesting," he breathed, one hand

sliding to the lace band of my undergarments.

I blushed, unable to say a word.

"So this is how I make you quiet." He smirked. I opened my mouth to snap at him, but he was already nibbling on my lower lip, slipping his hand beneath my underwear and along that spot that made my knees weak.

His tongue swept into my mouth, just as one finger slid inside me. I clenched around it, and he let out a rough groan as I pushed his shirt up, desperate to feel his skin. A second finger joined the first while his thumb teased my clit, and pleasure rippled through me. I let out a sound that would likely make my cheeks heat tomorrow.

He raised his head, his eyes on my face. "You like that."

Arrogance dripped from his voice, and I snarled.

He thrust his fingers again and smiled at me. "*I* like *you*," he said, and his voice was filled with something that sounded almost like wonder.

I opened my mouth, but a low moan came out, and Lorian cursed, his voice hoarse.

He pulled off my underwear, and then he was lowering his head in a way that made me squeak.

He just met my eyes, raising one dark eyebrow. I shivered at the sight of him, poised between my legs.

"I—"

He'd already leaned down once more, and I had to clamp my hand over my mouth to stifle the sounds I was making. His mouth was so warm, and he let out a growl as he slowly explored, his tongue teasing until I was panting, *begging* for more.

He lashed his tongue over my clit, and I bucked beneath him. He laughed, and the vibration, combined with his warm breath, almost sent me over. He caught my hips in his hands, holding me in place for him, and I slid my hands into his hair as I arched my neck, desperate, writhing…

"Knew you'd be like this," he growled. He lowered his mouth once again, his fingers thrusting deep as he flicked my clit with his tongue. Then *sucked.*

I shuddered, my pleasure cresting in a wave, until my breath caught and all I could do was gasp, trembling through my release. Lorian continued playing with me, continued that steady thrusting until I was boneless.

"You…" My voice was hoarse.

Did that just happen? While it was difficult to believe I was just that intimate with Lorian, at the same time, it felt strangely…inevitable.

Lorian met my gaze, his cheekbones flushed. Then his gaze swept over me, spread out for him, limp and satisfied, even as my body craved more.

"Yes," he murmured. "*Me.*"

I reached for him, but he was already pulling my dress back down, my underwear disappearing into his pocket.

"What—"

"I need you healthy for the things I want to do to you," he growled. "Now leave, before I can no longer control myself."

I took a shaky breath. The idea of *Lorian*—the man who was always in control—now having to fight for restraint…

"I feel fine."

"Out," he grumbled. I was standing before I realized I'd moved, hauled to my feet by the mercenary who glowered at me.

I couldn't help it. I grinned.

He shoved me out of his room, ignoring my delighted laugh.

26
PRISCA

Auria visited me the next morning, perching on the edge of my bed. "How are you feeling?" She smiled at me, her eyes alight with her usual good humor.

"Ready to get back to work." I almost winced when I said it. Calling my days of following the queen around *work* was an insult when Auria practically broke her back in the laundry.

"I think the queen probably wants you rested. Especially because the Gods Day ball is so close."

Just days away. Blood rushed into my ears at the thought.

"Setella?"

"Sorry, mind wandering."

"I'm glad you're okay."

"Thanks." She was studying me, and I raised one brow. "What is it?"

"The entire castle is talking about you and the prince."

I winced, and she just laughed.

"I'll leave you to rest." She scampered out the door before I could reply.

I spent the rest of the day in bed, visualizing leading over three hundred prisoners out of the king's tunnel only days from now. The tunnel he'd created to put them to death. My body broke out in a cold sweat, and I shuddered beneath my blankets.

By the time it was dark enough to risk going down to the dungeon, I felt more like myself. A little shaky, but ready to help Tibris hand out food. Since Tibris wanted to check Asinia's and Demos's wounds first, I got to work slipping pieces of bread, hunks of meat, and stolen fruit between cage bars.

Laurel held out her hand for her share, angling her head as she watched me.

She was a couple of years younger than me and had told me she thought she'd been here for at least six months. "Why are you doing this? At least when I was iron-crazed, I didn't know how bad this really was."

"Would you rather I didn't?"

She narrowed her eyes at me. "I want out. But…"

I understood. Now, she knew the reality of her situation. And it was grim. When she didn't know what she was missing, she didn't dare hope for more. The iron had kept her weak, dazed, easy for the guards to manage. Now, her eyes burned with retribution.

"Eat," I murmured. "And walk as much as you can. We need you strong."

She nodded, and I finished doling out the last of the food, making my way back toward Asinia.

"Finished sulking?" Tibris asked.

I winced, slowing my steps. That was the tone he most often used when speaking to either Lorian or Demos.

Shuffling sounded, as if someone was sitting down.

"My mental state is none of your business." Demos's voice was so cold, I almost shivered.

"What is your problem?"

Tibris had never been able to leave anything alone. When I was angry as a child, he would poke and prod at me until I exploded. Then he would laugh. Most of the time, his amusement would shake me from my fury. Or at least ensure I trained that fury on him instead.

"My problem?" Demos asked.

"You've found your sister. After all these years."

"She doesn't know me."

"So, spend time with her."

"Easy for you to say. You grew up with her. You got to see her turn from a child into a woman. You were able to be there for her. To protect her. To keep her safe."

My throat tightened, and I stopped walking completely.

"I wasn't able to protect her from the guards. Our mother tried and died for it."

"That woman—"

"I know how you feel about that," Tibris said. "And I can understand why. But *that woman* raised Prisca. She was the one who dried her tears after her nightmares. The one who taught her to hide her power and keep herself safe. My mother may be the villain in your story, but she died to protect our sister."

A long silence followed. Finally, Tibris sighed. "I need to see your shoulder." He let out a humming sound. "It looks good."

I resumed my footsteps, finding Asinia standing in her cage, stretching her legs.

"It's so good to see you moving." She still needed to gain her weight back, but she looked stronger than she had since I'd found her down here. And she practically radiated determination.

"I have to be ready to run if I need to."

I nodded. "I have a question. It's about your... power."

Her mouth curved in a faint smile. "You want to know what I can do."

Tibris and Demos stopped their sniping at that, and I glanced at them. Both of them had turned toward Asinia expectantly.

She rolled her eyes. "If you're hoping for some incredible offensive power, you can keep hoping. My power heightens my precision. I make incredibly neat stitches."

Tibris nodded at that, while Demos continued to watch her. "Precision can mean many things. Let's put a bow in your hand and see if you can let those arrows fly."

She raised one eyebrow. "I tried learning to use a bow when Prisca did. I was almost as bad as her."

"You were suppressing your power then, though, weren't you?" Demos asked.

After a moment, she nodded.

"Worth a try," I said. "As soon as you're free, you need to begin training and see if that precision can be used to aim."

She gave me a cool look, and I realized I was giving her orders. "Sorry."

She just smiled. "It's okay. You know, sometimes I barely recognize you."

I winced, and she reached through the bars and grabbed my hand. "In a good way. Some people break under pressure like this. You're using it to become strong."

I thought of Lorian and all the ways he'd prodded me into doing exactly that. "I'm working on it."

Tibris stepped out of Demos's cage. "We've been down here for a while now. We should go."

I nodded, and I squeezed Asinia's hand. "Not long now."

Glancing at Tibris, I gestured for him to follow me. He frowned but complied, and we walked toward the stone staircase. Hands on my hips, I examined it.

Tibris caught on immediately. "You think this is the tunnel entrance."

I held up my lantern between us. "My source insists it is."

He rolled his eyes at *my source*.

I scowled at him. "I've been down here every night, looking for this entrance. You can dislike Lorian as much as you want—and I can't blame you for any of it—but he helped us with this, Tibris."

"Fine. I guess I can thank him for that at least. I

wouldn't have thought to look here."

"Me neither. He even told me how it works."

"You're not an idiot, Pris. He's playing his own game here. If he gave you any information to help you, it's because it benefits him somehow."

"I know. I've spent more time with him than you have, after all. That doesn't mean we can't benefit from whatever *he's* up to." I circled the stairs and crouched in front of the second step from the bottom. The catch was tiny, created to look like just another crack in the stone. Shoving my finger into that crack, I pressed on the tiny metal latch.

Tibris pulled me off the stairs, and we both watched as a door slid open. Completely silent.

We glanced at each other and stepped into the tunnel.

PRISCA

As usual, I made my way to Lorian's rooms after I left the dungeon. This time, I was feeling exultant. The tunnel had led us all the way out to the main market. Just days from now, every person in the dungeon would be free.

I wanted to thank him. I knew Tibris was right. But Lorian was still helping us save the hybrids' lives.

My power came to me easily tonight, my mind on the mercenary. Lorian had the ability to both calm me and infuriate me. Either way, he was a distraction from the way my skin constantly felt too tight in this place, and I longed to run just to burn off some of the tension that consumed me.

The moment Lorian opened his door, it was evident he was in a filthy mood. He even seemed bigger somehow, like he was done hiding away and pretending to be the prince. It was a good thing no other courtiers were in this room right now.

I opened my mouth, but he was already speaking.

"Tell me where the amulet is."

My heart stuttered at the threat in his eyes. Once Lorian had what he wanted, he would have no reason to work with us to get the prisoners out. And we needed all the help we could get. I forced myself to raise my eyebrow with a smirk. "I don't think so."

"I could *make* you tell me." This time, I didn't think he was talking about the pleasurable kind of torture. I gave him the look that threat deserved.

"And *I* could leave you frozen at any time," I reminded him.

"For now." He smiled, and I barely suppressed a shiver. It was a scary smile.

Lorian had just confirmed all my suspicions. He had power, but I'd never seen it. And somehow, that power was tied to the amulet he wanted me to find. If I gave him that amulet, he could abandon all of us to our fates.

"How do I know you won't just kill everyone?"

"Oh, Prisca," he purred. "I would never kill *you*."

He was trying to unsettle me. Trying to ensure he had the upper hand in these negotiations. Unfortunately, it was working.

The blood pounded in my ears as we stared at each other. Finally, he sighed.

"We will make a blood vow."

My mouth dropped open, and his gaze dropped to my lips. "You've been spending too much time with the fae."

He gave a languid shrug. "They taught me a few things."

I'd heard about fae blood vows. The rumors about them had made it even to our tiny villages. The cost of breaking a blood vow was…death. If I was wrong, and the amulet wasn't where I thought it was, I would die screaming, begging for someone to end my suffering.

But if I was right…

I knew Lorian. If he agreed to get the prisoners to the city walls, that was what he would do. He and the rest of the mercenaries. If I died, it would be because I couldn't find the amulet. That would mean Lorian wouldn't have whatever dark power it would give him. I'd just have to warn Tibris and Vicer about the possibility, without letting them know about the death part. If I didn't appear, they would know to make sure the prisoners fled.

It would mean my life for over three hundred others.

A good deal.

"You look uncertain, wildcat."

"I'm not. We'll make the blood vow."

He studied me. "I will trust you to get the amulet." A flash of what might have been surprise flickered over his face at his own words. "But if you betray me…" His voice turned colder than I'd ever heard it. "None of your prisoners will live unless you give me that amulet."

I stared at him. Sometimes I'd forget who he was, until he reminded me.

He caught my chin in his hand. "Don't look at me like that. *Lives* depend on me."

"So you'd threaten over three hundred innocents?"

He leaned closer. "In. A. Heartbeat."

"Well." I swallowed. "I'm glad to know where we stand. From what I've heard, blood vows can't be broken anyway."

"They can't. But you're sneaky. Cunning. If anyone could betray me, it would be you."

I didn't know if I should feel satisfied or worried about that fact. Especially when it looked like Lorian was shaken by that little admission, and his expression had turned calculating.

"I agree. We'll vow right now," I blurted before he could change his mind.

Anyone with magic could complete a fae blood vow—as long as they'd learned the right steps and the correct incantation.

I swallowed. "You definitely know how to do this, right?"

Lorian just sighed. "Hold out your hand."

In the end, it wasn't as terrifying as I'd imagined. Lorian cut both of our palms, a thin slice that still stung and burned. He clasped our hands together, murmured a few words in a language I didn't know, then told me to repeat those words.

"I'm not vowing to anything I don't understand."

He gave me a slow smile. "A good choice."

I shivered. Would he have made me vow to something terrible?

"I could have made you my slave for the rest of your life," he whispered in my ear. "And you would have liked it."

I swallowed, my mouth bone-dry. "Switch to the common tongue."

He did, and I analyzed every word as he laid out our bargain. He would take the prisoners to the city gates, along with Rythos, Cavis, Galon, and Marth. They would wait for me there, and when I handed over the amulet, our deal would be complete.

Lorian said several more strange words, and I cried out as pain erupted from my hand, spreading up my arm and into my chest. He slid his hand to the back of my neck, holding me in place. When I looked down again, both of our cuts had sealed, leaving nothing but a thin line behind.

I went to step back, but he easily held me in place. His gaze examined my face, and then he was lowering his head, his mouth finding mine.

I sighed against his lips, and he let out a growl, backing me toward the wall.

"I have no desire to watch you scream as you die," he growled. "So you better be correct about where that amulet is."

I didn't want to think about that. Not now. All I wanted was for Lorian to make me forget. Just for a little while. I gazed up at him, and he cursed, his mouth capturing mine. Gods, he tasted good. Wild and a little feral and... I whimpered against his mouth, and he growled.

"You were designed to make me insane."

He flipped our positions, and this time, he was pushing me through the sitting room, toward his bed. I stumbled, and then I was in his arms, my back hitting his soft bed.

"Dreamed of seeing you here," he admitted, pressing a tender kiss to my lips. "Better than I could have imagined. Tell me you don't want this, wildcat, but tell me now."

I gazed up at him. He looked half crazed with lust. But beneath the lust was something else. Something we were both trying to pretend didn't exist.

"I want this."

"Then this needs to go."

His hands found the clasp to my necklace, and he placed it on the bedside table.

Our eyes met—mine no longer hidden—and his mouth crashed down on mine. I slid my hand down his chest, unfastening his pants. Within a moment, I was stroking him, and he bucked into my hand. My stomach fluttered at the feel of him. "You're…big."

He just smiled against my lips. "You can take me."

I squeezed him lightly, and he let out a rough groan, hauling me to my knees on the bed. He turned me, slowly unfastening each button, in between kisses to the back of my neck that made me want to beg him for more. He pulled down my dress, trapping my arms at my sides, and that hot, wicked mouth kissed up the side of my neck until he gently nipped at my earlobe. I gasped.

"I like you like this," he purred. "Helpless against me."

"I'm never helpless," I reminded him, and he laughed.

"Oh wildcat, I plan to make you so insane with pleasure, you won't even know where to *find* your magic."

My skin prickled at the dark promise in his voice. He seemed to lose that control he valued so highly, and my dress was suddenly gone—victim to his clever hands. He let out a rough groan as he took in the scraps of lace I was wearing beneath it.

There was something incredibly arousing about hearing that groan. About knowing it was for *me*.

He flipped me, and his lips trailed down, across my breasts—distracting me while he did away with my underwear. And then I was bared for him, and he held my gaze as he ran one finger over the peak of my nipple.

"Do you like this?" He smiled at me. "Or this?" He roughly tweaked my other nipple, and I let out a choked moan.

"Ah," he said. "A little pain with your pleasure?"

I shook my head, and he smiled. My breath caught in my throat, and I raised my hand, cupping his cheek. His smiles were so infrequent—and usually tinged with sarcasm. Or they were the feral kind of smiles that warned me something vicious and cutting would soon come out of that mouth. But *this* smile…

He smiled at me like I made him happy.

"What are you thinking?"

"Nothing."

"Mm-hmm. Let's see if I can really make that busy little mind blank."

He lowered his head, taking one nipple in his mouth, sucking and rolling it until I was holding his head to me, writhing beneath him.

"So sensitive," he murmured, moving to my other breast and giving it the same attention. My core clenched, desperate, *needy* in a way I'd never felt before.

"I want to touch you," I demanded, pulling his shirt up.

He ripped off his shirt, and my mouth watered at the smooth expanse of skin. I let my hands wander, learning his body the way I'd fantasized about that day when I'd watched him bathe.

"These too." I tugged at his waistband. He laughed against my breast.

"Demanding creature." But he stripped them off, and my body heated further at the feel of his skin against mine.

I attempted to twine my legs around him, *desperate* to finally feel him inside me. He cursed as I rubbed myself against the thick length of him, too needy to feel even a hint of shame at the act.

"I don't think so. I need to get you ready."

"I've *been* ready."

He ignored that, kissing his way down my belly. And if I'd thought the sight of his head between my thighs was erotic before, this was...

This was...

His naked back, his skin so warm against mine, the way he perused the heat of me as if I was *his* and he was deciding just how he'd best use me.

I gasped. He slowly lifted his head.

"I haven't touched you yet, Prisca."

"I need you."

"I know."

I would have scowled at his smug tone, except I could see the way he touched me with such careful restraint. The way he closed his eyes as his fingers found my slick core and he pushed my desire higher. And higher.

"Lorian."

"Gods, when you beg. It's the prettiest sound I've ever heard. Do it some more for me, and I'll give you what you want."

My cheeks blazed, but I met his gaze. He waited for me.

"There's no shame between us," he murmured. "Never. Now, tell me what you want."

"I want you inside me."

He smiled, flicking my clit with his finger. I clenched, and his smile widened. Then that same finger slid inside me. Gods, he made me *want* to beg.

"You want me here?"

"You know I do."

"Then you'll have me here. And you'll know no other man can make you feel the way I do."

He slowly kissed his way back up my body, until our lips met. I trembled as he positioned himself at my entrance, slowly thrusting inside me.

He got about halfway in, and I was suddenly *too* full. Maybe this was a bad idea.

"Uh, Lorian."

He just raised his head. Those green eyes were so dark, they were almost black, his pupils blown. "Take me, Prisca."

His hand slipped down to stroke me, and I opened for him, writhing at the dual sensation.

"That's it, wildcat," he murmured. And then he removed his hand, slowly thrusting once more. His pelvic bone hit my clit with each thrust, and I wrapped my legs around him, already on the edge.

Oh gods, the feel of him. It was better than I'd imagined in even my most secret fantasies—and yet, not enough. I needed more.

"Harder," I demanded.

"Made for me," he purred. But he complied, thrusting so deep I saw stars. There was pain, simply because he was so big and it had been so long…but the pleasure…

I had no words for the pleasure. For the way my body was already tightening around him. For the way my every nerve seemed to cry out for more. For the way my breath caught in my throat, and every muscle in my body clenched, on the verge of something incredible.

"Come for me, wildcat." Lorian leaned down to nip at my bottom lip. "And let me feel it."

I had no choice. My body was already tensing, my breath catching. He cursed as I clamped down around him. My climax roared through me, so strong, the edges of my vision darkened until all I could see was Lorian and the possessive lust in his eyes as he watched me fall apart for him.

When I was limp, he continued to move, his eyes still filled with that feral lust. "We're not done."

He might not be, but I certainly was.

He gave me a slow smile. Obviously, he knew exactly what I was thinking, because he pulled out of me and flipped me onto my knees, thrusting into me once more. He felt even larger in this position, and I clenched around him.

"So fucking beautiful," he growled in my ear.

He wrapped one of his hands around my throat. Not squeezing, just a dark threat. His other hand had slipped down until he thrust in time with that hand as it caressed my clit.

And just like that, I was on the edge again.

"Come for me," he ordered.

And I did. I let out a moan so filthy, he laughed. But it was a strained laugh. And then he was slamming into me, ensuring my climax went on and on, until he held me close and shuddered, emptying himself inside me.

LORIAN

I was strangely content, lying here in my enemy's castle, as Prisca watched me with those eyes that were hers once more. I'd found myself missing their strange color, but the calculation in them, at least, was always the same—whether disguised or not.

Her gaze turned intent. "Why did you leave me that day? At the river?"

She'd never asked me that before.

I wasn't a man who was used to feeling emotions like guilt or regret. And yet, when I thought of what could have happened to her, all alone by that river...

I quashed the urge to give her a glib answer. I was quiet for so long, she looked away. Finally, I sighed.

"I have been doing the kinds of tasks that would break many men for a very long time. When you live such a life, you eventually have to make a choice. Allow your deeds to stack up on your shoulders with every movement, crippling you with their weight, or turn that part of you—

the part that cares about right and wrong and good and bad—off. When I first saw you, I didn't see a *person*. I saw a problem I had no answer to. And then you looked at me, and I knew you'd survive."

"How could you know that?"

"You forget—I'm older and wiser than you." She rolled her eyes at that, and I couldn't help but smile. "It wasn't just fear and desperation in your eyes that day."

She snorted. "Is that right? Tell me what else you believe you saw."

I caught her wrist. It was so small in my hand. So fragile. And yet, this woman had already gotten closer to the king than any rebel before her.

"I saw a burning rage. A wrath and retribution within you, just waiting to be freed. You killed two men."

She flinched and attempted to free her hand, but I held on. "You fought for your survival. You made it through that forest until you found me again. When I saw you—and your poor attempt to sneak up on us—I wanted you so badly, I was enraged. So I buried it down deep, vowing to never even think of acting on it. And then I realized what power you had, and even as I loathed myself for it, I was relieved."

Her brow creased. "Why?"

The words were difficult to say, but she deserved to hear them. "Because I would get to keep you for a little while. And I vowed that even if you hated me for it, I would make sure you were able to survive."

She was quiet for a long time. Then she leaned down

and pressed a kiss to the hand I had wrapped around her wrist.

"Can I ask you something?" Her voice was drowsy.

"Yes."

"How much power do hybrids have?"

"Hybrids are more powerful than humans. Which is one of the reasons why they are a threat to the king. They recover faster from injuries and sickness. If you'd been human, you would have died from that poison." Ice spread through my veins at the thought. Even with her hybrid blood, she'd come incredibly close to death.

And it had taken all my self-control not to slaughter the woman responsible. My instincts urged me to remove the threat she still presented.

"What about the fae? How much more powerful are they than humans and hybrids?"

"The fae are their own creatures. But there are so many different types of fae that it would be difficult to compare them accurately. Some of them are so long-lived, they're almost ancient compared to humans. They see humans as little more than pests that should have been eradicated long before they became a threat. I've met fae who enjoy humans—not just sexually and not to *eat*, as Sabium likes to suggest. But as friends."

She thought about that. "Do you consider the fae your friends?"

"Some of them," I said honestly. "Some of them, I stay away from as much as possible. But you asked about their power. Most humans have one gift. One ability.

Hybrids have the same, but that one ability can rival the fae."

"And the fae?"

"They have one main ability, similar to the hybrids. But they also have various small magics. Simple things that would seem incredible to humans."

She was quiet for a while. "You're so knowledgeable. Clearly, you've been traveling for a long time. What's it like?"

She meant what was it like being a mercenary. "I enjoy the freedom. But it can be…lonely."

"Even with Marth and the rest keeping you company?"

I chuckled. "We've been together for so long, we're mostly tired of one another."

She yawned. "I should get back to my room before I fall asleep here."

I tamped down my instant denial. Becoming possessive of this woman would be a mistake. Even if I wanted to soak up her scent and chain her to this bed where she would stay safe.

So I helped her dress, distracting her with long kisses and murmured suggestions, until she was laughing, her eyes lit with lust.

Then I practically pushed her out of my room before I could do something stupid like order her to stay.

PRISCA

The next two days flew by. Vicer was making his plans, and I was making mine. Lorian spent most of the time away with the king on another hunting trip, and I'd spent my time helping Tibris in the dungeon, going over and over every part of our plan.

Meals with the other ladies had become…awkward. Caraceli's usual seat was empty, but since she'd taken to sitting next to me so she could hiss threats in my ear, I wasn't exactly upset about that. Lisveth had taken her seat back, although even she was quiet.

Pelopia and Alcandre sent me occasional wary looks. Obviously, Caraceli had managed to convince them of my scheming ways.

But I could barely focus on them. Instead, I was continually daydreaming about the way Lorian had taken me the other night. I'd been right about one thing when I'd fantasized about his body—even as I'd loathed him. He'd likely ruined me for any other man. And yet I couldn't find it in me to regret it.

Lorian was currently lounging next to the king, laughing at something Farrow said. I couldn't help but be entranced by the way he'd transformed from mercenary to prince.

He caught my eye, and I swallowed at the hard glint in his eye. Something was wrong. I gave him the tiniest nod and went back to my food.

But I could no longer eat.

By the time I met him back in his room, my lungs were heavy with dread.

"What is it?" I asked when he opened the door.

His expression was serious, and he kept his eyes on mine. "I just learned that Sabium has filled in the tunnel to the market."

A dull roaring sounded in my ears. Lorian cursed and pulled me farther into the room, hauling me onto the sofa.

"I'm sorry, Prisca."

"The king knows of our plans."

"If he did, we would all be burning. But it's possible someone reminded him that the tunnel was still there and unused. Perhaps a guard noticed dust disturbed near the entrance. Or Sabium had simply always planned to fill it in and it's a coincidence."

"You don't believe in coincidences."

He just shook his head. "You'd be surprised what I believe in. But there's another possibility."

I nodded. "That Sabium knows someone was in his dungeon and he's setting some kind of trap." I got up to pace. The tunnel wasn't the only way. It couldn't be. "I'll figure something else out."

"Prisca."

"This isn't the end."

Lorian caught my hand. For the first time, his eyes were dark with sorrow. I wrenched my hand away.

"Don't look like that. You promised to help if I found

your amulet. You *vowed* it."

He frowned. "And I'll complete my vow. But right now, you don't have a plan."

"I will." I attempted to keep my voice steady, but from the pity in Lorian's eyes, I wasn't successful. He stood and brushed my hair behind my ear. My eyes burned at the tenderness, and I pulled away, unable to handle kindness from him right now.

"I've got to go."

"Prisca."

I stalked out. With the tunnel no longer an option, how was I going to get the prisoners out? The Gods Day ball was in just four days, and the king was clearly being careful.

My mind raced with possibilities. The servants' halls connected to the back exit of the castle. But anyone leaving the grounds still had to go through the front gates. Even with the amount I'd practiced with my magic, I couldn't freeze time long enough for over three hundred prisoners to make their way down the paved road leading to the gates.

Maybe Vicer could arrange for the rebels to steal whatever conveyance they could find and meet us somewhere close enough to the castle that we could load the hybrids into that transportation.

I snorted. Even if they could somehow steal enough for everyone, what were the chances that the guards wouldn't notice hundreds of horses, carriages, and carts all heading toward the castle? I'd seen the guards stationed at various points throughout the city. Paid attention to their alert demeanor and the random searches they insisted upon. The city guards were bound to be on high alert for Gods Day, especially with so many prisoners due to be executed at dawn.

A hollow ache settled in my stomach, and I couldn't hear anything over the ringing in my ears. I'd already failed Wila. Failed Asinia's mother. Failed my own. I couldn't fail anyone else. Couldn't let anyone else die because of me.

I took a deep breath and buried my shaking hands in my gown. Right now, I had to get to the queen's chambers before she noticed I was missing. After my poisoning, she would likely pay closer attention to all of us, and the last thing I needed was for her to begin asking questions.

My mind raced as I walked toward the queen's chambers. There was a way to free the prisoners. I knew there was. This couldn't be it. It *wouldn't* be it.

The queen was withdrawn today. Servants brought in tea, along with tiny, perfectly crafted pastries, but the queen was staring out the window.

So many lives on the line, and I was watching the queen daydream.

"Is everything all right, Your Majesty?" Lisveth asked, after at least an hour of us making stilted conversation while she ignored us.

The queen gave Lisveth a small smile. But it immediately disappeared, and she heaved a sigh. "My husband has been absent lately. He refused my request for our son to come home for Gods Day." Those freckles stood out on her pale face as she turned her head to the window once more. Clearly, that was as much as the queen was prepared to divulge. "Oh, you don't need to sit in here all day with me," she sighed again. "Go take one of the carriages to the market or take a walk around the grounds."

Her tone was almost accusatory, as if our presence— at her request—was an imposition.

I was on my feet before the words finished leaving her mouth. She raised one eyebrow, and I merely bowed my head. "Thank you, Your Majesty."

Madinia caught up to me the moment we left the queen's chambers.

"What's wrong?"

"Nothing."

She caught my arm, and I shook my head. "Not here."

Madinia followed me out of the castle and onto the grounds. Even more guards were stationed than usual. To our west, across what had to be several hundred foot-spans of grass, the royal stables were situated next to the sprawling brick building where the carriages were stored.

"We can't use the tunnel from the dungeons to get the prisoners out."

Horror slid into Madinia's eyes as she stared at me. "What do you *mean*? That's how we're getting out."

"Not anymore. The king filled it in."

"What will we do?" To her credit, the words weren't

dripping panic. It seemed to be a genuine question, and the frown on her face told me she wanted to talk options.

"I don't know." My voice broke. Admitting such a thing when Madinia had put her faith in me…when they'd *all* put their faith in me…

"You have some scheme up your sleeve, I know you do. Prisca, I want to help."

As usual, her voice was haughty. Because Madinia wasn't used to *asking* for anything. Even when we wanted something from the queen, it was usually Lisveth who asked.

I opened my mouth to snarl at her, and something moved in the corner of my eye. I turned, feeling Madinia do the same next to me.

Davis stood outside the stables. He lifted his hand in a wave, that easy smile on his face as if we were all good friends. I glanced at Madinia, who was struggling not to curl her lip at him.

"You want to help?"

She sighed. "I'm not going to like this, am I?"

27
PRISCA

Madinia didn't like it. Within moments after I'd waved back at Davis, Madinia and I were standing next to him, gazing at hundreds of horseless carriages. It hadn't taken more than the mere suggestion from Madinia for him to offer us a tour.

"As you can see, this is where we keep them," he murmured, smiling at Madinia.

To her credit, she beamed brainlessly at him. Davis's eyes widened slightly, before crinkling at the corners.

If I hadn't known that he'd terrorized at least three of the women I'd once shared a room with, I might have believed the almost embarrassed way he scuffed his feet.

Not to mention, Auria had told me that the day I was poisoned—when half the court had seen Lorian hauling a drunk woman back to her room—she'd seen Davis *wink* at the "prince."

I wanted Davis dead.

Lorian's voice echoed in my head.

"Just weeks away from your village, and you're already turning into a little savage."

"How are the carriages controlled?" Madinia murmured. "It must require a lot of power to ensure they travel where you wish them to go."

Davis's chest puffed, and he shot her a grin. "I'll show you."

Satisfaction tempered my wrath, and we trailed after him, deeper into the huge space. At the back of the room was a door I'd assumed was a closet. He opened it to reveal a city map so large, it stretched across an entire wall.

"Wow," Madinia marveled. Davis was ignoring me, which was exactly what I'd hoped for. Taking a step closer, I attempted to memorize as many details as I could. My breath caught. The map was so incredibly detailed it was like a work of art—encompassing every part of the city. On the map, tiny replicas of the carriages were fastened, currently moving as if alive.

The king's favorites enjoyed magic like this every day, while even our village healers were stripped of most of their magic. Magic that could have saved lives.

Madinia placed her hand on Davis's arm, leaning close. "How does it work?"

Davis held one of his hands over the corner of the map where a stone lay on top of the parchment. I went still. It wasn't an oceartus stone—it was a dull yellow color—but the stone glowed slightly, and Davis reached for one of the tiny carriages positioned at our backs. He nudged it with one finger, until the carriage was outside the castle gates.

"Come with me," he said.

We followed him out to the gates, where the carriage was waiting. The nudge of his finger had moved it into place.

Ah. I glanced at Madinia. Thankfully, she wasn't an idiot.

"There's one thing I don't understand," she asked, her voice light. "How do the carriages know when to stop for people and other carriages and horses?"

"That's part of my father's magic. He gave the carriages a level of sentience. Just enough to ensure those within the carriages are protected."

"And as someone who spends a lot of time in those carriages, I appreciate that." Madinia's laugh sounded like a hundred tiny bells all ringing at once. "But what stops someone from sneaking into that map room and making a carriage go wherever they like?" She bit her lip as if genuinely worried about such a possibility.

"You don't need to concern yourself with that," Davis said. "Not only is the map secured by some of the king's most trusted guards, but other than my father, I'm the only one who can change the carriage routes."

Madinia linked her arm through his. "Now, that's a relief."

I cleared my throat, and Madinia turned that lifeless smile on me. "Setella has an errand to run in the city," she said. "But you'll entertain me, won't you, Davis?"

I'd always wondered how some women managed to purr their words in a way that made males lose their senses. If we lived through the next few days, perhaps I could convince Madinia to teach me.

Davis gave her a dark look that would have worried me if I didn't know Madinia could burn him alive with just a thought.

Actually, maybe *that* was what I should really be concerned about. I gave Madinia a warning look, and she smirked at me, turning to walk back toward the carriages with Davis.

"Where are you going, Setella?" a voice called.

I sighed. I'd been so close. I turned to find Pelopia and Alcandre strolling toward me.

"I thought I might go to the market," I lied. Hopefully they wouldn't ask to come with me.

Pelopia opened her mouth, but her eyes heated as she glanced over my shoulder. I turned to look. Lorian was walking out of the castle, surrounded by several men dressed in Gromalian colors. Marth was one of them. It was strange seeing his expression so distant, his eyes so bored. As I watched, he waited for Lorian to get several steps ahead and then winked at one of the maids, who gave him a saucy grin.

Lorian turned, giving Marth a hard stare, and I barely suppressed my own grin.

"I heard about how the prince attended to you when you were sick, Setella," Pelopia murmured.

I didn't know what to say to that. Any denial would likely just stoke her curiosity further.

"Don't worry," she said when I didn't reply. "I understand. He *is* a handsome devil, with his long red hair and that roguish smirk."

My smile froze.

I turned to the man whose hair was neither red nor long. Lorian sent us a wink, playing the part.

I understood now just why the king had allowed him to sit next to him.

He was wearing another man's face.

But for some reason, I could only see Lorian.

Why? Was it because I'd known him before the charm he must be wearing worked?

No. Tibris and Vicer could still see my darker eyes.

Was it because Lorian was a hybrid? I needed to ask Tibris what he saw when he looked at the Gromalian prince.

My pulse thumped as I stared at him, putting the pieces into place. This was how he'd been trusted to go where he pleased and to do whatever he liked in the castle. Could he wear *other* faces if he chose?

Was the face I knew even the real Lorian?

"Setella?"

I jolted. "Sorry. Just thinking." It didn't matter. It couldn't. What was important was that I could see through whatever magic Lorian had used. If I hadn't been able to, he would've known who I was the minute he'd stepped into this castle, and I wouldn't have known who he was.

I shuddered at the thought.

"We're going to take a walk on the grounds." Alcandre said. "Enjoy your time at the market."

"Thank you."

Tibris walked past, carrying a crate of wine. I caught his eye and he jerked his head, gesturing for me to follow him. He'd been busier than ever, healing the prisoners at night and working long hours during the day to ensure the king's visitors had their favorite wines. The dark circles beneath his eyes seemed to be permanent.

I froze time long enough for us to have a whispered conversation next to the cellar. His face drained of color. "The bastard filled it in? What are we going to do, Pris?"

"I'm going to go talk to Vicer now."

"He's going to say it's too dangerous."

"I know." We were both silent for a long, miserable moment. "I have another plan. I'll slip you a note once it starts falling in place."

Tibris nodded. "I'll do some thinking too. This isn't it, Pris. We're not leaving them there."

I knew what he was thinking. Had we ensured the hybrids were more alert, stronger, healthier, all so they would understand what was happening to them when they walked to their death in a few days?

"No. We're not."

I walked to Vicer's, keeping a lookout for anyone following me—which involved doing several loops past the house, ducking down alleyways, and hiding in door stoops.

Finally, when I was certain I was alone, I knocked, blinking as Vicer immediately opened the door, reached for my arm, and pulled me straight inside.

"Hello to you too."

He was obviously in a dark mood. Well, I was about to make it darker.

Following him upstairs to the common room—which was surprisingly empty—I took a deep breath.

"The tunnel has been filled in."

He looked into the distance, and I could practically see him calculating our chances.

Those calculations obviously weren't good, because he began cursing in at least six different languages, his face growing flushed, hands fisted. Finally, Margie came up from the kitchen and told him to calm down.

I'd told him the same, but he'd ignored me. When Margie gave him that stern look, he listened.

I'd never seen that kind of reaction from Vicer before. But we were all on edge.

"We can still do this," I insisted, ignoring the way he immediately shook his head. "Margie, are you coming with us?"

She hesitated. "I have a place here in the city."

"The prisoners will need you."

They were traumatized, half starved. But more importantly, I thought Margie needed them.

Grief flickered in her eyes, and I knew she was wishing her daughter was one of those prisoners. That Rosin been arrested just a few days later and missed the last Gods Day burning. She would have spent a year in the king's dungeon, but she'd still be alive.

"I'll think about it."

Thankfully, Vicer had arranged for Chava to meet me at his headquarters. She was as quiet as usual, but she took care of the lighter hair that had begun to grow in at my roots.

By the time Chava was finished, more of the rebels had gathered in the common room—all with various thoughts on the worthiness of our plan. Many of them would be helping Vicer to move the prisoners once they were finally outside the city walls—if we managed to get them out. So, I listened, even when most of them told me the hybrids were going to die. When I began pacing, Margie pulled me aside.

"Let me ask you one thing," she murmured with a faint smile. "If Vicer decided it was too dangerous to get the hybrids out, what would you do?"

"I'd ignore him and try anyway."

She smiled at me. "Then his thoughts on the matter are irrelevant."

I raised one eyebrow at her, and she waved a hand. "I love Vicer like he is my own son. But this many rebels means many, many opinions. And you can't afford to feel any doubt if you're going to succeed."

I'd had enough of my own doubts. And they were crippling me. Margie was right. If I was going to do this, I had to *believe* I could get the prisoners out.

"Thank you."

Vicer looked up from where he was talking to Ameri. I nodded at him. He studied my face, and after a long moment, he nodded back.

All I could do was take care of my part of the plan and hope Vicer changed his mind.

It took me twice as long to get back to the castle, but Madinia following me had taught me to be careful. The moment I returned, I asked Daselis to see if Telean would pay me a visit. She sniffed and said the seamstress was an extremely busy woman, but she would see that a message was passed on.

If I didn't hear back from her, I'd find another way to contact her.

Thankfully, Telean visited before dinner. Her eyes met mine, and even though I had a new necklace, I had a feeling she was remembering the true color of my eyes—her best friend's eyes—beneath the charm. I patted the spot on the bed next to me, and in a voice barely louder than a whisper, I told her what I needed.

"I will help you," Telean said. "It will be my honor to give my life for such a cause."

Give her life? It took me a long moment to understand what she was saying. She thought I was asking her to sacrifice herself. And she was willing to do such a thing.

"You're coming with us."

She blinked at that. "You would...want me?"

Did she truly think I would leave her here to die? "You're my aunt, Telean," I said gently. "Of course I want you with me. And even if we weren't family, I would get you out with everyone else."

Her smile was a beautiful, brilliant thing. And I realized then just how little she'd come to expect from life. From the people around her.

"You've been in this fucking castle for too long."

She laughed. "I have."

She squeezed my hand. I squeezed back.

We were getting over three hundred people out of the dungeons. Together.

LORIAN

If my brother knew I was trusting Prisca with the amulet we needed so badly—even with a fae vow in place—he would lose his mind.

"Are you sure about this?" Marth asked, echoing my own thoughts.

We stood in my sitting room. Stood, because I couldn't look at the sofa next to the door without seeing Prisca spread out and moaning for me. Just the thought of the little wildcat drove me to distraction.

I couldn't blame Marth for questioning my decisions. I'd questioned those decisions myself over and over again.

It had been two days since I told Prisca the tunnel was filled in. Two days since I watched the life drain from her eyes. She hadn't come to me since. But each glimpse

I'd caught of her around the castle had told me everything I needed to know.

Her expression was always thoughtful, eyes distant. It was as if she wasn't truly here anymore, her mind continually working on her new plan. The plan that no longer hinged on the rebels. Instead, *I* featured heavily in her plan, just as she featured in mine.

I would help her save the hybrids, and she would find my amulet. She'd refused to tell me where it was, and even if I could bring myself to torture Prisca until she revealed the location, she would likely freeze time and castrate me if I attempted such a thing.

Pride unfurled in my chest, despite the fact that the wildcat was the biggest inconvenience I had encountered in my plans—and potentially my life—so far.

Ultimately, she was right. If we were to split up and help each other, we could both win.

Despite the risk, I knew Prisca would do everything she could to fulfill her end of the bargain to me. Even if it meant she died trying.

That thought didn't make me feel any kind of satisfaction. No, it just made me want to slit the throat of the closest guard so there would be one fewer alive when she was hunted tomorrow.

"Lorian?"

I forced myself to focus on Marth. "I trust Prisca to get the amulet."

Marth's eyebrows shot up. "Who *are* you?"

I ground my teeth. But I couldn't blame him for his

shock. Just weeks ago, I would have laughed at the idea that I'd trust anyone outside of Galon, Marth, Rythos, or Cavis with anything this important. And yet...I *knew* Prisca. Knew she would cut off a limb before she left this place without the hybrids in the dungeon below us. Which meant she was trusting me, too.

"If she doesn't bring the amulet to me, the hybrids die." Prisca knew she would die herself, but I knew that she'd value those three hundred lives over her own. Which was why I'd informed her of that extra little part of our agreement.

Her eyes had turned wounded at my proclamation. But I had more at risk than she could even imagine.

"Just tell the others of the plan," I instructed Marth. "This is the only way for all of us to get what we want."

He nodded, and I turned at the knock on the door. Somehow I knew Prisca was standing there even before Marth opened the door.

She smiled at him, and that strange, feral jealousy crept into my gut. Marth raised his eyebrow at me and smiled back at Prisca, although he was stepping out into the hall within a second.

"Where is he going in such a hurry?"

"Nowhere that concerns you," I said, that irritation still prickling along my spine.

Prisca raised one eyebrow. "Ah. It's time for some brooding. I'll leave you alone."

I'd caught her hand and trapped her against the door before I was aware I'd moved. Irritation turned to fury.

This was never supposed to happen. This woman was never supposed to make me question *everything*.

"Why are you in such a good mood?" I asked.

Prisca beamed up at me. "Vicer agreed to help. The rebels are back in."

"Now is not the time to say another man's name."

She let out a breathless laugh. "I can come back later…"

"You're not going anywhere."

My mouth slammed down on hers, capturing her moan, as I pushed her dress high, sliding my hand to her hot core.

"Already slick for me. You *enjoy* making me lose control, don't you?"

Her next laugh turned into a moan as I slid one finger inside her and then another. She clamped around my fingers, her hips arching, and I scraped my teeth down her neck. She tasted like sweet poison. Like everything I shouldn't want…and would kill to keep anyway. But she moaned once more—just as desperate for me as I was for her. That thought soothed the worst of my fury. At least in this, we were the same.

I wanted to tease her some more. Enjoyed making her beg. But I needed to feel her. I was desperate with the need to—

"Now, Lorian," she gasped, and I pulled my fingers free, almost fumbling as I loosened my pants just enough. My hands found her ass, and I lifted her, pressing her into the wall. She opened for me, and I sank all the way to the hilt. There were no words for the pleasure I felt while right here. Inside her. Prisca let out one of those rough groans, and I caught it with my mouth, stealing it from her.

Holding her in place, I thrust, my vision narrowing, until all I could see was her. I let out a growl of my own when she writhed for me, her hands finding my shoulders, my back, her nails digging in as she attempted to spur me on.

"My pace," I reminded her, and I felt her tighten around me. My laugh was more of a breathless grunt. Prisca loathed being told what to do more than anyone I'd ever met—except maybe *me*. And yet here, when I was inside her, she *wanted* my dominance. My orders made her come alive.

I slammed into her, and she gasped, angling her hips for me, taking me deeper. Picking up the pace, I slid my hand down to her clit, tensing at the way her inner muscles clamped down on me. At the way they began to flutter around me.

I pounded into her, flicking her little nub as her breath caught in her throat. The moan she let out...combined with the hot press of her around my cock, as if she never wanted to let me go...

I came so hard, I had to steady myself with a hand against the wall, grinding my teeth at the pleasure. Prisca shook against me, tiny aftershocks that I wanted to feel every fucking day.

I felt her slowly coming back to herself and lifted my

head. Her eyes were at half-mast, glinting amber despite the charm. She opened her mouth, but I took her lips—not yet ready to return to reality.

I'd told her she was mine, but she hadn't truly accepted it. Soon, she would learn exactly what that meant.

28

PRISCA

The morning of the Gods Day ball, I woke up the moment Daselis opened my door.

Sitting up, I swung my legs over the side of my bed and bolted for the bathing room.

Daselis followed me in as I heaved. "Are you okay?"

She was kind enough to put a damp washcloth on my neck. I shuddered and closed my eyes.

"Is it… Are you…pregnant?"

"What? No." I was filled with a dread so all-encompassing, I felt like someone was sitting on my chest while someone else played with my intestines.

Three hundred and nine lives. And that wasn't counting the rebels. Once Vicer had agreed with my plan, they'd all fallen in line. If I failed…

We were all dead.

I leaned over and retched again. Daselis held the back of her hand to my forehead—the first time I'd ever seen concern on her face. "You're not feverish."

"Something I ate," I got out.

"Back to bed with you. You can't miss the ball tonight, so you need to rest. I'll tell the queen."

I allowed her to push me back to bed, if only because the thought of sitting with the others over breakfast made me want to hide in a closet somewhere.

And yet lying in bed thinking about everything that could go wrong just made it worse. So much so that an hour later when Daselis returned to check on me, I was out of bed and pacing.

"What is wrong with you?" Daselis demanded.

I needed to make sure Daselis didn't get suspicious. And if I stayed in this room all day, I would lose my mind. "I feel better now. I'll go attend to the queen."

"She wants to be left alone. If you're determined to pace, you can walk outside."

I pulled on a thick woolen dress and fled, making my way down to the gardens. I kept to the outskirts of the gardens, where the trees were closer together and I could be assured of privacy.

The rest of the day crawled by slowly, torturously, until Daselis came to find me again where I'd been sitting beneath a shady tree, stewing in my worries.

"It's time."

I got to my feet, and my head spun once more. Everything hinged on the next few hours.

Daselis leaned close. "I don't know why you're so worked up today, but tell me this. Should I inform the servants to stay away from the castle tonight?"

My heart stumbled, a cold sweat breaking out on the back of my neck. Daselis had always seen more than she was given credit for. We stared at each other for a long moment. There was no rancor left on her face. Just a kind of grim knowledge.

"Anyone who doesn't need to be here should stay away."

The color drained from her face. It might be reckless, but…

"Do you want to leave here, Daselis?"

I should have thought of her and Erea. Would they be punished when I left? For not knowing what I was up to or—in Daselis's case—for not reporting her suspicions? I'd been so busy focusing on the prisoners, I'd forgotten about the innocent women who helped me every day.

Shame crawled through my body until I had to fight not to throw up again.

Daselis took a deep breath. "I don't wish to leave. My family lives in the city."

"I can get them out too."

Her eyes widened. "You're one of the…"

Had I just ruined everything? I didn't want to hurt Daselis, but I would knock her out if it meant delaying her accusations until after I left. "Please, Daselis."

"No wonder you're throwing up your breakfast!"

She backed away a step. The blood was draining from my face so fast I swayed on my feet. But she seemed to shake herself. "I won't say a word. But…I have a niece. Her name is Hanish. Tell me you'll get her out, too."

My knees turned weak, and I managed to take a full breath. "Can you arrange for her to be here? Tonight?"

"Yes."

"Then yes. But you should come with us. Please. You'll be interrogated once I leave. This could be your only chance for freedom. Tell Erea, too."

She nodded. "I understand. I'll think about it. But Hanish will be here. You get her out, and I'll owe you my life."

I nodded. "It's done."

She looked at me, and her eyes warmed. "One of the queen's ladies. And how I resented you for it. A social climber, to be sure, but for a reason."

"Yes."

"But who—" She went ashen, and I could see her calculating exactly why I would have snuck into the castle. "You're getting one of the prisoners out. Before dawn."

The words were so quiet I could barely hear her over the sound of my panting breaths, but I glanced around us anyway.

"I'm getting *all* of the prisoners out."

Her hand shook as she pushed back her hair. "Well, then. If you're going to humiliate the king, you should at least look good doing it."

I smiled and followed her into the castle.

29
PRISCA

I gazed at myself in the mirror. My aunt had outdone herself.

The dress was a deep, midnight black, shot through with silver thread, which caught the light. The sleeves of the dress covered most of my arms in sheer fabric, but most importantly, beneath the skirt, my legs were encased in tight leather breeches that fell to my calves. The front of the dress dipped low enough to show off my necklace—and the tops of my breasts—while distracting from the panels at each side, which hid slits in the fabric. Beneath those slits, I had a knife in a sheath wrapped around each of my thighs.

Erea had put my hair up tonight, using long silver pins to keep it in place. The braids wound across one another in a complicated pattern that had kept her busy while Daselis paced my room.

Erea hadn't yet agreed to come with us. She'd seemed strangely unconcerned when we told her, and it infuriated Daselis.

"They will *kill* you," Daselis hissed.

Erea sat on the edge of my bed and bit into her lower lip. "Surely if I explain, the king will know I had nothing to do with…anything." She slid me a look that begged me to agree. But I couldn't lie to her.

I sighed. "He'll use his truth-seekers, Erea." And because Daselis had explained the situation to her, if Erea did nothing now, she was just as guilty as us. I shouldn't have told her anything. I should have known she'd prefer to stay here where she was content with her life.

"You've seen what happens in this place," Daselis said. "It's worth a little inconvenience for three hundred lives."

"I could use you," I said. "We need people to help with the prisoners. Especially the younger ones."

Erea lit up at that. "You truly need my help?"

"Of course."

"Enough of this," Daselis snapped. "You have three choices. Either come with us, *don't* come and burn when the truth-seekers tell the king about how you knew what Setella was doing, or tell the king and watch three hundred people burn at dawn."

Erea's lower lip trembled. I opened my mouth, but Daselis sent me a fierce look.

Erea got to her feet. "I understand. I won't let you down."

"I know you won't," I murmured, guilt and relief warring within me. "Thank you."

I would make this up to her somehow. When I'd first

decided I could free the prisoners, I hadn't even thought of the women who woke me each morning. Who picked out my dresses and did my hair. Of course they would be targeted by the king. The thought made me nauseated once more.

"Don't you dare," Daselis snarled at me. "If I have to slap you to put some color back in your face, I will."

I stared at her. And burst out laughing. Her lips trembled, but she ruthlessly firmed them.

"Time to meet the queen."

I followed Daselis to the queen's chambers, where the other women were gathered. Madinia's expression was a cold mask of amusement, which she turned on me when I arrived. I was so anxious, my tongue had begun to itch, and she looked calm, relaxed, and haughty as always.

"I like your dress," she said. The first nice thing she'd ever said to me. She'd have to be careful, or the queen's ladies would become suspicious just from that.

"Thank you."

Madinia's dress was crimson, cut off her shoulders and low enough to bare the top of her breasts. She looked like exactly what she was pretending to be—a confident, beautiful woman without a care in the world.

The queen perused me. "Very nice. My seamstress has always done good work, but she has outdone herself for us tonight."

Just hearing her talk about my aunt in that proprietary tone made me want to punch her, but I forced myself to smile, bowing my head.

She was wearing a deep-blue gown cut in layers and sparkling with jewels of the same color. Her lips were painted the color of blood, while a diamond and sapphire necklace encircled her neck—matching the crown on her head.

We all filed down to the ballroom. Since the queen enjoyed making an entrance, the ball was already underway. The marble floors had been polished until they gleamed, reflecting the glow of thousands of candles. The king had chosen a forest theme—likely a mockery of the fae and their love of the wild. Ivy draped from the roof in long strands, with maroon and gold baubles hanging from it. The chandeliers reflected off their glassy surfaces, bathing everything in warm light. My hands began to tingle, my heart tripped, my mouth turned dry. This was it.

The music stopped, and everyone bowed to the queen. She made them wait, the hint of a smile on her face. Finally, she nodded, and the dancing resumed once more.

Marth was just foot-spans away, flirting with a courier. Lorian stood to the side, and his eyes met mine, cool and steady. I took a deep breath, and a strange calm filled me.

We could do this.

"Where is His Majesty?" I muttered to Madinia.

"The queen said he's feeling unwell and will be here later."

A shiver of apprehension made its way up my spine. I turned to find the king's assessor watching us walk in, the High Priestess next to him. I gave them a nod, quickly glancing away as something cold and oily settled in my stomach. The king was evil, but the assessors were just as bad. And *this* assessor—

"There's Davis," Madinia announced airily. "We may take a walk in the moonlight later."

Her tone made it clear what exactly she meant by that. Pelopia sent her a grin. "I do so love the *moonlight*."

Lorian was striding toward us. "You look lovely as always, Your Majesty," he purred, and the queen put her hand in his.

"As do you, Prince Rekja," she said. "That color suits you."

While she saw red hair and pale skin, she still wasn't wrong. Lorian had always suited black.

"You're too kind."

The queen merely nodded, slipped her hand from his, and strolled away. Lorian turned to me.

"Will you dance with me…Setella?"

I nodded, heart in my throat as I took his arm and allowed him to lead me to the center of the ballroom.

"You look delicious."

"Would you be serious? We're about to—"

He slid his hand up to the bottom of my ribs, his thumb caressing just beneath my breast. I shivered, and his eyes heated. "So responsive," he murmured. "I *know* what we're about to do. It doesn't change the fact that I want to strip that dress off you and see what I find beneath it."

"You'll find knives," I said, narrowing my eyes at him.

His smile was dark—almost feral. "Wicked women are my weakness."

I couldn't help but grin up at him.

He squeezed my other hand lightly, and his expression turned serious. "Are you ready?"

"Of course."

I glanced at Madinia, who was smiling coyly at Davis across the ballroom. She murmured something to him, and he took her hand, leading her out of the ballroom and into the gardens outside. Good.

Tibris would be in place near the cellar. Vicer... Gods, I hoped he'd managed to sneak in.

It all came down to this. Everything rested on how well I could hold time stagnant. And for how long.

I sucked in a deep, steadying breath.

And grabbed my power with everything I had.

The music stopped. Everyone froze. Relief flashed through me, but we didn't have time for me to reflect on it.

Across the room, Marth continued moving, already heading toward the door. Lorian did the same, dragging me with him. But first, he reached out and unhooked the queen's necklace with those quick hands. It was around my own neck before I realized he'd moved.

"I believe I owed you jewels," he said.

I just shook my head at him.

Telean stood waiting. When she saw us, her shoulders

sank a little in obvious relief. She swept past us into the ballroom, ready to unclasp bracelets and necklaces. To unhook earrings and remove tiaras and diadems. All of which would be tucked into thick, stolen cloaks.

By the time we got to the dungeon entrance, Tibris had already unlocked the door and was gone. Vicer stood next to the unlocked door, handing out keys for the cells. That replication magic again. Lorian and I each took one, Rythos, Cavis, and Galon appearing behind us, expressions grim, eyes alight. Just seeing them all together, ready to help free the hybrids... Something loosened in my chest. We *could* do this.

I hauled up my dress and shot down the stairs. Already, I could feel my grip on my power loosening slightly. I sucked in a panicked breath and held tighter. I'd trained so hard, again and again, but time wasn't *meant* to be stopped. Not even for this.

In the dungeon, the prisoners were already waiting for us to step out of the way so they could begin moving up the stairs. All of them had stopped eating the food they were given days ago and had eaten the food we managed to smuggle down instead. All of them had a healed scar where their oozing, iron-infected wounds had been. Many of them had been pacing their cells in intervals, building up their stamina for this one chance.

Those who were still too weak to move were carried.

Tibris had gone over the plan with the prisoners over and over again. And so we opened each cell in the best possible order to ensure the prisoners got up the stairs as efficiently as they could. By now, Tibris knew each of their names. Knew who would be able to help the others. Knew who could use their powers to create a ball of light to guide their group or who could be counted on to use their gifts to keep their carriages safe from guards.

I held tightly to my magic, but blood began to drip from my nose. Already, my body was rebelling. My throat constricted, but I forced myself to keep holding on. Lorian was convinced I could do this, convinced I had much more magic than I'd ever thought. And it was that hope I clung to as I grabbed the arm of a young boy, no more than thirteen winters old, and hauled him up the remaining stairs with me.

Daselis stood at the top of those stairs, a young girl with her—obviously her niece. She was helping my aunt, and together they handed each prisoner a cloak with a pocketful of jewelry and gold coins—stolen from the nobles in the ballroom, the bedrooms of the courtiers who lived in the castle, and the room where their cloaks had been stored.

The prisoners wearing little more than rags were given the dresses, shirts, and breeches that Telean had spent the past two days stealing—with Daselis's help today. As the queen's seamstress, Telean had unrestrained access to every closet and drawer in the castle.

The prisoners each took a bundle, ready to change once they were in their carriages. Shoes were a problem—but one we'd had no solution to. They'd have to use their coins to buy shoes as soon as they were away from here.

"Pris." Asinia was suddenly next to me, her eyes glistening. "I wish you could come with us."

"I'll be fine. Promise me you'll be careful."

"I will."

I glanced at Demos, who was standing behind Asinia, wild anticipation in his eyes. "See you soon," he said.

"Soon," I promised, my heart light as Demos grabbed Asinia's arm, hauling her away.

Asinia would have her life back. And Demos... Demos would get to smell the grass while he gazed at those clouds he loved. We'd watch the sun set together and get to know each other properly. I just had to get through the next part of our plan.

"You did it." Dashiel grabbed my hand as he reached the top of the stairs behind me. I squeezed his hand back.

"I did the first part. It's up to all of you to work together for the rest of it."

The prisoners were running now, some of them stumbling, a few falling—only to be hauled up by the others. They moved as a group, splitting off as we'd planned and piling into the carriages that waited. Madinia had done it. She'd managed to convince Davis to let her into that map room, where she'd taken control. Even now, she would be with him. Hopefully, he was unconscious and she'd already ordered these carriages to go to the city walls.

If he wasn't unconscious...

No. I would figure that out if it happened. For now, I had to believe Madinia had done her part.

Blood poured from my nose now. So much that it was only a matter of time before I would collapse. If that happened…

It was all over.

Lorian took my arm.

"Go," I told him. "You have to take them and go. Now."

He didn't look pleased. His eyes were molten in a face that was set in hard lines. I held up my hand. "Blood vow, remember?"

He cursed, capturing my hand and bringing it to his cheek. "Stay alive. Just stay alive, Prisca."

I attempted a smile. "You think I can't handle it?"

"I *know* you can handle it. Because I trained you to handle it. That doesn't mean I won't wait with my gut in knots until I see you're still breathing." He pressed a kiss to my forehead, and then he was handing me a piece of his shirt for my bleeding nose once more. Only this time, I didn't resent the way his scent engulfed me. No, this time, that familiar, wild scent steadied me in a way that few things could.

We didn't have time for any more words. With a nod, he was gone.

Now it was time for me to do my part. But first…

I darted back into the ballroom. I had to release my grasp on my magic soon, or time would resume with no input from me. And I'd have no power left for my own desperate retreat from the castle.

But the king's assessor? This was *personal*.

He stood just foot-spans away. I smiled, stalking up behind him. And then I released him, allowing him to know a tiny hint of the confusion and terror that his victims had felt.

He stiffened, but I was already swinging my blade. My knife sank into his side, and he screamed. "This is for Ardaric," I hissed. "And his parents."

I ripped the knife free and stabbed again. "This is for Thayer and Dashiel."

He fell to his knees, and I dropped with him.

"And this? This is for everyone else you *murdered.*" I slashed my knife over his throat, something in me awakening at the sound of his gurgles. Something vicious and deadly.

Something that *craved* the blood of my enemies.

LORIAN

Prisca would owe me for this. Not only was I on horseback, along with Rythos, Marth, Galon, and Cavis—all of us killing anyone who attempted to stop the carriages from reaching the city walls—but behind me, Tibris and Demos bickered relentlessly on the horses Marth had stolen for them. I should have locked them in a carriage together.

"You seriously think Prisca's going to stay in the

city?" Demos laughed.

"I think I know her better than you," Tibris ground out. "She won't leave. Not while there are other hybrids needing help."

Demos went quiet. "Then you should be convincing her to leave. She needs to stay *safe*."

I shook my head, barely restraining myself from informing the two idiots behind me that Prisca wasn't going with either of them.

I was taking her with *me*.

"What makes you think we can't keep her safe here?" Tibris asked.

I caught Galon rolling his eyes at that. Meanwhile, Demos had lowered his voice, although I could still hear every word.

"Are you insane? Prisca will be hunted night and day. You know why? Because not only is she the only one who has ever managed to humiliate the king, but she's also the heir to the hybrid kingdom."

My hands tightened on the reins, and I fought to keep my face blank. The heir to the hybrid kingdom.

She didn't know.

But *my brother* must have known. The way he had insisted on learning about her magic...

Some magic was hereditary.

He had *known,* and he hadn't told me.

Tibris didn't say a word. Likely, he was too stunned to speak.

Rythos threw me a look before turning his attention

back to the guards ahead. One of them jumped out in front of Galon's horse, and Galon used his power to fill his lungs with water. The guard fell to his knees, and I directed my horse around his body.

The heir to the hybrid kingdom.

I ground my teeth. Ultimately, it didn't change my plans. But it did mean I had new considerations.

The next guard who got in our way was dispatched with my sword. Rythos sent me a look. "Bad mood?"

"You have *no* idea." My brother had always dealt in information. But this? This felt like a betrayal.

The seamstress stuck her head out of her carriage. I narrowed my eyes at her. "And why didn't *you* tell Prisca the truth about her heritage?"

She looked down her nose at me, which was impressive, given she was half my size and I was on horseback.

"That was a conversation I had planned to have with Prisca in private," she said, turning her head to where Tibris and Demos trotted behind her carriage. Both of them went silent.

I would have to think about it later. Because the city walls were just a few hundred foot-spans ahead of us. And they were surrounded by the king's guards. Next to the guards, several stone hags stood waiting.

I should have turned those bitches to rubble when I had the chance.

30
PRISCA

Tore through the servants' halls, wishing I could slam my hands over my ears to drown out the screams from downstairs. I'd dropped the thread of time the moment I'd made it to the first set of stairs. I wouldn't be surprised if the nobility were screaming over the loss of their jewels and not the sudden appearance of the king's assessor's corpse.

By the time I got close to the queen's chambers, the guards had already abandoned their post, likely rushing downstairs in an attempt to protect the queen.

Pushing open her door, I crossed the sitting room in three steps and dragged an armchair over to the queen's mirror. Hopping up onto the chair, I studied the blue stone. The middle of the jewel was a blue so dark it looked almost black, while the outside was so light, it seemed to melt into the whorled silver of the mirror's edge. I pushed it out of the silver casing, and it slipped free easily. The mirror's edge had cleverly hidden the top of the stone and the long silver chain connected to it. The stone glinted in the light, strangely warm in my hand.

"I knew you would come here."

I jolted, almost falling off the chair.

Auria stood between me and the door. The innocent smile was gone, and in its place was a wide grin that didn't reach her eyes.

She'd…changed. Her face was almost unrecognizable without its guileless, good-humored expression.

My head spun. This was very, very bad. I needed to kill time. Needed to find a way out of this. "What do you mean?" I slowly climbed down from the chair.

"Did you think I wouldn't notice your hair growing in a lighter color at the roots? Or your eyes turning that strange shade before you changed your necklace?" She took a step closer. "I notice *everything*," she hissed. "The king has already rewarded me for my loyalty. And I look forward to watching you burn."

Panic clawed at me. I pulled on the threads of time.

But nothing happened.

Auria smiled. "Attempting your corrupt tricks? They don't work on me. *I've* been truly blessed by the gods."

A null. Auria was a null. That was why magic didn't work on her. Because her own power was always bubbling under the surface, repelling other magic like a living shield.

"There's a cell waiting for you, Setella. It's the same one Wila sat in before she died. I thought you'd enjoy feeling close to her during your final hours."

I caught a trace of movement in the hall behind her. My heart was so loud in my ears, I could barely hear her words. But I kept my gaze on her face.

Distract her.

"You're one of the king's spiders."

She laughed. "Like in the old stories? King's spiders don't *know* they're spiders, idiot. And they're positioned in foreign courts until they're needed. *I* knew what I was doing the whole time. Because the corrupt need to burn for their sins."

She crumpled to the floor.

I pulled my knife, but it was Madinia who stood behind Auria's unconscious form, a vase in her hand.

For a moment, the world went dark at the edges, and I leaned against the wall. Alive. Madinia was alive. And she'd just saved *my* life.

She was supposed to have gotten in one of the carriages with the others. But instead, she stood in front of me with a black eye, her face and neck covered in blood.

"What happened?"

Madinia stepped over Auria. "Davis knew I was planning something. The moment we got near the carriages, he *changed*." She shuddered, and for a moment, I thought she might cry. But her eyes narrowed instead. "I killed him." Her eyes fired, and pure challenge drenched her voice.

"I hope you made him suffer." I slipped the amulet over my head and tucked it into my dress.

She hiccupped out a laugh. "I asked him to show

me how the carriages worked, just like we planned. And once the map was keyed to his power, I was able send the carriages wherever I chose. He even let me practice on one of the carriages near the stables."

"Then he was an idiot as well as a predator." And he'd gotten what he'd had coming to him.

"We need to go," she said, and it was clear that was the end of the discussion. "The hybrids are halfway to the city walls already."

"I know. One moment." I bolted to the queen's bedroom and threw open her door. Most of her jewels were kept locked in a room with guards posted permanently outside. But the queen liked to have a few of her favorites within reach.

I hesitated.

But my memory kindly provided me with a reminder of the way the queen had slapped Wila across the face. The way she had allowed her to burn for what had appeared to be an accident.

I ripped a satchel from the queen's closet and swept my hand over the dresser. Necklaces, earrings, bracelets, a ruby the size of a duck's egg, diamond and sapphire hair combs, an emerald diadem, even a heavy jeweled crown went into the bag. I slung it crosswise over my shoulder and grinned at the portrait of the queen on the wall. "The rebellion thanks you for your donation to our cause."

"Hurry, Prisca." Madinia tugged on my arm. Downstairs, the screaming was continuing. But it had changed—enough that it was evident the guards were establishing some level of order.

That meant we needed to move.

"Are you ready?" I asked.

Madinia nodded. "Horses are saddled." She threw open the door, and we hurtled down the main hall, toward the servants' quarters. We took the back stairs—the ones Daselis had ensured would be clear, the servants nowhere to be seen.

Now.

I reached for the last tiny thread of my power. It was slippery—as if covered in blood. But I clasped it tightly.

Just a little longer.

Madinia had made certain two horses were tied directly outside of the back entrance, and I launched myself toward the closest mare.

The black panels of my dress parted easily as I mounted. I wished I'd remembered boots, but there was nothing I could do except turn the horse toward the gate and hold on, the outside of my vision dotted with dark spots.

"If I fall from this horse, you get to the Gromalian prince," I called to Madinia.

She sent me a horrified look, her horse breaking into a canter next to mine. I threw her the satchel holding the jewels, and she caught them, tucking them away beneath her own cloak. I trusted her enough now. Knew if I went down, she would make sure the other hybrids could start a new life.

That thread of my power slipped again. Thankfully,

we'd made it out of the castle grounds. But my chances of making it to the city walls were not high. I felt as if I was looking at the world from thousands of foot-spans away. My ears rang incessantly, and my breaths were shallow, weak.

I would hide here in the city if I had to. As long as I could crawl into an alley somewhere to rest, I could get back to the—

"The slums are burning!" Screams sounded as we tore through the streets. My horse reared, pawing at the air as someone darted in front, a bucket of water in his hand. I slid, almost losing my seat. "You can't go that way," he shouted. "Someone lit a building on fire."

"Which building?"

"The old orphanage."

Nausea swept through me in a wave. Madinia's eyes met mine. "The rebels," she said. "That's their building, isn't it?"

Yes. And it was no coincidence that it was burning. "We need to get there."

"It's too late. If the king ordered it destroyed, it will be heavily guarded."

"I can't just leave them there!"

"They might have gotten out."

My mind provided me images of Margie, trapped in her kitchen—of the others, burning to death in their common room.

No. No, no, no. We had to go back.

Someone grabbed Madinia's reins. We were both

dressed in finery, riding the king's best horses on the outskirts of the slums. That made us targets. I yanked the thread of time toward me, leaned over, and ripped the reins from his hand.

Time resumed before I could do much more.

The man choked out a scream, turning to flee. I wavered on the horse, all sound dimming. Then we were moving once more. "Stop," I croaked out.

"You're about to pass out," Madinia snarled. "Just hold on."

She'd taken my reins, spurring my horse on. I buried my hands in the horse's mane and clutched tightly as Madinia took over our escape.

I had a bad feeling.

If the king had been in the castle, he would have been summoned by all the screaming.

That meant that he was at the city walls.

Madinia whirled as we cantered down a side street, only to find the next street we needed was blocked. For someone who spent most of her time in the castle, she'd managed to memorize plenty of routes to the city walls. Time and time again, we reached streets that were blocked, and she was able to take us in a new direction, until the city gates finally came into sight. My horse broke into a gallop with no encouragement from me, and the click-clack of hooves on stone was the only sound for the next few moments. I swayed once more, forcing myself to bend low, almost hugging the horse.

Sabium would be waiting at those walls. Where

everyone I loved was gathered in one place.

I crouched in the saddle, my heart beating hard enough to crack my ribs.

We hurtled through the gates and into chaos.

PRISCA

The world narrowed, but I saw everything with my next breath.

The king, surrounded by guards, Farrow kneeling at his feet. Strange, tall women who looked like they were made of stone, standing behind the king. Lorian, fifty foot-spans away, positioned shoulder-to-shoulder with the other mercenaries. My brothers—both of them— flanking Asinia. Three hundred other prisoners positioned behind them, all of them standing next to their carriages with their hands in the air.

Among them were Vicer, Margie, and some of the other rebels.

I turned my attention back to the king.

Farrow's eyes met mine, and then his gaze slid to Madinia's, wide and filled with sorrow.

"Please," Madinia choked out, and the king smiled.

With the swing of his guard's sword, Farrow's head rolled to the ground.

Madinia screamed and screamed.

I was out of energy. Out of magic. Out of *everything*. But I snatched my reins from Madinia's hands, turned my horse, and galloped across the wide expanse in front of the city. Toward Lorian.

"Aim!" the king shouted, and I felt hundreds of arrows turned on me. Any moment now, they would fire, and if I was lucky, I would die instantly. If I wasn't, I would be pierced through, forced to choke on my last breaths.

Lorian roared my name. It was a sound that seemed to be ripped from his soul.

All I could see was his face. All I could feel was the amulet I ripped from my neck, the stone heating up in my hand. All I could hear was Sabium laughing, that rough chuckle I'd always loathed.

But the king's laugh was drowned out by the memory of Lorian's voice in my head. Of our vow. *"None of your prisoners will live unless you give me that amulet."*

I lifted my hand. Lorian's eyes blazed into mine.

The amulet seemed to suck in the light. Behind me, the king's laughter turned to a wrathful scream.

I threw the amulet toward Lorian with everything I had, hunching my shoulders against the pain I knew would encompass my final moments.

Lorian caught the amulet in his hand. And he laughed—a wild, exultant laugh.

Dread exploded in my stomach.

Lorian was somehow growing *bigger* before my eyes. Distantly, I could hear Asinia screaming something.

But I couldn't make it out over the sound of thunder.

Lightning lit up the sky.

Lorian's ears grew longer. Longer and pointed. His eyes were no longer that familiar forest green. No, they blazed emerald, his irises silver.

Fae.

He was fae.

I'd thought he was a hybrid. Like me. Thought we were fighting for the same cause.

Something deep inside my chest cracked open, and I gasped at the pain. Lorian's eyes met mine once more. As if he'd somehow heard that intake of breath.

"Fae scum," the king roared. "You will burn for your deception!"

Lorian smiled—that slow, feral *killing* smile. I slid off the horse and turned back toward King Sabium, my knees so weak I stumbled.

I should be dead by now. But—

Lightning flashed, hitting each arrow as they flew toward us. The kind of power rumored to be nothing more than myth.

My gaze found the other mercenaries. Except they weren't mercenaries at all. All of them were taller, broader. All had pointed ears and eyes that glowed.

It suddenly made sense. Why they were so closed-mouthed about their powers.

Rythos couldn't just make people like him. Marth didn't only have the ability to see glimpses of the past. These men didn't have just one magical ability. They had many. But their power had been hugely diminished for some reason. And they wanted it back.

Because they were fae. That was why they were here. They'd each only ever told me about their main power. I'd believed them, because I'd never expected otherwise.

A crown of lightning wreathed Lorian's head before it became a ball of sparks, shooting at the guards once more.

"It's the Bloodthirsty Prince!"

I bent in two, hands on my knees. It was my heart that had cracked open. It had broken so violently, I could have sworn I was bleeding out.

Lorian wasn't *just* fae. He was the fae prince who had leveled Crawyth. The fae prince who had murdered my real parents.

The hole inside me, the one I hadn't even realized had begun to fill…it was empty once more.

"You can't kill him yet, Lorian!" Galon roared.

The guards were still firing arrows at us. Arrows that Lorian continued to destroy with his lightning. The guards began to scatter, backing away despite the king's roaring orders.

The stone women…*exploded.* Small rocks flew into the guards, causing several of them to fall to their knees.

Lorian slowly turned his head in that strange…*fae* way of his. I'd noticed those differences and ignored them. Ignored them, because I didn't want to see. Ignored them, because I'd been close to falling in love with him.

The air crackled. Thunder roared. Lorian lifted a hand. And the closest guards—the ones who'd listened to the king and stayed…Lorian's bolts struck them with one blow. A gruesome, instant death.

The king turned and kicked his horse, fleeing. Most of his guards followed him.

Lorian's gaze was almost wistful as he watched them go. His mind likely on murder once more. But he turned away, dismounted, and prowled toward me. I felt like a rabbit that could sense a hawk circling above her, ready to strike.

Prey.

Around us, everyone was silent. It had also become strangely silent in my head, as if my thoughts were far away.

"That was a good throw," Lorian said. As if we were in training and he was giving me advice on my form.

I ignored the compliment. "Why didn't you tell me?"

His expression tightened. "I wanted to. But I couldn't. It was too important."

He gestured at Rythos and the others, who were now radiating power. Power I'd given them with that amulet.

"I have a gift for you, Prisca." Even Lorian's voice sounded different. Colder than ever.

Something in me recoiled. "I don't want anything from you."

A faint smile appeared on his face, and for a second, he looked so much like *my* Lorian that my chest ached.

"Oh, I think you want *this*."

He leaned over to the closest prisoner, a young man who went still in the way of a terrified animal. Lorian put one finger to the man's temple and burned a blue mark into it.

One identical to the priestess's mark.

I stared at Lorian. Turned out I wasn't too proud to take that gift.

"Everyone, line up," I called to the prisoners, my gaze still on the fae prince.

In the end, Rythos, Marth, Galon, and Cavis helped too. With the jewels we'd stolen, and the blue marks on their temples, the hybrids could start a new life.

Tibris appeared next to me, his face white. "Did you know?"

"Of course not."

His gaze searched my face, and he gave a sharp nod. "There's something else you need to know. Something Demos hasn't yet told you."

Another man in my life lying to me. But I couldn't take much more. I'd reached my limit. "Do I need to know this information right now?"

Tibris's gaze flicked to Lorian, and he nodded.

"Tell me."

"You're the heir to the hybrid kingdom."

What was he talking about? Impatience clawed at me. We didn't have time for this. "There *is* no hybrid kingdom. Not anymore."

Lorian was still watching me with those wild green eyes. "But it still existed. Your parents were the rulers."

The hybrid kingdom was located on what was now a barren continent. Only…

"That continent was never barren. No, the hybrid kingdom was beautiful. When your kingdom was invaded, many fled north, to the mountains. Some fled across the Sleeping Sea on merchant ships and winged creatures, landing on this continent where they crossed the Asric Pass. Thousands died. Those who lived made it to cities and villages on this continent. And they've remained hidden ever since."

I fixed my gaze on Tibris in an attempt to block out Lorian's presence.

"If…if my parents were truly the rulers of the hybrid kingdom, I wouldn't be the heir. Demos is older than me."

Tibris swallowed, his expression almost apologetic. "Their rules of succession specify that only those with time magic can rule."

I'd never asked Demos about his power. I'd just assumed it was the same as mine.

My lips went numb. I turned and stared at Demos.

But he was already moving, shoving Tibris into me.

Tibris let loose a vicious curse as both of us fell to the ground. Demos made a choked sound.

I pushed Tibris off me. Demos lay on the cold stone. An arrow jutted from his chest.

A high, keening sound left my throat, and I crawled toward Demos. Sobbing, *begging*.

"No, no, no." I pressed my hands against his chest, attempting to keep his blood inside his body.

I couldn't lose him. Refused to consider the possibility. He'd spent so much time shut away from the world, freezing and hungry and in pain.

Tibris was already dropping to his knees at my side. He held his hand to Demos's chest, his face turning gray from the strain. "I'm out. Oh gods, I'm out."

Tibris had been healing the prisoners. I should have prepared better. Should have made sure he wasn't drained.

"Healer!" I screamed. "Someone get a healer!"

Demos attempted a smile, but it was fractured with his pain. "It's okay," he mouthed.

"Don't try to talk."

Tibris was watching Demos, his face stark-white. "Why would you do that?"

"She loves you. She needs you. Protect her. For me."

"You know I will."

"No deathbed confessions," I hissed. "No deals. You're going to be okay."

Demos looked at me as if he was memorizing my face. "Already so fucking proud."

I buried my head in his neck, my tears dripping onto his skin. "Please."

He was supposed to see the clouds. To smell the grass. To watch the sunset. He was supposed to *live*.

"Please," I begged again.

A hand came down on my shoulder, and I stared up at the Bloodthirsty Prince. Lorian casually lifted his hand, aiming his lightning at the guard who'd appeared out of nowhere, crouched in the shadows behind one of the carriages.

The guard screamed as he died.

Lorian's expression was blank, but I'd seen that look before, and it had never boded well for me.

"I have a healer," he said.

Hope exploded throughout my chest.

"Where?"

He gestured, and a man stepped forward. I recognized him. The healer who'd saved me from the poison.

"Heal him," I begged as more blood spilled from the wound in Demos's chest. My brother's eyes were fluttering now, as if it was too difficult to keep them open.

"Not quite yet," the fae prince said. I knew that tone. He wanted to negotiate.

Demos let out a strange gurgling sound, and I choked on a sob. "What do you want?"

Anything. I would give him anything.

From the way Lorian's eyes glittered, it was clear he knew exactly that.

"I will heal your brother. In return, you will come with me to my kingdom."

Instant denial flashed through me. Oh, how I *loathed* this man.

"No." Two voices said at once. My brothers. So different, but alike in so many ways. But Demos's voice was a mere gurgle, and blood was slipping from his lips.

"Yes," I said, ignoring them both. "Heal him."

Lorian's eyes widened slightly. Had he really expected me to negotiate with him while my brother choked on his own blood?

Lorian pulled me away so the healer could get to

work. I wrenched my arm free of his hand. There could be no sound worse than Demos's screams as the arrow was pulled from his chest. But then he went silent. And that *was* worse.

The wound was slowly closing. The blood was no longer pooling beneath him. My knees turned weak, and I stumbled. Lorian caught my arm once more.

"Remember what you said when we parted at the city walls?"

It took me a moment to understand what he was speaking of. *"In another life."*

It was as if he'd reached into my chest, clamped down on my heart, and squeezed. "This isn't another life! This is the *same* life."

"Truly? Because you're not the same woman I met that day at the river."

"*You* didn't meet me. Galon did."

"Are you going to throw that in my face for the rest of my life?"

It hurt, sniping with him like this. Because it felt like nothing had changed. In reality, everything had.

"Yes. Every day. So, you should let me go."

"We made a deal."

I should have known he was fae just from the number of bargains we'd made together. I knew what this was about. Now that Lorian knew I was the hybrid heir, he wanted to use me against the king.

"Why didn't you kill Sabium?"

That muscle ticked in his cheek. "It's not his time to

die yet."

"Why not? After everything he's done…"

He smiled. "There's my wicked little savage."

I just waited him out. He angled his head. "The king won't die until I have everything I need."

"That's not a real answer."

He gave a languid shrug. Those strange silver-green eyes watched me.

"How did you do it? How did you hide…yourself?"

He lifted his hand to touch my cheek, and I stiffened. He dropped his hand, his fingers curling into a fist. "You can't even say the word. Is the fact that I'm fae really that horrifying?"

"If you didn't expect this response, you would have told me earlier."

"You're right." His expression shuttered. "I knew you would react like this."

How *dare* he? As if I were a bigot.

"You killed my parents."

Confusion swept over his face, and I took a step back. As usual, he just followed me.

"Crawyth," I hissed. "I lived in Crawyth when I was just three winters old."

His expression turned carefully neutral, and I shook my head, disgust roaring through me. "How did you hide your true form?"

He studied my face. "The vial we picked up at the Gromalian border. It was the Gromalian prince's blood. Powerful fae can wear glamour to tamp down our appearances." A sharp smile stretched his lips. "There are more of us in this kingdom than Sabium can imagine. But to wear the glamour of someone else? It requires blood."

"Is the real Gromalian prince still alive?"

"Yes."

"Why did you need me to get through the city walls?"

"Even my glamoured human form would be recognizable to those who know what they're looking for. Those who have specific instructions from Sabium. We would have figured out a plan, but it would have been risky. You made it much, much easier."

If I went with Lorian, it would prevent me from helping the hybrids. From building a life with my friends and family. From joining the rebellion.

It would also be torture, seeing him every day.

"Please don't make me go with you."

His expression hardened. "We made a deal."

"This is because people believe I'm the hybrid heir, isn't it? You and your brother...the fae *king*..." I choked on the words. "You want to use me somehow."

He just watched me. "Remember how you told me you used to see me in your dreams?"

If I thought about that, I would humiliate myself and burst into tears right here. "No."

The hint of a smile curved his lips. "Liar." He held out his hand. "Come, Prisca. Your brother lives. Now it's time to fulfill your end of the bargain."

I forced myself to ignore the commotion around me. Forced myself to block out Demos's cursing, Tibris's frantic denials, Asinia's weeping.

Keeping my gaze on Lorian's face, I made a silent vow to any gods who happened to be listening. I would make the Bloodthirsty Prince pay for his lies. For everything he'd done to my family and my people.

I took a deep, steadying breath.

And put my hand in his.

THE END

Thank you for reading a Court This Cruel and Lovely. I hope you enjoyed it! The adventure continues in book two: A Kingdom This Cursed and Empty.

I also have a *free bonus scene* which is Lorian's POV of his meeting with Prisca by the river. I ended up switching to Prisca narrating, as Lorian wouldn't stop sliding in information I didn't want readers to know until later ;) You can find it at staciastark.com.

Acknowledgments:

Mum: It goes without saying that I wouldn't be where I am today without your support... only this time I'm actually saying it.

Thank you for *not* insisting I go to university when I had no idea what I wanted to do with my life, and giving me the time and space to figure it out instead.

Thank you for reading to me so much when I was little and encouraging a life-long love of words.

And thank you for busting ass as a single mother... and showing me just a hint of what a woman can achieve on her own when properly motivated.

To my editors Dawn, Fay, Lisa, and Kristen– thank you so much for your wise, honest, and helpful feedback throughout this process.

To Petra, who has supported me in this career from day one and continues to cheer me on even from thousands of miles away, I can't even imagine having started this journey without you.

Deb and Angela: thank you for all your hard work, initiative, and putting up with my shoddy communication followed by a series of desperate emails as I attempt to catch up on the balls I've dropped while writing. You're both amazing and I already have no idea what I'd do without you.

Elli: Thank you so much for our brainstorming sessions and your unwavering support. And for calling me out when I plan spin-offs while still plotting my first book in a series.

To Amy: Thank you for your formatting, and for turning it around so quickly!

Thank you to Sarah, who somehow took my geographically challenged version of a map from Inkarnate and made my world come to life.

Thank you to @Samaiya.art for your incredible artwork!

Thank you to Bianca at Moonpress Covers for my gorgeous cover. I'm still obsessed.

Finally, to my incredible readers: There aren't enough words to express how grateful I am that I get to do this every day–and that you guys love my worlds and characters as much as I do. You keep me writing even on the hard days. Thank you, thank you, thank you.

www.ingramcontent.com/pod-product-compliance
Lightning Source LLC
LaVergne TN
LVHW090318280125
802334LV00002B/27